Keithan Quintero

AND THE SKY PHANTOMS

(A Story from the Future)

—Author's Edition—

FRANCISCO MUNIZ

Hidden Spark
BOOKS

KEITHAN QUINTERO AND THE SKY PHANTOMS
(A STORY FROM THE FUTURE)
Book 1
– Author's Edition –
Copyright © 2020 by Francisco Muniz

First Edition Copyright © 2015 by Francisco Muniz

This is a work of fiction. All characters, names, incidents, organizations, and dialogue in this novel are either the products of the author's imagination or are used fictitiously.

Front cover illustration by Andros Martínez
Front cover concept by Francisco Muniz
Interior illustrations by Francisco Muniz

ISBN 978-1-7360694-0-0 (hardcover)
ISBN 978-1-7360694-1-7 (paperback)
ISBN 978-1-7360694-2-4 (ebook)

www.hiddensparkbooks.com

I dedicate this book to

37738-V51

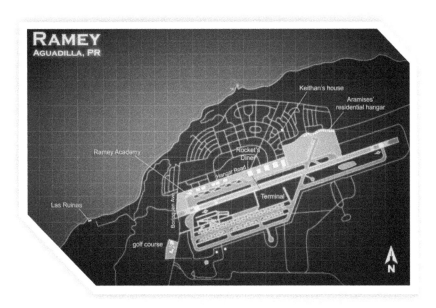

CHAPTER 1

3:47 p.m.
Forty-one miles off the west coast of Puerto Rico

K laxons resounded, and red lights flashed throughout the labyrinth of tunnels that ran deep beneath the flat, dry surface of Mona Island. They made men and women clad in high-tech black bodysuits hurry to their designated areas. Among them was Lieutenant Colonel Codec Lanzard, a man close to six feet, with a square jaw and a steely gaze that projected authority. Lanzard marched down the tunnel, anxious to reach the command center. He hated not being at his post when an emergency happened. The flashing red words "UNIDENTIFIED INCOMING" blinked on the left sleeve of his bodysuit, adding to his distress and pushing him to hurry up.

Within minutes, he reached the command center's double doors at the end of a tunnel. A sensor recognized the ID code on Lanzard's uniform and allowed him access to a dimly lit room that bustled with activity. Technicians rushed all over the place. Some worked busily at their console stations, which were aligned at either side of a raised steel walkway that stretched toward the center of the room. A few of them acknowledged the lieutenant colonel's presence while he marched down the raised walkway, though they remained focused on their duties.

Lanzard kept his gaze to the front as he headed straight toward a tall, broad-shouldered African American man who stood at the end of the walkway, working on an isolated holographic console. The man wore the same high-tech black uniform as everyone else, except his included the major rank lines insignia on his shoulders. He didn't hesitate when the lieutenant colonel stopped beside him.

"What's the status, Major?" Lanzard asked.

"Three UFOs coming our way from the northeast, sir," Major Theron O'Malley answered, his hands moving busily over the projected console in front of him. His gaze remained fixed on the movie-theater-sized holographic screen that hovered at the front of the room. "They're approaching at great speed at an altitude of 150 feet," he added.

Lanzard glanced at the holo screen. It showed a grid map with Mona Island at the bottom left and three red dots representing the UFOs at the top far right. According to the visual data, the dots were 15.3 miles away from the island and approaching fast.

"All right. Give me a closer visual," Lanzard ordered.

O'Malley tapped several keys, selecting the three red dots on the holo screen. A second later, the enhanced frame took over the whole projection, and the dots disappeared, revealing the images of the flying objects. They looked like small aircraft, but it was hard to tell if they were piloted or if they were drones.

"Where did they come from?" Lanzard asked.

"Based on their angle, they must have come out of Ramey Airport," O'Malley replied.

Lanzard grimaced, still staring at the image. "Ramey? Then why aren't they identified? Are they even piloted?"

"We don't know yet, sir, but we're working on it," O'Malley assured him. "Either way, a small squadron is armed and ready to intercept them."

Lanzard ran a wrinkled hand through his cropped white hair and frowned. Could it be what he feared? Had someone found his secret base? It wasn't probable, but not impossible, either.

Not letting his thoughts distract him from his responsibility, Lanzard shook his head and pressed the small microphone attached to his left ear.

"Attention, everyone. This is Lieutenant Colonel Lanzard." His voice was amplified throughout the room and across all the areas of the base. "On my mark, I'm ordering the assigned squadron to intercept the approaching bogeys. I repeat, I am ordering the assigned squadron to—"

"Lieutenant! *Wait!*" a voice interjected from a distance.

Lanzard and O'Malley turned around. The technicians at the stations raised their gazes to Natalia Salas, a uniformed woman with red hair tied in a businesslike bun. She was rushing down the raised walkway, toward the lieutenant colonel.

Salas paused to catch her breath before she spoke. "Lieutenant, Agent Venus is online from Ramey Airport. She strongly insists that you hold the squadron."

Lanzard frowned. "Agent Venus?" he repeated, acknowledging the code name of his secret agent. "Patch her in."

Salas nudged her way between Lanzard and O'Malley and tapped a code into the console in front of them. Then she stepped back.

"Venus?" Lanzard spoke into the console.

"Colonel, hold the squadron!" The insistent voice of Agent Venus crackled through the console's speaker. *"Do not send the squadron. I repeat, do not send the squadron!"*

Lanzard and O'Malley exchanged confused glances.

"Give me one good reason, Agent," Lanzard demanded.

"They're air racers, sir, and they're just kids!" Agent Venus responded.

Everyone in the room froze.

"Say again, Agent?" Lanzard leaned closer to the speaker. Had he heard wrong?

The reply was clear and reassuring. *"They're just kids!"*

CHAPTER 2

4:15 p.m.
A mile off the west coast of Aguadilla, Puerto Rico

It was a perfect day to be in the sky, with its brilliant azure color extending as far as the eye could see. Several cumulus clouds, white as cotton, moved peacefully northeastward, like silent creatures floating in the air. Most of them were small, yet one was so big it resembled a gigantic bloated mountain.

Suddenly, from the center of the giant cloud—*WHOOSH!*—two small aircraft shot out and raced through the sky. Both were T-shaped, had long sharp noses, and sported twin engines, curved wings at the back, and bottom rudders. The only difference between them was their paint jobs. One was metallic blue with small yellow accents, and the other was the opposite.

Their pilots, two fourteen-year-old identical twin boys, flew side by side and close to each other. Owen Viviani, who piloted the metallic-blue racer, pushed his tinted eye visor over his helmet and glanced left toward his brother in the other craft.

"Lance, do you see Keithan?"

"No," his brother replied through the helmet's integrated communicator piece. *"I've no idea where he went."*

Owen could see his brother looking left and right from his cockpit. "I don't get it. He was right in front of us a moment ago, right before we flew around Mona."

"*Forget about him,*" Lance insisted. "*Keithan must've gotten lost when we entered the clouds. Let's focus on winning the race.*"

Owen sneered and pulled his eye visor back over his eyes. "You got it. Let's make Keithan look like a fool this time."

The twins flipped their aircraft in perfect synchronization and dove straight into one of the small clouds, their engines disintegrating it instantly. It was then that the coast of Aguadilla came into view, along with the Atlantic Ocean, which stretched to the north and west. The entire coast was a combination of different green patches and residential grids, all of which surrounded the elongated area of an airport.

"There it is," Owen said into his communicator. "Ramey."

"*Okay, Owen. Locate the finish ring on the runway,*" his brother said.

"Copy that."

Owen activated his head-up display by pressing a blue circular button to his right. It made a small virtual screen appear on the glass of his canopy, showing him a much closer look of Ramey Airport's main runway. Owen moved the image, using a thumb-sized joystick on his left panel while keeping one hand on one of his steering yokes. Once he located the finish ring, he pressed the joystick down to zoom in on the image.

The finish ring, with its checkered pattern, was visible on the tiny screen. It hovered about ten feet from the ground at the free-landing area of Ramey Airport.

"Finish ring located and locked on my screen," Owen said into his helmet's microphone. "How about you, Lance?"

"*Locking it on my screen right now. Get ready to dive with full power. I'll let you pass through the ring first.*"

"Got it. We've just reached the 5,000-foot altitude limit. Wait a second ..."

"*What's wrong?*"

Owen glanced left and right. "Do you hear that?"

He could hear a third aircraft, but where was it coming from?

Then …

"Watch out!" Lance shouted.

The twins threw their aircraft hard to opposite sides as a third craft, a composition of orange and exposed metal, with battered parts all weathered and somewhat roughly joined, rushed past from underneath them. Its deafening sound was a mixture of crackling roars and thunder rumbling. It was a one-man racer but with triple engines, one at the back and the other two on top of its small wings, which angled downward behind the cockpit. Yet what stood out most about the craft were its two crab-like arms, which extended forward from the lower sides of the fuselage, holding a pair of independent steering vanes.

There was only one person who the twins knew would dare to fly such a machine …

"It's Keithan!" Lance yelled desperately. *"FULL POWER! FULL POWER!"*

The two boys, now furious, pushed their throttles, sending their craft down sharply after their opponent's.

"Hey, guys. Did you miss me?" Keithan's cocky voice said.

"Shut up, Keithan!" Lance's voice echoed in Owen's earpiece.

"Yeah! Shut up!" Owen repeated, full of anger. "We still have two thousand feet to go. We can still beat you."

It was easier said than done. Owen and Lance were having a hard time trying to gain on Keithan. Owen felt drops of sweat trickling down his forehead. He dove fast, gripping his yokes tighter as he felt the wind turbulence against his aircraft. He glanced at his brother to his left and noticed him looking straight ahead.

When Owen managed a glimpse, his altimeter read 2,700 feet in neon-green numbers. Yet the numbers were changing fast, much faster than the countdown of a bomb.

Owen clenched his teeth. He, Lance, and Keithan were only seconds away from reaching the airport's grounds. There was no need to keep looking at the finish ring from his head-up display anymore. The ring was visible ahead, the size of a quarter—and Keithan was about to reach it first.

"There's only one way we can win this, Bro," Lance told Owen, his heavy breathing noticeable through the communicator. *"We have to cross in front of Keithan."*

Owen hesitated. "Are you serious?"

"It's the only way."

One thousand feet, Owen noticed in his altimeter. It was either that or accept defeat.

"Let's do it," he answered. "I'll go for the ring. Just tell me when." He took a deep breath and braced himself.

They could do it. They *had* to do it, but they would only get one shot at it. Gradually leveling their racers with the ground, the twins flanked Keithan's silver-and-orange craft. Keithan looked from one twin to the other on either side of him from his cockpit. His face was half-hidden inside his helmet with tinted eye visor.

"Careful, guys. Don't try anything foolish just to win," he taunted them, not sounding the least threatened by the twins' plan.

Owen ignored the comment. "Lance?"

"Now!" Lance shouted.

At approximately 615 feet away from the finish ring, Owen and Lance arced their aircraft toward Keithan's front end. Yet, a split second before they could cross in front of him, blue-and-white flames burst out of Keithan's middle engine, accompanied by a powerful whine. Keithan passed them so fast he didn't even give the twins an instant to improvise.

Then—*SWOOSH!*—Keithan's aircraft shot straight through the finish ring.

"How did he—?" Owen cried, jerking his head back, but Lance cut him off when he noticed trouble ahead.

"Owen! The ring! You're gonna hit it!"

CHAPTER 3

"Woo-hoo!" thirteen-year-old Keithan Quintero shouted as his racing aircraft, the *d'Artagnan*, shot straight through the hovering finish ring like a bullet through a bull's-eye. To his right, a small crowd of boys and girls in orange and blue unisuits threw their hands in the air when he zoomed past them in a blur. Keithan saluted them from his cockpit even though he was already several yards away and had activated the antigravity force. In response, the *d'Artagnan* bounced slightly without touching the runway and continued rushing forward, hovering three feet above the ground.

Suddenly, the loud crash of metal against metal made Keithan jump. He turned his head, but because he was still unable to see, he rotated the twin steering yokes all the way to the right and made the craft pivot 180 degrees while still hovering down the runway. It was then that he saw what had happened.

Owen's aircraft had hit the finish ring with its left wing, sending metal pieces of both the ring and the wing in all directions. The impact forced the craft to stray off the runway toward the left, over the grass. Meanwhile, the ring threw sparks and made small explosions from its circuits before it lost all power and fell to the ground with a heavy thud.

Fortunately, Owen had managed to activate the antigravity force in time to prevent crashing, yet everyone in the crowd gasped in horror as Owen's damaged aircraft hovered out of control across the grass.

"Owen!" Keithan shouted in shock into his communicator. "Owen!

Are you all right?"

No reply.

The twin's craft continued hovering all the way to the pond beyond the main runway and fell nose-first into the water. About seventy feet away from it, Lance landed his aircraft and rushed out of it to get to his brother. Several boys were already hurrying to Owen's craft.

Keithan pulled the landing gear lever once the *d'Artagnan* came to a stop and quickly settled the craft on the ground. He took off his racing helmet and ran a hand through the jet-black hair plastered to his head while he allowed his honey eyes to adjust to the intense sunlight. Following that, he took off his seat restraints. As soon as his cockpit canopy swung open, he jumped out of the *d'Artagnan.*

He would have expected his best friends to come and congratulate him, but under the circumstances, Keithan headed to them instead. He spotted Fernando and Marianna at the locals' free-landing area along with the rest of the crowd. They were gazing far at Owen's ruined aircraft. Fernando, a blond and spiky-haired boy, sat on his customized powered wheelchair, shading his eyes with both hands. He glanced over his shoulder as Keithan approached before he returned his gaze to what was happening at the pond. His sister, Marianna, on the other hand, didn't notice Keithan coming. She kept staring at the pond, recording everything with a viewscreen headset and a small globe-shaped camera, which hovered at eye level next to her. It was hard not to notice her from a distance since she stood out from the crowd, not just because of her short brown-and-pink hair, which was layered and flicked out at the ends, but also because she was the only one there wearing casual clothes.

"You think Owen is okay?" Keithan asked as he stopped next to Marianna and Fernando.

"Man, I hope so," Fernando replied.

The three of them watched while Lance and several other boys tried to pull Owen's aircraft out of the pond without success. Seconds later, Owen's cockpit canopy opened. Keithan expected to see the twin hurt, but instead, he saw a furious Owen jump out of his aircraft and land in the pond with a splash. Lance, already half-submerged, tried to calm his brother down, but Owen pushed him away and started kicking his damaged craft.

"At least he doesn't seem to be hurt," Marianna said.

Fernando and Keithan snorted as the twins spotted them.

"Uh-oh. Here comes trouble," Fernando said.

"YOU!" Owen shouted from a distance, his face red with rage. He pointed toward them, though it was obvious that he was pointing at Keithan.

Marianna continued recording. She focused her small hover camera on Owen while he marched toward Keithan with his twin brother. The two were soaked up to their waists, and they left a trail of dripping water behind them as they crossed the main runway.

"Maybe you should start running, Keithan," Fernando suggested while he pushed his wheelchair back and turned to face his friend.

"Are you crazy? And miss Owen acting like that?" Keithan said. He turned to Fernando's sister. "Keep recording, Marianna."

"Shut that camera off, Marianna!" Owen snapped.

He tried to snatch the hovering camera, but Marianna managed to move it away in time. Still recording, she stepped back to get a better shot of the Viviani twins, who halted in front of Keithan. The crowd hurried to gather around them.

"This is all your fault, Quintero!" Owen shouted. He and Lance stood tall in front of Keithan, who, despite his slightly athletic-built body, was a whole foot shorter than the two. Their broad shoulders didn't allow Keithan to see behind them. It would have been hard to tell them apart for whoever didn't know them, for not only were Owen and Lance identical, with short curly black hair and pale pink skin, but they were also wearing identical blue pilot unisuits of Ramey Academy.

Their jock look didn't intimidate Keithan one bit even though they looked way too big to fit inside the cockpit of a one-man racing craft.

"*My* fault? I didn't crash your aircraft," Keithan shot back at Owen with a smirk that seemed to anger the twin even more.

Owen threw his hands at Keithan like a wild beast about to strangle him, but Lance held him back.

"Yeah! Fight! Fight!" shouted a few boys in the crowd, quickly making others join in.

"FIGHT! FIGHT! FIGHT! FIGHT!"

"You were lucky this time, Quintero!" Lance said over the loud chorus. He struggled to hold a furious Owen. "This isn't going to end like this!"

"Oh, I think it *does* end like this. Your brother broke the finish ring, remember?" And with that, Keithan walked away.

Most of the boys and girls watching the confrontation cheered while only a few remained silent. Gradually, the crowd dispersed.

On Keithan's way back to the *d'Artagnan*, several teens hurried up to congratulate him. One of them tapped Keithan on the back.

"Awesome race, Quintero," told him Cameron Brooks, who was a year older than Keithan, before he walked away.

"Yeah. Way better than the Aerial Nationals on TV," added a twelve-year-old girl with blonde hair and orange unisuit, but Keithan didn't know her name.

Moments later, it was Fernando and Marianna who caught up with him.

"Do you have to be that cocky when you win?" Marianna asked.

Keithan glanced at her over his shoulder as he unzipped the front of his blue flight suit down to his chest. "Oh, come on, Marianna. I'm not the bad guy. Owen and Lance were the ones who claimed to be the best air racers in our level. Somebody had to prove them wrong."

"Yeah. But now what? You're gonna claim that title?" Marianna said.

Keithan didn't answer. The thought had crossed his mind. He grinned, but it only made his two best friends grimace.

This wasn't something new to Fernando and Marianna; Keithan knew they were already used to his cockiness. After all, they'd known him since Keithan and Fernando were eight years old, Marianna a year younger. Keithan and Fernando had met first. It had been on their first day at Ramey Academy of Flight and Aeroengineering. Their relationship had eventually led Keithan to meet Marianna. She, however, wasn't a student at the academy. She went to a public school outside of Ramey.

"You know, I wonder if it would've been best if one of the twins had won instead of you," Marianna commented while watching Keithan continue alone toward the *d'Artagnan*.

Fernando stopped his wheelchair next to her. "I wonder that too, Sis. Still, you gotta admit, the Viviani twins had it coming even though Keithan acts like them sometimes." He said the last part loud enough for Keithan to hear.

"Remind me then why we hang out with him."

This time Keithan replied, "*Because*, unlike Owen and Lance, I'm a good guy."

Both Fernando and Marianna gave him sour looks while they stared at Keithan's cocky smile.

"Now, come on!" Keithan insisted. "Let's go to Rocket's Diner and celebrate my victory with three caramel cola floats—my treat."

CHAPTER 4

Rocket's Diner was a popular place, not just among Ramey locals but among foreigners as well. Located opposite to the airport's north entrance and the arched passenger terminal at Hangar Road, it was the main spot for many pilots to eat and relax while they exchanged stories to pass the time, whether after they had landed or before they left for what could be a long flight. Only on weekdays in the afternoons, though, if a pilot were to look for some peace and quiet, Rocket's Diner wasn't the ideal place, as it tended to be packed with students from Ramey Academy. The students gathered there to release stress after classes, either by enjoying burgers, pizzas, sandwiches, and milkshakes, or simply by spending their money playing different virtual video games there.

The diner, open 24/7, could be easily spotted due to its distinctive retro sign on top of it: a large copper rocket with the diner's name in lit art deco lettering. Sloping glass windows made up the building's elliptical façade. They provided customers a wide view of Ramey Airport and all types of aircraft arriving and taking off.

As expected, when Keithan, Fernando, and Marianna got there, they found the place already full of students from the academy. There were a few adults at several tables, some of them pilots, and a couple of short serving robots with wheels moving all around, bringing plates and beverages to customers.

"Well, well! The young illegal air racing champion has finally arrived!" said Mr. Rocket, the diner's owner, from behind the counter at the far end. He was a large yet friendly-looking man with a pouchy face and a Vandyke beard as white as his chef uniform, which included a traditional diner hat.

"Hi, Mr. Rocket," Keithan replied over the noise of the people talking and the music playing in the background.

He and Fernando headed to the counter while Marianna went over to a group of girls that were gathered around the octagonal hockey table.

"Save me a seat. I'll be right there," Marianna told Keithan and Fernando before she reached the girls.

Keithan pushed aside one of the metal stools so Fernando's wheelchair would fit. Meanwhile, Fernando pressed a button underneath his armrest, adjusting his seat so he could rest his elbows comfortably on the counter.

"So how are you doing, Fernando? Still watching your fearless pal break the rules?" Mr. Rocket asked. He shot a teasing glance at Keithan before he placed two plates with delicious-smelling burgers on the counter and let one of the serving robots pick them up.

"More or less," Fernando answered, glancing at Keithan.

"And from that smile on Keithan's face, I assume he dragged you and Marianna here to celebrate," Mr. Rocket added.

Fernando was about to answer, but Keithan spoke first. "Yep, with three caramel cola floats," he said proudly.

Mr. Rocket arched his eyebrows. "Ah, a young air racer's victory drink. Coming right up."

"With extra caramel," Fernando and Keithan added in unison.

"You got it," said Mr. Rocket, his back to the boys. He picked up three milkshake glasses, along with an ice cream scoop, and started working on the floats.

Mr. Rocket's floats and milkshakes were famous—not just at Ramey, but in many parts of the world. Even though it was 2055, Mr. Rocket was one of the few who still preferred to make them the old-fashioned way: by hand instead of using automatic shake machines or robots. Yet the main reason his shakes and floats were so famous was due to the numerous articles that had been published about them. It had all started five years ago, when a well-respected food critic from New York had arrived at Ramey, tried the beverages, and fascinated by them, insisted on writing about them. Copies of those articles were visible on the walls throughout the diner, highlighting the delicious beverages, as well as Mr. Rocket's success. Thanks to all that recognition, pilots from every part of the world made an effort to do a stopover at Ramey to enjoy the shakes and floats.

"So, Keithan," Mr. Rocket said while he filled half of the glasses with cola, "rumor has it that you and the Viviani twins managed to carry out an air race without permission and that one of the twins crashed into one of the academy's finish rings."

Keithan nodded. "I'm not happy about the accident, but you should have seen it, Mr. Rocket."

"It was a total mess," Fernando added.

"I'll say."

Both Keithan and Fernando turned their heads when Marianna got into the conversation. She placed her camera bag on the counter and sat next to Keithan.

"How did it happen?" Mr. Rocket gave Keithan a suspicious look while he poured caramel syrup into each of the float glasses.

"It wasn't my fault," Keithan said before Mr. Rocket had a chance to make him feel guilty about it. "Owen and Lance tried to cross in front of me at less than two hundred feet away from the finish ring but failed to do it. I tell you, Mr. Rocket, if it hadn't been for Fernando, who finished improving the *d'Artagnan*'s middle engine yesterday, the twins and I would have crashed—and the race would have ended a lot worse."

"I told you the middle engine would work better if I improved the afterburner's igniters," Fernando remarked.

"Luckily, nobody got hurt," Marianna told Mr. Rocket, "though Owen's aircraft lost its left wing. I got it all on video."

Mr. Rocket served the vanilla ice cream scoops into each of the glasses and poured whipped cream onto them. He placed the three floats in front of Keithan, Fernando, and Marianna and began pouring the extra caramel over the whipped cream. The three friends licked their lips while they watched. The three caramel cola floats looked like masterpieces.

"Well, my friends," said Mr. Rocket, finally sliding them their floats, "the only thing I can tell you is that you know pilot students are not allowed to air race outside class hours. So, Keithan, I hope you enjoy your victory drink because I have a feeling it could be the last one for a while. That is, once the headmaster and your father find out you were air racing illegally—again."

Keithan smirked, not worried at all. He was in such a great mood to let that thought ruin the moment. He remembered the first time he and the twins had gotten into trouble for air racing without permission. It had been nearly six months ago. That time, they weren't able to finish the race, all because the headmaster and several professors of the academy found out about it before Keithan and the twins could have been able to reach the finish ring. Fortunately, that hadn't been the case today. Today, Keithan had won an air race, and not only that, he had beaten the Viviani twins. He showed them they weren't as perfect as they annoyingly claimed. For now, that was all that mattered to Keithan.

Holding his caramel cola float with one hand and its red straw with the other, Keithan took a moment to forget about everything and everyone around him and simply drank his float with pure bliss. Its refreshing, sweet, and creamy taste relaxed him instantly. The float was so delicious Keithan had to concentrate on it for a few more seconds. He could even feel it filling him with energy as it went down his throat. An energy that only air racing champions could taste, Keithan imagined.

Fernando and Marianna also enjoyed their caramel cola floats passionately at either side of him. As the three of them continued drinking, they gazed to the far left of the diner where a group of boys and girls from the academy gathered. The boys and girls seemed to be all excited about a display on the wall.

"What's going on over there?" Keithan asked Mr. Rocket.

"Oh, *that*," Mr. Rocket said with a sudden look of excitement on his face. "That's the latest news at Ramey. Go ahead, take a look."

Deeply intrigued, Keithan took his caramel cola float with him and headed to the group of boys and girls. He gently pushed his way through them until he reached a digital poster screen on the wall. His honey eyes opened wide in disbelief when he saw what was on the screen.

The digital poster showed a 3-D animation of a rotating stallion bust in silver and gold with a long wing wide open. Underneath it, in a shiny metallic font, it read:

Experience the rush! Feel the adrenaline!
Live the excitement!
THE 2055 PEGASUS AIR RACE
at Ramey Airport
Aguadilla, Puerto Rico

Keithan immediately turned around and raised himself over the crowd as best he could to look at Mr. Rocket. "Are you serious?" he shouted to him.

"Very cool, eh?" Mr. Rocket replied over the noise, still behind the counter. "A man from Pegasus Company brought it in this morning and insisted on displaying it. Of course I had to say yes."

Keithan looked from Mr. Rocket to the poster screen and back to Mr. Rocket. "The Pegasus Air Race. *The* Pegasus Air Race?" He reread it and still couldn't believe it. "Here, in Puerto Rico—and at Ramey?"

"*What?*" Marianna and Fernando almost choked on their floats. Fernando immediately rotated his wheelchair and hurried to the digital ad. Marianna went right behind him.

"No way! How is it that it hasn't been announced anywhere else?" Fernando said rhetorically, staring at the poster.

"This is incredible!" Marianna grinned.

"I know. And you know what that means, right?" Keithan told her.

Marianna turned to him with a questioning look, though her expression changed when she realized what Keithan was thinking. "You want to be in it."

Keithan smirked. At first, he thought Marianna would oppose and tell him that he was crazy, but he noticed a slight look of approval while she stared at him thoughtfully, as if imagining how cool the idea actually sounded.

Fernando, on the other hand, didn't react the same way. "You can't possibly be serious about that, Keithan."

"Oh, come on, Fernando," Marianna interjected. She paused to take a sip from her float. "Why not?"

Fernando did his best to sound rational. "Um, I don't know if you guys are aware, but the Pegasus Air Race is a professional race. I mean, Keithan, think about it—"

"I *am* thinking about it!" Keithan cut him off, sure that his face glowed with excitement. "Being in the Pegasus Air Race, one of the coolest and most famous air races in the world, and the same in which my mom became famous … Fernando, I gotta participate with the *d'Artagnan!*"

"Whoa! Hold your thrusters, Keithan!" Mr. Rocket interrupted. He now stood behind the three of them like an erected polar bear with his white diner uniform. "Aren't you aware of what that race really involves? I have to say, I agree with Fernando. The Pegasus Air Race is for racers with well-respected backgrounds, and there's a good reason for that."

"Yeah. Like the numerous and deadly obstacles that they all must pass throughout the aerial racecourse," Fernando insisted, hoping to knock some sense into his best friend. "Keithan, being in that air race wouldn't be at all like competing against Owen and Lance. You would be competing against real air racers."

"That's exactly the kind of challenge I should be looking for if I want to become a real air racer too—just like my mom was." Keithan took a sip from his float. "Fernando, if I go for it, I'm definitely going to need your help. So think about it."

Mr. Rocket rolled his eyes, giving up on trying to reason with Keithan. The fact was Keithan had made it clear right away; he wasn't going to back down from this, especially when the digital poster behind them showed that the Pegasus Air Race was going to be held at Ramey and all around the island of Puerto Rico.

Keithan was well aware it was a dangerous race. The best pilots in the world dared to risk it all in it just to go beyond the limits of air racing, and more than that, to win the glory every one of them dreamed about. Keithan wanted to be part of that too. Sure, he was only a pilot student, but he was in the elite Air Racing Program of Ramey Academy, and to Keithan, that had to count for something. More than that, he couldn't let this opportunity pass when he and Fernando had the *d'Artagnan*—the fastest racing aircraft in the academy, at least to them.

Keithan needed to be in that race or participate in its preceding qualifier tournament at the very least. He couldn't explain it, but he felt it called to him. Air racing was in his blood, all thanks to his mother.

Keithan took another sip from his cola float before he said, "Come on, Fernando. We have to participate. You know I could never do this without your help. Right, Marianna?"

Marianna nodded, her lips puckered while she drank her float.

"Well," Fernando huffed, "we would have to prepare the *d'Artagnan* and make sure she has all the specifications required for the race. We could also make some improvements to her, like what I did with the middle engine's afterburner."

"Definitely," said Keithan, starting to sense hope in his friend. "We could even ask your dad to help us. I'm sure he would love to be part of it."

"And what about *me*? I want to be part of it too," Marianna cut in. "I may not know anything about improving a racing craft, but I could record the whole preparation process until the day of the race. You know what? I'll be right back."

Marianna handed Keithan her cola float and went back to the

counter to bring her camera bag. She pulled out her viewscreen headset and put it on. Then she took out her small globe-shaped camera and turned it on, making it hover in front of her.

"What are you doing?" Fernando asked.

"I'm going to start recording the process right now," she told him.

Keithan, Fernando, and Mr. Rocket watched as Marianna pressed a button on her headset and the hover camera turned its lens toward the digital poster announcing the Pegasus Air Race.

"Okay," said Marianna, already recording while she adjusted the tiny microphone attached to her headset. "Just a few minutes ago, Keithan, my older brother Fernando, and I found out that the famous Pegasus Air Race will be held here at Ramey Airport this year. We've been discussing whether Keithan should be in the race." Curiously, she spoke like a newscaster. "So far, Keithan and I agree that Keithan should go for it, and we look forward to becoming a team to get him and the *d'Artagnan* ready. The only one left to confirm is Fernando."

Marianna pressed another button on her headset and made the hover camera rotate on the spot to face her brother. "So what will it be, Fernando?"

Fernando hesitated. "Um …"

"Come on, Fernando," Keithan insisted. "We can do this. We can make the *d'Artagnan* the fastest aircraft in the Pegasus Air Race—and I can fly it!"

Fernando rubbed his forehead.

"Just say yes," Marianna urged.

Fernando stammered. Then he shook his head and sighed. "Oh, all right. I'm in."

"YES!" Keithan and Marianna shouted.

Twice as excited as he had been when he had gotten to the diner, Keithan handed Marianna her float back and raised his.

"And so, the next race … the Pegasus Air Race!" Keithan announced.

The trio clinked their float glasses.

Behind them, Mr. Rocket gave a deep sigh. "Well, good luck, then," he said in a warning tone, making them turn. "Especially to you, Keithan. Just hope that the headmaster or any of the professors from the academy don't take away your pilot certificate when they find out you were air racing without permission again."

Keithan snorted. "Don't worry. Just wait and see, Mr. Rocket. Nothing is going to stop me from being in that race. Nothing."

CHAPTER 5

There was little activity going on at the airfield, no departures or takeoffs. Only a few workers doing their routine inspections could be seen either at different parts of the main runway or on the group of twin-fuselage airliners that were parked in front of the passenger terminal and the main hangars. A metallic-red-and-black turbo hoverbike, however, caught some of the workers' attention as it rushed past the airliners at an acceleration of one hundred miles per hour, and it was driven by Ramey Academy professor Alexandria Dantés.

Dantés kept a straight course, satisfying her need for speed as she drove eastward. She could feel the intense heat of the Caribbean afternoon sun on her back even though the tinted visor of her helmet made the airfield look to her as if it were under a clouded sky.

Once Dantés passed the last of the main hangars with the twin-fuselage airliners, she leaned her body hard to the left, along with her vehicle, and made a sharp turn. It was then that a series of residential hangars aligned near the chain-link fence that surrounded the whole airport came into view. The hangars were arched and half the size of the main ones. Originally built for military purposes during the Aerial War of the 2020s, these old buildings had housed fighter pilots and tech crews along with their craft and mechanical equipment. Yet today, they belonged to civilians after the United States Air Force had decommissioned them at the end of the war.

Each residential hangar had a different number preceded by the letter H, and one by one, Dantés counted them as she zoomed past.

H1 … H2 … H3 …

With a squeeze of the decelerator on the right handlebar, the hoverbike came to a stop in front of the hangar marked H11. Alexandria Dantés removed her helmet, letting her tousled, light-brown sideswept hair cascade over her shoulders. She dismounted the hoverbike by swinging her right leg and brought her wrist communicator close to her mouth.

"Engine off," she spoke into the device, and in response, the bike's engine shut down, and the vehicle touched the ground.

The thirty-five-year-old British professor proceeded to walk toward the hangar in front of her. All the while, she kept her usual fierce look, which complemented her authoritative-looking, gray flight suit and calf-high boots, distinctive of all the professors of Ramey Academy.

Dantés couldn't help but stare with curiosity at Hangar H11. The building stood out from the rest of the residential hangars, not only because it looked as if it were the oldest one there, but mostly because of its unique design. At first glance, it resembled a giant and weathered armadillo carapace, segmented into three main divisions. Its middle section stood higher than the other two, and it consisted of a series of glass roof panels. To its left side stood a metal-plated annex shaped like an igloo. It included a terrace at its top enclosed with a metal railing. There, at that annex, Dantés spotted a small door. She decided to approach it since the main entrance of the hangar was closed.

The green light on a switch told Dantés that the door was unlocked, and so she opened it.

"Hello?" she called as she entered. It took a few seconds before someone responded.

"Yeah. I'll be right there," said a male voice through a hallway at the other end of the room.

Dantés was inside what appeared to be a small and unusual office. It was unlike any other she had ever seen, and everything there seemed to suggest only one thing: this was clearly the office of a huge science-fiction aficionado.

An alien-type flying saucer, like the ones that appeared in old black-and-white movies, hovered silently over the top-left corner of an aluminum desk in front of her. The desk itself caught Dantés's attention. It was made from the wing of an aircraft. On the opposite corner of the desk stood a metal, retro-style rocket lamp with tiny red fins like the ones that used to appear in the two-dimensional cartoons from the 1950s.

There were more science-fiction collectibles—a lot more. Behind the desk, dominating the wall, stood an aluminum and mahogany shelf with a display of over twenty spaceship model replicas and robot figures from famous movies. To the left, practically covering the entire concave wall adjacent to the shelf, was a collection of old science-fiction ship blueprints. A digital picture frame showed a slideshow of old movie poster prints of the same genre.

"Wow!" Dantés muttered. She couldn't keep her eyes on one thing. There was so much stuff to see in that small office it was overwhelming.

The entire collection seemed childish. Ironically, Dantés found it interesting. She had a certain respect for science fiction, though not in an extremely fanatic way as the owner of this office seemed to show. Dantés was aware of the impact science fiction had in modern society. After all, for years the genre had motivated and inspired many men and women to transform the world with many technological advances, especially in the field she knew best: aviation.

Dantés continued looking around the office, keeping a straight posture with her hands behind her back. She felt as if she were in a museum. Curiously, the wall at the right, the only flat wall there and which connected to the hangar, was the only thing in the room that lacked the decorative science-fiction theme. Instead, it had a large bulletin board with numerous old newspaper clippings that shared the same topic: sightings of unidentified flying objects throughout the island of Puerto Rico. There was something else that caught Dantés's attention, and she approached it.

It was an eighteen-by-thirty-six-inch electronic poster sheet about an upcoming event. Dantés immediately recognized the winged-stallion trophy that rotated within the digital image, yet she stared in disbelief at what was written underneath it in bold, metallic lettering.

"The 2055 Pegasus Air Race. This year at … *Ramey?*" she muttered, pausing. "Where did this come from?"

"Fascinating, isn't it?" someone said behind Dantés, making her jump.

Dantés turned around on the spot and found a man about her height. The man brought with him a strong scent of diesel and motor exhaust. He was wearing a pair of old welding goggles over his long and raggedy gray hair, which he had tied back in a ponytail. His calloused hands, as well as most of his clothes, were stained with black grease, and he rubbed them with a piece of cloth, though it didn't seem to do much to clean them.

The man nodded to the air race poster. "A man from Pegasus Company brought it in this morning," he told Dantés and chuckled. "Sorry if I startled you."

"It's all right. I didn't hear you come in," Dantés said in her British accent, embarrassed. "Are you Mr. Aramis?"

"Yes. William Aramis. How may I help you?"

"My name is—"

"Oh, I know very well who you are, Miss Dantés," Mr. Aramis cut her off. "Your advanced flight training courses at Ramey Academy are well known throughout this airport. Nevertheless, I know you better from your participation in the International Air Race Cup from 2037, in which you won the title of youngest pilot to have ever been allowed to participate in a pro air race."

Dantés gave a faint smile. The man's words made her think back to that year when—hard to believe—she was rebellious and stupidly daring.

Those were the good old days, she reminded herself.

"So how may I help you?" Mr. Aramis asked, bringing her back from her thoughts.

"I'm looking for your son Fernando."

Mr. Aramis frowned. "Is he in trouble?"

"Oh, no, sir. But his best friend Keithan Quintero is, and I was hoping that your son could tell me where I could—"

"Keithan! Of course," Mr. Aramis cut her off again, but this time with a sigh of relief. "That's what can be expected from that *chico* almost every time—him getting into trouble."

"Is your son here?" Dantés asked.

"Yep—and Keithan too. They got here half an hour ago with my daughter, Mari—"

At that moment, a digital voice coming from Mr. Aramis's desk interrupted him.

"Incoming call. Incoming call," the voice said. The next instant, a hologram appeared over a small projector on the desk.

Both Mr. Aramis and Dantés turned their heads. The hologram showed the small bust of an odd-looking man with a handlebar mustache as white as cotton and red-lensed glasses.

"Good afternoon, Mr. Aramis," said the man with a noticeable Dutch accent. *"This is Jeroen Luzier speaking. I am calling about the progress of the Daedalus Project—"*

"Oh! Excuse me," Mr. Aramis told Dantés. He hurried to his desk and tapped the holo projector to silence it. He looked back at Dantés. "Sorry about that. Um … feel free to go through that door behind you, Miss Dantés. Y-you'll find the boys at the far end of the hangar."

He pointed to the door next to the bulletin board and the air race poster. For some reason, he had a nervous look on his face now, and it was as if he were waiting for Dantés to leave so he could take the call in private. Not wanting to make him feel uncomfortable, Dantés smiled at Mr. Aramis, thanked him, and went through the door.

The air on the other side felt much warmer, and there was a strong smell of diesel and motor exhaust. The low humming of a generator somewhere nearby resounded all around due to the acoustics of the area. Steel girders, sheeted with galvanized steel, composed the arched interior of the hangar, and high above in the middle top section of the ceiling, a grid of curved and frosted glass panels provided the area with natural lighting.

Dantés walked across the hangar and couldn't help but notice a series of small aircraft not too far to her left. There were four in all, and they were all in different stages of completion. The strangest thing about them was that they were unlike any modern aircraft. They were prototypes, probably inventions Mr. Aramis was working on. One of them looked like a roughly built saucer about the size of a car, with a small jet engine at its top and a vertical stabilizer intersecting it at the back. Another one resembled a spider but with long wings at its top, extended to the sides.

All in all, the four prototypes looked as if they had come out of the mind of a wild and crazy inventor, which reflected Mr. Aramis's fascination with science fiction.

Just as Mr. Aramis had told her, Dantés found Keithan, Fernando, and Fernando's sister at the other end of the hangar. A sturdy, medium-sized golden retriever accompanied them, lying next to the girl with brown-and-pink hair. None of them noticed Dantés approaching. They were next to their silver-and-orange aircraft, watching a video hologram that was being projected from one of the armrests of Fernando's wheelchair. To Dantés's luck, it was the video proof she needed to see to confirm what Keithan Quintero had been doing this afternoon.

"Whoa!" the three youngsters exclaimed in a chorus when they saw the scene where Owen Viviani's craft hit the academy's finish ring. Even the golden retriever reacted, raising her head and barking.

Meanwhile, Dantés watched silently. She remained about five feet behind them with her arms folded.

"Hello, boys," she finally spoke.

The three friends and the golden retriever turned their heads simultaneously.

"—and girl," Dantés added when she saw the girl shoot her a sharp look.

"Professor Dantés!" Keithan exclaimed with his eyes wide open. He hesitated before he jumped to his feet. He reached for Fernando's armchair and turned off the holo projector, which flickered before it disappeared.

"Wha-what are you doing here? I mean, still at the airport," Keithan stammered. "It's five o'clock. Isn't the academy closed?"

"Closed to students," Dantés corrected him. She kept her deep gaze at Keithan, who was trying to keep his best innocent look though with not much success.

"Then … you probably know about this afternoon's race," Keithan said.

"That is correct, Mr. Quintero."

"Even who won?"

"Even how the academy's finish ring was broken, which I just saw on the video hologram."

Neither Keithan nor his friends dared to reply. Keithan's jaw dropped. It was priceless. He knew he was caught. Dantés even found it amusing, yet she did her best not to reveal a smile.

"Now, Mr. Quintero, if you would be kind enough to follow me … Oh, and bring your pilot certificate."

"You're in so much trouble, Keithan," said the girl with brown-and-pink hair in a low teasing voice.

Keithan looked as if he wanted to say something back, but instead, he shot the girl a look of annoyance over his shoulder. Without any other choice, he took a deep breath and silently followed Dantés out of the hangar.

CHAPTER 6

Keithan couldn't help feeling uncomfortable riding on Dantés's hoverbike, worse still, holding on to the fit waist of the professor while she drove back to the academy. *Man, I hope nobody sees me*, was all Keithan thought along the way. Fortunately, at the speed Dantés drove, it would be hard for anyone to recognize him behind his professor. Dantés drove so fast it only took her less than a minute to reach the academy.

Ramey Academy of Flight and Aeroengineering was located on the other side of the airport. As many people commented, it contrasted its plain surroundings beyond its architecture, for it was a vivid reflection of its prestigious reputation. Not that Keithan knew much about architecture, but he knew the academy was known for having trained some of the best pilots and aeroengineers in the world. The academy's main building, mostly flat white with several navy-blue and gray areas, consisted of a three-piece disk shape on a twenty-foot-high cylindrical base from which a wide stairway stood. At its northwest side was the bay's annex: an elongated and curved building where students parked their craft during classes. The academy even had its own control tower, though it stood at a distance, connected to the main building by an enclosed bridge made of a stretched web of steel tensors and curved glass panels.

Dantés parked the hoverbike in front of the entrance stairway and led Keithan inside the academy. They walked down a brightly lit corridor with concave walls that meshed with both the floor and the ceiling. All the while, Dantés and Keithan didn't say a word to each other. It made Keithan feel uncomfortable, especially since there was already a deathly silence in the corridor, but he preferred that than to talk to the professor. The fact was he didn't like Dantés much—and he was sure Dantés didn't like him much, either. As a flight instructor, she was excellent, probably the best professor the academy had (not that Keithan would admit that to her, though). As a person, however, Dantés was stone cold, to such extreme that some students had come to refer to her as Ice Woman without her knowing it.

Keithan had never understood how Dantés could live without the slightest sense of humor. Her seriousness was so natural Keithan could not even remember a single moment at the academy in which he had seen her smile.

It felt weird walking down the academy's corridor at this hour. Compared to when it was crowded with students during between classes, there was a ghostly emptiness now, the air much colder than usual.

At the far end, Dantés and Keithan entered a cylindrical elevator. It took them to the top level, and there the two of them headed down another corridor, only this one was much shorter. It led to a single white door framed in blue light. Up until now, Keithan had remained relaxed, but now he bit his lower lip as he approached the door, which had the words "HEADMASTER'S OFFICE" stenciled on it.

There was only one reason Keithan found himself in this office, and that was when he got into trouble. Today was no exception.

Dantés stopped in front of the door and pressed a button on a small panel next to it. A synthesized female voice spoke through a tiny speaker.

"Please identify yourself," it said.

"It's me, Sally. Dantés," Dantés replied.

The door slid open to the side, and Dantés and Keithan stepped into a small waiting room. Decorating the wall opposite to the entrance was the academy's name with its crest. It was like the one Keithan and

Dantés had on their left shoulder sleeves: a chromed propeller with a copper spinner hub and its twin blades shaped like art deco wings. A female-looking robot with glossy white coverings and blue lights for eyes stared at Keithan and the professor. Its humanoid appearance, however, was only from its waist up, for where its legs should be, there was nothing more than a desk.

The robot straightened as Dantés and Keithan approached. "Welcome back, Professor," it said. "I have informed Headmaster Viviani about your arrival. You may go in."

"Thank you, Sally," Dantés said. She headed to a door behind the robot and waited for it to open. Then she stepped aside and gestured for Keithan to enter.

Keithan went in without looking at Dantés. He passed below a white concept aircraft model that hung from the ceiling and continued toward the headmaster's desk, which stood in front of a wide circular window that gave a clear view of the airfield. Owen and Lance were already there in front of the desk, each one with his hands behind his back and his feet separated shoulder-width apart. They blocked the headmaster from view. The two of them glanced at Keithan over their shoulders and grimaced. Keithan ignored them but froze a few feet behind the twins when he saw the person he least expected to find there …

"Dad," said Keithan, doing his best to keep his cool. He looked from his father to the twins and back to his father.

Caleb Quintero, a tall man in his early forties with a stubble beard and a short Caesar cut almost as dark as his son's jet-black hair, turned to Keithan with an expressionless face but returned his gaze to the headmaster. Meanwhile, the headmaster waited for Keithan to approach. Unlike Keithan's dad, Headmaster Viviani had no hair. His shiny head didn't even show the slightest hint of having had any for a long time.

Viviani stared at Keithan through a pair of high-tech silver glasses shaped like coins. He looked intimidating seated behind his half-cone desk with his fingers laced and holding his chin. Yet it wasn't his appearance what worried Keithan at the moment, but rather the fact that Headmaster Viviani was none other than Owen and Lance's dad.

"Come closer," the headmaster told Keithan in his croaky yet neutral voice. He leaned his head to the side and gestured for Dantés to enter. The door closed behind her. "Keithan," he went on, "as I mentioned a few minutes ago, the airport cameras recorded what happened this afternoon, so there's no need to explain. Luckily, airport security decided to contact me so I would deal with the matter since it involved students from the academy."

"Headmaster, sir," Keithan interrupted. "With all due respect, your sons started it."

"What?" both twins exclaimed in unison, outraged.

Headmaster Viviani raised a hand, silencing them instantly. "I have no interest in knowing whose idea it was to air race without permission after classes. Whoever participated in it is just as responsible. Therefore, due to your actions, I want the three of you, Owen, Lance, and Keithan, to give me your pilot certificates. I'm going to keep them until further notice."

"Until further notice?" Owen protested. "But, Dad—I mean, sir—"

"We're in the middle of our training for our flight sequence test next month," Lance added. "Everyone in our level is getting ready for them."

The flight sequence test? What about the Pegasus Air Race? Keithan wanted to say. He instantly thought of the digital poster at Rocket's Diner. He didn't remember having seen an official date for the race, but he couldn't afford not being allowed to fly.

Still serious, the headmaster leaned forward over his desk. "I am well aware of that, Lance. You boys should have thought of that before you took the academy's finish ring to air race without permission, which, by the way, is illegal and extremely dangerous, as you experienced today. So, until further notice, none of you will leave the ground. You are not allowed to use your aircraft or any of the academy's craft—not even during flight classes."

"How are we supposed to practice?" Owen asked.

"You can use the 3-D simulators if you like," Dantés suggested.

"The *simulators?*" This time Keithan protested. "They're for first- and second-year students; pre-solo students."

"Keithan," his father said seriously. It was the first thing Keithan heard his dad say since he had entered the office.

Keithan wanted to keep protesting. He couldn't spend the following weeks practicing on simulators. How would he practice for the Pegasus Air Race? He wanted—no, needed—to practice with the *d'Artagnan*, with the real thing.

But there was no escape from the trouble he and the twins were in now. Marianna was right; he was in so much trouble.

Seeing his dad's look of disappointment, Keithan swallowed his anger and pulled his wallet from the back pocket of his flight uniform. He took out his pilot certificate from it and placed it on the headmaster's desk. The twins did the same and stepped back, doing their best to avoid Keithan's glance.

No one spoke while Headmaster Viviani took the three certificates. Then the headmaster concluded. "I hope this is the last time this happens. You three know students aren't allowed to air race without permission. Professor Dantés and I, or any other professor here at the academy, will not tolerate irresponsible pilot students. You should all be an example of what Ramey Academy stands for. Don't forget, you students are the few who have proven to be capable of learning to fly at an early age in the hopes of becoming the best pilots in the world. That's why you were accepted here—and in your case, in the Air Racing Program. So, from now on, *prove* it."

Keithan's dad and Dantés continued discussing what had happened that afternoon as they walked out of the academy. Meanwhile, Keithan followed them quietly, wondering how he would train for the Pegasus Air Race now that he wasn't allowed to fly for who knew how long.

The simulators, he repeated in his head, displeased. They were supposed to be for new students and those who had not yet built their own aircraft. Keithan remembered the first time he used them. He had been eight at the time, during his first year at the academy. By age ten, he had already mastered them much better than any other student in his level had, which had lit the fuse of jealousy in the Viviani twins and given the two boys more than enough reason to dislike Keithan. Now, however, the simulators didn't seem more to Keithan than any type of 3-D video game.

It'll have to do, then, he tried to convince himself.

At the bottom of the academy's main stairs, Keithan, his dad, and the professor headed to the metallic-red-and-black hoverbike. Then Keithan's dad turned to him.

"Son, give me your aircraft's key."

Keithan was taken completely by surprise. "What? Are you serious?"

"I am," his dad said.

Keithan's jaw dropped, but seeing the look on his father's face, he reached into his uniform's collar and pulled out a tube-shaped electronic key attached to a chain with silver pellets. Sighing deeply, he handed it to his dad.

Mr. Quintero turned to Dantés. "Professor, I may not know much about aviation. I'm sure you know Keithan's mother was the pilot in our family and who involved him in everything about flying when she was alive. As for me, I'm more the kind of person who prefers to keep his feet on the ground. That's why I think it would be best if you hold on to this."

Keithan watched horror-struck as his dad handed the *d'Artagnan's* key to Dantés. He was about to protest but decided not to.

"You should hold on to it until you think Keithan is ready to fly again," Mr. Quintero suggested.

Dantés nodded. "I understand, Mr. Quintero. I'll make sure to give it back to him when the time is right."

"Thank you," Keithan's dad said.

Dantés approached her bike and raised her wrist communicator to her mouth. "Engine on," she said into it, and instantly, like an obedient pet, her vehicle rumbled to life and rose from the floor. "Well, Keithan, I hope you learned your lesson," she said over the noise of the engine as she climbed onto the hoverbike.

Keithan wasn't sure, but he sensed a slight satisfaction in the professor's tone. Frustrated, he didn't take his eyes away from her while she put the *d'Artagnan*'s key in one of the pockets of her uniform.

"Oh, I did learn my lesson," he muttered under his breath. *I definitely have to change the* d'Artagnan*'s key for one of those voice activators.*

CHAPTER 7

9:07 p.m.
Mona Island

All operations and work areas inside the secret base had returned to normal after the afternoon's emergency. Fortunately, the event hadn't been a real threat. It had served as a drill for everybody in the base, which was why Lieutenant Colonel Lanzard hadn't given anyone a hard time afterward. Still, everyone remained alert in case another emergency came up.

Inside the control room, deep underground, technicians continued monitoring their radarscopes, which showed the base's surroundings and airspace. None of them had detected any other anomalies. The giant holo screen projected at the far end of the room showed a calm satellite image of Mona Island and its surrounding water, which covered a diameter of fifty miles. Major Theron O'Malley watched it from his usual work area at the center of the room. He stood in front of the main digital console as he fought against his tiredness to stay awake.

Only a few more hours before the colonel returns, O'Malley reminded himself. He wished he had retired for the night instead of his superior, but until then, O'Malley was in charge. He hoped the rest of the night went on as smoothly as it had so far, but just as a yawn escaped from his mouth, the alarm in the control room went off.

O'Malley opened his eyes wide when he saw once again the warning sign start to flash in red on the giant holo screen, accompanied by the sound of klaxons.

"UNIDENTIFIED INCOMING!"

"Oh no. Not again," O'Malley growled. He leaned over his console and started tapping keys.

The technicians at the lower consoles at either side of him were already moving as fast and as best they could to attend the emergency as well. The next second, the satellite image on the giant holo screen zoomed out, and a neon-green cross cursor started to move crazily over the satellite image. It stopped a second later when it detected three bogeys at the north of Mona Island.

"Sir, three bogeys approaching at an altitude of two hundred feet above sea level," reported a man from one of the consoles on the right side of the room.

"How far away are they?" O'Malley demanded.

"Four miles away from base," another technician replied.

"Great," O'Malley exhaled.

A younger technician with short brown hair hurried up to him and said, "Sir, should I inform Colonel Lanzard?"

"No need to yet," O'Malley answered over his shoulder. He then raised his voice so everyone in the control room could hear him. "Listen up, people. It's probable we have detected more young air racers—"

"Major, I don't think we are dealing with air racers this time," a technician cut him off.

O'Malley and the man next to him exchanged perplexed looks before they turned to the female technician who had spoken. It was Natalia Salas, the same woman who had alerted the colonel about the emergency call this afternoon.

"What makes you say that?" O'Malley asked.

"You better see for yourself, sir." The redheaded woman pressed several keys on her projected console and made a new satellite image appear on the giant holo screen.

Everyone in the control room saw a much closer look at the three bogeys from an aerial view on the main screen. The bogeys were flying in perfect horizontal line formation and heading south, straight to Mona. Their shapes, however, were what caught everyone's attention, for they were unlike any type of known aircraft.

"They're just ... circles," said the technician alongside O'Malley with a look of confusion.

Still not sure what he was staring at, O'Malley moved his hands over his console and zoomed in on the image more. It didn't help much; the three bogeys still looked the same, like mere flying circles speeding toward Mona Island.

Unexpectedly, the bogey at the left and the one at the right changed direction while the one in the middle continued its straight course.

"What the—?" O'Malley asked, but before he could finish the sentence, the three bogeys disappeared from the image.

O'Malley blinked twice, not believing what happened. "Where did they go?" he shouted. He spun around, expecting an explanation, though it never came.

Everyone in the room held their breath and stared blankly at the main holo screen, as if waiting for the circular bogeys to reappear. But seconds passed, and the satellite image remained the same—empty and silent.

"*Now* would be the time to inform the colonel," O'Malley told the officer behind him, doing his best not to sound too worried. "We will definitely have to send the knights now."

Keithan looked at the time on his wrist communicator. It was 9:20 p.m. His father, who was somewhere inside the house, would soon come out to the backyard terrace and tell him to wrap things up and go to bed, which was why Keithan did his best to hurry up with his schoolwork. He had been at the terrace for three and a half hours, working on a twenty-eight-inch drone for his Advanced Aeronautics class. The drone was part of a two-week project he and Fernando had been assigned to build together, and so far, the final touches were coming along nicely.

Keithan was testing the small camera he had installed on it. He wore a viewscreen headset over his eyes, which showed him what the camera was capturing. Noticing the image out of focus, he adjusted the camera's lens.

"There. That should do it," he said, taking off the headset.

All that was left to do was mount the counterthruster into the drone, which he and Fernando would do tomorrow since Fernando was finishing it at his home.

The project had kept Keithan busy during the night, although it hadn't distracted him completely from his new worries. Keithan couldn't stop thinking about the fact that he wasn't allowed to fly now. According to what Headmaster Viviani had said, he wasn't going to be able to fly even during his flight classes. Worse still, the fact that the headmaster had taken his pilot certificate, and Dantés the *d'Artagnan*'s key, added to his frustration. They would certainly keep him grounded for a week. But what if they kept him grounded for an entire month? Or two? Keithan wondered if he would have enough time to prepare for the Pegasus Air Race.

There was only one alternative for being able to fly the *d'Artagnan*, but it would be risky—with Fernando's key copy.

No! he told himself, already imagining the consequences if he got caught flying without permission.

Keithan scrubbed his hands down his face and took a moment to gaze out at the relaxing scenery of his backyard in the hopes of taking his mind off his worries. Glowing in front of him in bright blue was the pool, and around it, small mushroom-shaped lamps illuminating the grass, which still had its freshly cut smell. There was also a cool breeze softly swaying the fronds of the areca palm trees and dwarf palmettos.

As for the sky, it looked calm with barely any clouds and stars. The brightest lights up there, though closer to the horizon, were the red and blue lights of Ramey Airport's control tower, which Keithan could see blinking randomly and close to each other.

With a deep sigh, Keithan took his wrist communicator from the table and pressed a button on its side, changing the time display to digital dial keys.

"Keithan, what's up?" Fernando answered as soon as his image appeared on the communicator's mini screen. *"Did you finish assembling the drone's fuselage?"*

"Yep," Keithan said. "I assembled the wings about an hour ago. After that, I synchronized the controller with the drone. Oh, and I finished installing the micro camera about a minute ago."

"Good. Did you check the stabilizers too?"

"Uh-huh. They shouldn't be a problem. And what about you?"

"I finished the counterthruster a few hours ago. So tomorrow, before class, we'll put it into the fuselage," Fernando said.

"Great. Anyway, Fernando, did you find anything about the official date of the Pegasus Air Race?" Keithan said, changing the subject to what he wanted to discuss with him.

"Why did I have a feeling you were going to ask me that?" Fernando said with a snort. *"Well, I checked over the internet, and it seems there's no date announced for the race anywhere yet. There's not even a date announced on the Pegasus Company's website. But that's not all."*

"What do you mean?"

"There's not even anything about the Pegasus Air Race taking place this year at either Ramey or in Puerto Rico."

Keithan shook his head. "How can that be?"

He reached for his *laptube* and turned it on. The laptube, a truncated cylindrical computer no bigger than a spray can, flipped up two mini projectors from its sides, which generated a small holo touchscreen on top of the device. At the same time, the laptube projected a cyan-lit keyboard at its front, over the table.

Touching the holo screen, Keithan opened an online window and looked for the Pegasus Air Race official website.

"That's weird. Why wouldn't the website show anything about the date and location of the race yet?"

"Beats me," Fernando replied. *"Look at the bottom of the page. It only says*

that the race's date and location will be announced soon."

Keithan stared at the Pegasus's homepage. It showed the famous silver-and-gold Pegasus logo in the background, along with two animated racing aircraft flying toward the screen every five seconds. Other than that, the website had nothing else except what Fernando mentioned.

Keithan opened a small calendar window by touching the lower right corner of the projected touchscreen. "Man, I need that date," he exhaled, looking at the calendar. "I wanna know if I'll have enough time to get ready when I'm allowed to fly again."

"Allowed to fly again?"

Keithan was about to explain everything about his punishment when he started smelling a familiar woodsy fragrance accompanied by the soft aroma of hot tea. It warned him his father was approaching.

"I don't wanna talk about it right now," he told Fernando. "Listen, I have to go. I'll see you tomorrow."

"All right, then. Don't be late."

"I won't," Keithan reassured him. He hung up and went on to shut down his laptube. He was packing up his set of tools when he heard his father step into the terrace. Keithan didn't have to look over his shoulder; the strong woodsy smell of his father's cologne was more than enough to confirm he was there.

"Are you still upset I gave your aircraft's key to your professor?" his father asked, breaking the cold silence that had been kept between them during the rest of the day and that evening.

Keithan kept his head down, still with his back to his father. He didn't want to answer. He continued putting his tools away in their small toolbox. He was unable to keep the silent treatment up for too long, though.

"You didn't have to do that." Keithan turned around.

His father stopped in front of the sloped glass that divided the terrace from the rest of the house. He had a red cup with hot tea in his hands.

"You didn't have to give the key to Dantés," Keithan specified.

His father narrowed his eyes. "Knowing you so well, Son, I think I did have to."

"Come on, Dad! I know it was stupid to race against Lance and Owen—"

"But you're not fully aware of the danger that you put yourself into," his father interjected, moving closer. "What if there had been an airliner on the way? Or if it had been you who had crashed with the academy's hover ring? You could have gotten yourself killed—you could have killed someone else, Keithan!"

Keithan flared his nostrils. "That wouldn't have happened, Dad. You know how I fly."

"Yes. I know very well how you fly. You're cocky, extremely competitive, and you rely too much on your instincts, never taking the time to think before acting. Those are the same things that got your mother …" His father held his breath.

Keithan waited, watching him struggle to control his emotions, just like every time either one of them talked about Keithan's mother.

His father sighed deeply. "Son, it was always your mother's dream that you would become a great air racer someday. Thanks to her you were accepted at Ramey Academy. So, please, don't waste that opportunity—but more than for her, for yourself. Don't waste it." He leaned his head back and took the last sip of his tea. "Now, please go to bed; it's still a school night."

Keithan watched his father head back to the house. He dared not say anything else; he knew how hard all this was for his father. Keithan was following his mother's footsteps, even in his behavior, which Keithan knew was what worried his father most. Keithan, however, always tried to avoid thinking about that too much. He didn't like getting too emotional, especially because he didn't like people feeling sorry for him. He shook his head and went on to pack up the drone and the rest of his stuff to go into the house.

He was about to turn around, but when he gave one last glimpse at the night sky, he spotted a tiny white light. It fell straight down as fast as a shooting star, but right before it got closer to the control tower lights, it changed direction abruptly, as if tracing a perfect L.

And just like that, it shot out of sight.

Keithan froze, mouth open. He had never seen anything change direction that fast. For a moment, Keithan wondered if it had been a flying insect or something similar. *It couldn't have been,* he told himself.

All of a sudden, two other lights shot straight down from the night sky and changed direction, also making a right-angle turn before they shot out of sight.

"Keithan, hurry up. I'm going to turn off the lights," his father called out from inside the house.

Keithan glanced at the house but returned his gaze to the control tower lights far away.

"What were those things?" he murmured. He moved forward unconsciously, stepping out of the terrace while wondering if he had been the only one who had seen the lights.

His wrist communicator rang. Keithan jumped. Still staring at the sky, he pressed the answer button, and instantly the live image of a shocked Fernando appeared on the mini screen.

"Keithan, did you see that?"

CHAPTER 8

Early the following morning, Keithan rushed out of his house on his hubless magnetic bicycle. He was anxious to get to Fernando and Marianna's house. He'd barely slept, marveling at the mysterious lights that he'd seen the previous night. As far as he could remember, he had never woken up so early and with so much energy to go to the academy. In less than an hour, he showered, put on his flight suit, brushed his teeth, and even had breakfast. Yet he left his home in such a hurry that it wasn't until he got to the corner of the street that he realized he had forgotten the most important thing for today …

"The drone!"

Keithan had to hurry back to his house. He found his father having breakfast at the dining table while he watched the morning news on a floating holo screen. He offered Keithan a ride to the academy, but Keithan refused.

Soon Keithan was on his bicycle again, his laptube strapped to his back and the drone in its box, which Keithan had attached over the rear fender. He pedaled hard down Hangar Road, parallel to the chain-link fence that enclosed Ramey Airport, and past *El Taíno*—the neighborhood's local mini-market. The twin hubless wheels spun in a blur while held in place by the bike's magnetic locks.

Keithan turned right with the bike and continued straight until he finally reached the guardhouse at the airport's main entrance. There,

Sergio, the security guard, had reactivated the blue control access beam after letting a vehicle pass. The man, who was as tall as a basketball star and as skinny as a lamppost, saw Keithan approaching and raised a hand forward. Keithan, in response, pressed the brake hard, forcing his rear tire to skid sideways until he stopped barely two feet away from the guard.

"Whoa! Careful there, Keithan," Sergio said. "Any closer and you and I would have been shocked by the beam."

"Sorry, Sergio," said Keithan, panting.

Sergio held out a scanner touchpad for Keithan to place his thumb on, and the next second, Keithan's registered profile appeared on the device, confirming his pilot student number.

"All clear. *Now* you may pass," Sergio told him.

He had just deactivated the access beam when, all of a sudden, three bulky and turtle-shell-like vehicles painted in green camouflage surprised Keithan from behind. They didn't even honk a warning; they just rushed past him without slowing down.

"Hey!" Keithan shouted.

Each of the military vehicles, six-wheeled and with a long gunner on the roof like a tank, passed so close to Keithan it almost ran over him. Each one hurried down the airport's parking lot and entered the airfield through the second security checkpoint.

"What's their problem?" Keithan asked Sergio, though he didn't wait for the man to reply. Instead, Keithan pedaled again and hurried to the second security checkpoint as well.

Once he was inside the airfield, Keithan drove his bike behind the twin-fuselage airliners. He wasn't supposed to pass so closely from them, but he kept going since nobody seemed to notice. It turned out all the airport's guards and technicians out there were paying more attention to the military vehicles running down the main runway, as well as to the pair of white vertical helicraft that circled low in the air.

Once Keithan reached the area of the residential hangars, he found Marianna, along with her golden retriever, Laika, in front of Hangar H11. The two of them were gazing at the main runway, and as expected, Marianna was recording what was happening out there with her hover camera and viewscreen headset. There were other people in front of the other hangar residences too, all of them intrigued by what was happening on the main runway.

"Marianna!" said Keithan, pressing his brake and coming to an abrupt stop right next to her and Laika.

"Hey," Marianna replied, still gazing forward.

Shielding his eyes, Keithan turned in the same direction and saw what was happening. A crowd of security officials and military men, along with a dozen camouflaged vehicles like the ones that had almost run over Keithan, surrounded what appeared to be three round and shiny metal objects.

Keithan frowned, wondering if those things could be the same things he had seen last night. He had a feeling they were, but at the same time, something inside him said otherwise, for the round, metal objects out there didn't look like aircraft at all. They looked more like three giant pinball balls.

"What are those things?" Keithan asked.

"I've no idea," Marianna told him. "Whatever they are, no one there seems to dare to get too close to them."

She had just pressed a button on the side of her headset to adjust the image projected in her viewscreen when Fernando showed up. Like Keithan, he was already in his academy uniform, though instead of blue, his was orange, distinctive of all aeroengineer students.

"Did you get a good look at the spheres?" Fernando asked Keithan as he stopped his wheelchair beside him. He looked more excited than intrigued. "Almost all airport security is around them with the National Guard. Here."

He handed Keithan his digital binoculars. Keithan held them up to his eyes. With them, Keithan got a much closer look at the shiny metallic spheres, but he still couldn't see them completely due to all the uniformed men and military vehicles that blocked his view. The spheres looked as big as a one-man pod, with their chromed surfaces as smooth and shiny as mirrors. They hovered about four feet off the ground.

"You think those things might have something to do with what we saw last night?" Keithan asked Fernando.

"It's hard to tell," Fernando said. "The lights from last night had to be some type of aircraft, but those spheres out there don't seem to have any wings or anything else that could make them fly."

Keithan grimaced. "They don't seem to have antigravity plates underneath them, either, yet they're hovering."

"Do you think they might be some sort of military project?" Marianna asked.

Fernando shrugged. "Could be. Anyway, Dad told me he's gonna go there to try to get information. Let's hope they let him get closer."

Just then, Keithan, Fernando, and Marianna heard a car horn, and as they turned around, a scarlet minivan with transparent door surfaces pulled over behind them. The vehicle had the *d'Artagnan* attached to its rear by a hover trailer, and behind the wheel was Fernando and Marianna's mom, who called out to them.

"Come on you guys; you're going to be late—especially you, Marianna," she said while she gathered her golden hair in a quick bun. She opened the sliding side door behind her, and a ramp unfolded outward for Fernando to get in, yet Laika went in first when Mrs. Aramis whistled to her.

"Let your dad worry about those things out there," Mrs. Aramis told them. "I'm sure he'll tell you all about it when you get back from school." She turned to Keithan and said, "Better hurry up and take your bike inside the hangar if you want a ride with us, dear."

Keithan nodded, but before he went into the hangar, he said, "Um, I don't think we need to take the *d'Artagnan* to the academy today."

"Why not?" Fernando asked with a frown.

"Well, I'm not allowed to fly her until further notice."

Both Marianna and Fernando shook their heads in surprise. "*What?*"

—(-o-)—

On their way to the academy, Keithan told the Aramises about his punishment for having air raced with the Viviani twins yesterday. He did his best to hide his frustration, but Fernando, Marianna, and Mrs. Aramis were still able to sense it by the way he explained the whole thing.

"So how are you going to practice for the Peg—?" Marianna started to say before Fernando quickly cut her off by clearing his throat.

The deep look he shot at her warned Marianna and Keithan that he didn't want his mom to know about their plans to participate in the Pegasus Air Race.

Therefore, Keithan nodded and turned to Marianna.

"Honestly, I don't know what I'm going to do," he told her. "I could use the academy's simulators in the meantime, but it's definitely not going to be like practicing with the *d'Artagnan*."

Soon, they arrived at Ramey Academy. Mrs. Aramis drove the minivan under the bridge that connected the control tower to the main building and stopped in front of the hangar bay, where other students were bringing their aircraft as well. Fernando got down with his wheelchair, carrying the drone, while Keithan proceeded to detach the *d'Artagnan*'s hover trailer. Even though Keithan insisted that Mrs. Aramis take the *d'Artagnan* back with her, Mrs. Aramis and Fernando chose to leave it.

"Who knows? The headmaster might change his mind and allow you to fly at least during your flight class," Fernando said.

Keithan knew better; the headmaster wouldn't change his mind. Even if he did, Professor Dantés had the *d'Artagnan*'s key—and she would definitely not change her mind. No matter what.

As soon as Mrs. Aramis left with Marianna and Laika, Keithan turned back to the *d'Artagnan*. He stared at her with foolish longing while a one-armed, yellow tow robot with tractor treads hooked itself to the aircraft's trailer and took it inside the academy's hangar bay.

Next to him, Fernando looked back and forth from Keithan to the *d'Artagnan*. "Seriously? You're missing her?" he said with a snort in an attempt to bring Keithan back to his senses. "It's not like she's going anywhere, you know."

"I know. That's the sad part," Keithan said thoughtfully.

Fernando rolled his eyes. "Come on. Let's go to class."

He grabbed Keithan by the arm and forced him to move forward as he moved his wheelchair. Together, they entered the academy.

They were met with an unexpected atmosphere of excitement in the common hallways. It seemed as if nobody cared about what was happening outside with the mysterious spheres on the airport's runway, but it was clear that everybody already knew about the big news of the Pegasus Air Race. Pilot students and aeroengineer students talked about it as if it were the best thing about to happen at Ramey. It was, Keithan knew it, and the other students' faces clearly showed that they couldn't wait to know more about the event, either.

"Just imagine, the best air racers in the world will be competing here in Puerto Rico!" a boy in aeroengineer uniform told another student in pilot uniform.

"What I wonder is why they decided to do it here this year," said another student nearby.

"I know. That was so unexpected."

Keithan had also wondered about that. Why indeed had Pegasus Company decided to do its famous air race this year in Puerto Rico? As far as he and everyone else knew, Puerto Rico hadn't been announced as one of the places to be considered for the next Pegasus Air Race.

Throughout the hallways, a few students gave sidelong glances at Keithan.

"Hey! Congrats on winning yesterday," said Arthur Mendez, a pilot student who was a year younger than Keithan.

"That was some race, Quintero," another student said with a thumbs-up.

"Thanks," Keithan replied, grinning while walking beside Fernando.

The two of them turned left to another hallway. Above them, on the ceiling, a red floating hologram showing the time ran continuously for all students to see.

"Seven forty-five," Fernando noticed. "We better hurry up if we want to put the counterthruster into the drone before class begins."

They were heading to their Advanced Aeronautics class. Like History of Aviation and Atmospheric Science, among a few others, it was one of the classes that pilot students and aeroengineer students took together. The class took place inside one of the three concave hangars located at the back of the academy's main building. Keithan and Fernando had to cross the courtyard to get there. They entered the hangar in the middle, which had its entrance wide open.

The inside of the hangar was not exactly what most people would consider an ordinary classroom environment. It looked more like a mechanic's workshop, which it was too, with piles of all types of aircraft spare parts in metal boxes and a variety of metal-bending machines, cutters, and rollers, all aligned in different areas. Some of the machines moved without any assistance, making their loud, rhythmic sounds while they worked. The center of the hangar, however, was the area that looked more like a classroom. There, six worktables formed two rows, facing a wide blacktop desk. Keithan and Fernando's classmates were already gathered there, doing the finishing touches to their drones for the day's test.

"Good. Professor Steelsmith is not here yet," said Fernando, looking around the hangar.

He and Keithan hurried to their worktable. As they got ready to do the assembly, they turned their attention to the Viviani twins and their aeroengineer partners. The four boys stood around their tables with their two drones.

"Now, you *know* they couldn't have built those things from scratch," Fernando said. He sounded more outraged than surprised. "We all had only two weeks to come up with a design and build the drones, and those guys managed to have theirs painted? Even chromed?"

Keithan snorted. He agreed. The two drones the twins and their aeroengineer partners had with them didn't look at all as if they had been designed and built by them. They looked more as if they had been bought. They even showed some resemblance to the twins' real aircraft: T-shaped with bottom rudders. Yet, more than having been made to fly, they looked as if they had been built for display.

It didn't surprise Keithan, though. There was nothing unusual in seeing this in all the work Owen, Lance, and their aeroengineer partners did. The boys always seemed to rely only on brand-new and sometimes expensive parts to do their projects, as if that were the best way to prove how good they were. Curiously, in Keithan and Fernando's case, it was exactly the opposite, and their drone reflected that. Keithan and Fernando's drone was a composition of scrap parts without a particular design per se. It was more the result of all the ideas they had agreed on to create the fastest and most efficient craft they could have come up with. Just like their *d'Artagnan*.

"Forget about them," Keithan told Fernando as he opened his tool kit on the table. "I'm pretty sure they bought those drones already assembled, and all they did was add the counterthrusters to them."

"I know, but the instructions the professor gave us were to come up with our *own* aircraft designs, not to customize others," Fernando insisted. Aware that their professor would show up any moment, he shook his head and got to work with Keithan on their own drone.

Keithan unscrewed the small antigravity plate and took it off for Fernando to insert and connect the scaled counterthruster he had built. The counterthruster was similar to the drone's mini jet engine, though half its size and more compact. Once it was in place, the two of them put the antigravity plate back and tested it. It was working properly, so they moved on to do an overall check.

They were almost done when a black girl with a short curly afro and a tall brunette with freckles appeared in front of their worktable. The two girls were partners, like Keithan and Fernando, and it was evident since one wore the blue pilot uniform and the other the aeroengineer version.

"Hi, guys," said the black girl in pilot uniform.

"Hey, Genevieve," said Keithan and Fernando, glancing at the girl and her friend but still doing their overall check on their drone.

"So, Keithan, we heard Headmaster Viviani grounded you and the twins until further notice."

Keithan huffed. "Man! Does everybody know already?"

"Of course everybody knows," said Yari, the freckled girl in orange uniform. "We all knew you and the twins would get busted."

"Yeah, well, it's no big deal," said Keithan, though not sounding too convincing. He was rechecking the battery power of the drone's radio controller.

"Anyway, don't worry about that," Genevieve told Keithan. "That's not the main topic in the academy today."

"That's right," Yari went on. "In addition to the news about the Pegasus Air Race, everyone's also talking about the mysterious spheres that appeared on the main runway."

Keithan and Fernando raised their gazes, paying full attention to the girls.

"Has anyone found out what they are?" Fernando asked.

"Well, no one is quite sure," Genevieve said. "Some students believe the spheres could have something to do with the Pegasus Air Race, though others are saying that they may have something to do with some kind of military project that crashed there last night."

"Crashed? It couldn't have been," Keithan interjected. "There should've been smoke rising on the runway if it had been a crash, and there wasn't any out there."

"There should have been a crashing sound too, and I didn't hear a thing last night," Fernando added.

"Well, there's a third 'rumor' circling in the academy," Genevieve said, doing the air quotes gesture with her fingers when she said the word "rumor."

"What third rumor?" Keithan asked.

Genevieve and Yari exchanged uncertain looks before they turned to Fernando and Keithan again.

"That the spheres are … UFOs," Genevieve said.

There was a pause. Fernando and Keithan exchanged skeptical looks.

"UFOs. You mean like *alien* unidentified flying objects?" Fernando asked.

The girls nodded.

"Who's saying that?" Keithan asked, not at all convinced, either.

"Oddie there," Yari said.

She gestured over her shoulder toward a chubby red-cheeked boy in orange uniform. He was engaged in a conversation with three other classmates, and he was leading the conversation. From what Keithan could see, the boy was reenacting a deep-dive flight maneuver with his hands as he spoke.

"Winston Oddie? Really?" Keithan said. "I wouldn't find it hard to believe that he's the only one who believes that."

Genevieve shrugged. "He's even saying that his father believes the spheres are alien cocoons."

The thought of it made Fernando and Keithan chuckle.

Keithan didn't know Winston too well, but he knew him enough to be careful about taking the boy's rumor seriously. Winston Oddie was the kind of boy who always seemed to have an unusual explanation for everything. It had to do with the fact that he liked to read a lot. The problem was he believed almost everything he read, whether it was fact or fiction.

"Good morning, everyone!" said an adult voice.

The students turned their heads and saw Professor Steelsmith enter the hangar. They hurried to their seats at their respective tables. The professor, who was no taller than any of his students, looked dwarfed by the bunch of scrap metal parts he carried in front of him. It covered him from the waist up, making only his scruffy gray hair visible, which grew just at the lower back and sides of his head. Having some difficulty holding his stuff with both hands, the man hurried between the rows of tables and finally dropped everything with a loud clanking on the black desk at the front.

"Sorry I'm late," he said, wiping his hands on his shabby gray unisuit, which was already stained with old grease. "All right. Listen up. Before we begin our class, there are a few things that have happened at the airport during the past twenty-four hours that I need to clarify."

The students braced themselves. Finally, they were going to get real answers.

"As all of you already know," the professor said, "there were numerous digital posters found yesterday all over Ramey announcing that the well-known Pegasus Air Race will take place this year in Puerto Rico—but more than that, that it will be held here at Ramey."

The whole class cheered, but Professor Steelsmith raised his hands, demanding silence.

"I get it; you're all looking forward to this event. *However*," he paused before he dropped the bombshell, "I regret to say that such advertisement is not true."

That last part stunned the students. It was as if the professor had frozen them with his words, leaving a sudden silence save for the noise of the machines working in the background. It was worse for Keithan; to him it felt like taking a hit hard to the chest, making him lose the air in his lungs.

Not true? he repeated in his head.

It didn't take long for his classmates to react.

"*What?*" blurted one of them, outraged. "H-how can that be?"

"It can't be!" another exclaimed.

"I know. I know. It is disappointing," Professor Steelsmith went on. "The truth is nobody from Ramey Airport had any knowledge of an agreement for Pegasus Company to do its race here or in any other part of Puerto Rico. In fact, Pegasus Company hasn't even asked permission from the government of Puerto Rico. That is why the Ramey administration informed the faculty that those posters running around the airport are nothing more than a false advertisement of some sort."

"A false advertisement?" Keithan didn't want to believe it. He was still so shocked he didn't even blink; he just stared blankly at the professor.

"So that's some of the news," Professor Steelsmith said. "I also need to talk to you about this morning's event in the middle of the airport's main runway."

The students' buzzing stopped as they returned their full attention to the professor.

"I'm already aware several rumors are running around, but airport security has already informed Headmaster Viviani and all the professors about what happened. It turns out that the things that appeared in the middle of the runway are nothing more than military radars brought to the airport for testing." The professor paused. "So now you know. The metallic spheres have nothing to do with the alleged Pegasus Air Race, they did not crash—and *no*, Mr. Oddie, they are not alien UFOs."

Professor Steelsmith shot a sharp look at Winston Oddie, who had raised a chubby hand instantly, ready to counter.

"So that will be the end of it," he said.

"But, sir—"

"I said that will be the end of it, Mr. Oddie."

There were a few giggles among the students. Meanwhile, Keithan and Fernando exchanged confused looks, not convinced about the quick explanations the professor had given them.

"Now, let's begin. Shall we?" Professor Steelsmith said. He rubbed his hands together and picked up a small data pad from his desk. "We have an important evaluation today, and we can't let rumors and events not related to the class keep distracting us. So, everybody, grab your drones and follow me to the airfield."

CHAPTER 9

Professor Steelsmith must have regretted having told the students the disappointing news about the Pegasus Air Race because none of them showed much enthusiasm toward the upcoming evaluation. Keithan felt as if he had taken it the hardest, though he didn't express it. He still couldn't believe the posters announcing the race were nothing more than false advertisements. The mere thought of it seemed like a joke, a mean joke that the professor was playing on Keithan and his classmates. Despite this, Keithan wasn't willing to accept that as a fact, at least not until he could find out where exactly the Pegasus Air Race would take place this year. But that would have to wait for the time being.

Lost in his thoughts, Keithan followed Professor Steelsmith with Fernando and the rest of his classmates out of the academy. They headed to the open area in front of the hangar bay building where they found a tall metal structure curving upward like a concave five-story turret in the distance.

"The pull-up wall," said Keithan, realizing how they were going to be evaluated today.

Keithan knew the pull-up wall as the obstacle that the students from the higher levels used with their real aircraft to practice their vertical climb maneuvers. The structure stood approximately fifty feet away from Keithan and his classmates. Keithan noticed a figure standing in front of it, to which Professor Steelsmith beckoned.

Just Keithan's luck, it was Professor Dantés.

"Thank you for agreeing on helping me with today's evaluation," Steelsmith told the professor.

"Glad to do it," Dantés replied, nodding in greeting as she approached. She had her light-brown hair pulled back and gathered in a tight bun, which brought out her sharp features and particular stern look. Like Steelsmith, she had a data pad in her hands, and she tapped on it while the students settled with their drones in front of the two professors.

"Great," Keithan muttered, not happy at all about having Dantés as an evaluator.

"All right, students. Gather around," said Professor Steelsmith, raising his voice to get everyone's attention. "I know you're still disappointed about what we talked about before we came here, but let's try to focus on what we have to do, okay? Today's evaluation should be important to all of you. You will get to try out the first counterthruster prototypes that you assembled before you get to build the real thing next year for your aircraft, when you get to level six. Now, let's review. Who can tell me why the counterthruster is such an innovative feature, especially in air racing? … Miss Donnelly."

Genevieve lowered her hand. "Because it allows air racing pilots to change direction radically despite the forward thrust force and the aerodynamic designs of their aircraft."

"Correct. And by aerodynamic design we mean … Gutierrez."

"How the shape of an aircraft affects or interacts with the way it moves through the air," recited Manuel Gutierrez, Owen's aeroengineer partner.

The professor nodded. "Very good."

So far Keithan had been paying little attention to the review. He could hear the professor, but he was still half lost in his thoughts. Keithan gazed at the sky, looking for any aircraft that might be flying up there. He found none, which probably meant airport control wasn't allowing any craft to land or take off because of what might still be happening with the radar spheres at the airport's runway.

Fernando cleared his throat as a yawn escaped Keithan, who covered his mouth in the hopes that neither of their professors would notice.

Meanwhile, Steelsmith went on reviewing with the class. "And after making sure that your counterthrusters were well assembled, each pair, consisting of an aeroengineer student and a pilot student, built a drone to incorporate the counterthruster. So today we are going to put them to the test."

The short bald professor paused to look down at his data pad. He went on to explain how the evaluation would be graded. Seventy-five percent of the points would depend on how the counterthrusters worked with the drones, while the remaining twenty-five percent would depend on how the drones performed in the air.

"Now, your drones will be evaluated based on a flight sequence that I asked Professor Dantés to design for you. So, Professor …"

In response, Dantés tapped in a few keys on her data pad and turned around to gaze at the pull-up wall. Everyone looked in the same direction. The next second, the whole class witnessed three hover rings near the pull-up wall leave the ground like floating balloons. Unlike the real rings used in air races, these were half the size and no bigger than five feet in diameter. One of them ascended about twenty feet, hovering horizontally, like a basketball hoop. The other two went up close to ten feet higher, but vertically and close from one another, as if forming a figure eight. Some of the students raised their eyebrows, including Keithan, who thought the two rings were too close from each other for even a small drone to pass through them.

With her hands behind her back and still with her data pad, Dantés turned to face the students again. "Listen up, pilot students," she said in a military tone. "As you can see, the flight sequence will not be a common one for your level. Still, I think it is appropriate for this evaluation since your purpose is to show if your counterthruster prototypes work in the air. So pay careful attention to the instructions—especially *you*, Owen."

All eyes turned to the bulky twin standing at the back of the group.

He had been talking to his aeroengineer partner but instantly froze at the mention of his name.

"You wouldn't want to make a silly mistake like the one you did yesterday. You know, while air racing with your brother and Quintero." Dantés narrowed her eyes, looking straight at him, her lips tightening.

Owen had no comment or excuse. He sucked in his lips as his face turned almost as red as an apple. When Dantés looked away, he shot Keithan a glare as he noticed him trying to hold in a chuckle.

"First things first," Dantés said, addressing the pilot students again. "You will not air race with your drones. They will be evaluated one at a time."

Right away, there were low moans of disappointment among the students. Dantés ignored them.

"Second," the professor continued, "you will commence by flying your drones no higher than six feet and straight toward the wall, which, of course, will force you to pull them up. However, you will not fly them through the hover rings while they climb vertically. Once your drones pass the top of the pull-up wall, you will have them do a recovery and prepare them for a vertical drop."

"It'll be then that you will put the counterthrusters to the test," Steelsmith added, looking straight at the pilot students. "That'll be the moment in which you'll use them to pass the drones through each of the hover rings. Any questions?"

Both Steelsmith and Dantés gave a slightly taunting smirk at the students' sudden look of astonishment. They allowed them a few seconds to register the given instructions. The twelve students stared at the wall, though the six pilot students seemed to stare at it more deeply than the aeroengineers. A few of them couldn't even hide their nervousness, particularly Genevieve and Winston's pilot partner, Gabriel Ortiz. Their nervousness was noticeable on their frowns.

Keithan took his time to study the flight sequence in his mind. It was no easy challenge, that was for sure, but he felt confident he could do it.

No sweat, he told himself.

Professor Steelsmith clapped his hands together and gestured for the students to step forward and get their drones ready.

Each team placed its drone on the ground. Keithan placed his next to Genevieve and Yari's when he heard a few of his classmates chuckling nearby.

"Man, can that even be called a drone?" Owen commented, causing more chuckles from his twin brother and his aeroengineer partner. "Looks more like it was taken straight out of a junkyard."

It wasn't hard to realize the twin had referred to Keithan and Fernando's drone, but Keithan knew better than to reply to Owen's comment. He didn't even feel the need to do it after having beaten the twins yesterday in the air. Keithan, however, couldn't believe that Owen still felt the urge to make fun of him and his work even after having lost to Keithan yesterday.

"You have to admit, it looks like a smaller and uglier version of their *d'Artagnan*," Lance joked.

"Yeah, the same ugly aircraft that beat yours yesterday."

Keithan turned his head at Fernando's unexpected and straightforward comeback.

"Ouch!" chorused some of the other students. They couldn't help enjoying this.

Both Lance and Owen turned to Fernando with a glare. Still, Fernando moved his wheelchair forward and stared defiantly at the twins, waiting for them to answer back. They seemed to have run out of words, though. Their mouths tightened and their nostrils flared, clearly aware that they ended up looking like fools.

"That's enough, you guys," Professor Steelsmith said. "Don't make me take away points before the evaluation begins. Let's get on with it. Lance, you're up first."

Looking for Lance's profile in his data pad, the professor stopped in front of the twin and his partner's drone. So did Dantés.

"Hmm," said Steelsmith, examining the drone and making notes on his pad. "What do you think, Professor?"

Dantés leaned closer to the shiny and fancy-looking drone. "Looks pretty good."

"Of course it does. They bought it already built," Fernando whispered to Keithan, leaning closer.

"Okay, then. Fire it up," Steelsmith ordered.

Gustav Albrektson, Lance's Swedish techie partner, flipped a switch on the drone and made its scaled antigravity plate lift the drone six inches off the ground. Meanwhile, Lance, with the controller in hand, put on his viewscreen visor over his eyes and turned it on to get a picture of what was in front of the drone, as if he were in it.

"On my signal," Steelsmith told him.

Everyone except Lance stepped back.

"And … go!"

The drone shot out with a high-pitched whine straight toward the pull-up wall. On its way, it reflected Lance's nervousness as it wobbled. Right in front of the pull-up wall, it began its vertical climb, making some of the students gasp as they saw how close it had been to hit the wall.

"Keep it steady, Viviani," Dantés warned him without taking her eyes off the flying drone.

Keithan, too, followed the drone with his gaze, starting to feel the urge to try it with his own drone. He watched it pass the top of the pull-up wall. Lance made it lean backward, and the drone, now upside down, dropped vertically like a falling arrow.

"Very good. Wait," said Dantés, suddenly with a worried tone. "Better straighten it up faster."

Lance acknowledged her with a slight nod but kept the rest of his body as stiff as a statue. He bit his tongue and tightened his grip on the controller. He leaned forward to the right, as if he were flying the drone from inside the tiny cockpit.

For some reason, the craft wasn't doing it fast enough.

"Watch it, Lance. Watch it," Steelsmith warned.

"Argh!" Lance gritted his teeth.

Instead of passing through the highest hover ring, the drone hit the ring's top.

"Ow!" cried the students as the drone cartwheeled in the air and—
CRASH! It hit the ground and shattered like a plastic toy.

The accident left Lance and his aeroengineer partner immobile
for several seconds. To everyone's surprise, Steelsmith and Dantés didn't
show any reaction; they simply made some annotations in their data
pads, as if nothing serious had happened.

Once he finished making his annotations, Steelsmith looked up
toward the students. "Okay, Miss Donnelly and Miss Estremera, let's
see your drone."

Both Genevieve and Yari took a deep breath and stepped forward.
Meanwhile, an angry Lance stepped back, tightening his grip on his
controller, as if wanting to tear it apart. Yari turned on the drone while
Genevieve put on her viewscreen visor and set her controller.

This time, after she did a quick inspection of the drone, Dantés
gave the signal to take off.

Genevieve nodded, her eyes shielded by her viewscreen visor, and
giving it full throttle, she sent her drone flying straight toward the pull-
up wall. Her pose made her look as if she were playing in front of an
invisible arcade machine, standing with both hands on the controller,
her legs separated, and her shoulders leaned slightly forward. She
threw her shoulders back at the same time her drone flew upward at a
distance.

"Nice climb, Miss Donnelly. Keep it vertical," Dantés told her.

The drone shot past the top of the pull-up wall. As Lance's had
done, it leaned backward and began its dive. Unlike Lance, however,
Genevieve managed to make the drone's nose point downward as it
was supposed to. And without needing Dantés to remind her,
Genevieve activated the craft's counterthruster and—*SWOOSH!*—made
it pass through the first hover ring.

Her classmates were about to cheer for her, but before they could,
her drone failed to pass through the second hover ring and hit it with
its tail instead, which sent it out of control. An instant later, the drone
crashed.

The students who followed weren't successful, either. Gabriel

Ortiz, who had built a single-engine, maneuverable-looking drone with Winston Oddie, managed to pass it through the first ring but hit it with one of the wings. The drone spun out of control and slammed into the wall before it crashed. As for Aimi Murakami, the short Japanese girl who had transferred last year, she didn't even get the chance to attempt a vertical dive with her drone. She didn't manage to pull it up in time and crashed it against the top of the pull-up wall. By the time her drone hit the ground, it was already in pieces.

Meanwhile, Professors Dantés and Steelsmith watched each performance and graded them in their data pads. Neither showed any sympathy for the crashed drones. Instead, they had a slight hint of satisfaction on their faces, which made Keithan and his classmates realize this evaluation was something the two professors were used to seeing and enjoying every year.

Now the only pilot students left to fly their drones were Owen and Keithan. Owen was called first. His partner, Manuel, turned on their drone and hurried next to Owen to give him a few last-minute pointers, yet Owen was so concentrated he forced him aside and lowered the viewscreen visor over his eyes.

"Ready, Viviani?" Steelsmith asked.

"Ready, sir," Owen replied, holding his controller tightly.

"And … go!"

The drone, which resembled Lance's in almost every way, took off with impressive speed. In a matter of seconds, it reached the pull-up wall and began its vertical climb.

"So far so good. Get ready to turn it around and dive," Dantés said to the twin.

Nervous, Manuel leaned closer to Owen and repeated what the professor had said.

"I heard her!" Owen snapped.

The twin loosened the throttle stick of the controller and made the drone drop backward. Meanwhile, the rest of the class watched in suspense as it approached the highest hover ring. To everyone's surprise, the drone did a tight barrel roll and passed successfully through the first two rings.

Several students cheered, still stunned by the fact that Owen hadn't needed to use the counterthruster to make the stunt. Right then, they held their breath again when they noticed Owen's mistake. The barrel roll maneuver had caused his drone to fly a bit too far from the third and last hover ring. If Owen didn't use the counterthruster now—and fast—his drone would not make it through the ring.

"Owen, the—" Manuel started to say.

"I know what I'm doing," Owen cut him off.

"But you're not using the counter—"

"Shut up!"

With the press of a button, the counterthruster forced the drone to a tight right turn, yet it pushed it so hard the drone shot past over the hover ring before it could have dived through it and continued straight down.

"NOO!" Owen cried, unable to pull it up in time.

Then …

CRASH! Owen's drone smashed with the ground, sending its pieces, along with those of the other drones that had already crashed, in all directions.

"Oh! So close, Mr. Viviani!" Professor Steelsmith said through gritted teeth. "Good try, though."

Owen didn't seem to hear the professor. His frustration and anger got the best of him, and without thinking, he yanked off his viewscreen visor and smashed it against the ground.

"Mr. Viviani!" snapped both Dantés and Steelsmith with full authority.

"You need to control that anger," Steelsmith told him sharply. "That will cost you five points from your evaluation."

Owen, who looked as if he were trying to hold the monster inside him, was about to answer back, but he saw the looks on the two professors' faces. So instead, he gave a loud huff and walked away to the rest of the group.

Nobody spoke while Dantés and Steelsmith made the last

annotations of Owen's evaluation. None of the students bothered to look at Owen, not even his brother. It was for the best, especially since they were all familiar with Owen's particular anger management problem.

"Now we have Mr. Aramis and Mr. Quintero's drone," Steelsmith said, looking at the students again.

Finally, Keithan thought, glad to push the awkward moment aside.

He and Fernando approached their drone. With the flip of a switch, its small engine came to life. It created a heavy and distinctive roar, much louder than the sound of the previous drones. It made the other students cover their ears. At the same time, the drone's low-powered antigravity plate lifted it six inches off the ground.

Keithan was about to put on his viewscreen visor when Steelsmith and Dantés stepped in front of the drone with perplexed looks.

"Um, are you boys sure you finished building that drone?" Professor Steelsmith asked.

"Of course," Fernando and Keithan answered in unison.

"Looks like it's still half-built," Dantés said in a low, sardonic tone.

Some of the students chuckled, but Fernando and Keithan kept their gazes at Dantés, twitching their lips, not amused.

"It'll fly, Professor. We guarantee it," Keithan reassured her with a challenging tone.

Dantés frowned, unconvinced. "It better," she told him. With that, she and Professor Steelsmith stepped aside and made annotations in their data pads.

Not letting her comment take his confidence away, Keithan proceeded to put on his viewscreen visor and turn it on. An image showing the pull-up wall from the drone's point of view appeared in front of his eyes. At the same time, a digital head-up display, like the one on the glass of the *d'Artagnan*'s cockpit, appeared on either side of the image. It showed the horizon line, as well as the airspeed, heading, and altitude indicators.

Fernando handed Keithan the controller.

"Ready, Quintero?" Steelsmith asked.

Keithan assured him by making the drone roar louder.

"Wait for it, Keithan," Dantés said. "And …"

But before the professor would say the word "go," Keithan pushed the throttle stick to the maximum and sent the drone off.

"Quintero!"

"Oops!" Keithan said with a mischievous smile.

Instantly, he forgot he was standing on the ground with people near him. He felt a rush of adrenaline run through his blood as he watched the live image projected on his viewscreen. The airspeed indicator at one of its corners had changed from zero to forty-four knots (the equivalent of nearly fifty miles per hour) almost at once. All the while, in the center of the image, the ground zoomed past in blurry gray as the flying drone under his control sped up toward the pull-up wall. It wasn't like flying with the *d'Artagnan*, yet Keithan felt the exhilaration, as if he were flying.

It didn't take five seconds for the drone to reach the curved wall. Instantly, Keithan made it climb vertically like a rocket. It shot past the top of the wall and ascended twenty more feet.

"Here we go," Keithan murmured, watching the airspeed numbers drop fast on the indicator. He applied full right aileron and turned the drone's front steering vanes to their limit. In response, the drone did an impressive quick, one-eighty arch without requiring either a backward or a forward drop.

"Wow! That was unexpected," Steelsmith said.

Keithan grinned at the comment but remained focused; he knew he hadn't reached the challenging part yet. He watched from his visor as the front steering vanes of the drone, now pointed to the ground, descended. Sure of what he was doing, he braced himself to send them through the three hover rings.

The trick was to do the maneuvers as if they were one. It was the only way; he had realized it after watching the other pilot students fly their drones. He executed the stunt in perfect timing.

The drone, while still dropping vertically, did a barrel roll, passing successfully through the two rings aligned as if forming a figure eight. And after that, Keithan activated the counterthruster and made the drone change direction abruptly. It went straight down the third ring like a snake, slithering with grace in the air.

Everyone behind him gasped in disbelief when they saw that one of them had finally accomplished the flight sequence. But then …

"Oh no. NO!" Keithan cried, desperately trying to recover from the dive, but the drone dropped too fast even to recover with the counterthruster. And just like the others—*CRASH!*

"Oh! Now *that* was close!" Steelsmith exclaimed, satisfaction in his tone.

The image in front of Keithan's eyes whited out, forcing him to take his visor off.

"That wasn't supposed to happen!" he blurted out. He stared ahead in disbelief at the pull-up wall.

"Mr. Quintero, that wasn't too bad."

"But, sir—!"

Professor Steelsmith didn't bother to listen. Instead, he turned his back to Keithan and went on to make his final notes on his data pad. So did Dantés.

Keithan scratched his head, exasperated. He turned to Fernando, not knowing what to say, what excuse to give him. Fernando didn't look upset, but he shot Keithan a warning look, which made Keithan realize what he was doing; he was acting almost the same way Owen had. Therefore, Keithan did his best to control himself and decided not to say another word.

"Well, that was fun," Steelsmith joked, addressing the whole class, though none of the students appreciated his humor. He, therefore, cleared his throat before continuing. "As you could see, to have a counterthruster doesn't necessarily mean that it'll be much easier for a pilot to maneuver in the air. Yes, it can allow him or her to execute drastic maneuvers, especially within short distances, as you pilot students experienced today. Still, you all witnessed that using a counterthruster requires that a pilot masters not only how to use it but, more importantly, how to control it according to his or her particular aircraft."

Steelsmith paused to look at his data pad. "I must point out, however, that of all the drones, Mr. Quintero and Mr. Aramis's showed the best balance between the use of the counterthruster and the aerodynamic design, which, I must also say, proved to us that aesthetics is not as important as efficiency."

Fernando glanced at Keithan with a slight smile, satisfied by the professor's last remark. Keithan, on the other hand, remained with his head down, still upset.

How could I have done it wrong? he kept telling himself.

"In conclusion," Professor Steelsmith said, "I hope that all of you have understood the purpose of this evaluation. And keep in mind this was only an introduction of what you will attempt next year—"

"With your real aircraft," Dantés finished for him.

How could I have done it wrong?

The question continued aggravating Keithan the rest of the morning. He knew it was dumb to keep thinking about it, but he couldn't accept the fact that he had crashed the drone. It bothered him so much he even had a hard time paying attention in the classes that followed.

After Advanced Aeronautics, Keithan went to Flight Risk Management, followed by Racing Precision and Techniques. They were part of the list of specialized courses that only pilot students took while the aeroengineer students took their own specialized courses. Because of that, Keithan and Fernando didn't see each other again until lunchtime.

They met at the circular courtyard, the only area at the academy with vegetation. The area included a couple of palm trees aligned in different curved patches of grass and a tall flamboyant tree, also known as a flame tree, which stood right at the center of the courtyard with its impressive, flaming-red crown. Few students were already there having lunch and relaxing under the shade of the palm trees. Keithan and Fernando settled at one of the tables under the flame tree. Of the two,

Fernando was the only one eating his lunch. He took another piece of fried tilapia with his fork and brought it to his mouth while he stared at Keithan, who sat opposite him without having touched his food yet.

Keithan held what was left of their broken drone's fuselage in his hands. He stared at it, as if trying to find a convincing explanation as to why he had failed to pull it up before he crashed it.

"I still can't figure out what went wrong?" he complained. "I know I could have pulled it up in time."

Fernando sighed. Clearly, he was tired of talking about the subject. "Jus' forg't 'bout it," he said with his mouth full, pausing to swallow. "You still did better than everybody else. Besides, you should be glad your first failed attempt with a counterthruster was with a drone and not with the *d'Artagnan*. Otherwise *I* would've been upset. Very upset."

Keithan nodded in agreement. Things could have been a lot worse if Keithan had crashed the *d'Artagnan* during the evaluation instead of the drone. As Professor Steelsmith had made the students realize at the end of the class, the purpose of the evaluation had been to prepare them for what they would be facing next year.

Keithan shook his frustration away and finally put the wrecked drone aside. He grabbed the tangerine next to his plate of chicken pasta and started peeling it. He was about to bring the first piece to his mouth when he and Fernando saw a bunch of students—pilots and aeroengineers—rush past them.

"What the …?" said Fernando, holding his fork halfway to his mouth.

Keithan called out to one of the running students. "Hey! What's going on?"

The boy, an aeroengineer with bushy blond hair, halted a few feet away in front of Keithan and Fernando. "Someone saw the metallic spheres take off to the sky!" he replied, panting. "You know, the ones that showed up on the main runway this morning." And with that he kept on running.

Keithan and Fernando exchanged looks. The next second, Keithan dropped the tangerine and jumped to his feet as Fernando dropped his fork on his plate, pushed back his wheelchair, and turned it around. They hurried together after the other students.

They rushed through the hangar bay and went out the other side, where they found over thirty students of all the different levels agglomerating. They were all gazing skyward with their eyes narrowed and shielded with their hands, most likely searching for the metallic spheres.

Keithan and Fernando did the same when they reached the group, yet they didn't see anything up there, aside from a few wispy strands of cirrus clouds. There weren't even contrails showing any evidence of a craft having flown by over the airport.

"There's nothing up there," complained somebody in the group. "Is this a joke?"

"It's not. I saw three shiny spheres fly away," a boy pilot replied. "I swear. I saw them about a minute ago."

"He's right. I saw them too," said a boy next to him.

"They shot off northwestward."

Everybody stood still, staring with intrigue at the sky.

"Are you sure they were flying spheres? Professor Steelsmith said they were military radars," said Fernando, looking to the northwest.

"They couldn't have been radars. They flew, and they flew fast," the first boy reassured him.

Keithan didn't know about Fernando, but he believed the boy. He kept searching the sky like everyone else. So far, he couldn't see anything unusual up there. The only thing he could spot was a small flock of white herons flying east. If the mysterious spheres had indeed flown away as the boys claimed, they were long gone now.

"What is the meaning of this?" the authoritative voice of Headmaster Viviani made the students jump. He marched straight toward them, a look of outrage behind his coin-size glasses moving from student to student, like a scanner identifying each one. Right behind him were five professors, among them Steelsmith and Dantés.

"What is going on here?" the headmaster demanded. He stopped in front of the crowd of students, his hands on his wide, round hips while he waited for somebody to answer.

The professors waited behind them, staring at the students.

"Sir, the three metallic spheres that appeared this morning on the main runway shot off into the sky," said one of the students.

"It's true, Headmaster," another said, "We—"

But the headmaster cut him short right away. "Is *that* what this is about?" he said, irritated. "For the hundredth time, no mysterious spheres are flying over Ramey. The spheres on the runway were military radars brought to the airport for testing. Now..." He took a strong breath, his large chest inflating before he continued. "...I want every student back inside the academy this instant, or I will give you all detention for an entire month."

His menacing look showed he meant business, yet none of the students reacted right away. Headmaster Viviani clapped his hands insistently. "That was an order!" he said sharply.

The crowd dissipated right away, and the students headed back inside. Keithan and Fernando looked one last time at the sky before they moved along with everyone else.

"You think it might have been the spheres?" Fernando asked Keithan as he rotated his wheelchair back to the academy.

"I'm not sure," Keithan said.

Keithan had to pass right in front of Headmaster Viviani, but he dared not look at the man. Instead, he turned his attention to Professor Dantés, who was beside the headmaster but looking skyward, as if searching for something. He kept walking but kept staring suspiciously at the professor until he was forced to look away when she noticed him watching her.

Keithan waited a few seconds before he dared to look back over his shoulder. This time, he saw Dantés walking away—but in the opposite direction of the academy.

"What's wrong?" Fernando asked when he noticed that Keithan had stopped.

Keithan turned to him and continued walking.

"Nothing," he lied.

CHAPTER 10

Time for flight class. Keithan could only wonder what he and the Viviani twins would be doing since they were grounded until further notice. He didn't see the point in going to the class if he wasn't allowed to fly, but he had had no choice. Dantés had instructed him to show up anyway.

The first two students had already taken off to the sky: Gabriel Ortiz, flying his single-engine racing craft, followed by Aimi Murakami in her double-engine racer. Keithan, who stood under the shade near the entrance of the hangar bay, watched them soar up and bank right to the west. He kept his arms folded and his back against the wall as he sighed, wishing he were flying too.

Not far from him, Owen and Lance looked as miserable as he did. Keithan looked away to avoid making eye contact with either one of them. He checked his wrist communicator and noticed that fifteen minutes had passed since the class had started. Still, there was no sign of Professor Dantés.

Something fishy is going on, Keithan thought. The professor never arrived late for class.

At the moment, Harley Swift, Dantés's twenty-three-year-old assistant, was the one in charge. The young man, redheaded and wearing aviator shades, stood on a circular hover platform that remained two feet off the ground by four low-powered antigravity plates. He was monitoring the students in the air from a console.

"Keep ascending and do a couple of laps over the airfield to warm up," Swift said, addressing Gabriel and Aimi through his headset.

Just then, a low rumbling, accompanied by a humming, became louder near Keithan as a dark-gray aircraft with purple linings came out hovering slowly from the hangar bay. The craft's side had the custom decal of a Goth fairy in a short black Victorian dress, along with the words *Rebel Fairy* in metallic purple.

"Genevieve," Keithan called at his friend, who saw him from inside the aircraft's cockpit.

The girl had her canopy open as she brought the craft to a halt next to Keithan. She raised her helmet visor and gazed down at him.

"You sure you're not going to be allowed to fly during class at least?" Genevieve asked him over the noise of the craft's engines.

"Pretty sure," Keithan said, grimacing. "I still have no idea what the twins and I will be doing in the meantime, though."

"Miss Donnelly!" Swift called. Both Genevieve and Keithan turned to see Dantés's assistant approach on his floating platform. "Miss Donnelly, please get ready to take off. I want all the students who are allowed to fly in the air before the professor arrives."

"Yes, sir," Genevieve replied with a nod.

"Good luck up there," Keithan told her.

"Thanks. You know, it's a shame you can't join us; I was hoping I could get a chance to beat you today in the air."

"Ha! As if that could happen," Keithan replied with a cocky smirk.

He watched her close the cockpit canopy and backed away as the *Rebel Fairy's* twin engines gained more power. Swift moved his platform to leave a clear path for Genevieve. The strong propulsion of the *Rebel Fairy* forced Keithan to cover his face with his forearm. He even had to place a foot back to prevent himself from losing his balance as the aircraft took off.

Not long after she was gone, Professor Dantés showed up. Keithan spotted her coming from under the academy's bridge that connected to the control tower. She marched fast as she approached. Keithan couldn't help but watch her suspiciously. He wondered why she had taken so long to show up. He was sure it had something to do with what had happened during lunch hour. He had a feeling the professor knew something the students didn't regarding the mysterious spheres that showed up at the airport.

"All right. Let's start this," Dantés said aloud, gesturing to Swift to pick her up. Before she climbed onto the moving platform to assume control of it, she turned to Keithan, Lance, and Owen. "You three, wait right there. This will only take a moment," she told them.

Swift, who remained beside her, took off the headset and handed it to the professor.

"All flying pilot students confirm communication," Dantés said right away into the headset's microphone.

The students replied one by one.

"Excellent. Listen carefully now," Dantés began. "You're going to practice several maneuvers while I go take care of something inside the academy. Begin by executing the split S maneuver, followed by the loop over and the loop under. Do not fly higher than two thousand feet—and no barrel rolls until I return. Is that clear?"

The students in the air acknowledged, their voices heard from the hover platform's console.

Dantés took a moment to work on the console before she addressed the students again. "I am finishing programming the hover rings' positions to raise them when I return. So warm up so we can carry out a short obstacle race." With that, she took off the headset and handed it back to Swift.

"What about them?" Swift asked, nodding at Keithan and the twins.

"I'm taking them to Professor Treweeke," Dantés told him.

Keithan, who wasn't far away from earshot, huffed silently, knowing what Dantés meant; she was going to take them to the simulators. "Oh man!"

He glanced at the twins and noticed they weren't too happy about it, either.

"I could take them if you prefer, Professor," Swift offered.

"That won't be necessary," Dantés told him. "I have to go inside anyway and deal with something else. I need you here to supervise the students until I return. Call me if there's any trouble."

"Yes, ma'am."

Dantés stepped down from the platform and marched straight to Keithan, Owen, and Lance.

"All right you three. Follow me."

It was uncomfortable enough to have to walk with Lance and Owen, but it was worse to do so in complete silence while Dantés led them down the hallways. Lance and Owen continued side by side, looking like two gorillas behind the professor, while Keithan brought up the rear like a kid being ignored. They walked until they reached the cylindrical elevator, which took them deep underground to the lowest floor of the academy.

After a bounce, the elevator opened, and the group stepped out to a narrow corridor that ran around an octagonal room enclosed by floor-to-ceiling glass walls. The room gave the impression of a giant fish tank, which was how the students had come to refer to it. Its door, also made of glass, had the word "Simulators" stenciled on it. Dantés opened it.

For Keithan, to enter the simulators room was like stepping into an arcade, deafened by all kinds of loud electronic sounds. It had no illumination except for a series of neon-blue lights on the black floor that intersected among themselves, creating one big lighted web design. Both left and right were students mounted on the simulator machines. Each simulator consisted of a single seat with an egg-shaped black capsule that enclosed the student from head to waist, leaving his or her legs exposed and stretched forward, along with the feet resting on a pair of pedals. The seat, however, didn't touch the floor; it was attached by the back to a big mechanical arm that hung from the ceiling, along with numerous wires. It was that mechanical arm that allowed the seat and its capsule to rotate upside down and sideways.

"Nice and easy, everybody. Nice and easy," the amplified voice of Professor Treweeke echoed over the non-rhythmic servo sounds.

Keithan remembered the first time he entered this room five years ago. Like his other pilot classmates, he had felt scared at first since it had been here where basically everything had started for him, where he had taken his first flight class. Back then, the simulators were the coolest things the academy had to offer him. Keithan remembered waiting anxiously every day for his flight training classes to use them. Of course, that was until the second half of his third year, when, after having received his pilot certificate, he was assigned to team up with Fernando to build their biggest accomplishment so far: the *d'Artagnan*. From that moment on, the simulators room was nothing more to Keithan than another classroom in the academy.

"Excuse me, Walter?" Dantés called out to Professor Treweeke, who stood at the center of the room, working inside a round, low-raised workstation.

Enclosing Treweeke were a pair of floating holo screens that allowed him to see each student's viewport.

"Ah, Alexandria! I'll be right with you," Treweeke replied in his amplified voice. He glanced at her through the yellow lenses of his rectangular-framed glasses but returned his attention to the holo screens. "Number Eight: Mendoza," he said to one of the students in the simulators, "check your attitude indicator to make sure your aircraft is leveled with the horizon bar. Don't forget, you need to keep it leveled unless you want to make a turn."

Soon after that, he got down from the workstation and went to Dantés. "Sorry about that, Alexandria."

"It's all right," Dantés said. "I'm here to see if, by any chance, you have three simulators available."

"I do. Headmaster Viviani already explained the situation with Quintero and the Vivianis."

"Perfect," Dantés said. "Here are the flight sequences I want them to practice."

Dantés handed Treweeke a data card and turned to Keithan and the twins. "Listen up and listen well. Until further notice, while the three of you are grounded, you're to come here and report to the professor during flight class. Understood?"

"Yes, ma'am," the three of them answered with a lack of enthusiasm.

Dantés nodded and turned to Treweeke. "They're all yours, Professor."

She turned and headed to the door. Keithan didn't take his eyes away from her until she was out of the room.

"Okay, rebel air racers. This way," said Treweeke, adjusting his yellow-lensed glasses.

Owen, Lance, and Keithan followed him in single file among the simulators to the other end of the room. There, the professor reached out to the ceiling, pressed a button, and stepped back. A metal hatch opened, and a simulator machine attached to a mechanical arm descended. Treweeke reached out to two other hatches next to the first one and brought down two other simulators.

"There we go," Treweeke said. "Lance, Owen, the first two are yours. Keithan, you take the third."

Both twins got into their assigned simulators, yet Keithan remained staring at his with a sour face.

"Um, Professor, could I go to the bathroom first?" Keithan dared to ask.

"Now?" Treweeke scowled and took a moment before he answered. "You have five minutes. Here."

He pulled out an electronic pen from one of his pockets and pressed it against the academy's digital insignia on Keithan's uniform. "Remember, five minutes."

"Yes, sir."

Keithan hurried out of the room to take the elevator. Before he pressed the "up" button, he looked up and noticed the number "4" lit up. Surely the last person who had used the elevator must have gotten out on that floor, and Keithan was confident it had been Dantés.

As soon as he entered the elevator, he told the command recognition system, "Fourth floor, please," and waited to be taken there.

Once he got out, he looked to the left. The bathroom signs were down the hallway, not too far away, but Keithan didn't go in that direction. He had no real intention to go to the bathroom; he had something else in mind. So instead, he went right—in the direction he had a feeling Dantés had gone.

The hallway took him counterclockwise around the building. It comprised a blue-gray convex wall with square panels and angled corners on one side and a concave wall of glass windows that faced the airfield on the other.

Keithan felt the need to run, but he preferred to walk to avoid making noise with his boots against the smooth gray floor. He heard someone ahead and slowed his pace. He moved closer to the wall on the left and waited a few seconds. He wasn't sure if it was best to keep running or to turn back. By the time he decided to do the latter, it was too late.

"Whoa!" Keithan jumped, staring at the figure that had found him. It wasn't a human, but an HM unit—one of the hall monitor robots that ran around each floor. Students hated them since they were good at catching students running in the hallways or walking around without permission during classes. The robot was nearly four feet tall, with a blue mushroom-shaped head with yellow linings, a dark lens, and no extremities, except for a mechanical bent arm that balanced over a spherical tire that allowed the robot to move. On its front, it had the number "4" glowing in blue, which indicated the floor it was programmed to monitor.

The HM robot stood in front of Keithan and straightened itself, becoming a foot taller. From its oval lens, it shot a red scanning fan at the insignia on Keithan's left shoulder sleeve.

"Keithan Quintero, age thirteen, level five," said the robot in a slightly distorted monotone voice. "Supposed to be in flight class with Professor Dantés."

"Yes. I know!" Keithan snapped in a whisper, looking at both ends of the hallway and hoping that nobody would hear them. He pressed his digital insignia and showed it to the robot, this time with the hall passcode Professor Treweeke had downloaded to it visible.

The robot scanned it a second time and said, "Hall pass confirmed. You may proceed." Lowering itself again, it continued down the hallway in the direction Keithan had come from.

Keithan only gave it a few seconds before he, too, took off. He walked fast and was about to go into the entryway of an ascending staircase to his left when he heard voices coming from there. They made him halt for a moment before he approached it. He dared not enter. Instead, he threw himself against the wall and leaned close enough to the entryway to eavesdrop.

"Airport security and its authorities confirmed it. The metallic spheres took off from the main runway around twelve o'clock," a female voice with a familiar British accent said in a hushed tone.

"Did they finally find out what they really were?" a male voice asked in the same tone.

"No, sir. They never did. They weren't even able to confirm where they came from."

Keithan's hearing sense heightened at that moment as he realized what the conversation was about. It didn't take him long to recognize the voices of Professor Dantés and Headmaster Viviani, either. Doing his best not to make the slightest sound, not even with his breathing, Keithan neared to the edge of the staircase entrance to listen more.

"Students believe those spheres are related to the Pegasus Air Race, which, by the way, it's being announced that it's going to take place here at Ramey this year," the headmaster said with a tone of concern.

"I know, sir. I saw some of the posters that announce it," Dantés replied. "I asked airport security about that too. They informed me that they've been trying to contact Pegasus Company since they found out about the poster ads yesterday. For some reason, they haven't been able to get a response."

There was a moment of silence. Keithan held his breath. Once again, he looked both ways down the hallway. Sure that neither the HM robot nor anyone else was near, he attempted to peek into the staircase.

It was then, at the worst possible moment, that his stomach growled. Keithan was forced to back away immediately.

Man! I should've eaten something at lunch, he grumbled in his head.

"Still, I don't think the spheres have something to do with the race, and airport security seems to think the same," Professor Dantés went on.

"What are you saying, then, Professor? Are you implying we have unidentified flying objects over Ramey?" the headmaster asked.

Another pause.

"I don't want to jump to conclusions, sir, but it is a possibility," Dantés said.

Keithan, still with his back against the wall, frowned while he tried to make sense of that last comment. It reminded him of Winston Oddie, who, according to Genevieve and Yari, had been telling everyone at the academy that the mysterious spheres were UFOs. Keithan found the idea absurd at first, but now he couldn't help but wonder.

What if Winston hadn't been mistaken?

CHAPTER 11

Keithan couldn't wait to tell Fernando about the secret conversation between Dantés and the headmaster, yet as soon as the bell of the last period rang, he left the academy without meeting with him. There was something more important he needed to do first—and fast …

He needed to get something to eat.

His stomach kept grumbling like a grouchy dog inside him. It hadn't even let him focus while he did the flight sequence he had been assigned to practice in the simulator. So once Keithan was outside the academy, he hurried out of the airport and crossed the street, straight to Rocket's Diner. There, he ordered two Wing Burger combos (one for him and one for Fernando), and as soon as he paid, he hurried back to the airport, to Fernando's residential hangar.

His best friend was working on the *d'Artagnan* by the time Keithan got there. Mrs. Aramis had brought him before she left to pick up Marianna at her school. As for Mr. Aramis, he could be heard working far at the back of the hangar.

Keithan, who was finishing his burger, tossed Fernando the bag with the other one and went on to tell him about Dantés and the headmaster's conversation.

"Thrr s'r tha'?" said Fernando, half swallowing a bite of his burger.

"Mhmm," Keithan replied after taking a sip from his bottled water. "I don't get it, though. It's as if nobody at the airport knows what's happening. First, we see posters throughout Ramey announcing that the Pegasus Air Race will be held this year in Puerto Rico, but they turn out to be false advertisements, according to airport security. Then the three flying metallic spheres mysteriously show up at Ramey, and nobody knows where they came from."

"Then the spheres fly away, just like that," Fernando added.

"Exactly," Keithan said. "I'm telling you, something weird is going on at this airport."

"Maybe somebody isn't telling the whole truth."

Keithan frowned. "You think so?"

Fernando was about to answer when a loud and high-pitched whine, like a jet engine about to explode, interrupted them. It resounded over the hangar, causing Keithan and Fernando to jump and cover their ears. As they turned their heads toward the back of the hangar, a small weird-looking engine rocketed upward from Mr. Aramis's private workshop. It hit the metal ceiling with a clank and kept shaking abruptly against it as if trying to break through it.

All of a sudden, the thing shut down and crashed with another clank.

There was a moment of silence. The next instant, a muffled explosion.

"Dad!" Fernando shouted. "Are you okay?"

"Mr. Aramis!" Keithan shouted.

A thin, black cloud rose from the workshop, accompanied by a stench of burnt metal.

Keithan and Fernando rushed there, but before they could get to the entrance of the workshop, Mr. Aramis came out through the PVC strip curtain, his whole body and clothes covered in soot.

"What has he been doing in there?" Keithan asked Fernando.

"One of his crazy inventions."

Fernando moved his wheelchair toward his father.

"I'm okay," said his dad, coughing a cloud of smoke as big as his face. "It's ... no problem. Just a malfunction with the ... um ... something I'm working on."

"What was that thing?" Fernando asked.

Mr. Aramis didn't reply. Instead, he went to his left and pushed a button on the wall, activating the extractors on the ceiling. He headed over to a panel on the wall and pulled down a lever, making the giant door of the hangar open upward.

Meanwhile, Keithan took the opportunity to move closer to the entrance of the workshop. He barely got enough time to push aside one of the curtain's strips to peer inside when …

"Don't go in there!" Mr. Aramis shouted. "I'm sorry, Keithan, but you can't. I'm working on something top secret."

He didn't take his eyes off Keithan while he headed to the nearby sink and started scooping water with both hands to throw on his face.

"Top secret?" Keithan murmured. Now he was more intrigued to know what Fernando's dad was hiding in there.

"Dad, did you find out anything about the things that appeared on the main runway this morning?" Fernando asked, changing the subject. He seemed to know there was no point in trying to make his dad tell them what he was working on.

"Oh! The metallic spheres? I did," his dad replied. "Pretty neat things, eh?"

All the water Mr. Aramis threw on his face seemed to do little to clean it. He was so covered in soot that he looked as if he had come out of a chimney.

"I found more about them when I came back," Mr. Aramis explained. "I tried to get close to the spheres, but neither airport security nor the military officers allowed me. They even threatened to arrest me if I so much as took a picture with my phone." He paused to wipe his face with an old cloth. "Anyway, as soon as I got back, I made several sketches of the spheres. Come and see."

He threw the cloth aside, which was now as dirty as he was, and led the way to his office on the left side of the hangar.

Inside the office, Mr. Aramis went to his desk and organized a bunch of loose papers while Keithan and Fernando settled at the other side of the desk. The papers were filled with sketches of the metallic spheres, some drawn with a pencil, others with blue ink. Some of them were hard to understand, yet they all showed Mr. Aramis's attempt to figure out what the spheres could be and how they worked.

"See this one here?" said Mr. Aramis, picking up one of the pencil sketches. "Each sphere had a propulsion engine that seemed capable of rotating in multiple axes."

Keithan and Fernando leaned closer. The sketch showed what Mr. Aramis had told them, the rear view of one of the spheres with an engine nozzle and several guide arrows around it, which seemed to explain how the engine, in theory, could rotate.

"So if their engines can rotate like that ..." Keithan started to say.

"They can change direction abruptly while they fly?" Fernando finished for him.

"That's right," Mr. Aramis said.

Keithan picked up a sketch. This one was a front view of a sphere and showed only a dark glossy area in which Mr. Aramis had written over it the words "not metal."

"What's this?" Keithan asked, pointing at the glossy area drawn.

Mr. Aramis leaned closer. "I'm not sure, but that thing seemed to be the clear panel from which a camera could see through."

"So they're not piloted?" Fernando asked.

"I doubt it," his dad said. "They weren't big enough to fit both a pilot *and* an engine. They seemed more like drones, but without any wings or tails."

"It doesn't make sense," Fernando interjected. "Professor Steelsmith told us the spheres were nothing more than military radars."

"Radars? I don't think so. At least not from what I saw—and what I found," his father told him.

"What do you mean?"

"I mean the spheres that showed up on the runway looked like something more maneuverable than radars. I did some research after I saw them, through many of my books—the digital ones and the old paper ones. I found out they looked like the kind that I have seen where you—and probably most people—would least expect to look."

"Where?" asked Keithan, becoming more intrigued.

Mr. Aramis grinned. He bent down behind his desk and came back up with a small pile of old books, along with a bunch of old comic books and magazines that he dropped over the desktop.

"Here," he said.

There were over forty pieces and all of them about one genre in particular: science fiction.

Both Keithan and Fernando exchanged perplexed looks, unsure if Mr. Aramis was serious.

"Flying spheres aren't something new," Fernando's dad told them when he noticed the look on their faces. "People have talked about them for years, though not as real things … at least not publicly. Look at some of these covers."

Keithan had already picked up one of the magazines. It was dated 1953. Its deteriorated cover showed the illustration of several robotic spheres floating over a New York-type city and shooting out straight lines of fire over numerous tiny civilians who were screaming and running for their lives. Curiously, the spheres in the illustrations looked like the ones that appeared on the runway.

Meanwhile, Fernando picked up one of the old paperback books. Its half-loose old cover showed the invasion of a greater number of metallic spheres, also similar to the ones that had appeared on the runway, except that the ones on the cover were descending from outer space with some sort of green alien creature inside each of them.

"*Attack of Utopia*," Fernando read the title.

"*Earthmen, Beware!*" Keithan read his.

The two of them studied the other covers lying on the desk. They were trying to understand what Mr. Aramis was driving at with all this. Suddenly, Keithan noticed what was so particular about them. Besides having illustrations about flying spheres, the covers were all about alien invasions.

"Um, Mr. Aramis, correct me if I'm wrong, but are you implying that the spheres that appeared on the runway might have been … alien?" Keithan asked with a frown.

Next to him, Fernando couldn't help but give an exaggerated skeptical look.

"It's probable," Mr. Aramis said with a shrug. "Hey, but that's what I think. I went to Rocket's Diner at midday and heard other rumors too. Some folks there were debating whether the spheres were part of some military project or had something to do with the upcoming Pegasus Air Race."

"Well, they're not related to the Pegasus Air Race. The rumors of the race being held here aren't true," Keithan remarked.

"What?" Mr. Aramis raised an eyebrow. "Why do you say that?"

"Professor Steelsmith told us that the digital posters announcing the race all over Ramey are fake," Fernando clarified.

"That's impossible. Why would anybody waste time and money handing out false advertisements about the air race?" Mr. Aramis insisted. He moved toward the air race digital poster on his bulletin board. "The guy who brought this one yesterday was a representative from Pegasus Company. Trust me, the Pegasus Air Race *is* going to take place here in Puerto Rico this year, *and* it's going to be held here at Ramey."

Keithan felt his hope return when he heard those words. They filled him with the same excitement he felt when he saw the air race poster for the first time at Rocket's Diner. He had been looking forward to hearing somebody say that.

"Trust me. Don't believe otherwise," Mr. Aramis reassured them.

All of a sudden, the familiar horn of Mrs. Aramis's minivan interrupted the conversation. It honked in an insistent and annoying rhythm, making Keithan, Fernando, and Mr. Aramis hurry back to the hangar.

They saw the van enter, and though Mrs. Aramis was the one driving, it was Marianna who kept honking from the passenger seat.

"What's wrong with her?" said Fernando, stopping his wheelchair in the middle of the hangar.

The van hadn't come to a full stop, but Marianna didn't wait to open the door and jump out. Right behind her, Laika did the same, barking as if Marianna were running playfully.

"Guys, you have to see this! You're not going to believe it!" Marianna held up a small memory drive in one hand.

"What is it?" Keithan asked.

"Something I managed to record earlier today during lunch. Here, Fernando, project it."

Fernando took the memory drive and inserted it into a slot on the side of his left armrest. Meanwhile, his dad, Marianna, Keithan, and Laika, gathered behind him. Mrs. Aramis joined them seconds later.

"Okay. All set," Fernando said. With the flick of a switch on his armrest, a holo screen appeared four feet in front of him. The screen showed the image of a female reporter with glossy hair as black as her blazer. She was accompanied by the semitransparent number two logo of Channel 2, which floated at the bottom right of the screen, along with the recorded time: 11:35 a.m.

"Good day to all our viewers," the reporter began. "I'm at Ramey, Aguadilla, where residents are gazing at the sky after several mysterious sightings that have taken place. According to witnesses, the sightings began around nine and nine-thirty last night when three strange lights appeared at incredible speed but then disappeared. We were able to interview some of the witnesses this morning. This is what they had to say …"

The image switched to a man in his sixties with a wide double chin and a big round nose.

"I'm telling you, they were unlike anything I've ever seen flying over Ramey," the man told the reporter with a hoarse voice while looking skyward. "It was kind of impressive the way they changed direction before they disappeared."

The image changed again, but this time to a couple in their mid-thirties.

"Well, it was around nine and nine-fifteen. My husband and I were chatting on the patio in our backyard when we saw a small white light in the sky, like a shooting star, only it fell downward. Then it changed direction super fast! Like, without even arcing."

"That's right," the husband added. "Three seconds later, two more appeared and did the same before they shot out of sight."

Keithan glanced at Fernando, who gave him a perplexed look. It turned out they hadn't been the only ones who had seen the strange lights last night after all.

"Spotting lights in the sky isn't unusual here at Ramey," the female reporter went on. "After all, Ramey has its own airport, which operates twenty-four hours a day, seven days a week. Nevertheless, the residents interviewed seemed convinced that what they saw last night were not the lights of ordinary aircraft. The question is, what exactly were they?"

The woman paused. "In an attempt to get some answers, we headed to Ramey Airport, and to our surprise, we found a more intriguing scene. It turned out the airport had canceled all its flights, closed its entrance to civilians, and asked for the intervention of the military. Apparently this was because of the unexpected appearance of a trio of unidentified objects on the airport's main runway."

Keithan and the Aramises were so hooked on the report they didn't say a word. They kept watching, almost without blinking.

"As you can see, I'm outside Ramey Airport, in front of its surrounding fence," the reporter continued. "Unfortunately, we were denied entry, but still we attempted to get information about the things that appeared this morning on the main runway. The only person who was able to give us information was one of the security guards at the airport's entrance."

"Hey, look! It's Sergio!" said Keithan, recognizing the tall and skinny man on the holo screen.

Sergio stood in front of the blue control access beam. He struggled to hold his composure against a tight group of hover cameras and story-thirsty reporters who swarmed in front of him, their microphones aimed at his face, as if trying to suck the words out of him.

"Poor Sergio," Fernando said.

"Poor Sergio indeed," Mrs. Aramis added. "Those reporters look like hungry vultures all around him."

Sergio raised his hands in front of him in an effort to calm the crowd. "People, people! Airport security and the National Guard are still handling the situation," he said over the questions the reporters shot at him. "We still don't know what they are or where they came from."

Keithan turned to Marianna. "So it's true, then? Nobody knows what they really—" he started to say, but Marianna cut him short.

"Shh! Now comes the best part," she told him.

"Are those things related to the mysterious lights that some people saw last night?" shouted one of the reporters.

"And are they a threat?" another managed to ask.

"I'm in no position to make further comments about the matter," Sergio replied, his nervousness more noticeable.

The image returned to the female reporter. "There you have it, ladies and gentlemen," she said, staring directly at the camera. "Strange sightings in the sky, followed by unusual behaviors and secrets within Ramey Airport. Incidents that have led locals to believe it could all be a new case of unidentified flying objects, or UFOs, as many call them. We will continue following on these particular events, and we'll provide full coverage of it during this evening's news edition. Until then, I am Rebecca Knight, reporting live for Channel 2 News."

The holo screen flickered before it turned blue and faded away. A long silence followed.

Keithan, not sure how to react, turned to Fernando, who also didn't know what to say. Together, they turned to Mr. Aramis. Unable to hide his smirk, the man said, "So you boys still believe they could have been military radars?"

Far off the west coast of Aguadilla, among the stone cliff walls of the isolated Mona Island, a rock-camouflaged opening revealed itself—and from it, three fighter aircraft shot out at sonic speed. The only thing visible about them, though, were the blue-white flames of their exhausts; the rest remained stealthy even to the naked eye.

Keeping a perfect V formation, the three fighters banked

northeastward. Its squadron leader, Captain John Ravena, better known to his wingmen as Phantom One, cracked his neck and gripped his steering yokes hard, preparing himself to begin the hunt they had been ordered to carry out.

"Phantom Two and Phantom Three," Ravena said into the microphone piece inserted in his helmet, "we should be intercepting the bogeys at a low altitude, so get ready to reduce speed on my command. Remember, no matter what happens, our mission is to stop them from entering Puerto Rico's airspace."

"Roger that, Phantom One," his wingmen acknowledged.

In less than five minutes, the three fighters covered eighty miles, past the Mona Passage, before they reduced speed. The scanner display on Ravena's main console was doing its job, but so far it hadn't picked up any signals near him and his companions.

"Come on. Where are you?" Ravena muttered, confident that there was something else flying out there over the open sea.

No more than fourteen minutes ago, home base had detected three bogeys heading in this direction, but somehow, they had disappeared from radar's scope, just as it had happened the previous night. So now it was up to Ravena and his squadron to find them.

"Phantom One, my scanner doesn't detect any company," Phantom Two's voice came in from Ravena's hearing device.

"Stay sharp," Ravena insisted. "They may be invisible to radar but not from plain sight. Only our aircraft can—"

"Sir! I see them!" Phantom Two cut him off. *"Three UFOs at nine o'clock—flying straight south!"*

Ravena looked left and rolled his fighter into a dive right behind Phantom Two, who had already taken the lead when he broke left and dove. Not too far, Phantom Three followed.

The three UFOs came into view right away. They flew in aligned formation and at a low altitude over the sea level. As Ravena had expected, they were three metallic spheres.

"All right, squadron. Let's show ourselves and drive them away," Ravena ordered. Cracking his neck a second time, he braced himself for the chase.

The squadron leveled to the same altitude as the UFOs and at the same time deactivated their cloaking devices. The next instant, their semitranslucent, half-chromed super aircraft came into solid view, their vertical and amorphous wings pulling to the middle of their pointed capsule fuselages in attack position.

In response, the spheres broke their formation like a bomb burst.

"Whoa!" Phantom Three exclaimed, clearly not expecting such a move.

"Let the chase begin, men!" Ravena exclaimed, and as he said that, he pushed his thrusters to the maximum.

Phantoms Two and Three broke formation, shooting after the flying spheres that went left and right, thus leaving Ravena with the one in the middle.

To Ravena's surprise, his sphere shot downward and passed beneath his fighter, forcing him to make a sharp turn.

"Don't let them reach Puerto Rico!" he reminded his fellow pilots.

It was an intense chase. Keeping up with the flying spheres didn't turn out to be an easy task. Not because of their speed, but because of their incredible ability to change direction. The spheres didn't keep a straight path. Instead, they continued zigzagging like flies. So fast that one moment they were on the left, then they appeared on the right.

"They're playing with us!" said Phantom Two, annoyed.

Ravena couldn't agree more. He, too, was having a hard time with his own sphere. He couldn't find a way to remain steady on its tail. Now flying approximately three hundred feet above sea level, he watched the sphere make sudden climbs, dives, and sharp turns in every direction but without any pattern. Was it trying to confuse him? Ravena could only wonder.

He heard Phantom Three's agitated voice.

"Sir, my sphere is about to reach Puerto Rico's airspace."

Seconds later, Phantom Two echoed the same words.

"That does it!" Ravena said through gritted teeth. "You know what to do, Phantoms. Ranged weapons ready!"

He flipped open the covers of the firing triggers on each of his steering yokes with his index fingers. In response, the green target display on his helmet visor turned on. With it, Ravena aimed at the sphere in front of him. The sphere changed direction so fast it didn't allow him to get a lock on the darn thing. A moment later, Ravena clenched his teeth and opened fire anyway.

A rain of white and purple energy bolts shot out from under his fighter's wings, only to be evaded by the sphere, which broke hard to the left, arcing away. Ravena pulled his yokes and banked, doing his best not to lose sight of his target. To his surprise, the sphere was flying away from Puerto Rico's airspace and accelerating north.

Ravena considered accelerating too, and so he closed in on it. But a split second later, he let it go. He did a half loop upward to turn back and rejoin his comrades.

"One sphere just left," he told Phantoms Two and Three. "I'm heading in your direction to give you men a hand."

"Yeah!—What!—NO!" Phantom Two shouted, first with excitement but then with frustration.

"Phantom Two, what's wrong?"

"Thought I had it, Captain, but that thing is changing direction way too fast."

"I'm on my way. Stay on its tail."

Captain Ravena pushed his thrusters harder, heading south. He spotted Phantom Two chasing after the sphere and shooting crazily at it.

"Hold your fire. Get ready to break to your right," he ordered. "I'm going to jump in front of you."

"Sir, are you sure?"

"Get ready," Ravena said sharply, already setting his jump coordinates on the control panel to his right. "Brake!"

Phantom Two did as he was told and broke the chase. There was no way for the sphere or its pilot (if there was any flying it) to have predicted what happened next. Like an apparition, Ravena's fighter materialized right in front of it with an overwhelming shower of bright purple laser bolts that hit their mark.

"Finally!" Ravena exclaimed as he rushed through the space where the metallic sphere had been hit. He wasted no time and turned around fast, expecting to see the sphere falling in flames to the sea.

To his shock, it was still flying. Badly hit, but still flying.

"How in the world—?"

"*Sir, look!*" Phantom Two cut him off. "*It changed course.*"

The sphere left a black trail of smoke and threw sparks. It headed north, away from Puerto Rico's airspace, though with some difficulty.

"*Do we go after it?*"

"Negative. Let it go," Ravena answered. He had already turned his attention to Phantom Three on his radarscope and was flying in his direction. "Phantom Three, what's your status?" he asked.

"*Still trying to get a clear shot, sir,*" Phantom Three replied with frustration. "*Can't fire freely at it; it's getting too close to Aguadilla's coastline. And I can't even get a lock on it. It doesn't stop zigzagging.*"

"Stay close behind it," Ravena said. "Phantom Two and I are coming your way. Phantom Two, are you with me?"

"*Right behind you, Captain.*"

Captain Ravena checked Phantom Three on his radar and set the coordinates to make the jump. He and Phantom Two needed to be no farther than one thousand feet from Phantom Three's range, which was as far as their teleport jumps would work. Considering how fast the two were flying, a thousand feet was a short distance and meant there was no room or time for error.

"Phantom Two, get ready to jump with me," Ravena ordered. "Phantom Three, prepare to break away on my command. We're going to appear in front of you and the sphere."

"*Roger that,*" Phantom Three responded.

Ravena and Phantom Two bulleted their fighters at only three hundred feet above sea level, the water rushing past them in a blue blur. They were nearing a small archipelago of tall rock formations close to the coast of Aguadilla, which was on the horizon.

Also in front of the horizon was Phantom Three, still struggling to get a clear shot at the flying sphere.

"*Sir, fifteen seconds to reach Puerto Rico,*" Phantom Three warned. "*That sphere is going to make it.*"

"*No, it won't.*"

The response took the three fighter pilots by surprise. It didn't come from any of them, but from a female voice.

Captain Ravena hesitated before he was about to make the teleport jump. By the time he realized whose voice it was, he saw Phantom Three engage his counterthruster and bank abruptly to his left. A second after, the metallic sphere got hit by a wide and bright ball of energy that came out of nowhere. The energy ball didn't blast the sphere; it engulfed it in a web of live electricity bolts that shut it down.

Ravena felt a sudden vibration in his fighter, as if another craft had swooshed close past him from the opposite direction.

"Agent Venus, is that you?" he shouted at the new female voice.

"*Affirmative. I figured you would need my help,*" the female voice responded.

Ravena released a heavy sigh and shook his head in disbelief. It had been an impressive stunt by his female comrade even though Ravena didn't get to see her since Agent Venus remained invisible. His radar, however, showed her as a third green dot among Ravena's other companions.

"*Excellent shot, Agent Venus!*" Phantom Three said.

"*Thanks,*" the woman replied.

The green dot representing Agent Venus in Ravena's radar was heading to Aguadilla, where he was sure she had come from. Meanwhile, Ravena and his two wingmen reduced their thrusters and arced with their craft, each from his own direction, to see what had become of the sphere. Ravena stretched his head to the side and looked down, expecting to see the sphere floating on the water and still intact. Hopefully, a team would be able to take it to the base.

Unfortunately, the sphere had crashed in the small archipelago against one of the rock pillars that rose out of the water, and what was left of the sphere was dispersed and dragged to the sea as strong waves smashed against the rock formation.

CHAPTER 12

The days that followed turned out to be very unusual at Ramey as the news about the UFO sightings continued to make headlines. It appeared in the newscasts of almost every network (local and international), as well as in the most visited news websites on the internet. Even on the local radio, people didn't stop talking about the sightings. They continued to either theorize or come up with their own presumptions of what they believed the UFOs had really been.

The news had attracted so much attention overnight that curious people from different parts of the island, and even from other parts of the world, started to arrive at Ramey. They agglomerated on the outskirts of the airport just to see if they could spot one of the mysterious flying spheres or any other type of unidentified flying object in the sky.

To Keithan, it all seemed like madness as more and more people continued to arrive each day. What seemed crazier for him, as well as to other Ramey residents, was the lot of UFO and alien aficionados that showed up.

Aside from the numerous news vehicles with their transmission satellite dishes mounted on their roofs, there were other cars, vans, and trailers with rough versions of satellite dishes on them to try to make contact with the UFOs, or so Keithan and his friends thought. Weirder still were the cars and trailers with all kinds of alien-themed stuff on them.

Keithan noticed a gray van while he headed back home one afternoon. It had a cheaply built aluminum saucer mounted on its roof and was decorated with what looked like Christmas lights all around it. There was also an olive-green hybrid car with a big pear-shaped alien head made of glow-in-the-dark fiberglass. A few other vehicles had custom paint jobs and metal fins attached to them to make them look as if they could actually fly into outer space. There were many others with banners—if not painted, with holographic animation—that showed different phrases welcoming aliens to land and make contact with them.

And those were just the vehicles. There were also people out there wearing spacesuits and alien costumes among others who showed up wearing T-shirts with alien creatures and spaceships from famous movies. It looked like a big science-fiction convention had taken over Ramey grounds.

It was all amusing at first, but soon Keithan realized it was becoming too much. He knew this was more the result of exaggerated propaganda created by the media. In fact, Keithan eventually didn't pay much attention to all this new craziness going on at Ramey. He had other things that bothered him.

Keithan was still not allowed to fly, which was becoming aggravating. It made the days pass too slowly for him. Aside from that, he kept wondering about the Pegasus Air Race, for the days kept coming and going, but neither he nor his friends and classmates had heard anything else about it. So far, not even the Pegasus Company's website showed an official date or a location for the event. Had all the digital posters of the race placed throughout Ramey been fake? Keithan still didn't know, but as much as he wanted to believe otherwise, he was starting to accept that the race wasn't going to be held on the island after all.

"Think about it, Mr. Aramis," Keithan had told Fernando's dad. "Why, then, is the air race being announced only at Ramey and not all over the media, like the news about the spheres?" To which Mr. Aramis had only shrugged, unable to give a logical or convincing answer.

—–(·O·)—–

At least classes ran as usual at Ramey Academy, though all the professors did their best to make the students take their minds off everything that was going on outside the airport. Their best strategy was to not make any comments about it or let the students bring up the topic.

Keithan and Fernando hadn't talked much about it. By the second week since it had all started, the two of them were determined to focus on all the extra work the professors gave them, which they thought was also the professors' way to keep the students' minds busy.

During flight class, Keithan and the Viviani twins were still forced to go to the simulators room while the other pilot students from their level practiced in the sky. To the boys' annoyance, the sequences assigned didn't involve anything new. They varied in order of maneuvers on certain occasions, but other than that, it was all about repeating the same aerobatic tricks Professor Dantés had been teaching them since the beginning of the year, which was why it didn't take long for Keithan, Owen, and Lance to grow tired of them.

"Practice makes perfect. That's why Dantés wants you to keep using those flight sequences," Professor Treweeke told the three of them after they complained about it.

Keithan couldn't help but roll his eyes, especially because of the cliché saying. He had already mastered the maneuvers Dantés wanted them to keep practicing—or at least he believed he had. The sharp turns, the barrel roll, the Derry turn, the loop, the horizontal eight, and the split S, among a few others; he had executed them so many times with the *d'Artagnan*, both at low and high speeds. There was only one maneuver Keithan didn't mind continuing practicing, and that was the sharp pull up—the same he had failed to do effectively with the drone in Advanced Aeronautics.

Keithan needed to find a better way to make the most of his flight class period, especially since he still had no idea how long Professor Dantés and Headmaster Viviani had planned to keep him and the twins grounded.

So one day, Keithan decided to do something about it without telling anyone.

After settling into his assigned simulator at the back of the room and next to the twins, he waited for Professor Treweeke to download the flight sequence into his virtual screen. Treweeke, who stood on his control area, downloaded a flight sequence for his first-year students. Moments later, Keithan, now enclosed to his waist by the simulator's egg-shaped capsule, saw his download and immediately reached out to a holographic button at the top of the virtual screen, which returned him to the flight program's main menu. A three-dimensional sphere zoomed in from the center of the empty virtual black space in front of him. The sphere consisted of hundreds of tiny squared viewscreens. Each one was a different flight sequence file. They were all organized in different frame colors, according to each level.

Keithan knew he would get into trouble if he got caught changing Dantés's flight sequences for another, but as always, he wasn't afraid of taking risks. Swinging his hand in front of him, he made the floating 3-D sphere spin. He stopped it with his hands and zoomed in on one of the files framed in gold.

"Now *this* is what I'm talking about," Keithan murmured, smiling as he touched the Download holographic key.

The file was much better than the ones Dantés had prepared for him and the twins. Not only did it let him practice the maneuvers the professor wanted him to do, but it also allowed him to practice many others. Even better, it let him test himself in what he had been craving for: air racing.

Of course, it wasn't as cool and didn't feel as real as air racing with the *d'Artagnan*, but at least it gave Keithan a chance to make his favorite class fun and exhilarating again. To Keithan, air racing was the best way to test his intuition and reflexes as a pilot. Without racing, there was no competition and no challenge for him. He considered it his motivation, and he believed it always determined what he needed to improve.

Not caught the first time, Keithan continued doing it the days that followed. He changed the flight sequences Professor Treweeke downloaded into his simulator for others that included air racing modes. He felt confident he wouldn't get caught, for once the sequences were downloaded into his simulator and the twins', Professor Treweeke always went on to work with his first-year students, barely noticing what Keithan, Owen, and Lance did. Keithan even got so used to this that, as the days went by, he opened the rest of the air racing practice files from the Gold level, the most advanced files the academy had to offer.

"Gee, I don't know, Keithan. I would be more careful if I were you," Fernando told him during one of their lunch hours. "Sooner or later you're gonna get caught. Wait and see."

"Nah. No way," Keithan assured him. "Besides, it's not like I'm not practicing what Dantés wants. I'm simply spicing things up a bit."

Fernando gave him an unconvinced look, and Keithan grinned.

"Anyway, how are you doing with the *d'Artagnan*?" Keithan said as he put a spoonful of mashed potatoes into his mouth. "Th'nk'n 'bout plann'g ter add 'ome new featu's ter 'er?"

It took a moment for Fernando to understand what Keithan said. "I'm already working on some new features for her. In Experimental Mechanics, for example, we're learning about different theories and possible ways to increase the power of an engine by twenty percent without overheating it. I'm making several theories to see how I can apply that to the *d'Artagnan*'s engines."

"So, you can make her faster?"

"Much faster."

"Awesome!"

"And that's not all," Fernando added, leaning closer to Keithan and lowering his voice. "Don't tell anybody, but *if* we qualify for the Pegasus Air Race, I think I can incorporate a counterthruster to the *d'Artagnan*."

Keithan's eyes widened, and quickly he swallowed his food. "Are you serious?"

"Only if we qualify," Fernando reassured him. "Remember, we're not supposed to put a counterthruster to our aircraft until next year when we reach level six."

Keithan and Fernando talked about this for the next few days during their lunch hour. They also discussed possible ideas to improve the *d'Artagnan*'s aerodynamic features after they watched a series of pictures and 3-D schematics that Professor Steelsmith had brought for Advanced Aeronautics. The pictures showed some of the best racing aircraft that had been designed through different decades. This affected Keithan since it also reminded him that, whether they made the changes or not to the *d'Artagnan*, he still couldn't fly her until he got his pilot certificate back.

Unexpectedly, one day the wait was over.

It was Friday afternoon, and Keithan had jumped out of his simulator machine when Professor Treweeke told him and the Viviani twins that they were to go to the headmaster's office. The three boys looked at each other, wondering if they had done something wrong. Treweeke didn't even explain why they were to go, but none dared to ask. They simply did as they were told.

"Come on. Let's hurry up," Owen murmured to Lance before they rushed past Keithan. They ran into the cylindrical elevator, and before Keithan could get in, they made the door slide shut. Their laughs faded behind the door as the elevator went up.

"Jerks," Keithan hissed.

He shook his head. After all, it wasn't as if he were in any hurry to reach the headmaster's office to be lectured for whatever he and the twins had done. Therefore, Keithan waited for the elevator to return.

To his surprise, when Keithan arrived at the headmaster's office, he found out neither he nor the twins were in trouble. They had been summoned to have their pilot student certificates returned.

"Even though I don't think enough time has passed to return them to each of you," Headmaster Viviani said while seated behind his desk with his fingers laced near his chin, "I'm aware of how essential they are for you to continue to train with your aircraft for your flight sequence test. Especially since Professor Dantés informed me that the test will be in a month. Nevertheless," he pointed threateningly at them and leaning forward, "I warn you, if any of you dare to make or participate in any other illegal air race, I will make sure that you never pilot an aircraft ever again. Do I make myself clear?"

It couldn't have been clearer. As far as any of them knew, no student had ever gone through what Headmaster Viviani had warned them about, but Keithan—and he was sure that Owen and Lance, despite being the headmaster's sons—didn't want to be the first to go through that, and so they answered without hesitation.

"Yes, sir."

"Oh, and Keithan, I almost forgot this." Headmaster Viviani reached inside the pocket of his vest and pulled out a silver pellet chain with a tube-shaped electronic key. Keithan recognized it right away. It was his aircraft key.

Almost by instinct, and as if attracted to it like a magnet, Keithan stepped forward to take it, yet the headmaster held it back.

"I must tell you," said Viviani, staring at him, "Professor Dantés had no intention to give it back to you yet. So consider yourself fortunate, if not lucky, that I convinced her to accept since Lance and Owen already have their keys."

Keithan barely acknowledged what the headmaster told him. His mind was already on one thing, and that was to take the key and run straight to the *d'Artagnan* to fly her. So as soon as Keithan left the office, he rushed to the hangar bay, but when he got there, he found that the *d'Artagnan* wasn't there. Fernando and his mom had already left with it.

Keithan quickly activated his wrist communicator and called Fernando.

"Mom and I waited for you for about twenty minutes, but you didn't show up," said the tiny image of his best friend on the screen.

"Sorry, I had to go to the headmaster's office," Keithan explained. "But I have great news. He gave me my pilot certificate back—and the *d'Artagnan*'s key."

"*That's great!*"

"I know. So I was planning to fly the *d'Artagnan* before the sun goes down. Is she ready for takeoff? I really need to fly again."

There was a short pause.

"*Um … I don't think you're going to be able to do that today, Keithan.*"

Keithan frowned. "Why not?"

"*Did you look outside? It's pouring rain,*" Fernando said.

Keithan hadn't looked out the wide and tall opening of the hangar bay until now. Fernando hadn't exaggerated; it was pouring heavy rain. The sky was so gray it looked depressing and threatening at the same time. The worst part was that it seemed as if the rain had no intention to stop any time soon, which guaranteed that Keithan wouldn't be able to fly today.

"Oh man," Keithan sighed, staring at the loud rain.

"*I was planning to work on the* d'Artagnan*'s middle engine for a while,*" Fernando told him. "*I wanna check if I can start modifying it to improve its power performance as I've been learning to do in my Experimental Mechanics class. You wanna help me?*"

"Fernando, it's Friday," Keithan emphasized. "You're asking too much of me. I don't do schoolwork on Fridays after classes."

In the end, Keithan settled for a calmer afternoon. Instead of going to Fernando's house, he decided to go to Rocket's Diner and spend time by himself. He arrived with his jet-black hair and flight suit uniform soaking wet and settled at one of the tables near the front glass windows. The air was cold and moist in the diner, which kept the windows foggy. A relaxing instrumental tune played in the background, accompanied by the low bleeps, beeps, and buzzes of the arcade machines located at the far right.

There weren't many people in the diner, two men with different pilot insignias on their shirts chatting at one of the tables and a few others eating at the main counter where Mr. Rocket stood, preparing one of his famous shakes. As for the two short serving robots, they kept themselves busy, moving silently among the tables, sweeping the floor.

"Welcome," a gentle, metallic voice said, addressing Keithan. "May I get you anything from the menu?"

Keithan, who had been staring outside, turned his head, startled. He hadn't heard the serving robot approach. "Um, no. I'm all right for now. Thank you."

The wheeled robot leaned its pillar-shaped body forward, as if in acknowledgment, before it rolled away to continue sweeping the floor.

Keithan took out his laptube and placed it on the table. He remained there for the next hour, entertaining himself by downloading air race videos. But these weren't just any air race videos. They were the best of the Pegasus Air Races in which his mother had participated.

It didn't matter if he had seen them hundreds of times, Keithan still didn't tire of them. He didn't stop being impressed by watching his mother fly with her legendary racing aircraft, the *Milady 18*—the same craft that inspired Keithan and Fernando to build their *d'Artagnan*. No pilot, as far as Keithan knew, had done the kind of crazy and almost unbelievable maneuvers at incredible speeds while competing against the best in the sport the way his mother had.

The videos showed her racing through the series of elaborate and highly dangerous slalom courses that distinguished the Pegasus Air Race from any other race. These courses consisted of numerous hover rings and pylons arranged in different angles, strategic places, and even different altitudes, depending on the landscape where each race took place.

Keithan was watching the second half of the last video when Mr. Rocket came.

"Ah, the 2046 Pegasus Air Race in Italy," said Mr. Rocket, staring down at the holo screen.

"Yep," said Keithan, glancing up. "The one that made Mom a legend, though it was also the one where she … you know."

Mr. Rocket nodded bitterly. "Oh, your mother was a legend before that, Keithan, don't you forget that. Before she won that last race, she'd been the Pegasus Air Race champion two years in a row. Her performance in each of them, hmm. Now *that's* what made her a legend."

Keithan smiled, still staring at the holo screen.

"So," said Mr. Rocket, getting Keithan's attention again, "are you planning to order something?"

Keithan hesitated and glanced at the digital menu board at the opposite end of the diner. "I'll have a … mango-vanilla shake," he said.

It was the first thing he had seen on the menu board. He wasn't thirsty or hungry, but he ordered it anyway since he knew how Mr. Rocket felt about people who came to the diner and didn't buy anything.

"That's it? You sure you don't want anything else?" The wide bear of a man added, sounding a bit insisting, yet in a teasing way.

"I'm sure, Mr. Rocket. Thanks."

"*Okay.* One mango-vanilla shake coming right up."

Mr. Rocket half turned to head back to the serving area but stopped and faced Keithan again. "You know, it's too bad the Pegasus Air Race isn't going to take place here. I know it meant a great deal to you, especially since you were hoping to follow your mother's footsteps."

Keithan looked up at him and sighed. "Yeah, well …"

"Don't get me wrong. I still don't think it would've been a good idea for you to be in it—after all, you're only thirteen."

"What about you, Mr. Rocket?" Keithan asked. "It would have been a great opportunity to have a lot of customers if the air race had been planned to take place at Ramey. So you must've been looking forward to it being held here too."

"True. Luckily, many people *have* been coming here thanks to all the news about the UFO sightings. It's been slow only today, but that's because of the rain."

Mr. Rocket was walking away when Keithan's wrist communicator sounded. Keithan pressed its tiny circular screen.

"Hey, guys," he said when he saw the image of Fernando and Marianna appear on the device.

"Keithan, where are you?" Marianna asked insistently.

"I'm at Rocket's. Wh‑ ‑?"

"Well, hurry up and get your butt to our house!" Fernando cut him short. *"You're not gonna believe what's happening inside the airport!"*

"What do you mean?" Keithan said.

"Take a look at this!"

Fernando moved his wrist communicator, and the expression on Keithan's face changed automatically from one of confusion to one of complete surprise. On his communicator's screen, he saw the airport's pond at the other side of the main runway but with what appeared to be two metallic spheres hovering over the water.

Sirens started to sound at a distance. At first, it seemed to come from the tiny speaker on Keithan's wrist communicator, but as the sound ascended, it turned deafening. Keithan raised his gaze and noticed that it was coming from outside the diner. A row of approximately a dozen military vehicles, just like the turtle-shell-like tanks with six wheels that had almost run over Keithan two weeks ago, started to enter the airport's main entrance without reducing speed.

Everyone in the diner turned their heads and looked out the glass windows, wondering what was going on. Neither Marianna nor Fernando had to say more. Keithan leaped to his feet the next instant, pushing his chair back. He shut down his laptube before he grabbed it and hurried to the double glass doors.

"Gonna have to cancel that shake, Mr. Rocket!" Keithan shouted as he ran out of the diner. He heard the man call out to him, but Keithan was already crossing the street, heading toward the airport's main entrance.

It was only drizzling, but that didn't slow Keithan down. To his luck, Sergio, the security guard, still had the control access beam turned off as the heavy military vehicles continued passing. Keithan sneaked behind the last one.

"Hey! Hey— Keithan!" Sergio shouted, but he was too late.

Keithan's laptube bounced against his back as he ran. He hurried past the parking lot, then past the airliners in front of the terminal and the large hangars. The entire airport had been paralyzed because of what was happening. No landings or takeoffs were happening. At a distance, outside the airfield, the groups of curious onlookers who had been gathering there for days had already noticed that something was going on in the airport, and they were already crowding the high chain-link fences. There were a few news crews also trying to get a good spot to see.

Meanwhile, inside Ramey Airport, more military vehicles, now mixed with the red-and-white cars and hoverbikes from airport security, rushed to the main runway in the same direction as Keithan.

"Fernando! Marianna!" Keithan shouted when he saw his friends in front of their hangar.

Marianna was recording everything with her hover camera and visual headset. Fernando waved at him to hurry up. Mr. and Mrs. Aramis were also there, along with Laika, who was staring toward the runway and the pond, her tongue out and going up and down nonstop.

Keithan reached them and looked at what was happening beyond the runway. He saw two metallic spheres still hovering in the middle of the pond. All around the pond, the entire group of military and airport security vehicles, as well as dozens of men and women in uniforms, pointed loaded weapons at the spheres. It was a tense scene. Keithan and his friends, as well as the rest of the civilians watching, had no idea what it would lead to. Not too high up in the sky, two white vertical helicraft circled over the pond, their guns pointed down at the spheres.

"When did those spheres get here?" Keithan asked.

"Nearly ten or fifteen minutes ago," Mr. Aramis replied.

"They were already there when we came out to see," Fernando explained. "We didn't know something was happening until we heard the sirens."

He handed Keithan his digital binoculars.

Based on what Keithan could see, it was obvious the spheres weren't military. Why, then, would all the military officers keep their weapons pointed at them? Plus, if the military feared them, that proved that the spheres weren't radars, either. The question now was, could they be a threat?

"Don't scare them away!" shouted the people watching from outside the airport.

"Aliens are our friends!"

"They come in peace!"

Keithan still wasn't sure what exactly to make of it all. Lowering the binoculars, he turned to Fernando and Marianna's dad and said, "Do you still believe the spheres are alien?"

Mr. Aramis nodded with a smirk. He was about to say something but hesitated when the entire airfield began to darken.

"Whoa! What's going on?" he said, his smile disappearing.

Everybody looked up to the sky, which was covered with gray clouds from end to end, and witnessed it start to darken. Neither Keithan nor the Aramises could make sense of what was happening now, but it looked as if the sun far behind the clouds was losing its light.

Chills ran down Keithan's spine as uncertainty grew inside him. He had a strong feeling everybody else was feeling scared too. The entire airfield, as well as outside of it, had turned deathly quiet.

With the fading of daylight, a deep humming began, slowly becoming louder.

"Um … maybe we should get inside," Mrs. Aramis suggested with a trembling voice.

She grabbed Laika's collar and paced back toward the hangar. Nobody else followed her. Keithan and the rest of the Aramises remained unmoving, still gazing skyward with their mouths open.

Outside the airport, however, things turned out of control. Most of the curious onlookers panicked. Crying and shouting, they retreated and scattered, starting a mob among the numerous parked vehicles and the reporters who were still capturing the sudden anomaly in the sky.

"They're here! The aliens are here!" a terrified voice cried out.

"Let's get out of here!" another cried.

"No! They mean no harm. Let's see them land!" another shouted.

Keithan and his friends considered Mrs. Aramis's suggestion to rush inside the hangar while the sky continued to darken, but they remained where they were when they saw the silhouette of what was making the heavy humming. It descended from the colorless clouds. Whatever it was, it was gigantic, each second darkening the wide shadow it had already cast on the airfield and its nearby outskirts.

At the pond, where the military and airport security officers still stood, sharp voices shouted out orders, making the group switch target from the two metallic spheres to the thing in the sky. Keithan saw this with the digital binoculars. The officers looked as perplexed and worried as everyone else did.

In a matter of seconds, the bottom part of the large object in the sky became visible as it appeared through the clouds. Keithan shook his head. He realized it was no UFO, but an impressive man-made machine.

"It's an airship!" Marianna gasped. She kept her hover camera steady in front of her, pointed upward.

Keithan, Fernando, and Mr. Aramis gaped.

"What the blazes?" Fernando breathed, snatching the digital binoculars from Keithan's hands.

By now the machine was so low there was no need to use binoculars anymore. It was like watching a god-like monster descend from the clouds. Most of it was white, but it had a few black areas too and what appeared to be a series of golden embellishments that resembled the rich style of the Baroque era.

The machine continued descending. Whoever was flying it didn't seem to be aware of the two vertical helicraft still hovering low over the pond. The helicraft were forced to fly away to avoid being pushed down to the ground.

"I don't get it. Who owns that thing?" Marianna said while she captured it with her camera.

No sooner did she say this than a digital image appeared on the side of the airship, showing the colossal gold-and-silver logo of a stallion bust with an impressive wide-open wing that moved up and down like a bird's.

Keithan gasped and froze. "Oh … my … You *have* to be kidding me!"

Like him, Fernando, Marianna, and Mr. Aramis didn't take their eyes off the image. Their jaws also dropped, except for Mr. Aramis's. Instead, he wore a wide smile that stretched from ear to ear. For one thing was clear at that moment …

Pegasus Company had arrived at Ramey.

CHAPTER 13

Keithan couldn't believe it, and neither could anybody else. Inside and outside the airfield, people remained openmouthed and gazing skyward while the giant airship made its grand yet unexpected descent. It took a while for them to realize that it was the real deal, the actual Pegasus Company airship. The silence of intrigue and puzzlement, however, broke when the crowd of spectators returning to the chain-link fences burst out in cheers of excitement and applause.

The people didn't seem to care about UFOs at the moment. Pegasus Company had stolen the show. The reporters trapped among the crowd did their best to keep narrating what was happening while their news cameras hovered over them, capturing everything nonstop. Keithan noticed all this from inside the airfield and felt glad he wasn't cramped among all those people out there.

The airship stopped its descent over the pond, though it didn't touch the water or the ground. Its massive body was much wider at its front, like a bloated white whale with golden accents. It remained low over the surface of the water and behind the spheres, which, compared to the airship, looked like chrome marbles.

"So the spheres are from Pegasus?" Marianna pondered.

"So it seems. But what exactly are they?" Keithan said.

He lowered his gaze to the group of military and airport security officers who, underneath the airship, looked like tiny military action figures. They kept a perimeter around the pond with their weapons still pointed at the airship and the spheres when something happened.

Below the wide and curved screen of the airship, which still showed the animated Pegasus logo, a rectangular hatch with rounded corners opened forward and downward. From its opening, three figures came into view. They stepped onto the hatch door, which had settled horizontally to serve as a platform. At the same time, one of the metallic spheres moved over the water and settled in front of them. The next moment, the Pegasus logo flickered and was replaced by the enlarged live image of the three figures for everyone to see.

Keithan didn't recognize the one on the left who stood with his hands behind his back. The man had the weirdest mustache Keithan had ever seen. It was shiny, white as snow, and curled to the tips like tiny fish hooks. He seemed to be in his sixties, with an expressionless face, thin red-lensed glasses, and a gray-and-black suit. As for the other two figures, Keithan recognized them right away. He caught his breath at the sight of their faces. The one at the right, a tall young and model type with a self-assured look and perfect long hair as golden as the sun, was none other than Drostan Luzier, the famous air racing champion of the last two Pegasus Air Races. He was wearing the coolest leather flight suit Keithan had ever seen, which reflected the white, black, and gold of Pegasus Company.

Yet it was the broad-shouldered man in the middle who stood out from the group, for everything about him indicated that he was a figure of importance—and power. From his immaculate one-sided panel white suit, which was adorned with golden epaulets and a series of black and gold stripes at the end of the sleeves, to the matching captain's hat, from which stood out a shiny, gold winged stallion brooch. Even the man's beard, which was as black as a crow, gave him an authoritative appearance, perfectly squared, like the beard of a Greek god. It was on this man that the camera auto drone, which was what the metallic spheres had turned out to be, remained focused on.

"Keithan, t-that's …" Fernando stammered, pointing to the man in the middle. He took a hold of Keithan's left arm and shook it, struggling to control his excitement.

"I know! I *know!*" Keithan reassured him, holding back his friend's arm.

Curiously, the three men on the platform didn't seem the least intimidated by the officers pointing weapons at them. They were relaxed and in perfect control of the situation while they gazed at the spectators. The man in the extravagant white suit placed a small microphone on his right ear, took a deep breath, and spoke.

"Good afternoon," boomed his amplified voice from the airship in a clear Italian accent. "I am Captain Giovanni Colani, CEO of Pegasus Company."

Those simple words were all it took for the crowd to respond with loud cheers and applause. Keithan, however, didn't react at all. He was flabbergasted that the chief executive officer of Pegasus Company was there at Ramey.

Captain Giovanni Colani, an incredible aeroengineer and inventor, was a world-renowned figure who had even been named Man of the Year on several occasions by respectable magazines due to the great contributions he had made in the aviation industry. Such contributions dated back to long before Keithan had been born. They included the super thrust vector control nozzle, which was capable of rotating in any direction up to ninety degrees while flying at great speeds. More important than that was the best of his inventions, which had taken the way air racers and air fighters flew to a whole new level (after the invention of the antigravity plates)—the counterthruster.

In simple terms, as *Time* magazine had stated in a 2025 article, the man was a grand innovator, if not an aviation god.

Showing a dazzling smile, the CEO of Pegasus Company gestured with his hands extended forward for the crowd to allow him to speak again. "Thank you. Thank you so much," he said. "I want everybody to know this is being broadcast live all over the world. I have a big announcement to make. Some of you might imagine what it is, and so I will get straight to the point."

Keithan held a deep breath and tightened his fists, holding his excitement.

"I have arrived here at Ramey Airport, located at Aguadilla, Puerto Rico, to officially announce..." Colani paused intentionally. "...that the 2055 Pegasus Air Race will be held here!"

Keithan wasn't sure if it was the man's words or the people's reaction, but the hairs on his arms prickled. There was a moment of complete awe before he felt it, right before the excitement in the air intensified with deafening applause and cheers that lasted for a whole minute. It was such a reaction from the crowd that all the military and airport security officers had no choice but to lower their weapons.

"That's right, ladies and gentlemen, boys and girls!" Giovanni Colani went on, still with a broad smile. He gestured with his hands again to request silence. "I have chosen the island of Puerto Rico to host my great air race."

"See? I told you it was true," Mr. Aramis said behind Fernando and Keithan. Marianna shushed him, wanting to keep listening.

"As many of you know," Captain Colani continued, "the Pegasus Air Race, besides being an amazing event that takes place every three years, has also served as a way to show the world that the technological advances in the aviation industry—especially those made by Pegasus Company—can be used for good and not for war. As a matter of fact, it was because of that that I created the race twenty-seven years ago. Since then, air racers and aeroengineers from all over the globe, and from all kinds of backgrounds—professional and nonprofessional—have participated in it to show their potential, as well as their latest racing aircraft designs.

"But that's not all," Colani added. "The Pegasus Air Race has become such a success since the first one held in Greece in 2028 that it has even created the opportunity to improve relations among the countries affected by the Aerial War and opened their doors again for international trading, thus playing a significant role in the restoration of the global economy. Thanks to that, the air race was held successfully at such places like Shanghai in 2040 and Cairo in 2052, among others."

While he said this, several images of the past Pegasus Air Race locations flashed in sequence above him on the airship's giant screen.

"And so this year is Puerto Rico's turn!" Colani exclaimed.

The audience went wild. This time Keithan and the Aramises joined in, shouting and raising their hands above their heads in celebration. Meanwhile, Giovanni Colani watched with delight. He waited for everybody to settle down again before he continued his speech.

"Now, 'Why Puerto Rico?' some of you might wonder. Well, this small Caribbean island, besides being famous for its impressive natural wonders and beautiful historical landmarks, is also well known as a place of numerous intriguing sightings in the sky. This is according to many rumors about superfast yet unidentified flying objects—or UFOs as some refer to them—that have been spotted here. This was what motivated me to choose the island. I mean, let's face it," Colani snorted, "if such superfast objects are real, I would very much like them to be in my air race. Who knows? Perhaps this year we'll get to see a new type of air race.

"Therefore, to all those daredevil air racers out there, if you think you have what it takes to compete against the best of the best, I look forward to seeing you prove it. As you can see behind me, we have a familiar face that will be joining us again to defend his title. Mr. Champion himself, Drostan Luzier!"

Captain Colani glanced over his shoulder at Drostan. Drostan, modest but with a proud and self-assured gaze, as if he already knew he would win, stepped forward and nodded in response to the audience's applause.

"So that is it, people," said the captain, extending his arms to the sides. "I invite you all to this year's Pegasus Air Race, which will be held on Saturday, May 1. And don't miss its preceding qualifier tournament on April 25, where we will see who will get to compete in the race. For more information, you may visit the Pegasus's official website. I assure you this year's race will be unforgettable!"

Keithan and his friends watched Colani turn with Drostan and the man with the red-lensed glasses and head back inside the airship. The platform rose and shut, as the Pegasus logo reappeared on the giant screen above, accompanied by the location and the official date of the air race.

"April 25, the day of the race's qualifier tournament," Marianna noted, grimacing. "That's only a month from today."

Neither Keithan nor Fernando replied, though they realized how soon the qualifier tournament was going to be. Keithan didn't care. He was about to burst out shouting with joy, but he knew he would need to save that energy for later. Now he had work to do. His plan to train could be put back into motion. Now he was going to train for the Pegasus Air Race, for now it was no rumor.

The race was officially going to be held in Puerto Rico. It couldn't get any better than that.

CHAPTER 14

C aleb Quintero had just gotten home after a hard day's work at the university where he taught. Without stopping, he placed his carbon-fiber briefcase on the dining table and did a quick scan of the house. He noticed no shoes lying on the floor, no smell of burnt food or dirty dishes in the sink. Everything looked the way he had left it this morning, which confirmed that his son had not arrived yet. Therefore, Caleb went to the living room, and releasing a deep sigh, he let himself fall backward on the red faux-leather sofa.

"Turn on TV," he pronounced while he loosened his tie and neck button. A holo screen appeared at the opposite end of the living room, accompanied by a brief introductory tune. "Show multiple channels. Topics: news."

The holo screen followed his command and divided itself into six viewports, each one showing a different news channel. A diverse group of anchorpersons and field correspondents, along with their channel logos, showed up on the viewports. All of them talked at the same time, yet Caleb was able to make out they were discussing the same thing.

"It is the news of the day here at Aguadilla and all over Puerto Rico," said a black male reporter from CNN.

"People are still excited about what happened this afternoon at Ramey Airport," a female reporter said in a second viewport.

A third showed a male anchor behind a curved desk, addressing the camera. "...as the mystery about the unidentified flying objects sighted over Aguadilla was finally resolved this afternoon after two weeks of intrigue—but with an interesting turn of events."

One of the viewports caught Caleb's attention from the rest as it showed unedited footage of the event.

"Enhance viewport five," he told the command recognizer. The viewport at the lower center expanded to cover the whole screen.

Caleb leaned forward with his fingers laced in front of his lips and paid full attention. The image showed a large group of airport security officers and vehicles mixed with an even larger group of military men and women with their heavily armed and turtle-shell-looking vehicles. They rushed down the main runway of Ramey Airport, their weapons at the ready, gathering around what appeared to be two metallic spheres that hovered over the airport's pond. A male voice narrated a summary of the situation.

"It was like a science-fiction movie; that was how it was perceived," the voice said. "Curious onlookers and UFO enthusiasts who came from near and far watched from the outskirts of the airport as security officers, along with the National Guard, formed a perimeter around the two mysterious spheres that appeared unexpectedly at the airfield around 4:30 p.m."

The holo screen cut to a woman in a crowd of onlookers that was near the airport's chain-link fence. "They're UFOs!" she said to the camera over the loud noise. "My husband and I have always believed they existed!"

Caleb rolled his eyes.

The screen cut to another spectator, a teenage boy with bushy brown hair who was wearing alien-eyes sunglasses. Fooling around behind him were a group of extroverted teens, also wearing whacky alien accessories. "Can't wait to meet 'em, man! My pals and I love ETs!" he said while his friends gestured toward the camera with Vulcan salutes and rock 'n' roll hand signs.

Soon after, the image returned to the uniformed officers surrounding the metallic spheres. Caleb's eyes widened when he saw the scene where the Pegasus airship made its impressive arrival.

"As you can see from the footage, the airship wasn't expected by airport officials," the reporter explained. "Nevertheless, it was allowed to land. Captain Giovanni Colani, Chief Executive Officer of Pegasus Company, stepped out from the lower part of the flying vessel and addressed the spectators with a big announcement."

"I have arrived here at Ramey Airport, located at Aguadilla, Puerto Rico, to officially announce … that the 2055 Pegasus Air Race will be held here!" said the image of the Pegasus CEO, which was projected from the giant screen on the side of the airship.

"Oh no," Caleb breathed with dread, his expression changing.

The reporter went on to talk about the people's reaction to Captain Colani's announcement when the front door opened. Caleb didn't have to look over his shoulder to see if it was Keithan; he heard the boy coming toward the living room.

"Quite an interesting day, eh?" Caleb said without turning around. He made an effort to sound as casual as possible.

"*Awesome* day," Keithan corrected him. He leaned over his father, resting both hands on the back of the sofa. "And it's just the beginning."

"I know," said his father, more to himself than to Keithan. *That's what worries me.*

An awkward moment of silence followed between them while the news broadcast continued. Caleb wasn't paying attention to what the narrator was saying anymore. He sensed Keithan retreat, but before the boy was out of sight, he said, "I assume you have plans to participate in the race?"

It was the first thing that came to mind. He intended to show enthusiasm in what he knew Keithan was already thinking, but his tone betrayed him.

Keithan, who was heading to the kitchen, stopped and turned. "Absolutely," he replied. "I mean, come on, Dad. The Pegasus Air Race is being held this year at Ramey. Why *wouldn't* I participate in it?"

With that particular smirk of his, the boy left.

Caleb watched him disappear into the kitchen and sighed in regret.

He couldn't help worrying about what Keithan's smirk implied. He knew his son too well. That smirk told him Keithan would try to be in the Pegasus Air Race no matter what. If only there were some way to convince the boy to change his mind and wait until he was older and more experienced. But there wasn't. Keithan was just too stubborn and too blinded by his desire to become an air racing star as soon as possible.

It was that way of thinking, that desire, and that fearless attitude of Keithan that Caleb still found so hard to relate to.

Deep in those thoughts, Caleb turned his gaze to the collection of air racing trophies, medals, and plaques displayed at the right side of the living room. He paced in that direction. A low neon-blue light behind the floor-to-ceiling shelf accentuated the shine of all the priceless mementos. Caleb stared only at one thing there, a digital frame at the center of the shelf, which played a nonstop slideshow of his late wife's most memorable racing moments.

Adalina, or "Milady" as she had been known, wearing her trademark scarlet uniform with pearl-white linings, appeared on every photo as beautiful as Caleb remembered her, with her natural tanned skin and light-brown hair that she used to wear in a messy updo almost all the time, highlighting her sweet yet confident-looking smile, that smile so similar to the one Caleb saw many times on his son.

Caleb exhaled, staring with nostalgia at his wife's photos. "Why does he have to be so much like you, Adalina?"

It only took Keithan minutes to prepare himself a grilled ham sandwich with swiss cheese. As soon as he gobbled it up, he went to his bedroom on the north side of the house. His bedroom wasn't so different from that of any other teenager, at least in the sense that it reflected the style, interests, and tastes of its young owner—in Keithan's case, his passion for flying and air racing. This was evident from the 1/18 scale aircraft models at the top of the drawers at either side of the mirrored closet to the numerous, old editions of *Fast in the Sky* magazine that lay scattered on the floor and on a corner of the bed, mixed with several used shirts and trousers. Even the walls displayed how much he was into flying and air racing. Especially the one behind the queen platform bed, where he had two digital posters that displayed a random slideshow of the coolest racing aircraft from the early years of air racing and today.

The light and the cooling system turned on when Keithan entered the room. He took off his laptube and sat it down on his desk at the front of the wide concave glass window. He headed to the closet at the other end of the room. He opened it, pressing a button on the wall and watching his clothes on hangers move from left to right. Seconds later, he let go of the button, and his clothes stopped.

In front of him hung his racing jacket. Made of light-brown leather, with a stand collar and twin silver stripes around the left sleeve, it was the one piece of clothing that made Keithan feel like a pro air racer. It didn't matter if he was flying or not, every time he wore the jacket, he felt transformed. He wasn't sure why, maybe because it made him see himself more like the real deal. After all, as he and many pilots thought, no pro air racer looked like a real one without a racing jacket or suit.

Keithan took out the jacket and raised his chest with pride. Nearly a whole month had passed since the last time he had worn it. A series of images formed in his mind. He imagined himself wearing it while he flew the *d'Artagnan* at full speed against the fastest and most skilled air racers in the world, doing all kinds of crazy maneuvers in the sky as he passed through many challenging rings spread throughout the Pegasus aerial racecourse. He imagined himself making it through the finish ring first, becoming the youngest champion in the history of the Pegasus Air Race, stepping onto the first-place stand to receive the trophy, and holding it up for everyone to see.

Keithan couldn't wait to put on the racing jacket again for when he participated in the race. Until that day came, he would at least wear it during his training, which, luckily, no longer had to be in the academy's simulators.

Keithan placed the jacket on his desk chair. While he took off his shoes, he drew his attention to a black digital frame on the left corner of his desktop. At the moment, it displayed a picture of him at age five, embraced in a warm hug with his mother in the Air and Space Museum at Washington, D.C. The two stood in front of the one and only bright-red Lockheed 5B Vega that had been flown by Amelia Earhart.

Staring at the picture with nostalgia, Keithan couldn't help but think about how great it would have been if his mother were still alive. He tried not to think about this most of the time, for it still hurt, but at this moment, he found it inevitable. He wondered what a great feeling it would have been to run to his mother, heart racing, and tell her that he was going to try out for the Pegasus Air Race. To follow her footsteps of becoming one of the best air racers in the world. It would have been exciting news for her, especially since she had dreamed about watching him become even better than she had been.

Keithan remembered the first time his mother had told him about her dream. It was at the precise moment before his father took that picture he was staring at, which made it even more valuable to Keithan.

"I'll make you so proud, Mom," he sighed, holding the frame and hoping that somewhere, wherever that was, she had heard him.

CHAPTER 15

Saturday's weather turned out to be a lot different than Friday's. Though it drizzled at dawn, every gray cloud had gone westward around eight o'clock, leaving a brilliant azure sky over Ramey.

It was that morning brilliance that woke Keithan. He saw it coming through the space between the curtains at the concave window opposite the bed. Though it bothered him at first, Keithan ended up welcoming it to force himself to get out of bed.

After a good stretch, Keithan got ready to begin his day. First, he put on a pair of jeans and a short-sleeved blue shirt. Next, he jumped into his white power-strapped sneakers, and grabbing his leather racing jacket, along with the *d'Artagnan's* key, he hurried straight to the kitchen.

His father was still sleeping. It wasn't the silence inside the house that made Keithan assume that, but rather the coffee maker next to the stove, which was still turned off and clean. Keithan knew the first thing his dad always did when he got up was serve himself a cup of coffee, even before he got dressed to go to work.

Not wanting to waste too much time cooking breakfast, Keithan took out a banana and a handful of strawberries from the refrigerator, sliced them all up, and dropped them into a bowl. He accompanied it with a glass of chocolate milk and another with orange juice. Yet, when he got ready to eat, he took his time to savor it all, more importantly because he knew he shouldn't eat in a hurry if he was going to fly today. The last thing he wanted was to puke his entire breakfast while he performed aerobatics at over 173 knots (translated as over 200 miles per hour) in the sky.

After eating, Keithan rode his hubless magnetic bike straight to Fernando and Marianna's home. It was impossible for him not to see the white whale-looking airship of Pegasus Company in the distance. It looked impressively monumental, even imposing, compared to the largest of the hangars at the airport. The airship floated on the same area it had descended yesterday, over the pond next to the main runway.

Everything had returned to normal inside Ramey Airport. There was no sign of the National Guard anymore. A few vehicles from airport security were making rounds but nothing out of the ordinary. Even air traffic was working as usual, with two twin-fuselage airliners settled at the gates and a third one about to take off from the main runway.

Keithan hurried down the airfield to reach the Aramises' hangar while he felt the intense heat of the morning sun. To his luck, the wide rusty door of the hangar was already raised. Keithan continued pedaling, passing through the entrance, and finally pressed his brake, making the rear tire of his bike skid before it stopped right in front of the *d'Artagnan*.

Fernando's head popped up from behind the aircraft at the shriek of the tires. "Hey! You made it early!" he told Keithan then turned back to what he was working on.

Keithan flipped out his bike's kickstand, dismounted, and headed to his friend. Fernando was in front of the worktable with his back to him. A holo screen with a series of blue-and-white schematics projected from the armrest of Fernando's wheelchair, and Fernando kept looking at it while he worked on a bunch of sketches that covered the whole table.

"Man, like father, like son," Keithan said, alluding to all the sketches that similarly cluttered the desktop of Fernando's dad's office.

"So is the *d'Artagnan* ready to take her out?" he asked, opening the craft's cockpit.

"Not so fast," Fernando said. "There are a few things we need to check first."

"Like what?"

Fernando rotated his wheelchair. "For starters, we need to determine what modifications we're going to have to make to the *d'Artagnan* so she can pass the inspection in the Pegasus qualifier tournament. Check this out …"

He pressed several keys on his right armrest, and the holo screen still projected in front of him changed its schematics to a list.

"I downloaded this from the official website of the Pegasus Air Race," Fernando explained. "It's the list of requirements and specifications that all participating aircraft must have to qualify. Fortunately, the *d'Artagnan* meets most of them, but we're gonna have to work on the engine to make her fly a lot faster. And, um, we have a slight problem."

Keithan furrowed his brow. He didn't like the sound of that. "What slight problem?"

"We need to do something about the *d'Artagnan*'s weight."

Keithan shook his head. "What's wrong with her weight?"

Fernando reached out to the holo screen and scrolled down the list to requirement number twenty-seven.

"See here?" he pointed. "The weight limit for each competing aircraft can't exceed three thousand pounds, and the *d'Artagnan* weights—"

"Close to thirty-five hundred pounds," Keithan remembered. He stared at the screen, biting his lower lip.

"Well, that's what she used to weigh two months ago, before we installed the middle engine. Right now she weighs about a hundred pounds more."

Keithan turned to the *d'Artagnan* and studied her from end to end. How could they possibly make her lighter without making too many alterations to her? They couldn't even afford taking her apart just to see how much they could remove from her. That would take too much time.

"What could we take out from her that doesn't affect any other feature—and that doesn't take away time for me to practice with her?" Keithan wondered.

He paced around the aircraft and considered removing some of her coverings. The problem was the *d'Artagnan* didn't have many coverings already. That was one of the things that made her so different from the other racing aircraft at the academy. Most of her wirings and inner mechanisms were exposed, from the forward mechanical arms that held the steering vanes to practically the whole belly of the fuselage— and the recently added middle engine.

Most of the students at Ramey Academy, and even some of the professors, criticized that a lot about the *d'Artagnan*. Not that Keithan and Fernando cared. As everybody knew, for the two of them, aesthetics had nothing to do with making a racing craft fast and highly maneuverable. The *d'Artagnan*, along with Keithan's flying skills, had proven that well. Bottom line, the few coverings the *d'Artagnan* had, mainly old and roughly modified ones, which Fernando and Keithan had found, worked specifically to make her aerodynamic. So it wasn't a good idea to remove any of them.

"Don't sweat it. We'll figure it out," Fernando reassured him, noticing Keithan starting to worry. "I've been working on a few ideas for it while you were grounded these past two weeks. By the way, remember what I told you about what I've been learning in Experimental Mechanics?"

"The thing about improving an engine's performance?"

"To improve it up to twenty percent without making it overheat. Well, I've been brainstorming on that too. We can do that with the *d'Artagnan*'s engines."

Keithan raised an eyebrow. "Great! Can't wait."

The two of them turned to the worktable and looked over the many sketches lying there. There were over thirty sketches, and while most of them were drawn on tracing paper, there were others—especially tiny sketches—drawn on napkins and torn notebook pages.

This was one of the things that made Fernando so different from the other aeroengineer students. Like his father, instead of using 3-D virtual programs, he preferred designing the old-fashioned way—freehand. It was messier, and twice the work, but it seemed to work best for Fernando. As he insisted, it allowed him to be spontaneous and creative without having to delete any initial ideas, which usually came in handy when the design developed far off the wrong way and he needed to get back to the basic concept.

Keithan picked up a few sketches. "These look pretty good," he told Fernando. "They look a bit complicated to work on, though. Maybe we could ask your dad to help us."

Fernando pressed his lips into a fine line, making his expression turn skeptical. "I wouldn't count too much on that, Keithan. I've been trying to get him to help me figure out a couple of these details, but he hasn't paid much attention to me. He's still too busy working on that so-called secret project of his. Did I tell you he even fell asleep in his workshop last night?"

Keithan chuckled. "No."

"He woke up this morning and kept working. When Mom found out, she threatened not to cook him any breakfast if he didn't take a shower first. Anyway, Dad's already back in there, getting all sweaty and dirty again."

Fernando was showing Keithan his latest sketches when they heard the sound of a heavy engine coming from outside. They raised their heads to look in that direction and saw a brand-new black tractor trailer appear in front of the entrance of the hangar. They both gaped, for at the side of the truck's shiny, enclosed cargo trailer, they saw the distinguished Pegasus logo.

"Um, Fernando?" said Keithan, momentarily frozen. "What is a Pegasus truck doing here?"

Fernando looked stunned. "I've no idea."

The glossy, black sixteen-wheeler had a tinted glass and a steel-framed cabin shaped like an elongated bubble, which rested on top of the engine's compartment and the first tire axle, as if it were on a pedestal.

The circular glass doors on either side of the cabin slid open, and the driver and a passenger climbed down. The two of them wore short-sleeved black unisuits with matching mid-calf boots. One of them walked to the back of the tractor trailer and pulled down a lever that slowly opened the side.

Just then, another vehicle arrived at the entrance of the hangar. It stopped in front of the Pegasus Company truck. This one was a much smaller vehicle, a roadster sports car with covered spherical tires and the sleekest and fanciest-looking body Keithan had ever seen. It also had to belong to someone from Pegasus, Keithan guessed, because it had the same white, black, and gold as the company's logo.

But if seeing this car and the tractor trailer wasn't surprising enough, more surprising was when Keithan and Fernando saw who stepped out from the driver's side of the sports car.

"Oh my gosh! It's Drostan Luzier!" Fernando blurted out in a whisper, doing his best to compose himself.

Keithan felt his pulse quicken at the sight of the air racing star standing outside the hangar. He bit his tongue to hold his composure as he realized that, despite the man being the champion of the last two Pegasus Air Races, this year Keithan was going to be his opponent. That meant it was best for Keithan not to show any reaction that could make him look inferior to Drostan. Keithan needed to see him as if he were just another air racer. He needed to avoid feeling even the least intimidated by the man.

Drostan Luzier was a figure who radiated perfect class and style. He was dressed in a silver side-buttoned suit and glossy shoes that looked more appropriate for walking on a red carpet. His skin was flawless, ageless, and so pale that, from a distance, it gleamed like porcelain under the sunlight. And his long golden hair was pulled back perfectly in a ponytail.

Drostan was accompanied by the same man with the unusual white handlebar mustache from yesterday during Colani's presentation. The man, who Keithan still had no idea who he was, also had an elegant suit, though his was the same dark red of the lenses of his glasses. He stepped out of the sports car from the passenger side and approached the two men who had arrived in the truck.

In the meantime, Drostan paid no attention to them. He removed his shades, tucked them inside his suit, and paced toward the hangar entrance. Seconds later, the man in the dark-red suit followed him.

It took a moment for Fernando and Keithan to react before they approached the men to receive them.

"Good morning," Drostan Luzier said in his Dutch accent. "Is this William Aramis's hangar?"

Fernando hesitated as he halted his wheelchair in front of Drostan. "Y-yes. He's my dad. Um, please come in."

Next to him, Keithan gave a funny look. He noticed Fernando was so nervous he had invited the two men in even though they were already inside the hangar.

As Fernando pressed his wrist communicator to call his father, Drostan gestured to the two men that had arrived in the truck. The men had taken out a tall black-and-white fiberglass crate from the trailer. Keithan and Fernando watched them with intrigue while they brought it in on top of a base with an antigravity plate that kept it hovering about eighteen inches from the floor.

Meanwhile, Drostan glanced around the hangar. Then …

"What is *that?*" he said with a puzzled tone yet wrinkling his nose as if in disgust. He was looking to his right, straight at the *d'Artagnan*. The silent man with the red-lensed glasses turned his head in the same direction.

"Oh, that's our racing craft. My friend Keithan and I built it," Fernando replied. He exchanged looks with Keithan, who had also noticed the mocking intonation in Drostan's question.

"Really?" Drostan asked rhetorically, clearly not sounding impressed. Still staring at the aircraft, he narrowed his eyes and read the decal on the side of her forwarded mechanical arms. "*D'Artagnan*," he said, nodding. "Hmm. Like the legendary musketeer, destined for glory yet underestimated by most of its opponents." He turned to Keithan and Fernando with a slightly skeptical smirk. "Is it as great as the name suggests?"

Keithan tensed his jaw. *What a jerk!* he thought, but instead, he said, "Take our word for it; she's fast. Really fast."

"And we're going to make her even faster," Fernando added.

The tension was palpable, especially between Keithan and Drostan. But Keithan wasn't going to let it get to him. He glared at the Pegasus champion with his arms folded. He was certain he didn't like the guy now. Not one bit. Drostan had only been talking to them for nearly three minutes, and already Keithan could tell that Drostan was the snobbiest and most obnoxious guy he had ever met. *He's even worse than the Viviani twins.*

Drostan, however, as well as his companion in the dark-red suit, simply grinned, evidently not taking the boys' words seriously.

"Mr. Luzier, welcome!" suddenly said a familiar voice from the far end of the hangar.

Everybody turned in that direction to see Mr. Aramis approaching at a quick pace.

"Mr. Luzier, it is such a pleasure—and an honor—to finally meet you in person." Mr. Aramis extended a nervous hand to Drostan and his companion. "I've been working hard day and night on our project, though I'm still working with a prototype. I'm sure you'll be very impressed with what I've got so far. Mr. Colani will—"

"Take us to it," Drostan cut him off.

Both he and the man beside him kept a fixed haughty look that Keithan could barely stand. Drostan gestured toward the large black-and-white crate the two men in the Pegasus uniforms had brought and spoke to Mr. Aramis again.

"We brought you this to help you speed things up," he told him.

Mr. Aramis, Fernando, and Keithan stared with intrigue at the fiberglass crate. It had the Pegasus logo at its front and below it a set of numbers.

23-9-14-7-19

"What is it?" Mr. Aramis asked with a frown.

Drostan was about to answer, but seeing Fernando and Keithan still listening, he moved closer to Mr. Aramis and said instead, "Perhaps we can continue talking somewhere … more private."

Mr. Aramis hesitated and shook his head. "Oh, sure. L-let's go inside my workshop. That's where I am—"

"Lead us," Drostan urged.

Fernando's dad led the group to the back of the hangar and held aside the yellow PVC strip curtain of his workshop so his guests could enter. When the two uniformed men pushing the black-and-white crate passed, Mr. Aramis went in, the strips of the curtain dropping behind him.

Now Keithan and Fernando were on their own.

"So your dad is doing a project for Drostan Luzier," Keithan told Fernando, still staring at the curtain.

"Looks more like it's for Pegasus, and Drostan is supervising it."

"What do you think it is?"

Fernando shrugged. "No idea. Right now, I can't help but wonder what was in that crate those guys brought."

Keithan turned to Fernando. "Do you think it could be something to help Drostan in the air race?"

"I hope not." Fernando held his breath and bit his upper lip. "I'd rather have Dad help *us* for the race."

Keithan pressed his lips in a tight grimace and shook his head. "Well, let's not worry too much about that, shall we? Whether your dad helps us or not, we can do well on our own to get the *d'Artagnan* ready. Plus, don't forget, I'm going to be the one flying her."

"Yeah, as if that were enough to guarantee that you'll win the race," said Fernando, already knowing where Keithan was going with this.

"What? There's nothing wrong with being confident."

Keithan shot Fernando a teasing smirk. He was acting cocky on purpose, aware that he was also sounding stupid. It was just his way to keep his hopes up.

"Keithan, don't forget you're gonna be competing against *real* air racers—some of the best in the world. Including Luzier."

"I know, I know. And we have a lot of work to do before we even consider that the *d'Artagnan* and I are ready."

Keithan grabbed his leather jacket from his bicycle, put it on, and headed to the *d'Artagnan*. He opened the oval canopy and climbed into the cockpit. It was such a great feeling to settle in it again after not having been able to for two weeks. Keithan removed his key from the silver pellet chain that hung from his neck. He inserted it into the ignition, and tingling with anticipation, gave it a turn.

The *d'Artagnan* came to life with the roar and vibration of her engines, like a furious monster that had just been forced to wake. She rose slowly, the antigravity plates under her fuselage keeping her five feet off the floor.

"Fernando, can you hear me?" Keithan said after putting on his racing helmet and turning on its communicator piece.

"Loud and clear."

Keithan closed the canopy and did a quick check of his console and head-up display. Meanwhile, Fernando, wearing a communicator headset, took out his laptube and moved his wheelchair to the hangar's entrance.

"All right," Keithan said. He grabbed the twin yokes, feeling the power of the aircraft in his hands. "Let's see how well our girl here performs today and if there's something we need to fix from her before we do any modifications."

He pulled down his visor and fastened his seat restraints. Pushing the yokes slightly forward, he made the *d'Artagnan* move, carefully making her face the opening.

"Wait for my command. I'm checking air traffic," he heard Fernando tell him.

Keithan watched from his cockpit as his best friend worked on his laptube not too far away to make sure there were no aircraft flying nearby or about to take off. *Come on. Come on. Come on.*

"Okay. You're all clear."

"Roger that." Keithan nodded. He wet his lips and exhaled deeply through his nostrils. "Ready for takeoff. And off ... we ... *go*!"

CHAPTER 16

The roaring *d'Artagnan* shot out of the hangar so fast it made the Pegasus truck shake like a boat on choppy water. It even activated the alarm of Drostan's roadster sports car, though Keithan didn't hear it. He laughed when Fernando told him through his communicator.

In seconds, Keithan left Ramey far behind. He sped westward, the altimeter marking one thousand feet above sea level.

"Okay, Keithan," Fernando's voice came from inside Keithan's helmet. *"I have you on radarscope on my laptube. It seems the sky is yours within a thirty-mile-diameter range. Just don't climb over twenty thousand feet."*

"Roger that," Keithan replied.

"I'm also watching the readouts of the d'Artagnan. *So far, everything about her looks good."*

"She feels good too. Engines, steering vanes, ailerons, you name it."

"Good. Then you're all set. You should be able to access an advanced flight sequence that I uploaded on her computer. Look it up."

"Hold on...."

Keithan reached for the small touchscreen on the console and pressed the digital button labeled "Practice Sequences." In response, a list of numbered files appeared, organized from recent to oldest ones used.

"Gold level sequence 3B-7?"

"*That's the one,*" Fernando said. "*I copied it from the academy's archives a few days ago, but don't tell anyone. I think it'll help you a lot in your training. Now go easy on the* d'Artagnan. *Don't forget, she's my aircraft too you're flying.*"

Keithan snorted. "Got it."

He pulled back on the steering yokes and made a sharp climb. As soon as he zoomed into the clouds, the scenery changed, as if transporting Keithan into another world. The Atlantic Ocean was no longer in view, and all around him and the *d'Artagnan* now was nothing more but clouds of all shapes and sizes. Wide, puffy cumulus seemed to generate their own light due to their intense brightness. As for the cumulonimbus, they looked as broad as the Grand Canyon in Arizona. And there were even much smaller clouds—yet still bigger than a six-story building—shaped like mystical, dominating beasts that were herding a group of altocumulus clouds.

It was such an amazing view Keithan couldn't help but feel enthralled by its ever-changing nature, which didn't stop showing him a new and completely different way to perceive the sky. It was like seeing a morphing canvas that made every flight a unique experience.

Keithan reached sixteen thousand feet and leveled the aircraft over an extensive layer of stratocumulus. He continued flying straight, enjoying the moment. A few minutes later, he readied himself to start practicing. Keithan reached for the touchscreen and selected the advanced flight sequence Fernando had uploaded for him.

"Gold level sequence 3B-7 activated," said an automated voice, and instantly the entire concave canopy glass turned into a head-up display. With it appeared a series of digital, neon-green rings of different sizes, similar to the ones in a video game but as if they were spread outside throughout the foreground and background of the skyscape.

"Music media player on," Keithan said, addressing the craft's computer.

In response, the touchscreen on his console changed into the media player display. Keithan browsed over the playlist and selected the one titled "Racing Soundtrack Collection."

"Let's see if all that hard work in the simulators was worth something," he thought aloud.

He tightened his grip on the yokes. The music started, and Keithan pushed the throttles all the way.

At the rhythm of the smooth rocking chord changes and the fast, melodic, and crunching guitar riffs, Keithan maneuvered with the *d'Artagnan* as if he owned the sky. He banked, he looped, he rocked and rolled, feeling the freedom he had longed for so many days.

"Wahoo! Yeah!"

With a broad smile on his face, Keithan zoomed and soared through every one of the digital rings floating on the head-up display. He even used some of the clouds as obstacles to make the flight sequence more interesting—and daring. Every turn, every dive, and every climb made him feel the g-forces press his whole body and force him to clench his teeth. It didn't bother Keithan. He was used to it, as all air racers were. He enjoyed feeling the g-forces again, which made a big difference compared to when he used the academy's simulators.

"How is she doing?" Fernando's voice came over the loud music.

"She's doing awesome!" Keithan exclaimed as he made a half-barrel roll and passed through another ring. Flying at 391 knots, he felt one with the *d'Artagnan*. "To tell you the truth, I don't think we have to make too many modifications to her."

"Yeah, well, we'll make sure when you bring her—"

"Hold on!"

Keithan braced himself and made an ascending half-loop, remaining upside down through the last of the digital rings, then half-rolled to level the *d'Artagnan* again.

"Sorry," Keithan said. He turned the music down and exhaled deeply. "Just finished the flight sequence. I'm gonna head back to—Wait a second...."

"What is it?"

Keithan was gradually descending when he noticed a white streak trail not far away in the sky. It was the same type of white streak left behind by aircraft exhausts, better known as contrails. Keithan was sure it wasn't from the *d'Artagnan*; he hadn't been flying with her that low. Plus, the *d'Artagnan* had three engines, though Keithan was only using two at the moment. If it had been the *d'Artagnan*, there should have been two white streaks, not one.

Still, that wasn't what intrigued Keithan about it, but rather the fact that the single contrail was extended southward, and farther ahead it changed direction straight upward in a right angle.

"Keithan?" Fernando called.

Keithan didn't answer. He just stared in wonder at the contrail in the sky. As far as he knew, no aircraft could change direction as abruptly as that contrail showed. Even a racing craft with the best counterthruster on the market would still not be able to do such a perfect turn.

Then Keithan remembered when he had seen something similar. It had been on the night he saw the three mysterious lights in the sky. He still didn't know what those lights had been, but they had descended from the sky and changed direction the same way before they had disappeared.

"Keithan. What's going on?"

Keithan shook his head. "Fernando, is there any other aircraft flying near my coordinates?"

"No. Why?"

"There's a contrail approximately six or seven thousand feet above sea level stretching southward but turning abruptly upward—and by 'abruptly' I mean like in a perfect ninety-degree angle."

There was a short moment of silence on the other end of the communicator before Fernando spoke again. *"You mean like the lights we saw at night two weeks ago?"*

"Exactly," Keithan said. "I'm gonna go check it out."

He heard Fernando hiss. *"Just come back to Ramey, will you?"*

Keithan had already accelerated in the direction of the white streak. He kept a steady flight over it, hoping to catch up with whatever had made it. If there was a new type of aircraft that could change direction the way that contrail suggested, Keithan definitely wanted to get at least a glimpse of it.

He got in seconds to where the contrail turned upward, and immediately, he pulled back both independent yokes to make a steep climb, plunging like a bullet into a pack of stratocumulus clouds. As soon as he got out, he spotted the contrail again, and this time, Keithan's jaw dropped. Up there, the contrail continued but with a series of wild and crazy turns. It looked as if someone had scrawled the sky with an aircraft. The contrail turned left. Then it dove straight down and spiraled up again. It did a couple of more turns until it disappeared into a mountain-like cloud.

It didn't make sense at all, especially since it didn't even seem to have a logical path.

Keithan was still trying to imagine what could have done that when something shiny appeared from the clouds. He shook his head and narrowed his eyes.

To Keithan's surprise, it was no aircraft.

"It's one of those spherical drones from Pegasus!"

He banked hard to the right and shot straight after it.

Keithan managed to gain on the sphere. He flew only with two engines while he tried to figure out where it was headed. The drone, which was still leaving a contrail behind, now kept a straight path, piercing through clouds along the way. Then, all of a sudden, its engine rotated right and—*SWOOSH!*—the sphere shot left. It did it so fast Keithan almost lost it from sight. Thanks to his quick reflexes, he made a sharp left in time, though not as sharply as the sphere did, and continued the chase.

"Thought you were going to get away. Whoa!"

The sphere turned abruptly right, as if it had heard him.

"Keithan," again came in Fernando's voice, sounding irritated. *"Would you please stop fooling around up there? You're supposed to be practicing with the* d'Artagnan *and testing her."*

"Trust me. This flying pinball ball is putting me and the *d'Artagnan* to the test," Keithan said. "You should see how that thing moves!"

It looked as if the sphere were toying with him. It continued making all kinds of crazy and superfast turns and dives, which Keithan did his best to imitate, though with much difficulty. Despite this, Keithan had to admit he was also having fun. It was a great practice challenge, after all.

"Where do you think you're going?" he said in a competitive tone, his eyes fixed on the spherical drone. "You're not gonna beat me that easily."

Once again, the sphere dove straight down. Keithan rolled and dove too. Both went into the clouds one last time and were met on the other side by the Atlantic Ocean, which appeared right in front of them like an endless navy-blue wall.

4,000 feet … 3,000 feet … 2,000 feet …

Keithan started to worry as he watched the numbers start to change rapidly in his altimeter. He and the drone were approaching the ocean so fast Keithan considered giving up the chase. Yet, at merely eight hundred feet, the sphere rotated its engine once again and pulled up. Right on its tail, Keithan began to recover.

The pull-up stunt that he and his pilot classmates had failed to do at Professor Steelsmith's class with their drones instantly came back to Keithan's mind. Even the same tension he had felt that moment came back too, only this time Keithan wasn't making the craft dive by remote control; he was diving *with* the craft.

Keithan held the steering yokes with all his might, feeling them shake hard as the *d'Artagnan* fought against the turbulence of the wind. He leveled her gradually, with great effort, but he didn't seem to be doing it fast enough. The water got closer and closer. Keithan was running out of time. He only had seconds to decide, eject before the *d'Artagnan* crashed on the water or keep hoping to recover from the dive at the last instant.

"Pull up, girl! Pull up!" Keithan mumbled insistently to the *d'Artagnan*. His arms and grip were locked, still forcing the yokes all the way back.

And just when he was about to grab and pull the eject lever, at barely fifty feet above the sea level, the *d'Artagnan* recovered completely.

"Whew! *That* was close!" Keithan caught his breath and continued his pursuit.

A small piece of land loomed on the horizon. It seemed far away. Keithan, however, remained focused again on the spherical drone, which flew close to thirty feet in front of him but increased speed. He worked the thrusters and gained on it. He didn't understand why, but the sphere now flew straight. It kept a low altitude, no more than fifty feet above the water.

"Okay, you're good at making sharp turns," Keithan admitted, "but let's see how fast you *really* are."

He moistened his lips, savoring the challenging competition, and feeling his adrenaline rise, he activated the *d'Artagnan*'s middle engine.

The next instant, Keithan was forced back hard against the seat as the aircraft rocketed almost twice as fast as it had been flying, a water trail forming underneath it. In the blink of an eye, he reached the speeding sphere.

Then something weird happened. A ball of bright purple-and-white energy engulfed the sphere and made it shoot out sparks.

Startled, Keithan pulled away from it a second before the sphere lost power and plunged into the sea.

"What the …?" Keithan started to say, but his words trailed off when he saw something new flying next to the *d'Artagnan*'s left wing. It was unlike anything Keithan had seen in the sky—at least anything concrete or logical. Whether he was hallucinating or not, Keithan wasn't sure, but all he could make out of the thing that flew low beside him now was an intense, blue-and-white flame, just like the ones that come out of the afterburners of turbo jets—only it wasn't coming out of any afterburner, but out of nothing at all.

Keithan couldn't help but stare dumbfounded at the thing as he tried to make some sense of it. Suddenly, like a tiny insect that has just been spotted, the strange flame rocketed upward and vanished into the clouds. It happened so fast Keithan didn't react. He just kept staring openmouthed at the space where the flame had been.

"Um, Fernando? … There's something …"

"PULL UP, KEITHAN!"

Fernando's shout of terror brought Keithan back to his senses at the same time an insistent beeping began, accompanied by a flashing red light. It wasn't until Keithan returned his gaze to the front that he realized what was happening. His eyes bulged with horror.

The small piece of land he had seen a few seconds ago on the horizon was less than a mile ahead and approaching incredibly fast. Worse still, before it, was a white forest of helical structured wind turbines that grew out of the sea and stood as tall as the piece of land.

"Mona Island!" Keithan gasped. As if feeling a current of electricity run through his whole body, Keithan reacted.

He didn't get the chance to do what Fernando had shouted to him, though. Already too close to evade the threatening forest of wind turbines, and still flying less than a hundred feet above the water, Keithan did the craziest thing any daredevil pilot would have done …

He shot straight into the forest of wind turbines.

It was an instinctive response that didn't even allow Keithan to reduce speed. He evaded each of the white vertical structures in motion by mere inches with astonishing grace. He didn't even think about what he was doing or that he had dared to do it. It was all about relying on his reflexes, which were in full control of him now, guiding him.

In seconds, the *d'Artagnan* shot out of the forest of wind turbines—only to come face-to-face with the enormous limestone cliff wall of Mona Island. *That* was when Keithan pulled up.

"C'mon! C'mon! C'mon!" he growled through gritted teeth, the centrifugal force holding back his head and torso. Still, Keithan resisted and held the steering yokes to the maximum as he watched the rocky wall rush past him in a blur under the *d'Artagnan*. Then …

CLANK!

"Argh!"

"Are you all right?"

Keithan felt the hit underneath the fuselage. It made him lose control for a moment. The *d'Artagnan* did a spin, but Keithan leveled her quickly.

"I'm all right. I'm all right," he responded, feeling his heart in his throat from the fright. He leaned closer to the side of the canopy glass and looked down at the island, which shrank in the distance. He couldn't believe how close he had been from crashing. Keithan threw his head against the seat and released a deep sigh.

"Okay. *Now* I'm heading back home."

CHAPTER 17

The red warning light inside the cockpit console of the *d'Artagnan* blinked all the way back to Ramey, accompanied by an annoying beeping sound. It indicated damage in two areas: the rear left landing gear and one of the four antigravity plates beneath the fuselage. Neither had meant immediate danger, but they became a problem for Keithan when he got to the airport, causing the *d'Artagnan* to tilt and scrape the left wing on the runway. Sparks shot out from under the wing while the screeching of metal against concrete filled the cockpit.

Keithan forced both yokes to the right and managed to level the aircraft before any of the sparks could reach the fuel tank. Slowly, he brought the *d'Artagnan* into the Aramises' hangar and kept her hovering low until he pulled up to the sidewall, where Fernando and Marianna waited. He extracted the landing gears, and as soon as he shut down the antigravity plates, the *d'Artagnan* fell with a thud, leaning heavily on the damaged left wing.

"Oops!" said Keithan, feeling the impact hard on his butt.

"Nice landing." Marianna mouthed, standing in front of the craft.

Keithan gave her a look of sarcastic amusement.

He took off his helmet, then his seat restraints, and opened the canopy.

"Oh man!" Fernando moaned. He moved his wheelchair closer to the left wing. "You hit the top of the cliff when you pulled up, didn't you?"

"Um, yeah," said Keithan, trying to sound apologetic. He climbed out of the cockpit and dropped next to Fernando.

"Whoa," said Marianna, joining them. She knelt next to the underside of the wing.

"Come on. It's not as bad as it looks. Right, Fernando?" Keithan said.

Fernando sighed. "Boy, I'm not sure. That landing gear underneath the wing looks pretty mangled. That aileron took a beating too. Probably more when you landed than when you hit the cliff. As for the antigravity plate, that looks busted. We'll definitely have to replace it."

Keithan scratched his head as he stared at the damaged area of the *d'Artagnan*. He felt guilty over what happened but didn't dwell on it. He was too preoccupied with what occurred before the accident.

"Listen, did you see on radar what I saw in the sky?" he asked Fernando. "Right before the Pegasus sphere crashed on the water?"

Fernando turned to Marianna, who returned his perplexed look.

"What are you talking about? I wasn't even able to see the Pegasus sphere on my radar. It only showed you flying alone at all times."

"There *was* something else flying up there, aside from the sphere," Keithan said. "I saw it right before the sphere fell into the water. It kind of ... appeared out of nowhere. It looked like the flame of a power-jet engine, only I couldn't see the engine—or the rest of the aircraft."

"What do you mean, like an invisible aircraft?" Marianna asked.

"Actually, yes," Keithan nodded, finding it hard to admit.

"An invisible aircraft," Fernando repeated with a single raised eyebrow.

"Look. I know it sounds crazy, but I think it was something more. I mean, it took off incredibly fast, like a—"

"Like an alien UFO?"

This time it was Keithan who gave Fernando a skeptical look. "The last time 'alien' UFOs were said to have shown up in our airspace, they turned out to be nothing more than a neat stunt by Pegasus to get everyone's attention and announce its air race. So I'm pretty sure it wasn't alien." Keithan paused. "I would first buy the idea that it was some sort of secret military project or something."

Both Marianna and Fernando stared at him blankly, unsure what to say.

"Anyway," Keithan added, more to himself than to his friends, "whatever that thing was, I think it made the Pegasus sphere hit the water. I think that thing attacked it."

Keithan remained thoughtful for a moment. He headed to the worktable behind the *d'Artagnan* and took the digital binoculars from underneath some of Fernando's sketches.

"Mind if I borrow these?" he turned to Fernando.

Fernando frowned. "Where are you going with those?"

"To *Las Ruinas*. I don't know, maybe I can see that flying thing again with these from there. You guys wanna come?"

"I'll go," Marianna said. "Let me get my camera."

Fernando shook his head. "Keithan, it might've been nothing—"

"Oh, come on, Fernando," Marianna cut him off. "Let's just get out and get some fresh air."

"Yeah. Come with us," Keithan insisted. He took off his leather jacket and got onto his bike. "Tell you what, I'll race you there."

Fernando tilted his head with a challenging smirk. "Please. As if you stood a chance against me."

He ended up giving in to Keithan's and Marianna's insistence. The next second, he flipped a switch beneath his seat, igniting his wheelchair's custom motor.

The three of them left the airport and headed west, racing down Hangar Road. Keithan and Marianna pedaled on their hubless magnetic bikes as fast as they could, though they were no match for Fernando in his powered wheelchair. Fernando was in the lead right from the beginning, about fifteen feet ahead. Every now and then he glanced over his shoulder at Marianna and Keithan with a teasing grin.

"He's messing with us, isn't he?" Marianna said to Keithan between heavy breaths.

"I'm pretty sure he is," said Keithan, leaning over his handlebars.

Keithan knew Fernando could make the wheelchair go faster if he wanted to, but it seemed Fernando was keeping a reasonable distance so Keithan and Marianna wouldn't feel humiliated. Still, Keithan didn't give up; he gave it all he had with his pedaling, trying to gain on his best friend.

Once the trio got to the end of Hangar Road, they crossed Borinquen Avenue, which ran perpendicular to the former and went straight into the well-tended grassy areas of Ramey's golf course. Not too far away to their left, two white domes that resembled giant golf balls rested over a pair of cylindrical structures. Their appearance, however, deceived people into believing that they were related to the sport when, actually, they were radars—property of the United States National Guard.

Inside the golf course, Keithan, Fernando, and Marianna followed a narrow, paved road that crossed the course and continued through a cluster of tropical trees. They continued down a dirt path until they reached an open cliff area half surrounded by palm trees and sea grape shrubs. There, they found the remains of what had once been a lighthouse.

The colonial-style brick structure had been built more than a century ago by the Spaniards, yet due to a major earthquake in 1918, it had been damaged beyond repair, which had led to its abandonment and to the construction of a new concrete lighthouse a few years later at a nearby location. Today, what remained of the original lighthouse wasn't much to look at, mostly its foundation covered in moss and shrubs but still defining what had been the interior, along with the front façade with its main hollow entrance and hollow windows that overlooked the ocean. This was what people had come to call *Las Ruinas*, and it was still considered a tourist attraction.

There were no tourists this afternoon, though. The strong wind whirred and whistled continuously due to the height of the place, bringing with it a salty scent as it swayed the fronds of the palm trees. Among these palm trees stood one that had no crown, only its arched, pole-like trunk with a weathered Puerto Rican flag tied at its top.

Fernando, who arrived there first, settled next to the ruins' front façade. He took out his laptube while Keithan and Marianna settled their bicycles nearby and climbed onto the ruins' foundation. Keithan had the digital binoculars, and Marianna held her viewscreen headset and hover camera.

They looked west, toward the vast extension of water. Of the three, Keithan was the one who could see the farthest, thanks to the digital binoculars. The device allowed him to see up to a thousand feet, the inner viewscreen showing him the distance readouts on the lower-left corner. Far on the horizon, he made out the outline of the small island of Desecheo. It was the closest island to the coast of Aguadilla, but Keithan wanted to see beyond it. He wanted to see where he had seen the strange flame flying next to him, but that was too far away since that had happened much closer to Mona Island.

"How exactly are we supposed to spot an invisible aircraft?" Marianna asked, focusing on the tiny screen of her headset. Beside her, the round hover camera remained floating and oriented westward. "I mean, it's not like we're trying to see a stealth craft, which, though it's invisible to radars, can at least be spotted with the naked eye."

"See if you can spot any anomaly moving in the sky," Keithan suggested with the binoculars over his eyes. He turned to Fernando. "Is there still nothing showing up on your radarscope out there to the west?"

"Nothing out of the ordinary," Fernando answered without looking up from his laptube. "Radar shows a few aircraft, but they're way up in the sky, over twenty-eight thousand feet. Each one is identified with flight codes."

Keithan sighed in frustration. He felt they were wasting their time, but he didn't want to leave yet.

Carefully, he stepped down from the chunk of deteriorated foundation and descended to a group of rocks encrusted to the ledge of the cliff. He had just raised the binoculars over his eyes again when he heard an unfamiliar voice call to him.

"Hi there!"

Keithan jumped, almost losing his balance. A few feet behind, Marianna yelped. Neither of them knew where the voice had come from until Keithan looked down below the rocks. There, he found a plump man with a wide grin staring up at him, waving. The man wore khaki shorts, a short-sleeved shirt with a palm-trees print, and an aqua visor hat with the Ramey Gulf Club insignia over his curly black hair. He wasn't alone. Behind the man, a woman was seated on one of two folding chairs, gazing up at Keithan, along with a girl about nine or ten who was seated on the rocks with her legs crossed. The girl had dark hair tied in a braid and a big pair of headphones over her head. She was pointing an old-looking, handheld radar dish toward the sea.

"Are you guys looking for UFOs too?" the man asked Keithan and Marianna.

"Um, well …" said Keithan, not feeling comfortable admitting it.

"We are, actually," Marianna finished for him. She jumped onto the rocks where Keithan stood.

"Really?" The man beamed at them, turning to the woman behind him. "Did you hear that, honey? We're not the only ones."

Fernando appeared near the rocks where Keithan and Marianna stood. "Who are you talking to?" he asked them as he moved his chair through a group of grape shrubs.

Keithan looked at him over his shoulder and shrugged.

Below the rocks, the woman behind the plump man stood up and approached. "Hello." She waved at them, smiling.

"This is my wife, Lucy. Over there is our daughter Gabriela, and I'm Marcus. Marcus Oddie."

"Oddie?" Keithan repeated, recognizing the name. "Are you Winston's parents?"

Mr. and Mrs. Oddie nodded. "Yes. Winston, too, comes here often, although he had to stay home today. He said he had a lot of work to do with his aircraft. How do you know Winston, by the way?"

"We're from Ramey Academy too," Keithan replied.

"Well, *they* are," Marianna corrected him. "I'm Marianna. That's my brother Fernando, and this is our friend Keithan."

"Nice to meet you," Mrs. Oddie said. "So are you aeroengineer students like Winston?"

"I am," Fernando said.

"I'm a pilot student—a racing pilot student," Keithan added.

"Wait a second," Mr. Oddie said with a frown. "Keithan … Quintero?"

Keithan jerked his head back before nodding.

"I *have* heard of you," Mr. Oddie said.

The little girl with the big headphones set her handheld radar dish on the rocks and hurried to her father. She seemed to have also recognized Keithan's name. She pulled her father down to whisper something to him in his ear.

"That's right," Mr. Oddie told the girl, looking back at Keithan. "Winston has told us about you. He says you're quite an air racer, especially when you raced—without permission, as I was told—against the twin sons of the academy's headmaster."

"Oh. Yeah …" Keithan scratched his head, his face turning red.

"So do you come to *Las Ruinas* often?" said Marianna, changing the subject when she noticed Keithan's smirk.

"Some weekends. We try to spot the UFOs that are seen from time to time out there at the Mona Passage," Mr. Oddie replied.

Keithan raised his eyebrows. "UFOs?"

"That's right," Mr. Oddie said. "Either extraterrestrial or any that might be part of a secret military project. I strongly believe they are extraterrestrial."

Next to him, his wife rolled her eyes. "Here he goes again."

"They *have* to be extraterrestrial," the man insisted, still looking up at Keithan and his friends. "UFO sightings aren't something new here in Puerto Rico. If I remember correctly, that was even one of the reasons the Pegasus CEO mentioned that he wanted to do his air race here. I bet all those legends about alien craft flying in our sky got his

Francisco Muniz

attention. *Plus*, let's not forget that our island is one of the three points of the Bermuda Triangle, which everybody knows is related to all kinds of alien activity."

Keithan couldn't help but purse his lips. Without the man noticing, he exchanged skeptical looks with Fernando and Marianna.

"Now, you know that hasn't been confirmed," Mrs. Oddie interjected, shooting Keithan, Marianna, and Fernando a sympathetic look. "It would be fascinating if it were true. I almost believed it all when I saw the fuss about the flying spheres that started showing up—before anybody knew they belonged to Pegasus. Nevertheless, I think it's much more likely that the real unidentified flying objects spotted in our sky are military inventions kept under wraps."

"That seems more logical to me," Fernando said, getting everyone's attention. "I mean, Ramey used to be a military air base up to the early 1970s, I think. It wouldn't be strange if the military still had things hidden here somewhere."

"Yeah. Our dad has told us a few things about that too," Marianna told the Oddies.

"Really?" Mr. Oddie asked, intrigued.

"They're more like legends," Marianna clarified. "Like the one about the submarines from World War II that are supposedly still hidden in a cave somewhere under Ramey."

"Oh, that's right," Keithan said. He had heard the urban legend many times. It so happened Fernando and Marianna's dad wasn't the only one who had talked about it. The first time Keithan heard about the legend was at Rocket's Diner and from Mr. Rocket himself while the old man told it to a pair of foreign pilots that were having lunch there. As far as Keithan knew, however, this and other urban legends were nothing more than stories made up by locals to either attract or fool around with tourists. But while listening to the Oddies' theories about the UFOs that they were searching for, Keithan wondered if those legends he had heard about could be true.

"Have you ever spotted a UFO out there at the west?" Keithan asked.

The man and his wife hesitated.

"Not really," Gabriela said with a shy tone, half-hidden behind her mom.

"Well, not yet. But we've heard strange radio sounds a few times coming from that direction," Marcus Oddie explained, pointing west.

Keithan gazed in that direction and grimaced.

"It's not much. We know, but they are unusual sounds," Mrs. Oddie added. "Winston even came up with a name for them. Sky ... something."

"Sky ghosts," both Mr. Oddie and the little girl corrected her.

"Sky ghosts. Right. Anyway, at least with our equipment—which might not seem like much—we've managed to hear those sounds a few times coming from out there at the Mona Passage. It's weird, though, because the times we've heard them, we haven't seen anything in the sky or on the water."

As if the sounds were coming from something invisible? Keithan felt the urge to ask.

"The truth is," said Marcus Oddie, looking out to the sea, "whatever might be going on out there, it's something mysterious—and no doubt secret."

Deep beneath the surface of Mona Island, Lieutenant Colonel Codec Lanzard stood like a statue in front of the main console of the control room. He did his best to restrain his impatience and fought the urge to fiddle with his fingers, which was why he held one hand firmly under his chin. He stared blankly at the console's holographic panel, yet his hearing was on full alert while he waited for an update on the capture of the flying spherical drone that had fallen into the sea.

Around him, Lanzard sensed the men and women under his command radiating an aura of anxiety and anticipation from their different workstations. They, too, were waiting for an update. The few that were talking kept their voices to a murmur while they continued with their duties. They watched their radarscopes in case another bogey appeared near the base's coordinates.

Lanzard noticed the time displayed at the top of the console. Ten minutes had passed since the last update was received, nearly fifteen minutes after he sent an underwater team to capture the fallen sphere. Suddenly, the low and continuous static sound coming from the enclosed room's speakers was interrupted by a man's voice.

"Phantom Base, this is Sea Phantom Leader. The package has been securely contained. I repeat, the package has been securely contained."

Finally. Lanzard exhaled through his nostrils with satisfaction. "Good work, Sea Phantom Leader. Bring it to base at once. I'll meet you and your team at the main docking bay."

"Roger that, sir, over."

Lanzard turned to Major O'Malley, who stood next to him, and gave his instructions. Neither of them had noticed the woman who had entered the control room and was marching in a hurry down the platform that led to them.

"Hold it right there, miss," a heavy voice said.

"Excuse me. I need to speak to Lieutenant Colonel—"

"I'm sorry, but you cannot be in this room without authoriza—"

"Lieutenant—Lieutenant Colonel. *Please.*"

Both Lanzard and O'Malley turned to where the argument was taking place. They saw Dr. Griselle Bates, the senior director of the Research and Analysis Department, blocked by two security officers halfway down the platform. The doctor, whose facial features were as sharp as her white cat-eye glasses, was trying to force her way between the two officers. She wore her dark hair tight in a bun. Instead of wearing the high-tech black uniform as everyone else in the room, she wore a tagged, white lab coat with gray shoulders.

"Colonel, I've brought something important for you to see," Dr. Bates said insistently between the two towering officers. "It's regarding the recovered pieces of the flying spherical drone our knights intercepted two weeks ago."

Lanzard noticed the technicians at the workstations staring with intrigue at him and the doctor. With a single gesture, he ordered the two officers to step aside and allow the doctor to approach.

"Let's hope your information doesn't take much of my precious time, Doctor," Lanzard said with a deep look. "I'm sure you're aware that we have finally captured one of those spherical drones intact."

"All the more reason for you to see this, Colonel," Dr. Bates said. Without wasting more time, she handed him the small data pad.

Lanzard sighed and turned on the device. Next to him, Major O'Malley leaned closer to get a glimpse. It took a few seconds for Lanzard to realize what he was staring at, but the next second, his expression changed to one of worry.

"Is that what I think it is?" he asked, his eyes never leaving the data pad.

"I'm afraid so, sir," Dr. Bates assured him. "The robotic flying spheres are much more than what Pegasus Company claims."

CHAPTER 18

T he rest of the weekend passed, and Keithan didn't stop thinking about the invisible aircraft he saw—or rather "didn't see"—on Saturday. He didn't even stop thinking about what Winston Oddie's parents told him and his friends at *Las Ruinas*.

Could it be possible strange things were happening with UFOs off the west coast of Aguadilla? And more than that, could those UFOs really be extraterrestrial, if not part of some military project, as Mr. and Mrs. Oddie believed?

As intrigued as Keithan was, he couldn't dedicate enough time to research it due to all he had to study, not to mention the time he also had to dedicate with Fernando to fix (at least partially) the *d'Artagnan*'s left landing gear and aileron. Which was why, on Monday at the academy, during lunch hour, Keithan skipped lunch and went to one of the places of the academy he had never imagined visiting of his own free will: the multimedia library.

It certainly wasn't the kind of place where Keithan would hang out during his free time. He even felt weird going in there since he wasn't much of a reader. He'd rather be outside learning things through experience and practice, through trial and error. Despite this, Keithan knew it was in the library where he would likely find something that would help him figure out (at least a bit) what the thing he saw flying next to him on Saturday had really been.

The multimedia library was located on the third underground floor of Ramey Academy. Like the rest of the floors, it was reached mainly through the central cylindrical elevator. Its main area was wide and circular, with cubicles (each one with its own computer) aligned in a series of arcs and an information counter at the north side. On the left wing, there were four round holographic tables for students to work in small groups. On the right wing, which was twice as big as the left one, a series of narrow corridors separated by shelves were filled with old books about everything related to aviation.

Keithan felt like an outsider walking there. As he passed down the curved lines of cubicles, he noticed the faces of the few students who stared at him as if he were a stranger. All because Keithan happened to be the only pilot student in the library, which was evident since he was the only one in blue flight suit uniform.

Hoping not to draw more attention to himself, Keithan settled quietly in one of the empty cubicles at the far end of the library. He waved one hand over the desktop's glass. The next instant, the computer turned on and projected a digital keyboard on the glass with a holo screen at eye level. As soon as the computer uploaded, Keithan reached for the search engine icon on the screen with his forefinger and opened it, but before he placed his hands on the projected keyboard, Keithan halted and stared blankly at the holo screen.

What do I start searching for? He typed the first thing that came to mind.

INVISIBLE AIRCRAFT

The two words were simple and straightforward, the best Keithan could think of to begin with.

Keithan was about to press the Enter key when a tall, long-necked woman appeared over the front of the cubicle.

"Keithan? Well, isn't this a surprise," the woman said in a low voice.

"Oh, hi, Mrs. Peebley," said Keithan, looking up at the academy's librarian.

Mrs. Peebley was in her early forties with a short blonde bob haircut resembling a golden helmet. Unlike all the professors at the academy, she didn't wear a uniform. She was dressed in a slim-fitting black skirt and a tight white shirt with a glossy black scarf wrapped around her neck. Her warm smile told Keithan she had no intention of making him feel uncomfortable. It was the kind of smile that made students feel welcome.

"It's been a while since the last time I saw a pilot student visit the library—at least during lunch hour. All of you usually spend most of your time practicing either in the simulators room or in the sky."

If only she knew I didn't come here to do any schoolwork, Keithan thought.

"Is there something I can help you with?" she asked him.

"It's okay. I just need to browse the online database for a … a thing for one of my classes."

Keithan did his best not to sound or look suspicious as he waited for Mrs. Peebley to leave. As soon as she walked away, he pressed the Enter key.

Thirty minutes later, Keithan was still browsing the thousands of results that came up related to invisible aircraft. Moving both hands around the holographic touch screen, he opened, extracted, copied, and pasted numerous files, as well as articles and videos related to the topic.

Despite all the information that appeared, Keithan didn't find the search as effective as he had hoped. There was a lot of information related to stealth technology, both in the virtual library's database and on the internet. Keithan read about different experiments and prototypes tests. He even read about the theories of the origins of such technology. It turned out all that information was based only on radar invisibility, but what Keithan was looking for was *total* invisibility.

The closest he got to what he was searching for appeared in web pages about science fiction. As he had anticipated, under this genre, he found a whole bunch of examples from invisible aircraft described in novels to detailed illustrations of those that appeared in comic books and movies dating as far back as the 1930s. Yet Keithan didn't find all this helpful. After all, it was just science fiction.

Frustrated, Keithan squeezed his eyes tightly and pinched the bridge of his nose. He was about to give up on the search when, like a flash, he remembered Fernando and Marianna's dad. Mr. Aramis loved to look for inspiring ideas within the science-fiction genre. Many of his crazy ideas and inventions were proof of that. It was by looking through his collection of sci-fi books and magazines that the man had come to believe the flying spheres from Pegasus were extraterrestrial. The curious thing was that Mr. Aramis had come close to his beliefs, at least in the sphere's alien-like design, which showed that, as Mr. Aramis believed, sometimes science fiction influenced reality and not the other way around.

With this in mind, Keithan wondered if that could be the case with what he had seen last Saturday. Could such thing as an invisible aircraft have originated from the stuff found in science fiction? It seemed plausible. Therefore, Keithan continued with his search in the holographic computer, only this time he kept the search limited to the field of science fiction.

Browsing through the results, he stopped in the middle of one web page when he noticed two words that caught his attention ...

"Sky Phantoms," he read silently. They took him back to last Saturday when he met Winston Oddie's family. According to them, Winston had come up with a similar name for the strange sounds they had detected several times far off the west coast of Aguadilla. "Sky ghosts" was how Winston referred to them, which was why Keithan was intrigued and opened the link with his fingertips.

The new web page turned out to be a tribute to several science-fiction books between the 1930s and 1950s. It included a list of a hundred out-of-print titles Keithan had never heard of. The list ran downward on the left side of the screen, and each title included a tiny image of its book cover. The biggest of those book cover images was in the middle of the page. Its title caught Keithan's attention, for it consisted of the same two words he'd noticed in the search engine results: *Sky Phantoms*.

"*Sky Phantoms*, by Hamilton Stargland." He read it several times, seeing if it rang a bell. It didn't.

The most interesting thing about the cover was its illustration.

It had a cool, retro style reminiscent of the 1940s and the 1950s. It showed a giant tentacled machine in the middle fighting five silhouettes of futuristic aircraft above a half-burnt skyscraper city. Those aircraft, Keithan presumed, were the Sky Phantoms the title suggested. They reminded Keithan of the blue-and-white flame he saw flying next to him on Saturday.

The more Keithan stared at the book cover image, the more he wanted to know about the book. Barely blinking, he scrolled down the page and read the synopsis:

> *In 1946, a secret organization of pilots with highly advanced airplanes dares to risk it all to fight against alien machines invading our planet with the means to conquer it. Many wonder if the story is true, for it was inspired by one of the most famous legends that emerged from World War II.*

The last sentence kept Keithan thinking. *One of the most famous legends?* he repeated in his head. *What if that legend was true?*

Keithan was about to keep on reading when the time blinked in the middle of the holo screen. It showed 12:50 p.m. It meant lunch hour was over and students had ten minutes to get to their next classes. It showed up on every computer in the library, and though students began to get up and leave, Keithan remained in his cubicle.

He opened another search engine window without closing the first one and typed the title *Sky Phantoms* inside the search tab. He took out his personal data card drive from one of his pockets and inserted it into the computer. "Almost done. Almost done," he murmured, making the most of the few minutes he had left while he browsed through the new results on the screen as quickly as he could. He had just opened a document of what appeared to be an article from 1950, which made reference to the out-of-print book, when a familiar voice spoke to him.

"Is *this* a miracle?"

Keithan looked over his shoulder and hissed. Fernando had halted his wheelchair behind him. "You too, eh? Mrs. Peebley reacted the same way."

"And you can't blame her. *You*, in the library? What are you, in detention?"

Keithan gave Fernando a sour yet slightly amused look.

"I've been doing some research about invisible aircraft technology."

"Hmm. And did you find something?" Fernando moved the wheelchair closer.

"I'm not sure."

The time appeared on the holo screen again. It was now 12:55.

"You do know you're going to be late for flight class, right?" Fernando told Keithan.

"I know. I just need to save this page in my drive," Keithan replied, his eyes fixed on the screen as he saved the opened document. "And what about you?" he asked Fernando. "Aren't you supposed to go to Experimental Mechanics now?"

"That's why I'm here," Fernando said. "Professor Coverden is going to give the class in the library today. He wants us to look for different schematics of afterburner concepts from the pre-Aerial War era."

Fernando watched as Keithan moved his hands like two dancing spiders all around the holo screen. He jumped when Keithan threw himself back and clapped his hands.

"Done! See you after classes," Keithan told Fernando, and with that, he jumped to his feet, retrieved his data card drive, and rushed through the line of cubicles.

From the information counter, a startled Mrs. Peebley saw him running to the elevator. She tried to call his attention, but by the time Keithan turned to her, he was already inside the elevator, the door sliding shut in front of him.

The elevator took him to the ground floor, and there Keithan hurried down the main hallway. His breathing became deeper and faster as he ran. Keithan knew he was late for class, and he prepared himself mentally for when Dantés saw him arrive. He knew well how upset the professor turned when one of her students was late. There had been times in which she had prohibited students to fly as punishment. So far, it had never happened to Keithan, but now, while he ran, he wondered if today would be the day.

To his luck, most of the students were already in their respective classrooms. This allowed Keithan to rush easily past the few that were still in the hall and without tripping or bumping into them. At the end of the main hallway, Keithan turned right into another hall, and there he almost bumped hard into a quartet of older pilot and aeroengineer girls.

"Hey! Watch it, you little—"

"Sorry!" Keithan shouted back without turning his head. He didn't slow down, anxious to get to the hangar bay.

He shot past the last classroom door and was about twenty-five feet away from the bay entrance when one of the hall monitor robots appeared from the end of the curved hall.

"Oh no. Not now. *Not now!*"

There was no escape. The HM robot forced him to a stop so abruptly Keithan almost collided with it.

"Keithan Quintero, age thirteen, level five," the robot said in its monotone voice as it scanned the digital insignia on Keithan's left sleeve. "You are in violation of rule number two of the hallway rules for running …"

"Yes. I *know*. That's because I'm already late for—" Keithan began to explain but decided to hold his tongue when he realized how pointless it was to make the robot understand—or care.

"You are to be sanctioned …" the HM unit went on. As it kept talking, it printed the demerit on a small yellow piece of paper, which slid out from its front.

Keithan snatched it, irritated. He tapped his foot while the annoying robot recited how to avoid violating the hallway rules again. Yet Keithan's impatience didn't last long.

"Right. Thanks!" he snapped at the robot, and shoving the demerit into one of his pockets, he took off.

He could hear the robot still addressing him while he ran down the hall, but he didn't care. Finally, he reached the hangar bay and searched for the *d'Artagnan*. He found her parked at the far left, within a line of empty spaces where his classmates' aircraft should have been.

There was no time to lose. Keithan did a quick preflight check of the *d'Artagnan* to make sure she was ready to fly. Walking around her, he noticed that she still had the rear left landing gear damaged, yet Fernando had managed to finish repairing the aileron on the left wing, probably during one of his classes. Therefore, Keithan opened the cockpit canopy, climbed in, and turned on the engines.

"Come on. Come on. Let's go!" he murmured while he waited for the engines to stabilize their power.

Seconds later, Keithan forwarded the craft, carefully turning her to face the main opening. He was about to push the throttles and shoot out of the hangar when he noticed what was happening outside.

All his classmates' aircraft were there, but for some reason, none of his pilot classmates were inside any of them yet.

CHAPTER 19

Keithan didn't bother taking the *d'Artagnan* out of the hangar bay. Instead, he shut down her engines, got out of the cockpit, and hurried to his classmates. They were all with their respective aircraft at the takeoff area. There were five aircraft in all, including Owen's repaired Model-T racer, which was aligned with the others in standby mode forty feet from the hangar bay's opening.

Keithan spotted Genevieve in the middle of the line. She was seated on the right wing of her dark-gray-and-purple *Rebel Fairy* with her feet dangling. Her back was to him, but she must have sensed him coming because she looked over her shoulder and nodded to him.

"What's going on?" Keithan stopped behind her.

"We might not have flight class today," Genevieve replied.

She nodded ahead to where the rest of the students were looking. Twenty feet from them, stood an irritated Dantés and her assistant, Harley Swift, arguing with Headmaster Viviani. A young woman stood next to the headmaster, and she seemed to be from Pegasus Company. Keithan could tell by the impeccably white shirt with black short sleeves and gold linings that she was wearing. Dantés was doing most of the talking. Her cold, sharp attitude showed that she had no intention of backing down from giving her class. Meanwhile, Headmaster Viviani and the woman from Pegasus were trying to convince the professor to yield, though with not much success. The young woman kept looking down at her data pad, eyes hidden behind a shiny pair of golden aviator shades and a slight smile that seemed to irritate Dantés even more.

"Why do they want her to cancel the class?" Keithan asked Genevieve.

"It seems Pegasus wants to do a presentation at the academy," Genevieve said. "What bothers Dantés is that Pegasus showed up here unannounced."

Keithan, Genevieve, and their classmates could see how upset Dantés was. She hadn't burst out in anger, but they could tell their flight professor was having a hard time trying to control it from happening since she kept her arms tightly folded.

The argument lasted a few more minutes until Dantés walked away from the headmaster and the woman from Pegasus. She approached the students with a quick and heavy pace, Swift doing his best to keep up with her. Keithan had a feeling what was about to happen, for Dantés's deep look of restrained irritation spoke for itself. Still, neither he nor his classmates made a move.

"Class has just been canceled today," the professor exhaled uncomfortably. "We're to go to the theater, so return your craft to the hangar bay and meet me here so we all leave together. You have two minutes. No delays."

She turned, along with Swift while the students hurried and climbed into their aircraft. Keithan was halfway back to the *d'Artagnan* when he heard Dantés call out to him over the noise of the rumbling engines.

"Quintero!"

Keithan turned toward the professor.

"Don't think that I don't know you were late. That's ten points I'm taking away from your daily performance grade."

Having no counterargument, Keithan pursed his lips and clenched his jaw. *Great*, he wanted to answer back, but he knew it would be worthless.

Just then, two aircraft slowly hovered past him, their pilots, Owen and Lance, smirking at him as they did the forefinger rub gesture. Keithan was certain it had been they who had told Dantés he had arrived late.

Francisco Muniz

—(-o-)—

Almost the entire academy was already settled in the domed theater when Keithan and his pilot classmates arrived. The excitement was palpable as all the levels of students waited with eagerness to find out why Pegasus Company had shown up unannounced.

The curved tiers of seats sloping down toward the circular stage were almost full as the last groups arrived. Professor Dantés and Swift entered through the double doors located on the top of the theater. They led their students down the corridor behind the top row. As Keithan followed, he noticed the activity around the stage. A crowd of reporters with hover cameras from different channels prepared themselves to cover what would happen in a few minutes. Among the reporters were local news crews. To Keithan's surprise, a crew from ASC—the popular Air Sports Channel—was there. Even more impressive was the crew of the Entertainment Sports Programming Network, best known by its initials: ESPN, which made it clear that this was going to be big.

Not too far away, Keithan spotted Fernando who had settled his wheelchair at a small area that divided the top row in two. Fernando seemed to be saving him a seat.

"Hey," said Keithan, settling in the seat next to him.

Fernando nodded. "Hey. So much for trying not to be late for flight class, eh?"

"Tell me about it," Keithan said. "One of the hall monitor robots caught me as I ran to the hangar bay and gave me a demerit. All just to find out in the end that Headmaster Viviani forced Dantés to cancel today's class."

Fernando couldn't help but snort. "I assume Dantés didn't like that at all."

"Oh, you should have seen her," Keithan said. "She was furious, but I don't understand why. It's like none of this about Pegasus being at Ramey impresses her one bit."

"Well, at least *we* can't complain about it," Fernando said. "Whether

- 162 -

Dantés likes it or not, right now this is about Pegasus Company being at our academy. As for you and me," he leaned closer to Keithan, lowering his voice, "we should take advantage of it to prepare ourselves better for the race. You know what? I have an idea."

Fernando pressed a button on his armrest. A compact panel swung upward between his legs. He reached for his laptube behind his seat and placed it on the panel.

"What are you doing?" Keithan asked.

Fernando turned on the laptube. "I'm going to record the presentation."

Keithan arched his eyebrows, impressed.

Down at the lowest part of the theater, everything was ready to begin. The news crews and their respective hover cameras were set in position, waiting. The circular stage, with its concave black wall at the back, was clear and properly illuminated. A giant holo projector rose from underneath the center of the stage but didn't project any images yet.

"Oh." Keithan turned to Fernando again before the presentation began. "Do you think it'll be okay if I show your dad what I found in the library? You know, about invisible aircraft technology?"

Fernando gave him an uncertain look.

"I wanna see if he knows anything about the rare book title I found online," Keithan explained.

He could tell his best friend was tiring of the topic, but Fernando shrugged and replied, "I guess. If he's not too busy working on his secret project with his new stupid friend."

"New stupid friend?"

"Good afternoon, everyone," interrupted the amplified voice of Headmaster Viviani.

"You'll see when we get home," Fernando whispered and nodded toward the front of the stage.

The headmaster adjusted the tiny microphone piece attached to his collar and addressed the audience again. "You're all here because we have a special visitor. An unexpected visitor, I must say, yet one that honors us with his presence at Ramey Academy. He's looking forward to talking to you about the upcoming air race that will take place on our island on May 1. So, without further ado, I present to you—and let's welcome him with a big round of applause—the CEO and founder of Pegasus Company..." Viviani took a deep breath. "...Captain Giovanni Colani!"

There were loud gasps before the whole theater burst out cheering and applauding. Loud and fast-paced music started playing, and at the same time, bright multicolored lights burst out from the center of the stage, creating one giant holographic animation.

"Whoa!" both Keithan and Fernando exclaimed.

The students threw their heads back when the 3-D images of two rumbling, racing craft flew straight toward them through a holographic ring. They were followed by the chrome letters and numbers of the 2055 Pegasus Air Race, which, along with the Pegasus logo, zoomed in as if from far in the background. It all came to a stop high over the center of the stage.

It was then that Giovanni Colani appeared. Though the bearded man was dwarfed by the giant image above him, it was impossible to miss the gold embroidery and epaulets of his raven-black blazer. He stepped onto the stage, causing the applause and cheers to become louder. Some of the students even stood up to get a better look at him. Meanwhile, Colani smiled for the cameras and shook hands with the headmaster before the latter walked off the stage.

Nearly a minute later, the students were still clapping and cheering. It had been surprising enough to have Pegasus Company at the academy, but to have the company's founder and CEO was beyond their expectations. It was almost unbelievable. Now Keithan understood why all the reporters and news crews were here too. Most likely, Colani had persuaded them into coming along as part of his agenda to promote his air race.

"Thank you, thank you. That's quite a welcome," Colani's Italian voice resounded all around the theater. He had his microphone attached to his collar. He had to pause to wait for the applause to cease. "Well, I must say it is a pleasure to be here at Ramey Academy, one of the most prestigious academies of flight and aeroengineering, and where I understand great and respectable figures from the modern world of aviation have studied. Figures like the American Captain Thomas Hunt, better known as the number one flying ace of the Aerial War. Also, the great Argentine aeroengineer, Federico Marcel, who revolutionized the designs of many fighter and racing aircraft with his 2018 twin, front-steering vanes model. And, of course, who could forget the legendary air racer Adalina Zambrana?"

Keithan froze at the sudden mention of his mother's name.

"Winner of over a dozen aerobatic championships and air races, national *and* international. Among them," Colani emphasized, raising his forefinger, "the only *three* consecutive victories that have been accomplished in the history of the Pegasus Air Race."

Students around Keithan turned their heads to glance at him with excited looks. Fernando gave him a nudge. Keithan was only able to smile at them, blushing.

Like the rest of the other important figures mentioned, the image of Keithan's mom appeared high over the stage. It was one of her most famous photos in which she stood proudly in her racing uniform, beaming at the camera with that smile so similar to Keithan's, while she held the glorious silver-and-gold trophy of the Pegasus Air Race in front of her. Keithan felt the hairs on his arms stand on end as he stared at the image. He and everybody else knew how distinguished and famous his mother had become all over the world as an air racing champion, yet to hear the CEO of Pegasus recognizing her filled Keithan with even more pride as her son.

"Now, let's move on to the purpose of my visit, shall we?" Giovanni Colani said enthusiastically. "Aside from the fact that it will be here at Ramey Airport where the Pegasus Air Race will be held—preceded by its qualifier tournament—I've also come because I think it would be a great opportunity to show you young pilots and aeroengineers more about what my air race consists of. More importantly, what it takes to participate in it. You see, the Pegasus Air Race is unlike any other race—and it's not for any pilot. It's a race only for daredevils who have what it takes to go beyond their aerobatic skills at incredible speeds. Neat, right?"

The young audience cheered in approval. Keithan already wanted to prove that he had what it took to be in the race. He stared, fixed on Colani, leaning forward with his fingers laced in front of his mouth.

"But what does it take to become that kind of racing pilot?" Colani went on. "Some people say it takes a lot of experience. Others say it requires a certain level of madness. If you ask me, I would say it requires both." He paused as the audience laughed. "But who am I to judge? I might as well let one of the pros tell you in his words what it really takes. So I would like to invite to the stage right now the champion of the last two Pegasus Air Races, and who will defend his title once again this year … my good friend Drostan Luzier!"

The audience's reaction was unlike any other that had ever been seen in the theater. Not only did the cheers and applause come out much stronger than when Colani stepped onto the stage, but this time they were accompanied by the loud and high-pitched screams of all the girls present. They were so loud their screams came out like a deafening explosion of crazy fans at the opening of a concert.

Fernando clapped his hands to his ears. "Man! How can they scream like that?" he shouted; his voice barely audible.

Just then, Drostan Luzier came onto the stage. The girls' screams became even louder. Despite this, Keithan applauded while the racing star waved at everyone, smiling. He wasn't impressed seeing Drostan there, for after having met the man at the Aramises' hangar and seeing how arrogant and what a snob he was, Keithan just didn't think much of him anymore. Keithan had to admit, though, "Mr. Perfect" was the envy of many guys—and not just because he had earned wealth and fame due to his successful racing career, but also because he had the looks, which Keithan found irritating.

Drostan looked like a live version of one of those Greek sculptures found in art museums, with his pale skin glossy as marble while the spotlight followed him. It was even hard to tell where his forehead ended and his shiny, blond hairline began. His mainly white racing unisuit and matching leather jacket highlighted his god-like appearance even more. And there was no question about it, the racing unisuit, with several black areas and thin, reflective gold lines that ran down the sleeves, chest, and legs, was one of the coolest Keithan had ever seen.

"Don't judge him too much," Fernando said, leaning closer. He sensed what Keithan was thinking. "It wouldn't hurt to pay close attention to whatever he's going to say."

Keithan turned and frowned. "Why do you say that?"

"Because, who knows? He might reveal one or two of his particular tricks, which you could benefit from by practicing them too."

"Thank you," Drostan said in his low amplified voice with its clear Dutch accent. He took Colani's microphone and attached it to the collar of his jacket.

Keithan wasn't sure, but he sensed a lack of enthusiasm in Drostan's voice. He also noticed it on the man's expression; Drostan's smile, even from where Keithan was seated, looked somewhat forced. It was as if Drostan had been forced to come here.

The air racing celebrity gestured insistently with his hands so everyone would hush, but he began to speak anyway before they all did.

"Having air raced since I was seventeen, as well as having won many victories in numerous championships and exclusive races since then—among them the last two Pegasus Air Races—has taught me about what it takes to be one of the best pilots in the world."

"*Wow!* Could he be any more modest?" Keithan whispered.

Next to him, Fernando stopped himself from laughing. "Shhh."

"So as you can imagine," Drostan continued, "experience is indeed a determining factor. It is not about madness, as Captain Colani said, for I've seen throughout the years how such a thing like madness has led many competitors to recklessness.

"Now, when it comes to competing in the Pegasus Air Race, there are five things that every racing pilot candidate requires. The first one, as I already mentioned, is experience. The other four, you might say lead the pilot to the first one, and they are: speed, precision, skills, and control."

Students were hooked; there was no sound coming from where

they sat.

"Speed, of course, is of great importance," Luzier went on. "After all, I'm talking about air *racing*. And, for starters, in order to have speed, it is necessary to have a suitable aircraft."

Behind Drostan, the holographic image that had been projecting the date of the race transformed into a two-dimensional, rectangular screen from which a series of clips of different racing aircraft began to appear. Each of the superfast machines was shown in action yet flying in slow motion so the audience could see its distinctive design in detail. During this, Drostan talked briefly about the distinctions among different types of aircraft that participated in the Pegasus Air Race, as well as their advantages and disadvantages based on the craft's aerodynamic designs and engines.

Keithan watched each clip carefully. Meanwhile, Fernando made quick annotations, tapping like crazy on his projected keyboard. Among the clips, they saw the *Lightning Dragon*, the superfast, double turbo-engine craft painted in sparkling green scales with the Australian pilot, Tony LeVier, who had won the first Pegasus Air Race in 2028. There was also a clip of the *Milady 18*, the unmistakable scarlet-and-white racing craft with which Keithan's mom had won numerous races. And last, but not least, appeared Drostan's chrome, sleek, and intimidating racing craft, the *Sky Blade*, which, as expected, Drostan described as "flawless."

"These types of aircraft have proven to be among the best that have competed in the air race. However, don't think they're all a pilot needs to win," Drostan said pointedly, "for you could have the fastest and most responsive racing vehicle in the world, with the most advanced technology and best propulsion system, but that would only make you go fast. And for the Pegasus Air Race, you need much more than speed, which leads me to the next two requirements: precision and skills."

The giant holo screen flickered and changed to a new series of clips. These were from past Pegasus Air Races as well, yet they focused on the competing aircraft from a distance as they maneuvered through a variety of floating obstacles positioned in several well-known sites.

"It's true some pro pilots have shown to have them at some level already," Luzier went on, "but usually, precision and skills are developed gradually. In the Pegasus Air Race, it's essential that all competitors master both factors. That way they can execute any necessary aerobatic maneuver when they fly through the obstacles that they have to face in the aerial racecourse, as you can see in the footage."

Keithan was paying more attention to the footage on the holo screen than to what Drostan was saying. It was one of the best he'd ever seen, and it showed what the race was really about: flying at insane speeds and performing unbelievable stunts, all while the competitors raced against each other.

Keithan barely blinked. He was hooked. With each aerobatic stunt he saw, he took a deep breath while he imagined himself attempting them with the *d'Artagnan*. He was also impressed by how the selected sites added to the challenges of the race. Sites like the arid Grand Canyon in Arizona and the iconic skyscraper city of Dubai, where the race had been held in 2031 and 2043.

Keithan, however, realized something in particular. The clips that appeared showed only one aircraft doing all the aerobatic stunts, and it was none other than Drostan's *Sky Blade*.

"I don't believe this guy!" Fernando said in a whisper when he realized the same thing. "He's showing off!"

Keithan agreed. More than focusing on demonstrating what it took to be a great racing pilot, it seemed as if Drostan's intention with the clips were to prove to everyone that he was some sort of lord of the Pegasus Air Race.

Drostan kept on talking while more clips continued to appear on the screen. "But how can such things like precision and skills be mastered? You might be wondering. Well, there's one way, and that is by having the fourth and last of the requirements, which is *control*. Control in all its aspects, because that is the factor that determines the ability of a true racing pilot to react intelligently with the best tactics and split-second thinking when one flies for the win. *That*, I think is the ultimate test of the Pegasus Air Race and the main reason only the best daredevil pilots in the world get to be in it. Without control, it's not even worth trying to qualify for the Pegasus Air Race."

That last sentence made Keithan grip the armrest of his seat. He felt as if Drostan had spoken directly to him, warning him not to attempt being in the race. Usually, Keithan didn't take comments like those personally, but there was something about the way Drostan had said it that got on Keithan's nerves. If made him so uncomfortable that, for the first time since he had determined himself to be in the race, Keithan wondered if he really had what it took to be in it.

Of course, Keithan didn't have as much experience as most of the racing pilots that competed in the air race. His experience was based more on the races he had participated in during flight classes (not to mention the two illegal ones he had been in against the Viviani twins). Nevertheless, he had learned a lot from each one. As for speed, there was no doubt in his mind that he had it. After all, he didn't have any ordinary aircraft. He had the *d'Artagnan*. He also had precision and skills, and he was confident everyone who had seen him race knew that, especially those who had raced against him.

Now, control … well, at least *he* thought he had it, regardless of what his friends, his professors—and his dad—thought.

The presentation lasted twenty more minutes. Once Drostan finished, Colani stepped onto the stage again and reminded everyone about the official dates for the qualifier tournament and the air race. The students were in for a surprise when Colani announced he had brought more than enough free tickets for the day of the race. As expected, the audience went wild.

Afterward, the students gathered in front of the stage, along with reporters and news crews, in hopes of getting an autograph from Drostan. Keithan and Fernando, however, were now headed to the *d'Artagnan*.

"And all this time I thought *you* were the cockiest air racer I'd ever met," Fernando teased Keithan as they entered the tubed elevator. "Looks like you finally met your match."

Keithan frowned but then gave Fernando a slight smile. "I only see

Drostan as another opponent that'll be in the race." *Though I'm gonna have to practice a lot harder if I want to beat him.*

The elevator opened again but on the ground floor. On their way to the hangar bay, Fernando and Keithan discussed the special features that Drostan had mentioned about his racing craft.

"You know what got my attention the most about it?" Fernando said. "Some of its so-called special features are like those your mom's aircraft used to have."

Keithan nodded, grimacing. He'd noticed that too. "They're the type of features that we, ourselves, have added to the *d'Artagnan*. Still, that's not what worries me most about Drostan."

"What do you mean?"

They had just reached the hangar bay's entrance when Fernando halted his wheelchair and forced Keithan to stop.

"What worries me the most about him is that he has already won the last two Pegasus Air Races with that aircraft of his," Keithan explained. "And do you remember what Colani said about my mom? She's been the only one in the race's history who has accomplished *three* consecutive victories."

Fernando gave him a puzzled look, but then his eyes widened. "So, if Drostan wins this year, he'll …?"

"He'll match my mom's record, and I can't let that happen."

Keithan did his best to see this as a challenge and not as a threat. He needed to protect his mom's record. If someone were to match it— or break it—it should be him, not Drostan or any other air racer. At least that was how Keithan preferred to see it, which made one thing clear to him now. He needed to qualify for the Pegasus Air Race, no matter what.

CHAPTER 20

Mrs. Aramis was already waiting in front of the hangar bay when Fernando and Keithan came out. She waved at them from the driver's seat of her scarlet minivan and moved it in reverse while one of the bay's yellow tow robots brought the *d'Artagnan*. The tow robot released the racing craft once the minivan was close enough, and Keithan attached the trailer coupler to the van. Meanwhile, Mrs. Aramis slid open the side door, allowing the automatic ramp to lower for Fernando.

Laika, who accompanied Mrs. Aramis in the front passenger seat, barked and wagged her tail with excitement when she saw the two boys get in. She was so eager to jump to the back seats that Mrs. Aramis had to hold her.

"Easy, Laika. We're glad to see you too," Fernando told her while his mother calmed her down.

"So how was your day, guys?" Mrs. Aramis asked while she drove out of the academy.

"Great," Fernando replied. "Pegasus Company came to the academy to do a presentation."

"Really?"

"*And*, in the end, each student was given a ticket for the day of the air race," Keithan said. He took out his ticket and raised it so Mrs. Aramis could see it through the rearview mirror.

"That's great. Not that you boys will need them, right?"

Keithan and Fernando exchanged perplexed looks. Before any of them could ask Mrs. Aramis what she had meant, she said, "Aren't you planning to participate in the air race?"

There was a short moment of silence.

"How did you—?"

"Marianna told me," Mrs. Aramis answered before Fernando could finish the question. "Don't worry. I can't say I approve a hundred percent, but I think it might be a good experience for you boys. I just hope the two of you are sure of what you're getting yourselves into because, as far as everyone knows about the Pegasus Air Race, it is challenging—and quite dangerous."

Keithan noticed Mrs. Aramis shoot a glance straight at him in the rearview mirror when she said that last sentence, but he didn't show the slightest expression of worry.

"Does Dad know?" Fernando asked, biting his lower lip.

"Yep," his mother said casually, her eyes fixed to the front now. "I told him earlier today while we had lunch. He didn't believe it at first, and he also hopes you know what you're doing—especially you, Keithan. You should be well aware of the pro pilots you will be up against. By the way, did you hear the latest news? Some of them arrived at Ramey today."

Keithan and Fernando shook their heads. "What?" they said simultaneously.

"You'll see."

Mrs. Aramis kept driving down the airport, past the main hangars and the parked airliners. Yet, instead of turning toward the hangar residences, she kept going straight, parallel to the main runway. It was then that Keithan and Fernando saw what she wanted them to see. At a distance to the south, at the other side of the main runway and beyond the area where the large Pegasus airship floated, were two large and elongated cargo aircraft with raised, arched wings. They contrasted each other noticeably. One was painted in metallic-green scales, like those of a dragon, with a lightning bolt that ran on its side. The other had a dark look, all black with a huge bat wing design on its side, along with the words "Bat Fury" painted in dripping red, which simulated blood. Surrounding each of the cargo craft was a series of matching stationary modules and trailer vehicles, along with a crowd of people moving around.

"Those are Tony LeVier's and Leeson Lancaster's crews!" Keithan gasped as he and Fernando gazed out the window, their faces nearly pressed against the glass. They could see more than twenty people in each crew area. Somewhere among them had to be their well-known racing pilots. Tony LeVier, a native from Australia, was a veteran in the Pegasus Air Race. Not only was he the pro racer who won the first Pegasus Air Race held in 2028, but he had never gotten lower than third place in any air race. As for Leeson Lancaster—or "the Vampire," as he was best known—he, too, was a worthy competitor, though he had made his debut not long ago in the last Pegasus Air Race. However, the Vampire's reputation was more due to the many underground air races that were rumored he had won before he started his career as a professional racing pilot.

"Why did they get here so early?" Fernando asked his mother. "The race's qualifier tournament isn't until a month from now."

"Maybe they wanted to get a good area to settle in with their crews. You know, before the rest of the racers arrive," Keithan suggested.

Mrs. Aramis turned left. The minivan was about fifty feet from their hangar when—*BOOM!*—she and everyone else heard an explosion that made them jump in their seats. She pressed the brake and lurched forward as the van came to an abrupt stop. Soon after that, everybody looked to the front and noticed black smoke coming out of the open entrance of Hangar H11.

"Oh no. Not again," Mrs. Aramis moaned.

"That's the third time he's done that," Fernando complained.

Keithan knew they were referring to Mr. Aramis after having been present the first time something similar had happened.

"Don't tell me. That's your dad's secret project gone wrong again," said Keithan, exiting the minivan.

"Yep," Fernando and his mom replied at the same time.

Mrs. Aramis left the minivan parked in front of the hangar's entrance. A still-shaken Laika crossed over the driver's seat and jumped right behind Mrs. Aramis while Fernando moved his chair down the van's side ramp. As they approached the hangar, they heard the humming of the exhaust fans inside the building. Seconds later, more thick black smoke belched from the small openings at either side of the hangar.

"William?" Mrs. Aramis called to her husband.

"Dad?" Fernando bellowed.

The whole inside of the place was clouded with the black smoke swirling in the air while the exhaust fans on the lateral walls extracted it. It was like entering a blurry, spooky dream where nothing could be seen. The strong smell of something burning forced Fernando, his mom, and Keithan to cover their mouths and noses. Laika, on the other hand, dared not follow them. Instead, she remained several feet behind, barking insistently, as if calling for Mr. Aramis.

Keithan, Fernando, and Mrs. Aramis walked deeper into the hangar, barely able to see ahead of them. Somewhere inside the blur, they heard Mr. Aramis coughing. His silhouette became visible seconds later, moving toward them. At first glance, he looked like a hunched and disoriented creature. He still looked like a black silhouette covered from head to toe in soot and dust when he got close enough.

"Whew! That was fun," Mr. Aramis coughed, chuckling. He pulled up his goggles, revealing two clean circles around his eyes.

"What on earth went wrong this time?" Mrs. Aramis demanded, fanning the smoke in front of her with her hands.

"Just—*cough*—a miscalculation."

Mrs. Aramis wasn't amused at all. "*Little?* No. The first time, maybe. But look at *this*. All the aircraft, the prototypes, the high windows. They're all filthy!"

"And our stuff!" Fernando blurted out, staring at his and Keithan's work area covered in soot. It looked as colorless as the setting of a vintage silent film.

"I *know* you're planning to clean all of this right now," Mrs. Aramis told her husband with a bossy tone.

"I will. I *will*," Mr. Aramis replied without hesitation. The least he would dare to do was get his wife more upset.

Mrs. Aramis wasn't done with him, though. She followed him to the old aluminum sink nearby and kept scolding, telling him where he had to clean, what he should clean afterward, and so on while Mr. Aramis washed his face.

Meanwhile, Fernando and Keithan stared at their work area, trying to figure out how they were going to clean it. Aside from the floor and the fiberglass boxes filled with random spare parts, the table with Fernando's sketches and schematics was completely covered in soot. The first thing Fernando did was wipe the keyboard pad and the computer, carefully cleaning the soot off the holo projector's lens. Trying to avoid staining his uniform, he blew the soot off his hand, making it rise in a small cloud on his face.

"*Achooo!*"

"*Gesundheit!*" Keithan exclaimed, sneezing out the words.

"See? Now Fernando's gonna have an allergy attack because of this," Mrs. Aramis scolded her husband.

She returned to Fernando and Keithan. She took a deep breath and released it slowly, trying to calm herself. "I forgot to tell you boys. I bought you a used antigravity plate to replace the broken one on the *d'Artagnan*. I left it somewhere under all this mess."

That brightened things up a bit for Keithan and Fernando. "Thanks, Mom," Fernando told her.

The two of them wasted no time and started looking for the antigravity plate. It didn't turn out to be an easy job, as it was hard to distinguish everything covered in soot. To complicate things, the air was still blurry with dust. Fernando searched around the worktable while Keithan looked around the boxes of spare parts. Keithan checked them one by one, wiping the soot off some of the parts.

"Oww!" Keithan cried.

He had hit something hard with his foot. He looked down, and even though he couldn't make out what it was, it seemed to be what had caused the dirty mess in the hangar. Black smoke was still coming out of it. It was a small and weird-looking jet engine. Keithan leaned closer to it. He was about to touch it when a tall bipedal robot appeared in front of him from among the pile of spare-part boxes and extended its arms, as if to grab him.

"Ahhh!"

Keithan's scream was perfect for a horror movie. It was full of terror. But anyone would have screamed like that at the unexpected sight of the large robot that appeared in front of him.

"What? What is it?" Fernando cried, instantly rotating his wheelchair.

Keithan staggered backward and fell. He hadn't yet realized the robot wasn't after him. It didn't even pay attention to him. The robot simply leaned forward and covered the still-smoking thing that lay on the floor with a silver insulation drape.

"It's okay! It's okay, Keithan!"

"What the heck is that thing?" Keithan cried out, pale as a sheet.

"It's Dad's new robot."

"*What?*"

Mr. and Mrs. Aramis came rushing.

"What's going— Oh!" Mr. Aramis said.

"Keithan, are you okay?" Mrs. Aramis offered Keithan a hand to help him up.

"Yeah. I-I just— Never mind." Keithan got up, fully embarrassed. He couldn't believe he reacted that way. He glanced back at the robot. "Where did that thing come from?"

"That's an MA-7 unit. The latest mechanical assistant robot model from Pegasus Company," Mr. Aramis explained. "Courtesy of Captain Giovanni Colani himself."

Fernando moved his wheelchair closer to Keithan. "Remember the big crate Drostan and the other men from Pegasus brought last Saturday? That's what was inside it. They brought it to help Dad speed things up with his secret project."

"I call it Emmeiseven," Mr. Aramis said.

The MA unit, humanoid in shape, stood still and straight, like a soldier behind Mr. Aramis. It looked intimidating, not only because it was six-and-a-half feet tall, but also because of the many different mechanical tools that it had integrated into its forearm gauntlets. Keithan noticed it had a welding torch tip, a set of powered screwdrivers and wrenches, and several spiky saw blades of different sizes, among other stuff. Its main mechanisms were an elaborate composition of chips, wires, electrical valves, and hydraulics hidden under smooth coverings painted white, black, and gold—the colors of Pegasus Company.

Keithan stared at the robot, full of wonder. He approached it slowly, though he didn't dare get too close to it. The robot seemed capable to do any physical movement a human could do ... probably better. Its torso was smaller in proportion to its arms and legs, which started slender but gradually turned thicker from what functioned as its elbows and knees to its wide, mechanical hands and feet. Yet, unlike a human, its knees were bent drastically backward and upward. And its head—if it could be called a head—looked like a helmet with a curved glass screen that displayed what appeared to be numerous codes of some sort.

Staring at it, Keithan realized there was something particular about the robot's design.

"It's sleek coverings," he said. "They look ... aerodynamic."

Both Fernando and his mom grimaced and moved closer to the robot. They hadn't noticed that before.

"You're right." Fernando studied the sleek and wavy coverings on the robot's arms and legs.

"That's odd. Looks as if it had been designed to fly too," Mrs. Aramis added. She gave her husband a questioning look, but Mr. Aramis shook his head, confirming that flying wasn't one of the robot's capabilities.

"Wouldn't that be something?" Mr. Aramis chuckled. "No. That's just proof that Emmeiseven was designed by Pegasus."

He stepped forward and addressed the robot. "All right,

Emmeiseven, take the prototype back to the workshop."

The robot twitched its head, acknowledging the order, and responded in its metallic voice, "Order acknowledged." It picked up the metal object covered with the insulation drape and turned toward the back of the hangar.

Mr. Aramis followed behind it. He and the robot were met by Laika, who ran up to them and forced them to stop. Teeth showing, the golden retriever growled at the robot.

"Laika, stop it," Mr. Aramis told her sharply. He gestured for Emmeiseven to keep moving.

The robot forced Laika to step aside as it continued walking. Still, that didn't stop Laika from barking at Emmeiseven.

"What's with you, girl?" Mr. Aramis asked her before he kept walking.

"Laika! Come on," Mrs. Aramis called over the barking, snapping her fingers. "Come on. Let's go pick up Marianna at school."

The barking stopped. Without hesitating, Laika hurried to Mrs. Aramis, who was heading back to the van.

"See? Laika doesn't seem to like Emmeiseven, either," Fernando said.

Keithan turned to him. "I figure that's the new stupid friend you referred to back at the theater."

He noticed Fernando's look. He figured out why his friend didn't like the robot. Fernando was jealous.

"I just don't like to work with robots," said Fernando, more to himself than to Keithan. "I don't get it. Dad didn't like it either, until now. Now he's all about Emmeiseven this and Emmeiseven that. When the two of them are working nonstop, it's as if everything else becomes invisible to him."

"Invisible?" Keithan repeated. Then he remembered. He needed to talk to Fernando's dad. Shaking his head, he hurried to Mr. Aramis before the man disappeared behind the strip curtain of his private workshop.

"Mr. Aramis, *wait*."

Keithan reached him just in time. Mr. Aramis had dropped half of the yellow strip curtain after the robot went in. He looked at Keithan over his shoulder.

"Keithan, what's up?"

"Sir, I wanted to ask you, have you ever heard about an old science-fiction book called *Sky Phantoms*?"

Mr. Aramis's reaction was unexpected. "*Sky Phantoms*? How do *you* know about that book?"

"I found out about it today at the academy's library while searching for—" Keithan hesitated, aware that he was going to sound silly. He changed his choice of words. "Advanced stealth technology."

Mr. Aramis gave Keithan a questioning look. "Stealth?" He seemed to be intrigued.

"He claims he encountered an invisible aircraft last Saturday while he flew over the Mona Passage," Fernando clarified, appearing behind Keithan. He had found the antigravity plate his mom had gotten them and held it in his hands. "Kind of like the ones in science-fiction books and movies."

"Really?" said his father, looking from Fernando to Keithan. "How could you have possibly *seen* an invisible aircraft, Keithan?"

Fernando couldn't help but chuckle, even when he saw Keithan shoot him a serious look. "I asked him the same thing."

"Look, I don't know if it was really an aircraft, but I did see what looked like the fiery end of a jet engine flying next to me," Keithan explained. "Anyway, I spent my lunch hour inside the library, searching for information about advanced stealth technology. So far, the only thing that talked about something similar to what I saw was the science-fiction book *Sky Phantoms*."

Keithan waited for Mr. Aramis to respond. He hoped Mr. Aramis would help him, especially since he knew how much the man enjoyed talking about this type of mysterious thing.

"You know, I think I have a copy of that book," Fernando's dad replied. He caught Keithan trying to get a glimpse of the inside of the workshop and blocked his view, letting go of the yellow PVC curtain.

"You do?" Keithan's face lit up.

"I'm pretty sure. Somewhere in my office. Come on."

He drew Keithan and Fernando away from the entrance of his workshop. Fernando, however, turned his chair in the opposite direction.

"You go ahead," Fernando told Keithan. "I'm gonna clean the antigravity plate. Just don't take too long. I might need your help when I test it."

"I won't take long," Keithan reassured him and followed Mr. Aramis to the office.

Once they entered the office, Mr. Aramis headed to a corner behind his desk. He began looking into a group of dusty stacks of books and comics that lay on the floor. Meanwhile, Keithan stood waiting at the other side of the desk. Right away, he noticed all the books and comics in the stacks were about science fiction. They looked old, most likely older than Mr. Aramis. Especially the comic books, which Keithan knew didn't come in printed form these days.

"If I do have it, it should be here," Mr. Aramis told him while he dug deeper into his collection. He took out dusty books and wrinkled comics. He placed some on the floor and others on top of the desk. A small stack gradually formed in front of Keithan. Suddenly, Mr. Aramis got up and exclaimed, "Aha! Jackpot!"

Mr. Aramis now held an old paperback book, its cover half-loose and its pages as brown as dry leather. He wiped off the dust from the book and placed it on the desk in front of Keithan.

"Is this the one you were referring to?" he said.

Keithan smiled with satisfaction, recognizing the book's front cover. "It is." He leaned closer and looked up at Mr. Aramis, who nodded to him.

"Go ahead. You can open it. Careful, though."

The book looked fragile; Keithan wasn't sure he should pick it up. He was afraid to do something that might make its pages or what was left of its cover come loose. Still, Keithan was eager to open it. He picked it up carefully with both hands, as if the book were made of porcelain. He stared at the cover illustration of the giant tentacled machine fighting against the transparent fighter aircraft.

"Where did you get it?" he asked Mr. Aramis.

"It was part of my old man's collection," Mr. Aramis said proudly. "Most of these books and comics were his. He was the one who got me into all this sci-fi stuff, the same way his father—my grandpa—got him into it. In fact, I think it was my grandpa who got that book and later gave it to my old man, long before my old man gave it to me."

"Did you read it?"

"I started it sometime during my late teens—quite a while ago," Mr. Aramis chuckled, remembering. "It started as a really good book, but I wasn't able to read it completely because it was missing several pages. Many of them weren't legible anymore. I do remember it was about a secret group of fighter pilots with super-futuristic airplanes. What I remember most about it is that, supposedly, the book was one of the first in the science-fiction genre that talked in a convincing way about stealth technology."

"What do you mean?" Keithan asked.

"Well, the author explained how technology to make an aircraft invisible from plain sight worked but as if it could exist at its time. I think it was genius on the author's part. I mean, don't forget that that book came out in the late 1940s, when stuff like that didn't even exist."

"Kind of like what the author Jules Verne did in some of his science-fiction books?"

"That's right," said Mr. Aramis, surprised that Keithan knew about Jules Verne.

Keithan may not have read any of Verne's books, which dated far back to the 1800s, but he'd heard that the man had written about such things like powered submarines and rocket ships long before they became true.

Keithan still had the old book in his hands while he listened intently to Mr. Aramis. He wanted to read it, but because it was in such a delicate condition, he browsed slightly through the pages instead, making them turn by themselves to avoid touching them much.

He turned the book to the back cover. On it, he noticed the only other illustration beside the one on the front. It was an insignia of a triangle leaned slightly to the right, with each of its points enclosed in a small circle and an art deco-style wing at its right. Underneath this was the synopsis Keithan had read at the academy's library. It was the author's short biography, however, which was located at the bottom of the back cover, what caught Keithan's attention.

"Listen to this, sir." Keithan glanced at Mr. Aramis and read aloud,

> **Hamilton Stargland**, *a former engineer in the aviation field, has written numerous books based on his analytical yet controversial theories about futuristic technology. His knowledge, as well as his vast experience, served him as influence and inspiration for this, his first science-fiction work.*

"Hmm. It seems like the man was some sort of visionary in his time," Keithan said. He stared at the written biography for a few seconds before raising his gaze at Mr. Aramis. "Sir, do you think it might be possible that some of the ideas suggested in this book are real?"

Mr. Aramis frowned. "You mean about the invisible aircraft?"

Keithan nodded. "And about the secret legion of fighter pilots that flew them. I know you like to prove ideas about science fiction if possible. I mean, with most of the inventions and prototypes that you've built. What do you think, Mr. Aramis? Could it be possible a secret legion managed to make the invisibility technology mentioned in this book real?"

Mr. Aramis stood thoughtful. "It would be something amazing. There have been many attempts to accomplish that over the past hundred years. But as far as I know, to make an aircraft or anything else invisible—and I mean *literally* invisible—it's still only a matter of science fiction."

"Then what do you think I might've seen flying over the Mona Passage?" Keithan asked. "Whatever it was, it attacked the spherical drone from Pegasus I was racing against."

The intercom on the desk made a loud beep, startling Keithan and Mr. Aramis, before they heard Fernando's loud voice. *"Keithan, what's taking so long? I need your help to try out the antigravity plate."*

Keithan leaned forward and pressed the intercom button. "I'm coming." He didn't leave right away, though. He stared at Mr. Aramis, still with the rare old book in hand, waiting for him to answer his question. "Sir?"

Mr. Aramis shook his head. "Honestly, Keithan, you got me on that one. I doubt it was an invisible aircraft. I know you're trying to find some answers in that book, but you must be careful when you consider what things about science fiction could become real and what things couldn't. I do believe science fiction is not always just science fiction, but sometimes … I'm sorry to say, it just is."

"Keithan!"

Keithan hissed and pressed the intercom again. "I'm coming!"

CHAPTER 21

The used antigravity plate Mrs. Aramis had gotten Fernando and Keithan had turned out to be much better than the one Keithan had broken. It needed a few adjustments to make it fully functional again, but thanks to Fernando's skills, it ended up working as if it were brand new.

"See? All it needed was a good cleaning and to have its couplings changed," Fernando told Keithan while they watched the plate hover steadily three feet off the floor in front of them. "Whoever owned it before didn't realize it could have been fixed easily."

Keithan didn't say anything. He was half-lost in his thoughts while he held the jumper cable that connected the antigravity plate to the test battery. He had tried to put aside his disappointment after he left Mr. Aramis's office without much information, but more than that was his frustration for not having the slightest clue yet about the mysterious thing he had seen last Saturday.

"Keithan, are you listening to me?"

Keithan shook his head. "I'm sorry. I just …"

"Never mind. Let's install this. After that, we need to decide what modifications we're going to do to the *d'Artagnan* to get her ready for the qualifier tournament. So please work with me here."

Keithan sighed. "You're right. Let's get started."

They had no problem working underneath the *d'Artagnan*, which rested on a mechanical, arm-like lifter that came out in angle from the floor. They put the antigravity plate in place and adjusted its power to keep the aircraft hovering level with the rest of the plates. As soon as they were done, they went to their worktable, cleaned off the soot as best they could, and got to work on the most important thing on their checklist: figuring out what they were going to do to make the *d'Artagnan* much lighter.

Keithan and Fernando were discussing the possibility of removing a few of her coverings instead of some of the mechanical parts when each one felt a hand rest on their heads and ruffle their hairs.

"Hello, guys," Marianna said cheerfully behind them. She stepped to their right and pulled out one of the fiberglass boxes on the other side of the table to sit on it. Now facing the stationary computer, she turned it on and waited for the projected keyboard panel and the holo screen to appear. "So Mom told me two foreign air racers already arrived at Ramey with their crews. I also heard on the radio that two more are scheduled to arrive tonight."

"Two more?" said Fernando, fixing his spiky, blond hair. "So soon?"

"Do you know who they are?" Keithan asked Marianna.

"Nope," Marianna said. "Now, if you'll excuse me, I have work to do."

She faced the holo screen, which had just finished uploading. She opened the internet browser by touching the screen and started keying on the projected keyboard.

"What are you doing?" Keithan asked, curious.

"I'm a member of the *d'Artagnan* air racing team too. I'm doing my part," Marianna replied, beaming at Keithan and Fernando. "I'm going to research each of the air racers that we know will be in the qualifier tournament. That way you two can become familiar with their racing backgrounds. More than that, their strengths and weaknesses—both in their skills and in their aircraft."

"Awesome," said Keithan, impressed.

"Well thought, Sis," Fernando added.

Several profiles of different pro racing pilots came up on the screen.

"Like in every air race," Marianna told Keithan and Fernando, "it's much better to know your opponents in order to prepare. Keithan, you need to know what you're up against. Don't worry, though. Once I have the information, I'm going to help you study them. You'll need to learn their moves, see if they have any particular tricks, etcetera."

It wasn't until now, while he listened to Marianna and saw all of Fernando's sketches spread on the table, that Keithan realized just how much work he was going to have to do to get himself and the *d'Artagnan* ready. Deep inside, he started to worry.

Keithan rubbed his forehead. "Man. We're gonna have to work double-time from now on."

"I know," Fernando replied while he did a calculation on one of his sketches. "We must make as much time as possible, no matter how many hours it takes us."

"Actually, it's going to be triple-time," Marianna corrected them. "Don't forget, along with that, we also have to deal with our schoolwork."

Keithan and Fernando didn't reply; they gulped at the realization.

From that moment on, it was work, work, and more work for the three of them. Keithan, as expected, got the hardest part. Not only did he have to work on the *d'Artagnan* with Fernando, but he also had to learn with Marianna about the other racing pilots that were going to participate in the qualifier tournament. He even had to keep up with all he was given to study at the academy and do his most important role: practice, practice, and practice some more with the *d'Artagnan* in the sky. None of it was easy, yet Keithan knew there was no point in thinking about how much needed to be done. He, Fernando, and Marianna did it all. Their determination to participate in the Pegasus Air Race was all they needed to stay motivated and make the best of the limited time they had.

Ironically, it was during classes that Keithan and Fernando could take things easily. They knew it was after classes that they would get busy and their hands dirty. To their luck, their professors weren't drowning them with extra work as they had been doing so during the past two weeks. In Keithan's flight class, there wasn't much new stuff going on. Professor Dantés continued giving Keithan and his classmates a series of aerobatic sequences for them to do, each one more advanced than the last. Still, Keithan didn't feel challenged by any of them, not after he'd spent two weeks practicing with the most advanced flight sequences in the simulators room while he and the twins had been grounded. Meanwhile, in Advanced Aeronautics, Professor Steelsmith discussed how to improve the rotating mechanisms of the rudders, ailerons, and even the wings. This wasn't new to any of the students, just a deeper discussion about the topic. Only in their Aeronautical Chart Interpretation lessons, Keithan and Fernando had a rough time, and with good reason. It was a tough class since it involved a lot of time and distance calculating, not to mention memorizing a vast number of chart symbols.

Also, during those days Keithan had another responsibility, which Fernando and Marianna insisted upon, and that was to keep a low profile inside and outside the academy to avoid getting into any kind of trouble. He couldn't afford to be grounded again, which was why Keithan limited himself to act as calmly, quietly, and obediently as he could at all times. In other words, to be practically everything he wasn't. The best way he managed that was by staying as far away as he could from the Viviani twins and speaking in class only when the professors asked him something.

In the hallways, during class changes, and at lunch, if no one else was with him and Fernando, the two of them continued to talk about their progress with the *d'Artagnan* and Keithan's flight training. Not once did Keithan mention anything else about the invisible aircraft incident. He had finally realized it wasn't worth worrying about that. Yet the topic came up again on Thursday morning, though it wasn't Keithan or Fernando who brought it. The two of them were heading to their first class that day when Winston Oddie caught up to them in one of the hallways, a look of excitement on his face.

"Fernando! Keithan!"

"Winston, what's up?" said Keithan, still walking.

"Mom and Dad told me they met you guys last weekend at *Las Ruinas*. They say you were looking for UFOs. I didn't know you were into that too."

"Well, we, um—" Keithan started to say before Winston cut him short.

"I go there all the time! I even have several recordings of the strange sounds my family and I have captured there. You guys want to come to my house after classes and listen to them?"

"Maybe some other time, Winston," Fernando said when he noticed Keithan's look of interest. "We both have been busy lately. We have a lot to do today too. *Right*, Keithan?"

Keithan hesitated. He wanted to listen to Winston's recordings, but the look Fernando gave him made him realize he shouldn't be thinking about that. So Keithan also passed on the invitation.

The curly-haired boy shot them a look of disappointment before he left. It made Keithan and Fernando feel guilty—especially Fernando. He hadn't meant to cut Winston off like that. Keithan knew Fernando had simply wanted to avoid getting the two of them distracted from their preparation for the race.

The rest of the week and the one that followed went on without any other distraction or inconvenience. Still, it didn't mean that it was all boring at Ramey Academy. All over the classrooms and hallways, students kept an air of excitement while they continued talking about the upcoming qualifier tournament and the many pro air racers they hoped seeing there. So far, everyone knew about the new air racers that had arrived at Ramey. One was a Japanese rookie named Daiki Tamura and the other Italy's pride, Rosangela Sofio, who, like Leeson Lancaster (aka the Vampire), had made her debut in the last

Pegasus Air Race. These two racers, like LeVier and the Vampire, had officially announced their participation through the media. Drostan Luzier, however, had made it clear that he would only be a spectator in the tournament because, as champion of the last air race, he was already in this year's race.

Two other air racers appeared on the news on the second Tuesday announcing their participation in the qualifier tournament. They hadn't arrived at Ramey yet, though. And there were rumors that five more would be arriving soon, which kept Marianna stressed and busy while she researched their backgrounds.

As for Keithan, he became anxious and nervous as more air racers were announced. Fernando and Marianna were the first to notice when they saw Keithan start the disgusting habit of biting his nails every time he watched a new racing pilot appearing on the news. At least it wasn't the type of nervousness and anxiety he couldn't control, for aside from the nail biting, Keithan was confident he was as good as all those well-experienced racers. Even as good as Drostan Luzier.

The following Thursday, the rumor of a new racing pilot planning to participate in the qualifier tournament started to spread, but this time only in Ramey Academy. This one caught Keithan and Fernando by surprise.

"Gregory Paceley?" Keithan exclaimed in disbelief, his fork dropping on his plate of spaghetti and meatballs.

"The senior?" added Fernando.

"Yes," both Genevieve and Yari answered. The two were seated at the opposite side of the round table under the courtyard's flame tree.

"Isn't it great?" Genevieve went on. "We heard Headmaster Viviani is going to recommend him. That makes Gregory the only student from the academy to participate in the qualifier tournament. No other student here has tried to qualify for the Pegasus Air Race since— Well, since ..."

"Since my mom did," Keithan finished the thought.

Keithan didn't want either of the girls to know, but he wasn't excited about the news. No one at Ramey Academy, aside from

Fernando, knew he was planning to participate. He had hoped of being the only one there to do so. Then again, having Gregory Paceley as one of the opponents, and to beat him, would be great for Keithan's reputation at the academy. After all, Gregory was the best senior pilot student in the Air Racing Program. *It would be legendary if a level-five student beat a gold level in the air race*, Keithan thought.

As expected, the rumor about Gregory Paceley was confirmed early the next day. It was announced through the intercoms all over the academy. Soon, everyone was talking about how great Gregory was and how good his chances were to qualify for the Pegasus Air Race, and so on and on. It began to bother Keithan, though, and eventually it made him feel the urge to tell everyone about his plan to be in the qualifier tournament too. But as expected, Fernando insisted not to do it.

"Just be patient," Fernando repeated, aware of how much Keithan wanted to get the same attention Gregory was getting. "Trust me. The fewer people that know about our plans, the less distraction we'll have from everyone asking us questions and trying to find out more about you."

He didn't convince Keithan right away, but later Keithan thanked Fernando for talking some sense to him, which was why Keithan did his best to continue keeping their plans secret until the right moment arrived. That moment would be on the day of the qualifier tournament. That way they would take everyone by surprise.

Unfortunately, their plans didn't go as they expected. Somebody at the academy found out about them, and it turned out to be who Keithan least wanted, and at one of the least expected moments.

CHAPTER 22

"*Everyone, keep the rhythm. Do not lower your speed,*" Keithan and his classmates heard Professor Dantés say through their earpieces. "*Excellent precision, Miss Murakami. Lance, watch the third hover ring. And Donnelly, careful with the fourth.*"

One by one, the six pilot students from level five did the flight sequence the professor had prepared for them. It was 1:35 p.m., and they were all flying low, close to the north coast of Ramey while Dantés and Swift watched them from the top of the coastal cliff on their hover platform. The sequence was part of the usual warm-up exercises they did at the beginning of every flight class. It consisted of several hover rings strategically arranged in the sky so the students could practice different aerobatic maneuvers. With the hover rings' sensor system, Dantés could easily detect when her students flew through them accordingly, for every time one of them passed through a ring correctly, the ring would light up green, while if the students made a mistake, the ring would light up red.

So far, Keithan and his classmates had been doing fine with their aircraft. Only some of them failed to pass correctly through one or two of the hover rings. Genevieve, for example, flew through ring two, doing a right knife-edge maneuver when she was supposed to do a left knife-edge, and twice Gabriel Ortiz fell short in flying inverted through ring five.

Meanwhile, Keithan flew gracefully through all the rings. He was about to attempt the sequence a third time when Professor Dantés addressed everyone.

"That's enough, students," she said. *"Align your aircraft at a reasonable distance in front of ring one."*

Keithan angled the *d'Artagnan* upward, gradually arcing backward. At the top of the curved path, he reduced the thrust and leveled again. It allowed the craft to keep descending until it reached the same altitude as ring one, which he could now see nearly two hundred feet away from him. His classmates settled their aircraft also oriented to the ring.

"All right, everyone. Let's begin today's evaluation," Dantés said. *"Each of you was supposed to design a flight sequence for today. Therefore, I want each of you to send it to me so I can arrange the hover rings accordingly when your turn to fly comes. Understood?"*

"Yes, Professor," the class answered.

"Good. Send in the sequences."

Dantés gazed at her students in the air through her digital binoculars while she organized in her mind the order in which they would do their flight sequences. Swift, who stood beside her, downloaded their sequences on the hover platform's console and checked that each one met the given requirements.

"Wait a second," said Swift, frowning.

"What's wrong?" Dantés asked.

"This sequence here; it doesn't look like a sequence for a level-five student."

Dantés lowered her digital binoculars and looked at the sequences displayed on the console's screen. It took her less than three seconds to see what Swift had meant. The sequence looked so complex it could only be compared to those designed and attempted by pro air racers.

"Who sent this?" she asked.

Swift pressed a key on the touchscreen to open the sequence's properties. "Keithan Quintero."

Dantés couldn't help but sigh. "Quintero. Of course."

Like clouds moving with the wind, the five active hover rings rearranged themselves at different altitudes in front of the students' craft. They varied in the way they faced them; some had their openings toward the students, others floated horizontally or diagonally.

"Miss Donnelly, you're up first," Dantés said into the students' shared frequency. *"Remember, I will be evaluating time and performance. Ready?"*

Keithan turned his head toward Genevieve's craft, which hovered to his left. He watched her inside the cockpit as she pulled down her helmet visor.

"Ready," Genevieve replied.

The next second, Genevieve's *Rebel Fairy* shot out of the line of students' aircraft, its rumbling shaking the *d'Artagnan* as it sped off.

"All right, Genevieve!" Keithan rooted in his cockpit.

Genevieve began her sequence just like a pro. She did a fast wingover turn to the right, and as soon as she descended it, she made an unexpected ninety-degree turn to the left, zooming successfully in a knife-edge through the first ring. Following that, she turned again, but this time in the opposite direction and inverted, passing as she had planned through the second and third rings.

"Very good, Miss Donnelly," Dantés said. *"Careful with the last two rings."*

Right after the professor finished the sentence, Genevieve zoomed into the fourth hover ring and dove sideways into the fifth in a forty-five-degree angle, flawlessly completing her sequence.

The cheers from Keithan's classmates resounded in his earpiece while he, too, cheered for his friend, but Dantés cut them off.

"Settle down, everyone," she said. She wasted no time and started to rearrange the hover rings for the next sequence. *"Lance, you're up next."*

As soon as the rings were in place, Lance flew out of the line formed by the students' craft and accelerated. Unlike Genevieve, however, he began with a straight path, but then he turned steeply to the left, passing through the first hover ring, and immediately ascended high in a right wing-over maneuver until he shot through the second ring in a perfect knife-edge. In less than three minutes, Lance flew through the rest of the rings and completed his sequence.

His twin brother followed. Owen's sequence didn't seem much different from Lance's, at least at the beginning. It started the same way, with a straight path and a sharp left turn. The last maneuver, however, took everyone by surprise when Owen pulled up too high and dropped his new and still shiny Model-T to attempt a vertical recovery.

"Whoa. Control that drop, Viviani," Dantés warned him, her voice sounding worried now.

Owen's aircraft pitched backward and descended fast without thrust. From a distance, it looked like a toy craft falling from the sky. It had everyone holding their breath. Yet, right when its nose faced forward, Owen added thrust and dove straight into the fifth hover ring, then pulled up, successfully regaining control.

The students' cheers followed right away, preceded by loud sighs of relief. Keithan didn't join in, though he was impressed.

"Quintero, your turn." Dantés said.

Keithan took a deep breath and exhaled deeply. He laced his fingers and stretched them outward, cracking his knuckles. "Ready, Professor," he replied.

While Dantés prepared his flight sequence, Keithan took the time to do a quick scan over his console to make sure everything in the *d'Artagnan* was in order. He lowered his helmet visor and closed his eyes. Concentrated, he imagined being in a completely different and much more exciting environment, with hundreds of people watching from giant stands far on both sides and numerous cameras flashing pictures. He even tried to imagine hearing it all: the roaring engines of his opponents' racing craft next to him and the shouts of the crowd rooting.

He smirked, ready to give everyone a show. He opened his eyes again, and instantly his smirk disappeared.

"What the—?" he muttered, staring perplexed at the new arrangement of the hover rings at a distance. "Um, Professor, that's not my sequence."

"Yes, it is," Dantés reassured him. *"I just modified it a bit."*

"A *bit*?" Keithan gasped. "It's not even as complicated as the one I designed."

"It is the one I will evaluate you with. Now, commence your sequence."

"But, Professor—"

"Hurry up, Quintero!" an annoyed Lance shot at him.

"Yeah. We don't have all day," Owen added.

"Why don't you two mind your business?" Keithan shot back.

"Quintero," Professor Dantés said sharply. *"Commence the sequence."*

Keithan sucked in his lips and gripped his steering yokes hard, controlling his anger.

"Just do the sequence, Keithan. Get it over with," Genevieve's voice said with a calm tone.

"But that's *not* my sequence!" Keithan insisted.

"You're not going to do it? Fine," said Dantés, clearly tired of waiting. *"Is there anyone else who would like to try it?"*

There was a moment of silence before someone answered.

"I'll try it."

Owen's metallic-blue-and-silver Model-T moved forward in the air, but as soon as Keithan saw it, he throttled forward with all his might and shot past the twin's craft, straight to the first hover ring.

"Go, Keithan!" Genevieve shouted.

Keithan zoomed through the first ring with a hard, right roll. He rolled again but in the opposite direction and did a sharp U-turn from left to right to reach the second one. Soon after that, he shot straight up, never slowing down, and kept the *d'Artagnan* vertically toward the third hover ring, approaching it from below.

"Let's get this over with," he grumbled under his breath. He was piloting on instinct now, not caring about how well he flew. He was more focused on how angry he was at Dantés. *How could she do this to me?* he kept thinking in disbelief. The sequence he was doing was nothing compared to the one he had brought. He couldn't understand why she hadn't let him do his.

The third ring, positioned horizontally at two thousand feet above the sea, shook when Keithan shot through it with the *d'Artagnan*. Immediately after that, Keithan throttled right and did a wingover, completing a semicircle that sent him left. He inverted the *d'Artagnan*, shooting upside down through the fourth ring, and finally dove into the last one at a forty-five-degree angle.

In less than two minutes—1.37 seconds to be exact—Keithan completed the sequence, beating his classmates' time records.

"There. Done," said Keithan, leveling the *d'Artagnan* and reducing thrust.

He heard his classmates' cheers through his earpiece and waited for a response from Dantés, though it never came. Instead, the professor remained silent and moved on to arrange the rings once again for the next pilot student.

As soon as class ended, the students returned to Ramey and landed their aircraft one at a time. Keithan was the fourth. As he brought the *d'Artagnan* back to the academy's hangar bay, he couldn't take his mind off what Dantés had done to him. He kept wondering, holding the anger inside him, why the professor had altered his flight sequence and no one else's. It was obvious it was a complicated sequence, but Keithan had designed it that way on purpose.

Slowly, Keithan settled the *d'Artagnan* on his assigned area to the left of the bay. He had just turned off the engines and was climbing out of the cockpit when Dantés appeared in front of the bay's main entrance. She was visible only as a silhouette in front of the bright afternoon sunlight.

"Mr. Quintero," the professor called in a serious tone. "I want to see you in my office right away."

Keithan felt the urge to oppose. He wanted to confront her right there in the bay; he didn't care about his classmates watching. But aware that it wasn't such a good idea, he thought it best not to show even the slightest facial reaction. So he said, "Yes, Professor."

He hadn't even placed his second foot on the ground when he noticed that Dantés was already gone.

Going to Alexandria Dantés's office meant you were in serious trouble. At least that was what most students at Ramey Academy thought, especially because everyone who went always came out looking upset or worried. Some students even feared being sent to Dantés more than to the headmaster. Only a few had lost their fear of going there, but they were the ones who were no strangers to trouble. Among those students was Keithan.

The office was located above the hangar bay, and so Keithan had to take the elevator. It was a small windowless room, mostly flat white and with a wavy gray relief that ran throughout the walls. On the left side of the room stood a display of air racing trophies and medals that shined with the simulated sunlight that illuminated the office. The display, however, evidence of Dantés's respectable background, wasn't what caught Keithan's attention every time he was there; it was the glossy turquoise desk at the other end of the office. The desk, with its particularly organic shape, was the focal point as it contrasted with everything else in the room. Keithan found the professor behind it.

Dantés was seated on a high-backed armchair, working on two holographic screens that floated over the desktop. She studied them, looking from one to the other with an expressionless face. Keithan entered, yet she didn't glance at him as Keithan came to stand before the desk and waited silently with his hands behind his back. The uncomfortable silence between them, which made the sound of the air conditioner almost deafening, lasted nearly a whole minute before Dantés gazed up at him and finally spoke.

"I'm sure you know why I asked you to come."

Keithan cleared his throat. "I assume it's because you didn't like the flight sequence I designed, and, um, because I complained about the one you gave me instead."

Dantés leaned her head to the side as she held it with her index and middle fingers to her left temple. "I was very impressed by your sequence. What I would like you to explain, however, is why you, a level-five student, would dare to attempt one so complicated in my class and so far off from what I have taught."

Keithan chose his words carefully. "I just wanted to make my sequence a bit more interesting. You tend to push us to go the extra mile. This time, I decided to take the initiative."

"Take the initiative?"

"Yes."

Dantés tightened her lips and gave Keithan a deep look without blinking once. She had been tapping silently on the desktop with a slick silver pen, but then she put the pen aside. Leaning forward, she said, "You're planning to participate in the Pegasus qualifier tournament, aren't you?"

Keithan's serious expression changed automatically, caught off guard.

"Aren't you?" Dantés repeated more insistently yet keeping a controlled tone.

"What makes you say that?" Keithan struggled to maintain his composure.

Dantés pressed a key on her digital board, and one of the holo screens floating in front of her transformed into a digital, three-dimensional sphere the size of a soccer ball. Inside, it displayed the flight sequence Keithan had designed.

"Right from the beginning of your sequence I could see that what you came up with is way out of your level," Dantés explained. "Two hover rings practically touching each other at an altitude of two thousand feet—the first one arranged vertically and the second horizontally. Passing through them at over three hundred knots requires intense precision and practice. Now, as far as I know, I have not prepared you or your classmates to attempt such a stunt yet. As for the arrangement of the rest of the rings, it's obvious you got the idea from the Pegasus Air Races."

"Yes. So?" Keithan admitted, meaning to sound indifferent. "That doesn't necessarily mean I'm planning to participate—"

"Oh, I know, but when I added your sequence to the rest of the clues I collected, it wasn't hard for me to figure it all out."

Dantés pressed a few keys on her projected board again, and a window opened on the other holo screen. Keithan's jaw dropped. The digital window now showed a long list of familiar Gold level flight sequences—the same he had downloaded to practice in the simulators room during the two weeks he hadn't been allowed to fly.

"Twenty-seven flight sequences," Dantés pointed out. "Twenty-seven, and all of them from the Gold level files. Keithan, I don't think even the twins would have dared to try one of them—and they are the headmaster's sons. *And*, I found this …"

She pressed a key to open another window on the screen, which replaced the previous one. To Keithan's surprise, on this one there was a series of schematics that he immediately recognized as belonging to Fernando.

"Where did you get—?"

"Professor Coverden," Dantés cut him short. "He noticed several modification ideas that your aeroengineer partner has been secretly working on to incorporate into your aircraft during his Experimental Mechanics lessons."

There was no need for her to mention which modifications she was referring to. The evidence was right there, visible on the screen. From the different ideas to remove some parts of the *d'Artagnan* to make her much lighter to the counterthruster they weren't supposed to add until they were on level six.

Keithan realized there was no point in trying to hide it from Dantés anymore.

"You're right, Professor," Keithan admitted, regaining his confidence.

"I am planning to participate in the qualifier tournament. And, yes, Fernando is helping me. However, I don't see why it should be a problem. The Pegasus Air Race is a legal event. So I *can* participate in it."

"It might be a legal event, but you're not a pro air racer yet," Dantés said. "What can possibly make you think you have what it takes to race against air racers who are more experienced and highly trained than you?"

"The Gold level flight sequences that you found are my proof, Professor." Keithan hoped he hadn't sounded too challenging. "Check the scores I made in each of them. You'll see. I even managed to complete some of them flawlessly."

"That is still nothing compared to the Pegasus Air Race," Dantés shot back. "Believe me, Mr. Quintero, you're too young and still too reckless to be in that race."

Keithan looked away, his mouth twisted into a hard scowl before he returned his gaze to Dantés. He knew what she was trying to do, but Keithan wasn't going to back down from his plans. Not now, and definitely not because Dantés wanted him to. "Too young, you say? With all due respect, Professor, didn't you participate in a pro air race when you were still a pilot student? Which one was it? The 2037 International Air Race Cup, right?"

Dantés's brow furrowed. "I was a senior student when that happened," she told him. "And more than that, I was invited to compete in it after I won the Intercollegiate Air Race Championship that same year. So, unlike you, I had enough experience back then."

"We all have to get experience somehow," Keithan replied with a smirk. "I think it would be an excellent opportunity for me to start this year with the Pegasus Air Race."

Dantés sighed, irritated. "Keithan, like every other pilot student in this academy, you're here to become a great professional pilot. And in your case, to be in the Air Racing Program, you're being prepared to become a great air racer too—like your mother. But you must take things slowly. Success comes in due time, not necessarily when you want it. Remember what Drostan Luzier said? A true air racer must have experience, speed, precision—"

"Skills and control. I know," said Keithan, uninterested.

"And you have shown a certain level of those qualities so far. Still, that doesn't mean you have mastered them."

"Then I'll practice twice as hard, but believe me, Professor, I have every reason to participate in that race. Nobody beat Luzier in the last two Pegasus Air Races. That means that if he wins this year too, he'll match my mother's record."

Dantés raised her eyebrows and straightened up. "Oh. So that's it, then. That's one of the reasons. You want to beat Luzier to prevent him from matching your mother's record."

Keithan shrugged. "I have to try. I'm sure my mother would've wanted me to."

Dantés seemed amused by this, and it bothered Keithan. "I have to admit, it sounds … admirable, even heroic, but I get the feeling that's not the main reason you want to be in the race, is it?"

Keithan didn't answer; he wasn't even sure if she expected him to do so. Face frozen, he gulped.

"I know perfectly well how you fly, Keithan, and how competitive you are." Dantés kept her eyes locked on his. "So I guess that you're under the impression that winning this year's Pegasus Air Race could be the first step to the glory you so much desire as an air racing champion."

Once again, Keithan didn't know if he should reply. He could barely stand Dantés's penetrating gaze anymore. It made him feel almost as if it were forcing him back. He remained unmoving, his hands still behind his back, his fists tightened. He opened his mouth slightly to reply, but the professor didn't give him the chance.

"Don't you remember that it was in the Pegasus Air Race that your mother died?"

Oh no. She did not bring that up! Keithan thought, biting his tongue. He knew where the professor was going with this. "Of course I remember," he ended up saying flatly.

"Then you should have in mind that if she were still alive, she would not have approved what you're planning to do, either. I know as a fact that your mother wanted you to become an air racing champion at the right time, *not* when you still haven't learned what it takes to earn that title. Therefore, think about it well, Keithan." And with that, she nodded, gesturing him to leave. She pressed a button on her desk, which opened the frosted glass door at the other end of the room.

Keithan turned around and marched to the door with flared nostrils and his lips shut, but right before he passed through the door, he halted and turned to face Dantés one more time.

"I have already thought about it, Professor, long before I entered this office. But I *am* going to do it," he said with no regret at all. "I *am* going to participate in the Pegasus qualifier tournament. I'm sorry if you don't approve."

Keithan could tell the professor wasn't pleased. He shrugged. The last thing he saw before he turned away was the burning look on Dantés's face.

He couldn't believe what had just happened. For the first time in all his years at the academy, he had left Dantés's office feeling good—great, actually. As far as he knew, nobody else had ever accomplished that. He couldn't feel prouder of how he had handled it, especially his temper—and his mouth. He had simply made his point clear. He didn't let the professor convince him to back down from his plans. The fact was the Pegasus Air Race was an event that had nothing to do with the academy, and it wasn't at all like when he raced against the twins. It was legal for him to be in the Pegasus Air Race, and most importantly, it was his business, not Dantés's or the academy's.

Keithan walked straight to the elevator door. Once it opened, he stepped into the small cylindrical capsule, but right before the door would slide shut, a hand held it from outside, making it open again. Keithan raised his gaze and was surprised to see Professor Dantés now standing in front of him. Her hard expression told him that she wasn't done with him yet.

Keithan didn't react; he just stared back at her with no idea what to expect. He had been under the impression that the conversation had ended. Staring at Keithan with menacing eyes now, it was obvious she wasn't going to allow Keithan to leave with the last words. So she said them.

"You don't have what it takes to be in the Pegasus Air Race, and I am going to prove it. So make sure you get your aircraft ready because this afternoon, you and I are going to air race."

The elevator slid shut this time, and Keithan descended alone inside the capsule, all the while stunned by what Dantés had just told him.

CHAPTER 23

"**W**hat?"

It was the instant reaction chorused by Fernando, Yari, and Genevieve when Keithan told them what had happened with Professor Dantés. They stopped halfway to their next class on the second floor and couldn't help but stare at Keithan in complete shock.

"I'm not kidding, guys," Keithan insisted. "She challenged me to air race with her this afternoon."

"Nuh-uh. It can't be," Fernando said. "A few weeks ago, she and Headmaster Viviani took away your pilot certificate, along with Owen's and Lance's, just because the three of you raced illegally after classes—"

"And now she's encouraging you to practically do the same thing?" Genevieve finished the thought.

"Well, Dantés is a professor," Yari said. "Maybe she can bend the rule when she sees fits. In this case, to teach Keithan a lesson."

"Don't you guys think I have a chance against her?" Keithan asked.

"*No!*" The response was unanimous and so loud it made Keithan take a step back. It even made some of the students passing by in the hallway turn their heads.

"Keithan, you don't stand a chance. Dantés is going to cream you in the air," Genevieve reassured him.

"You *do* know she's a former air racing champion, right?" Yari remarked. "She's won international air races. She even broke records when she was a pilot student."

"I do know. That's what makes it all more exciting," Keithan replied. "I'll be honest with you, winning or losing against her is not what interests me most with this race."

The comment made it worse because, as if he'd just made a hilarious joke, his friends burst out with laughter.

"Yeah, right!" said Fernando, still laughing. "*You*, Keithan Quintero, aren't concerned about losing an air race? That'll be the day."

Keithan could only sigh. It wasn't worth explaining to them why he wasn't too concerned about air racing against Dantés. Keithan was aware of the odds, especially the ones against him. The professor could definitely "cream him," as Genevieve had said. That was almost a fact. And although it was also a fact that winning was usually the first thing in his mind every time he air raced, this time it was more than that. He wasn't going to race against rookies like Owen and Lance. This time he was going to fly against a real air racer—and legally.

What better way to warm up for the Pegasus qualifier tournament?

History of Modern Aviation was the last class of the day. Professor De Leon, a plump, little woman with a kind and good-humored personality, and who students considered a human encyclopedia due to the many curious and detailed facts she always brought up during her discussions, was leading a debate about the drastic transformation of the art and need of flight during the 2020s. So far, most students were engaged and attentive in the discussion while they enjoyed the images the professor showed to explain different facts. That, however, wasn't the case for Keithan.

The class didn't seem to be going by as fast as he had hoped. The time at the right corner of his laptube's holo screen confirmed it. What he thought had been forty minutes, his screen displayed it as only the first fifteen minutes of the class. It made Keithan tap his right heel rapidly without noticing as he stared almost hypnotized at the rhythmic change of the neon-green numbers in the seconds counter. Every now and then, he looked up to the front so Professor De Leon wouldn't catch him distracted, but as soon as she looked away, Keithan would stare at the time on his screen. Based on what little he'd been able to follow of the discussion, the debate around him was focused now on how the Aerial War from 2020 to 2026 had caused the great evolution of all aircraft worldwide.

Finally, the electric bell rang, and Keithan jumped to his feet. He didn't even wait for the professor to wrap it up; he just grabbed his laptube and his leather jacket and rushed out of the classroom. By the time the professor noticed it, Keithan was already out of sight.

Soon a crowd of students started to come out of the classrooms.

"Excuse me! Pardon me! Coming through!" Keithan repeated anxiously without slowing down and zigzagging among the students of all the levels.

"Ouch! Watch where you're going!" shouted an aeroengineer girl when Keithan accidentally stepped on her foot.

"Sorry!" Keithan shouted back.

He turned right and descended a metal staircase. A group of boys and girls appeared at the bottom, coming in his direction. They all moved hastily aside and against the walls when they saw Keithan approaching fast.

"Yo, Keithan!" called out Marco Hernandez, one of the boys from the group. "We heard you're racing against Professor Dantés!"

"Yeah! In a few minutes!" Keithan replied, rushing past the boy and skipping several steps.

"We definitely won't miss that!" Marco shouted back, though Keithan was already out of sight.

Keithan turned left at the end of the staircase and continued running down another hallway. Students crowded it just like in the previous one. Keithan was doing his best to move gracefully among them when he heard a distinctly familiar voice behind him.

"Halt. Halt. No running in the hallways," it repeated.

Keithan glanced over his shoulder and saw the HM robot making its way through the many students, the sound of its spherical tire a low whining as the robot accelerated.

"Oh, no, you won't. Not this time," Keithan muttered. He leaned forward, his jaw tightened, and ran faster.

He got to another staircase in seconds, and by descending it, he managed to escape the robot, which, due to its wheel, couldn't take the stairs. It wasn't until Keithan reached the bottom that he took a moment to catch his breath. He looked at either side of the new hallway to make sure there wasn't any other HM robot nearby. The coast was clear. He was about to start running again when a strong hand fell on his left shoulder.

"Hey, Quintero. Hold up."

Keithan's heart jumped. He thought a professor had caught him, but when he spun around, he found himself facing the chest of a tall black boy. Like Keithan, he wore a blue uniform, only the boy's included chromed linings over the gray areas on the shoulders, waist, and thighs, which classified him as a senior. And he was no ordinary senior. The boy was none other than Gregory Paceley—now the most popular senior at the academy for being the only student (as far as everyone knew) that was going to be participating in the Pegasus qualifier tournament.

Gregory's athletic-built body towered over Keithan. He had a firm, pointed jaw with a dimple on the chin, which, for some reason, drove girls crazy. There were four other seniors accompanying him: two boys and two girls. They all stared down at Keithan as if he were a boy who had gotten lost.

"Is it true what everybody is talking about?" Gregory asked. "You and Professor Dantés are going to air race?"

Keithan hissed. "It is, and I've to go. I have to get the *d'Artagnan* ready."

"Oh. You're gonna race with that *thing* against Dantés?"

Keithan sensed the mocking tone behind Gregory's comment; at the same time, the boy's friends giggled beside him.

"Yeah. With that *thing*," he shot back, not amused. "You can bring yours too if you like. There's still a spot for a third place."

"Oooo!" Gregory's friends said, not expecting a comeback.

"Are you challenging me?" Gregory said.

Keithan didn't back down despite the boy's intimidating height. "If you're up to it."

He and Gregory locked eyes fearlessly before Gregory snorted and said, "Take it easy, kid. I was just messing with you. Honestly, I've to say you've got guts. So good luck in the race. You're gonna need it."

Keithan wasn't sure how to take the comment. "Um, thanks," he said. And without wasting more time, he took off.

Outside, in the heat of the afternoon, past the entrance bridge, Dantés made the final touches to the flight course she and Keithan would soon fly. She stood mounted on the circular hover platform while her assistant, Swift, stood at a distance, setting the metal hover rings that would be used for the race.

"Ring four is not responding, Professor," Swift reported through the speaker on the console in front of Dantés. *"I'm checking the connections leading to its power cells, but they all seem to be in order."*

"Hold on. I'll see if I can activate it from here," Dantés told him.

She was still working on the platform's console when a hoarse voice called out to her with authority.

"Professor Dantés!" It was Headmaster Viviani. The large man, whose bald head and high-tech glasses gleamed with the sunlight, was marching straight toward her, his expression a mixture of controlled anger and incredulity.

Dantés glanced at him but continued working.

"Professor Dantés," Viviani repeated sharply. He stopped right in front of the hovering platform and folded his arms. "I would like to know the meaning of this."

"I'm preparing a racecourse, sir," Dantés replied, concentrated on what she was doing.

"I can see that, but is it true it's because you challenged a student?"

"That is correct, sir."

Just then, a group of professors appeared: Steelsmith, De Leon, and Treweeke. They were aware of what was going on, yet noticing the headmaster's seriousness, none of them dared to interrupt. They halted behind him and listened.

Viviani stepped closer to the platform. "Alexandria, professors don't challenge students to air race with them no matter the reason. Neither during classes nor, worse still, after classes."

Dantés didn't take her eyes off the console. "I know that, Headmaster, but it so happens young Keithan Quintero thinks he can participate in this year's Pegasus Air Race. I need to prove to him that he's not ready for such a dangerous event yet."

"Keithan Quinte—! Please tell me you're not serious." Viviani rubbed his forehead hard, as if beginning to feel a headache.

"I am, sir. Swift …" said Dantés, adjusting the microphone extended from her earpiece. "I activated ring four; it appears to be synchronized with the course design. Is it responding now?"

"It is. They're all set now," her assistant answered.

"Good. Stand by to raise the rings."

"Alexandria." Professor De Leon stepped forward. "Think about what you're doing."

"I have to agree, Alexandria," Treweeke added. The young professor with yellow-lensed glasses stepped forward as well. "I'm one who has wished for quite some time to see the moment in which a professor gets the opportunity to put Quintero in his rightful place— and a few other students too—but I don't think this is the correct way to do it."

"He's right," Professor Steelsmith added. "You wouldn't be setting a good example for the rest of the students."

Dantés made a quick and final check at everything displayed on her digital console: the designed air course for the race and the airspace clearance. All that was left to do now was press the Enter key to raise the hover rings into the air. Satisfied, she finally turned to face the headmaster and the rest of the company.

"Professors, please," she said, "I am well aware that this might not be the ideal way to deal with this matter, but I strongly believe that it would be the most effective one since we are dealing with Keithan Quintero."

"Is that so?" Viviani said skeptically.

"Yes. That boy is determined to make it to the Pegasus Air Race. Especially since he wants to prevent Drostan Luzier from matching his mother's unbeaten record. Keithan strongly believes he can accomplish that. Now, since I don't think there is anything any of us can do to stop him from participating in the Pegasus qualifier tournament, I should at least do everything I can to convince him that he could get himself killed if he does."

"So by racing with him today—"

"By *beating* him today," Dantés corrected Steelsmith.

"Right. You intend to make him realize that?"

"Exactly. Who knows? Perhaps this race against Quintero can serve as an example for the rest of the students, including Gregory Paceley, who is also planning to be in the Pegasus Air Race."

There was a moment of silence. The headmaster and the other professors considered her point.

"Well, I just hope you're not also using this race to quench your thirst to compete again after so many years," Viviani told Dantés. He narrowed his eyes as he adjusted his silver, coin-shaped glasses. "Don't forget, I know your background as an air racer."

"We all do," Professor De Leon said. "Your reputation, even when you were a mere pilot student, is well known for your competitive attitude and overconfidence, which, you have to admit—and I don't intend to offend you—resembles that of young Mr. Quintero."

The comment struck Dantés like a low blow to the stomach, making her clench her jaw. What she hated about it most was that De Leon was right. In some ways, Keithan was indeed like she had been at his age. That was something she would never admit to anyone, which was why she swallowed her discomfort. Looking at De Leon and the others, she said, "It's not like that at all."

"Good," Viviani said, though he didn't look convinced. "Then I guess what's left is for me to tell you, *Professor*, that you better win this race of yours and accomplish what you say you want. Otherwise I could be forced to reconsider your position as a professor of the academy's Air Racing Program."

Dantés gulped. "I understand, sir."

At a distance, behind the academy's bridge, a crowd of students started to form. Their cheers grew, getting the attention of the headmaster, Dantés, and the other professors. The next moment, Keithan's gray-and-orange racing craft appeared hovering low. It slowly made its way into the main runway with its particular humming.

Dantés stepped down from the hover platform and rubbed her hands. "Well, if you'll excuse me, my friends. It's race time."

CHAPTER 24

Refueling tank, check. Engines readouts, check. Cockpit air pressure, check.

One by one, Keithan reviewed each part of the *d'Artagnan* as he took her out of the hangar bay and onto the airfield. Though he had already done the pre-flight check before he climbed into the cockpit, he decided to go through everything one more time. After all, when it came to flying—and racing—there was no such thing as being too careful. Keithan tried the ailerons on the wings, making them move up and down, then the twin front steering vanes to make sure they were working properly.

Everything looked and felt normal. Now Keithan had nothing more to worry about except to fly fast and proficiently.

It was surprising to see how the news of him racing against Dantés had spread in the academy. Outside, almost the entire student body and faculty gathered to witness the race. The students got excited when they saw the *d'Artagnan* come out of the bay. Many of them waved at Keithan and gave him thumbs-up as he flew the craft slowly past them. Keithan saluted to them by tipping his forehead. He felt like a rock star, yet once he left the crowd behind and passed under the academy's bridge, he focused on the race ahead.

The airport's main runway was in front of him. Beyond it, Keithan saw the big metal hover rings beginning to move. They ascended high into the sky like floating bubbles in the air. Below, Swift controlled them from the hover platform. He noticed Keithan approaching and gestured to him, telling Keithan to settle his aircraft in front of the white exit line. Keithan acknowledged and headed right with the *d'Artagnan.*

Meanwhile, people approached the side of the runway. The ascending rings got everyone's attention. People were showing up from the airport's main terminal, the hangars, and even the racers' crew areas at the far southeast of the airfield. Among them, airport workers, pilots, and crew people who left everything behind to see what was going on. Even on the outskirts of the airport, curious civilians, either on foot or in vehicles, crowded the fences to see.

Taking all this in, Keithan felt butterflies in his stomach. He hadn't expected such a crowd. It didn't feel as he imagined it when he practiced. What should have felt like excitement now felt like nervousness. It took Keithan a moment to realize he couldn't let this make him lose his concentration. He needed to remain focused. If he couldn't stay in full control of himself now, how would he control the pressure in the Pegasus Air Race, where it would most likely be ten times as crowded?

Keithan tried to relax, accepting the pressure of having all eyes on him. Part of the big deal of air racing was also to put on a show for the spectators. Therefore, he shut his eyes and took deep, slow breaths, calming himself and clearing his mind. Keithan only thought about what he was about to do, regardless of how many people were watching. He was finally regaining control of his nerves when his wrist communicator rang.

"Fernando!" Keithan yelped, angry but also glad to speak with his best friend. "Why aren't you communicating through my headset?"

"Sorry, Keithan. You're on your own this time," Fernando told him. *"I don't want to be part of this particular race. This is between you and Professor Dantés."*

Keithan grinned. "Fair enough."

"Anyway, good luck, though, honestly, I'm not sure you should win this air race."

"Why not?"

"*Because, who knows? Dantés might try to get back at you later with your grade if you beat her today.*"

Keithan heard the loud cheers of the crowd through the tiny speaker of his wrist communicator. He saw what the commotion was all about when he turned his gaze to his left.

Dantés had finally arrived with her aircraft.

"Gotta go," he told Fernando, tapping the wrist communicator to end the call.

The students started the rooting, making the rest of the spectators follow when they saw the second racing craft enter the airfield. The craft made its way through the crowd and into the main runway. In appearance, it wasn't what any other racing pilot would consider impressive, at least in competitive terms, but it looked fast. It was an elongated, red-and-white Flapper air racer, well known for its particular wings, which could flap up and down just like those of a bird, allowing fast maneuverability. It had the Ramey Academy insignia on the side of its fuselage.

Keithan didn't feel intimidated by it, though. His *d'Artagnan* had proven to be faster and more maneuverable than similar aircraft despite her heavy weight and battered weathered look.

Dantés's aircraft hovered toward the *d'Artagnan* then turned and came to a smooth halt next to her. From the cockpit, the professor gazed at Keithan and tapped on the side of her helmet with her forefinger, gesturing Keithan to flip on his communication headset.

"*All right, Quintero,*" Dantés said once Keithan was able to hear her. "*Pay careful attention. I am only going to explain this once. There are six rings in the air, and each one is hovering at a different altitude and angle between one thousand and two thousand feet. Now, when Swift gives the signal, we take off, but we do not ascend until we pass between the pair of pylons located near the other end of the runway. Got that?*"

"Got it."

"*Once we ascend, we turn around and head for the rings. The goal is to fly through each of them, just like in the Pegasus Air Races, and the first one who*" *manages to do so and reach the seventh and final ring, which will be placed low, over the main runway after we take off, wins. Oh, and keep in mind that, just like in the Pegasus Air Races, some of the rings will be moving."*

That last part made Keithan raise his eyebrows. "What?"

"What?" Dantés repeated in a slightly mocking tone. *"Did you think I would take it easy on you? Think again, Quintero. If you cannot do this short air course, there is no way you will even make it through the Pegasus qualifier tournament. So you still think you have what it takes?"*

There was no need to answer. Dantés was giving him one last chance to reconsider, but there was no way Keithan would back down now, especially when there was a crowd waiting to see a great race. Therefore, Keithan lowered the visor over his eyes and made the burning engines roar, deafening the professor even from her headset. It was his way to hasten Dantés to start the race already. It seemed to work because she didn't say more.

Now facing forward, his arms and legs shaking with adrenaline, Keithan waited for Swift to give the signal.

Swift, still mounted on the circular platform, levitated overhead in front of Keithan and Dantés. He held an orange flag in one hand high over his head. Keithan didn't take his eyes off the flag. He narrowed them, and with each second that passed, he gripped the twin independent steering yokes harder, as if trying to control the strong trembling generated by the power of the engines.

"Come on, come on, come on," he murmured.

Swift swung the flag down, and like two ferocious beasts that had been released, the two racing aircraft blasted off.

Chapter 25

The crowd went wild, both inside and outside the airport, when they saw the two aircraft race down the main runway. Their screams, however, didn't compare to the roar of the racers' engines, which also showed their power through their blue flaming afterburners. Such a scene already built up the euphoria and excitement of the spectators, promising an intense race.

Keithan kept his thrusters to the maximum, his head leaned forward and his mind focused on remaining in control of himself and the *d'Artagnan*. Everything outside rushed past him: the airport's main buildings, the twin-fuselage airliners parked in front of them, the different crew areas of the pro racers, even the gigantic white-and-gold airship of Pegasus Company—all of it slowly becoming a blur as the *d'Artagnan* gained more speed. Only Dantés's aircraft remained clear beside him to his right. Keithan couldn't see the professor, but he could imagine her holding on tightly to her steering yokes with her deeply serious look of determination to beat him.

In a matter of seconds, the two inflated pylons Dantés had warned him about came into view. They emerged slowly from the horizon at the end of the runway, yet right behind them, Keithan spotted something else …

A concave steep ramp towering over the pylons—the same he and his classmates had used in Advanced Aeronautics with their drones. Yet, watching it now was a lot different because now, instead of flying the drone he and Fernando had built, Keithan was flying straight toward the ramp with the *d'Artagnan.*

Keithan braced himself for the challenge. He kept his speed to the maximum. Right when he passed between the two pylons, he pulled his twin yokes with all his strength, lifting the *d'Artagnan*'s wide front arms and steering vanes to the sky. The maneuver made the g-forces push his head and torso hard against the back of his seat. Still, Keithan held on, gritting his teeth. Right beside him, Dantés did the same and continued the abrupt climb all the way to the top of the ramp. As a result, the two ended up doing a half loop that pointed them back to the hover rings in an inverted position, followed by a half snap roll to straighten their flight.

Able to see the hover rings again, Keithan did a quick analysis of their positions. Three of the rings hovered close to one thousand feet while the other three hovered close to two thousand. Keithan glanced to his left and noticed Dantés had stopped ascending. That could only mean that she was planning to take the lower ones first. Keithan decided to do the same. He narrowed his eyes and stared straight at the first two rings as he rushed to them.

He automatically drew in his mind a flight path through the rings to figure out which maneuvers he would have to do. His only concern, however, was that he had to pass through the rings before Dantés, otherwise he could miss—or worse still, collide with—one of them. Keithan accelerated.

Ring one hovered vertically but with its opening faced sideways. That meant that at the speed Keithan was approaching it, he would have to fly into it sideways. Ring two, on the other hand, hovered horizontally, which meant that he would have to pass it either with a straight climb or by diving through it.

"Here we go," Keithan breathed. He twisted his steering yokes to the right and successfully shot the *d'Artagnan* straight into the ring— right before Dantés did. Soon after that, he banked and dove several feet, swung upward in a U-turn maneuver, and—*SWOOSH!*—he shot through ring two.

Not once did he dare to look back, but he knew Dantés was on his tail, gaining on him. Whether she managed to take the second ring or not, Keithan didn't know, but he doubted the professor would have missed it. As he shot out of the second ring, Keithan arced the *d'Artagnan* downward, as if he were descending the apex of a mountain. The stunt made his body rise slightly off his seat for an instant then drop back as he recovered and flew forward to the next ring.

Not too far from him, the professor did a different stunt. As soon as she shot out and upward from ring two, she made a backward loop, which allowed her to reduce minimum speed, and leveled her aircraft again.

Now it was time for ring three. Keithan flew straight toward it and realized things were going to get tougher. Unlike the first two rings, ring three was rotating vertically. To pass through it, Keithan needed to be precise and perfectly calculate the angle it would be when he got to it. Only then would he know which maneuver he would attempt. The truth was Keithan had no time to figure it out when he was just three seconds from reaching the ring. Even analyzing this was his mistake because it made him reduce speed without realizing it in time. By then, Dantés overtook him and swung her craft in front of him.

"NO!" Keithan cried, unable to see the hover ring.

Dantés shot through ring three like a bullet, and Keithan was forced to turn abruptly aside at the last second, missing it. He jammed the thrusters forward and made a sharp right turn, keeping the *d'Artagnan* in a knife-edge maneuver. As he did this, he stretched his head back all the way and got a glimpse of Dantés now ascending toward the higher rings.

Keithan pushed his frustration away. There was no time to be frustrated. *I can still win this,* he told himself, aware that he couldn't afford to make any more mistakes. Therefore, he changed his strategy.

No more calculating. It was all about trusting his instincts now, just as he used to fly.

Keithan gained speed and pointed the *d'Artagnan*'s front steering vanes back toward ring three. He followed its rotation without blinking.

Three ... two ... Then—*WHOOSH!*—he bulleted into it.

"Ha! Haaa!"

He pulled the yokes with all his might, and the roaring *d'Artagnan* turned straight up to the higher hover rings. He spotted Dantés close to five hundred feet above him. The skilled professor flew through ring four with impressive maneuverability. It would have been obvious for Keithan to give chase, but relying more on instincts, he attempted something more daring instead—he skipped ring four and went for ring number five.

Keithan didn't hesitate. He angled the aircraft in the same direction Dantés was heading and pushed on the thrusters. Ring five hovered vertically, yet it also rotated sideways, making it as challenging as the one Keithan had just passed. Luckily for him, Dantés didn't mention anything about taking the rings in order, which was why he kept his course. Keithan needed to reach ring five before Dantés did. He already knew what to do to accomplish it. He marked his timing carefully. The next instant, he took his shot.

Keithan passed through the ring with a sudden sharp wingover maneuver. He did it in time to force Dantés to evade the ring and him—just as he had hoped. The trick tied him again with the professor. Now each of them had three rings to go.

Without looking back, Keithan gunned the *d'Artagnan* toward ring four. He had no trouble with it. Meanwhile, several yards away, Dantés banked hard and flew back to pass through ring five. Almost simultaneously, the two of them shot straight up toward the last ring in the sky. After that, it would be crossing the finish ring that hovered low over the runway.

Sunlight half-blinded Keithan as it reflected on the glass of the cockpit and visor lens. Still, that didn't slow him down. The more altitude he gained, the more he pushed his thrusters. By doing so, his entire body pressed against his seat, wanting to sink in it.

Still flying vertically, Keithan half rolled to turn away from the sun. He was able to see ring six up ahead once again. He noticed its challenge instantly. The ring was positioned horizontally, but unlike the previous one, it had two bars raised on opposite sides flashing rhythmically downward. It meant the ring had to be taken only from above—and by doing one specific maneuver.

"An inverted flat drop?" Keithan gasped.

He hadn't expected this. As far as he knew, not many pro air racers had dared to do such a difficult maneuver while trying to pass through a hover ring, much less accomplish it. What was Dantés thinking when she came up with this? Was she crazy?

She's deadly serious, Keithan realized. Dantés was still climbing vertically at top speed, and so he kept on climbing too. At over 338 knots, the two shot past the ring and kept flying skyward over two thousand feet. Suddenly, a cold sensation took control of Keithan. It brought with it something he never imagined feeling—at least while flying. Insecurity.

Keithan couldn't believe it, but now he wasn't sure if he should go on. And the reason was valid. He had never attempted an inverted flat drop. The sensation was so intense it flashed a horrible image in his mind, of him ending the race as a loser—worse still, as a quitter. Such possible realization froze him for a split second.

"What am I going to do?" he managed to murmur.

He heard Dantés kill her thrusters. When Keithan turned his head, he saw her disappear behind him.

"She's going for it!"

Witnessing it was all it took for him to get his head back in the moment. As a result, Keithan shook his head and focused again. Without thinking twice, he shut down the thrusters and prepared for the fall.

The *d'Artagnan*, still vertical, slowly came to a standstill close to three thousand feet, according to the altimeter on the console. There was total silence for an instant, accompanied by a feeling of stillness and suspense … right before the craft pitched back and began its drop.

The seconds that followed became almost a battle between Keithan and the *d'Artagnan* as he struggled to control the steering yokes, which now trembled hard. Falling upside down, Keithan felt the violence of the airflow shaking the whole fuselage, as if the *d'Artagnan* were an angry beast that needed to be tamed. He had never had to struggle so much with her before, but the maneuver required it to keep the aircraft inverted as it accelerated downward.

Keithan craned his neck and saw the earth approaching. The elongated shape of Ramey's main runway, along with everything that surrounded it, made it look like an architectural model site—so well designed, yet unreal. Keithan didn't let the impressive view distract him. Instead, he stared straight at the small shapes of Professor Dantés's racing craft and the hover ring she was soon to reach. He glanced at his console only a few times as he dropped, checking that everything in the *d'Artagnan* was in order. He didn't want to miss when the professor passed through the hover ring. That way he could be sure how to do it too. In a matter of seconds, he saw it.

Dantés, who was also dropping inverted, went into ring six so fast, yet so gracefully it seemed to haven't been a challenge whatsoever for her. As soon as she passed it, she pitched downward, preparing to dive.

Now it was Keithan's turn. The ring rushed up to him. Hands sweating, Keithan worked his yokes carefully to keep the *d'Artagnan* inverted. He knew he only had one shot at this. There was no room for error.

2,500 feet … 2,300 feet …

The numbers changed rapidly on Keithan's altimeter. A drop of sweat trickled down his upside-down nose, between his eyebrows, and toward his forehead. Then, giving one last look at the rushing ring … he passed through it.

A heavy sigh of relief escaped Keithan, and he felt his confidence return tenfold.

"*Now* we're pro racing!" Keithan exclaimed.

Soon he pitched the *d'Artagnan* downward, as he had seen Dantés do, and began his dive. He spotted her aircraft diving as well approximately five hundred feet below. Her exhaust nozzles had just come to life again. It expelled furious blue flames, which was why Keithan wasted no time and turned on his thrusters too, making his *d'Artagnan* roar again.

And so the last part of the race began. Now it was all about reaching the finish ring. Both racing craft kept diving toward the earth. Keithan, however, still gained on Dantés, but he was running out of time to pass her.

1,300 feet … 1,200 feet … he noticed in his altimeter. He pushed the thrusters with all his might. In response, the *d'Artagnan* accelerated obediently, roaring much louder than Keithan had ever heard her before. But unexpectedly, the aircraft began to whine.

"What the …?" he said, trying to make some sense of the noise, which was becoming deafening.

800 feet … 600 feet … showed the altimeter in less than five seconds.

"Don't let me down now, girl. Just a little more!" Keithan cried to the *d'Artagnan* through gritted teeth.

Far below, at the airfield, people held their breath while they watched the two racers plummeting from the clear sky. They heard the sudden whining generated by Keithan's aircraft, and right away they could tell something was wrong when they saw it now leaving a wide trail of black smoke behind. Fernando, who was surrounded by his classmates, felt his breathing become heavier and his heart rate accelerate. He didn't blink; he continued following the *d'Artagnan* with his digital binoculars.

Come on, Keithan. Pull up. Pull up! He wished his best friend could hear him. Fernando didn't care about the *d'Artagnan*'s weird whining. All he cared about was that Keithan would recover without any problem.

A hand fell on his right shoulder and gripped hard.

"Keithan's not going to recover at that speed!" he heard a deeply worried Genevieve say.

"He will," Fernando reassured her, not taking his eyes off the *d'Artagnan*.

"Man, I don't know," said Winston, who was at Fernando's left.

Dantés's aircraft pulled up, recovering and leveling with the ground. Two seconds later, Keithan did the same. The crowd burst out with gasps but kept their eyes wide while they watched Keithan and Dantés now heading straight toward the finish ring. At that moment, confusion also overtook them when they all noticed that Keithan didn't recover in the direction he was supposed to.

"What in the blazes is Keithan doing?" Yari cried. Everybody else probably wondered the same thing.

Hard to believe, while Dantés had recovered from her drop and leveled her craft parallel to the runway, Keithan had recovered farther from and perpendicular to it.

Keithan hadn't planned it. It was how he had recovered from the drop. But he didn't care. All that mattered was he had recovered. Now flying low and level to the ground, he gunned the *d'Artagnan* with everything she had toward the checkered pattern finish ring.

The only thing he could hear was the whining of the engines due to overload thrust. It was so loud Keithan felt like he was inside a factory with hundreds of machines working at the same time. The noise forced Keithan to tighten every muscle in his face. His nose remained scrunched up, his jaw clenched, and his eyebrows ruffled downward. Yet his eyes remained fixed on the finish ring ahead. He ignored the red warning sign that blinked insistently on his console.

"Come on, girl! We're almost there!" Keithan murmured to the *d'Artagnan.*

Out of the corner of his eye, he spotted the rushing blur of Dantés's aircraft approaching from the east side of the runway while he raced northward to the middle of it. It was there where the finish ring hovered, no more than ten feet above the ground. Dantés had the advantage since she was facing the center of the ring, and for a moment Keithan wondered what he would have to do to beat her. Seeing how close they were, he started a quick countdown in his head.

Five, four, three, two ...

And that was when it happened. In an act of desperation, and at the last possible moment, Keithan rolled hard to the left and shot through the finish ring, spinning and spinning, right in front of Dantés, thus becoming the youngest air racer from Ramey Academy—and in history—to have beaten a professional air racing champion.

CHAPTER 26

The victory celebration took place at Rocket's Diner as soon as the race was over. Yari and Genevieve were the ones who spread the word, and it seemed to work because by 4:30 the place was packed with students from all levels of the academy. Whether with sodas or with one of Mr. Rocket's famous shakes, everyone had a drinking glass or cup in hand, and all around, the short serving robots continued bringing more.

Genevieve made her way through the middle of the crowd, trying not to spill the two caramel cola floats she held. She headed to one of the round tables where she handed Keithan one of the floats.

"There you go. This victory drink is on me," she told him.

"Wow! Thanks," Keithan replied over the noise.

"You deserve it."

Genevieve squeezed herself with Yari on the same chair, next to Keithan. Joining them around the table was Winston, his pilot partner Gabriel, and Fernando, all of them already with their own drinks.

"I gotta hand it to you, Keithan," Yari said, "I didn't expect you to beat Professor Dantés today."

"None of us did," Gabriel clarified. "Still, it was awesome seeing you do it. I bet Dantés was furious."

"And in trouble," Winston added. "I heard Headmaster Viviani and the other professors weren't too happy about her racing against you. Imagine their faces when they witnessed her lose."

Keithan took a sip from his cola float and licked his lips. "Well, she was the one who came up with the idea to air race, not me," he said. "She was so insistent in wanting to prove to me that I didn't have what it takes to be in the Pegasus Air Race, but I proved her wrong. So, Fernando..." He turned to his best friend, smiling. "...I guess our plans to participate are still on."

"Yeah, well, let's just hope we don't have serious problems repairing the *d'Artagnan*—again," Fernando said, frowning.

"What do you mean?" Genevieve asked.

"Keithan here almost incinerated the inside of the *d'Artagnan*'s middle engine when he gave it excessive thrust," Fernando explained. "I assure you, it's not going to be an easy fix, especially when we're only three weeks away from the Pegasus qualifier tournament."

"Then it's good it happened today. That way I can be aware of it during the tournament," Keithan replied. "Anyway, we'll worry about that later. For now, let's enjoy today's victory."

"That's right!" Genevieve said. She got up again and forced Keithan to do the same before she climbed onto his chair.

"Listen up, everyone!" she called out, taking Keithan and the rest by surprise. She raised her caramel cola float high to get the attention of the people around her. They turned their heads, and as soon as they quieted down, Genevieve went on. "I'd like to make a toast. To Keithan Quintero."

Keithan felt the hairs at the back of his neck rise.

"He achieved an air racing victory today, but more impressive still, he *won* against one of the most skilled professors at Ramey Acade—"

"Whoa! Whoa! Wait!" Keithan said. He climbed onto another chair with his cola float in hand to address the onlookers. "Today's victory wasn't mine alone, but also my best friend's, my aeroengineer partner: Fernando Aramis."

All eyes turned to Fernando who couldn't have turned any redder.

"If it hadn't been for him," Keithan went on, "the *d'Artagnan* wouldn't have flown as great as she did—even after one of her engines almost burned out. So..." He raised his float high. "...to the *d'Artagnan* team."

"The youngest team ever that will participate in the Pegasus Air Race," Genevieve added with a supporting smile. "Cheers!"

"Cheers!" Everyone raised their drinks in agreement.

Keithan looked at Fernando, who nodded to him in return before they clinked their glasses together. They slurped the rest of their cola floats. As Keithan finished his, he noticed Mr. Rocket over the crowd. The large man was staring at him behind the serving counter. He had a curious look on his face. He was smiling but frowning, as if happy for Keithan but at the same time not liking the idea of him participating in the Pegasus Air Race.

Things turned out to be different for Keithan in the days that followed, though not necessarily for the best in every aspect. The professors gave him the cold shoulder, speaking to him only objectively and when necessary. Not one of them even congratulated him for his victory against Dantés.

Gregory Paceley was another person who didn't seem happy about Keithan's victory. It wasn't hard for Keithan to notice it because now, every time the two saw each other in the hallways, Gregory gave him a serious look, evidently because he'd learned that Keithan also had plans to participate in the Pegasus qualifier tournament. And after watching Keithan air race against Dantés, it seemed that Gregory saw him as a threat rather than as another opponent.

Fortunately, this didn't bother Keithan much. His only concern about Gregory, however, was that the boy happened to be one of Headmaster Viviani's favorite students in the entire academy (probably even over his twin sons), which meant that, unlike Keithan, Gregory could get the headmaster to allow the academy to sponsor him. This was a big deal since Keithan knew that beginning an air racing career with a sponsor was more respectable than starting on your own.

Aside from that, not everything was uncomfortable for him at the academy. On the positive side, thanks to his victory against Dantés, Keithan gained a big group of supporters who were looking forward to seeing him in the qualifier tournament. Then there were the Viviani twins, Owen and Lance. As expected, they weren't enjoying Keithan's success so far, not one bit. Not that Keithan cared about what they thought, though. Still, it amused him how the two boys tried to avoid making eye contact with him. Having beaten Dantés made the race Keithan had with the twins a month ago look now like a training exercise—worse still for Owen and Lance, now that they, too, had learned about Keithan's plan to qualify for the Pegasus Air Race. Keithan could only imagine what was going through their heads.

As the days went by, throughout Ramey and the media, the news about more air racers arriving continued. There were three days left now before the qualifier tournament. So far, seventeen air racers had officially announced their participation, among them Gregory Paceley. Keithan hadn't announced his yet, at least officially. He stuck with the plan of waiting until the day of the event to avoid any distraction from the pack of nosy reporters that were already swarming the other racers. The plan allowed Keithan to continue to practice without interruptions and to work with Fernando on the *d'Artagnan*. It also allowed Marianna to show them important information about the other racers and their respective aircraft.

Marianna did an incredible job. She managed to gather an ample compilation of videos and background files on each of the racers. She told Keithan and Fernando about their strengths and weaknesses so Keithan would know who he would be racing against and Fernando would know if the *d'Artagnan* was missing something that she might need to compete against the other aircraft.

As a result, all that hard work and dedication consumed practically all their free time. They had to stay up late at night to finish their schoolwork. Of the three, Keithan went to bed the latest. He did his training exercises as soon as he finished his class assignments and changed into his pajamas. He did what was known as mental flying, and he did it in the middle of his bedroom. It was his way of practicing on the ground when he wasn't inside a cockpit or a simulator, the same way all pro air racers did. The exercises consisted of moving around and dipping his hands up, down, and sideways, mimicking maneuvers at the same time he pictured himself flying through an air course. Basically, it was a visualization of an improvised sequence walkthrough.

A loud classical symphony played in the background. The music allowed him to concentrate better. To anyone who didn't know what he was doing, it might have looked as if Keithan were dancing by himself and in a weird and eccentric way. At least nobody could see him since he was alone in his bedroom ... until his father opened the door.

Keithan didn't notice him there until he heard the music stop suddenly.

"Dad— Hey."

Keithan straightened up. His father stood next to the stereo system; it was he who had turned off the music.

"Son, it's midnight," his father said with a tired voice.

"Sorry. I was just practicing for, um ... an evaluation. For tomorrow's flight class."

"No, you weren't." His father sensed the lie right away.

He gave Keithan a don't-even-try-it look, tilting his head and revealing an amused smile. The smile faded when it was replaced by a look of worry, which Keithan understood well. It was that look that clearly showed his father was aware of Keithan's true plans. Since Pegasus Company had arrived at Ramey and announced the date of its air race, Keithan had sensed his father didn't approve the idea of him participating in it. Yet, for some reason, Caleb Quintero hadn't done anything to stop him. He seemed to have simply avoided the topic.

Keithan's dad sighed and said, "Go to bed, Keithan."

Keithan watched him leave the room, guilt burning inside him. He hated keeping his dad worried. But what could Keithan do? His dad knew what all this involved. Just like his late mother, Keithan was a daring air racer.

I won't end up like her, Keithan wanted to tell him, but instead, he turned to the digital photo frame on the desk and stared thoughtfully at his mother's image. *I won't. I promise.*

CHAPTER 27

Saturday, April 24. Just one day before the Pegasus qualifier tournament. Keithan had decided to stay at the Aramises' residential hangar to keep working on the *d'Artagnan* with Fernando since they were still behind schedule. The damaged engine had indeed not been an easy fix as Fernando had predicted, which was why the two of them had stayed up until midnight the night before, rewiring, remounting, riveting, and welding. Still, they hadn't been able to finish. Therefore, Fernando and Keithan had made sure to wake up early and make the most of the time they had left.

By 9 a.m., they were having breakfast along with Marianna. Mrs. Aramis had made them chocolate chip pancakes, which Fernando and Keithan drowned in maple syrup while Marianna spread a small amount of strawberry jam over hers.

"Laika! No!" Mrs. Aramis said sharply. She was bringing a jug of fresh, squeezed orange juice when she caught the golden retriever with both front paws on the table.

Laika barked, upset for failing to get one of the pancakes from Fernando's plate.

The door behind Fernando and Keithan opened, and Mr. Aramis entered.

"Good morning, everyone," the man said.

Everyone glanced at him. "G'morning."

Mr. Aramis looked wide awake but as if he had returned from a long day's work because already his clothes, arms, and face were stained with black grease. He had his welding goggles on his forehead, and as he approached the dining table, he began to take his working gloves off, which made Mrs. Aramis halt him.

"Honey, you're not going to put those on the table, right?" Mrs. Aramis said. It was more a warning than a question.

"Of course not," Mr. Aramis said with a snort. He stuffed the gloves into his back pockets with a mischievous smile, which revealed that he had unintentionally been about to put them on the table. Marianna, Fernando, and Keithan tried to hide their laughter while they continued eating.

"So are you three all set for tomorrow?" said Mr. Aramis, taking a seat at one end of the table.

"Mmm ... almost," Fernando struggled to say with his mouth full. He paused to swallow. "We still need to do more work on the *d'Artagnan*'s middle engine."

"And do one last test flight afterward to make sure everything about her is working properly," Keithan said.

"Good," Mr. Aramis said. He poured himself a glass of orange juice. "You know, I've been meaning to tell you how sorry I am for not having been able to help you. I know you boys have been working hard on making modifications to the *d'Artagnan*. It's just that this secret project for Pegasus has kept me ... isolated in the workshop."

"We understand," said Marianna, not wanting to make him feel guilty.

"Yeah, Dad," said Fernando, though not sounding as convincing as Marianna did.

Their mother gave them a kind smile from the other end of the table.

"What we don't get is why you have to hide it from us," Fernando said. "I mean, we are family—and Keithan ... he's practically part of it too."

"Why can't you tell anyone about it?" Keithan dared to ask.

"I'd like to tell you. Unfortunately, Pegasus made me sign a non-

disclosure contract, which included not to reveal anything to family members. Don't worry, it's just until the day of the race, when it'll be revealed to everyone. Anyway..." Mr. Aramis paused to drink some of his juice. "...today I'm taking a break from all that."

"How come?" his wife asked.

"Well, because I want to help them get the *d'Artagnan* ready for tomorrow."

Fernando's eyes widened. "Really?"

"Of course. I actually have a great idea for making her fly faster. It occurred to me a few days ago, shortly after your mom told me about your plans to be in the qualifier tournament. I just didn't have time to tell you about it because, as I said, I've been caught up with the project for Pegasus."

"What do you have in mind?" Keithan asked.

Mr. Aramis leaned forward. "It's a way to improve the performance of the engines. I know you've been working on the *d'Artagnan*'s engines to improve their performance by up to twenty percent. But what if I told you that I can help you increase their power up to forty?"

Both Fernando and Keithan froze, each one holding his fork right in front of his mouth.

"Forty percent?" Keithan repeated, looking as incredulous as his best friend did.

"Yeah. And without threatening their maximum capabilities," Mr. Aramis reassured them.

Fernando scratched the back of his neck. "Actually, Dad, I don't think we have enough time for that. We already managed to improve them twenty—"

"It's not that complicated," his father insisted. "We can work on one of them at least—the middle engine. It doesn't even require much dismantling. If we work together, we can have it done somewhere around one o'clock, along with anything else you have pending—and get the *d'Artagnan* all ready in good time for Keithan to do a last test flight. What do you say?"

Fernando, Marianna, and Keithan exchanged uncertain looks.

"It's your call, guys," said Marianna, looking from Fernando to Keithan.

"She's already fast … but it would be awesome if she flew faster," Keithan said with a shrug, letting Fernando make the final decision.

Fernando remained thoughtful for a few seconds. He turned to his father again and sighed. "Let's do it, then."

"Great!" Mr. Aramis gulped the rest of his orange juice and pushed his chair back to stand up. "Meet me at the hangar when you're done eating. I'll go get Emmeiseven to give us a hand—"

"NO!"

Everyone winced at Fernando's sudden outburst.

"I'm sorry," he said. "It's just that … I don't want Emmeiseven to help us."

"Why not?" Keithan and Marianna said together.

"I-I don't think it should. I mean, Drostan Luzier brought it to help Dad on the secret project, and Drostan … he's also going to compete."

"Emmeiseven is just a robot, Fernando. It's not like he's going to sabotage our work," Mr. Aramis assured him.

"I know," Fernando said, unconvinced, "but he's—*it's*—not part of the team … or family."

It was no surprise for Keithan and Fernando to find Mr. Aramis already working on the *d'Artagnan* when they got to the hangar. What did surprise them was seeing that he had taken the entire middle engine out after Keithan and Fernando had worked so hard on it. The *d'Artagnan* was raised five feet high with the mechanical arm that came out from the floor, and at its rear stood Mr. Aramis half-hidden inside the big hole where the middle engine should be.

"I thought you said it didn't require much dismantling," Fernando said, nearly aghast as he moved his wheelchair under the *d'Artagnan's* raised fuselage.

"Don't worry. We'll put the engine back in with no problem,"

Mr. Aramis said.

Fernando and Keithan exchanged uncertain looks, but since they didn't have much time left, they decided not to ask any questions and just follow Mr. Aramis's lead. Soon the two got their hands dirty too, which Fernando seemed to enjoy more than Keithan. And a while later, Keithan understood why. It seemed Fernando was glad to spend time with his father again. Both father and son worked a lot better than Fernando and Keithan together, and in such a way that, eventually, they didn't even seem to need Keithan's help.

"All right. Now we have to open the combustion chamber and analyze its low- and high-pressure shafts," Mr. Aramis told Fernando.

"What about improving the fuel burners?" Fernando asked.

"We can take care of that late— Wait a second." Mr. Aramis yanked a small metal box from the rear of the craft. "She's been flying with *this*? I have a much better one somewhere here in the hangar. Here, throw that away, Son."

"Are you sure?"

"Trust me."

Around fifteen minutes later, Keithan felt completely at a loss. Fernando and Mr. Aramis were talking about so many different parts and using so many engineering terms that he had no idea what they were doing to the engine anymore. So without being noticed, he turned away and let Fernando and his father continue to work together. Not having anything else to do in the meantime, he headed to the worktable and turned on the computer. He thought about browsing the internet for a while, checking his e-mails, and perhaps watching some air racing videos. Yet, as the projected holo screen and keyboard appeared in front of him, Keithan remembered the web pages he had saved at the academy's library a few days ago. Keithan had been planning to check out what he had copied there about invisible aircraft when he could finally find some free time. Therefore, he pulled out his personal data card drive from one of his pockets. He was about to plug it in when Marianna snatched it from his hand.

"Hey!"

"What are you doing?" Marianna said suspiciously, holding the small card drive away from Keithan's reach. "Aren't you supposed to be working on the *d'Artagnan* with my dad and Fernando?"

Keithan glanced at Fernando and Mr. Aramis over Marianna's shoulder. "They don't seem to need my help so far, so—"

"So let's get *you* ready," Marianna cut him short. "You need to stay focused on tomorrow's qualifier tournament."

Keithan tried to snatch back his data card drive from Marianna's hand but failed. So he sighed. "Fine. What do you have in mind?"

"Step aside …" She gave him a friendly push to take his place in front of the holo screen. Right away, she started tapping on it and the projected keyboard. "Aha! Here it is …" she said. Using her thumb and middle finger, she enlarged one of the viewports she had opened on the screen. "This here is an illustrated list of the different aerobatics you need to have in mind for tomorrow. Before you check them out, let's review the different sessions in which the tournament is going to be divided."

Marianna opened a few more viewports and organized them on the screen. Meanwhile, Keithan watched her work. He had to admit, he didn't stop being impressed by everything Marianna had done so far to help him get ready. All the research work she had done was so detailed and complete he felt overwhelmed, but also lucky to have her help.

Marianna turned to him. "What's wrong?"

"Nothing." He hadn't realized he had been staring at her.

"Concentrate," she insisted, forcing him to return his gaze to the screen. "Check this out. As you already know, after the inscriptions process, which will be the initial step tomorrow, the participants will move on to the inspection session in which they'll be evaluated along with their aircraft to see if they meet with all the required specifications and regulations for the Pegasus Air Race. You can see here that I already organized the *d'Artagnan*'s specifications according to what Fernando told me. I also prepared a file with your profile for the evaluators. Nevertheless, check it to make sure nothing is missing."

"Got it," Keithan said.

"Now, once all the participating aircraft pass inspection—"

"It's the speed test race," Keithan finished the sentence for her, still staring at the holo screen.

"That's right, which is going to be carried out with all the air racers simultaneously. Then the last session will be the obstacles course. Unlike the speed test race, it'll be individually." Marianna paused. "After that, the racers that qualify for the Pegasus Air Race—which should be a minimum of ten—will come out flying in aligned formation. That's how they will be presented to the public. Do you have any questions?"

"Nope," Keithan said confidently.

The two of them went on to do one last review of the other participants. Once again, Marianna showed Keithan their profiles, pointing out each of their strengths and weaknesses. By 12:40 they were discussing the last one when Fernando called out to them.

"She's ready!" he shouted.

Keithan turned to him all excited and hurried to the *d'Artagnan*. Mr. Aramis lowered the mechanical arm and detached it. Once the aircraft touched the ground, Keithan climbed into the cockpit with his key already in hand.

VRRRRROOOOMMM!

The *d'Artagnan* came to life with such power it reverberated all over the hangar. It even forced Keithan and the Aramises to cover their ears, for the sound was so loud it seemed as if it were coming from a monster.

"Now *that's* power!" Keithan shouted, his voice barely heard over the noise. He could definitely feel the difference in the *d'Artagnan*. She felt stronger and so full of power with her now-improved middle engine. Keithan had no idea how Fernando and his father had done it, but he didn't care. The new powerful sound reassured him the *d'Artagnan* was worthy to fly in the Pegasus Air Race.

"Forty-two percent!" a beaming Fernando exclaimed over the aircraft's roar, his laptube showing him the readouts.

"Of power improvement?" Keithan said in disbelief. "That's awesome!"

"I told you it would work!" Mr. Aramis shouted over the noise. "Go test her, Keithan! See how she flies!"

Keithan gave him a thumbs-up and closed the cockpit canopy. He moved the *d'Artagnan* toward the hangar's main door and waited for Marianna to open it. To his surprise, when he was able to see outside, an interesting scene caught his attention. The airfield was full of activity. Dozens of the Pegasus spherical drones hovered in the sky like metallic bubbles over the main runway. And from either side of the runway, more than a hundred men and women stood gazing skyward while a sleek chrome racing aircraft flew back and forth, doing a series of daredevil aerobatics.

Several spheres in the air were capturing the craft's every move, and it was all being broadcast beyond the main runway, on the gigantic screen on the side of the Pegasus airship. Keithan didn't have to look at the screen to recognize whose aircraft it was; the way it flew was more than enough for him to figure it out.

It was none other than Drostan Luzier in his shiny and famous *Sky Blade*.

CHAPTER 28

I t was only an aerobatics demonstration, yet the tall redheaded man with a short boxed beard who stood in front of a holo screen continued watching the scene carefully in case something unusual or unpredictable happened. He could only see what the holo screen revealed, for he was miles away from Ramey Airport, inside a small round room located at the top of a deteriorated iron structure that long ago had been known as the Mona Island Lighthouse.

The lighthouse—or what was left of it—was not much to look at from the outside. It was a rusted tower much browner than the arid land where it still stood, consisting of a central cylindrical shaft braced laterally with crisscross latticed beams, a few pieces of an outer catwalk without any railings left, and a nonfunctional lantern room. The few who were allowed to enter the structure nowadays, however, were the only ones who knew that it wasn't a nonfunctional lantern room anymore, but an active top-secret watchtower with highly advanced technology inside.

In there, the redheaded man known as Captain John Ravena stood with his arms folded and his green eyes narrowed while he gazed at the aerobatic show broadcast on the screen before him. He didn't pay much attention to the small racing craft that was performing, though. His attention was more on the numerous spherical drones that crowded the airspace over Ramey Airport.

Ravena had been keeping an eye on the drones since the first day he had seen them. At least now he knew they belonged to Pegasus Company. Yet that still hadn't eased his intrigue toward the spheres. He wanted—no, he needed—to know more about them.

Nearby, two men in high-tech black uniforms worked silently while they monitored different viewports of Mona's perimeter. They kept tapping on countless virtual buttons that were projected on the holographic glass panel walls that enclosed the entire room. There was a hiss behind them, and a cylindrical capsule rose from the floor, carrying inside an older man in a familiar uniform of much higher rank.

"Colonel," Ravena said, surprised by the man's presence. Automatically, he and his two companions straightened up and saluted.

"At ease, gentlemen," Lieutenant Colonel Lanzard said. He stepped out of the capsule and waited for it to descend. The shaft where the capsule disappeared closed, and Lanzard turned back to the men. He glanced around him with his hands clasped behind his back and halted right beside Ravena in front of the holo screen. "So, Captain, how does everything look out there at Ramey?"

"Everything seems to be in order at the moment, sir," said Ravena, not taking his eyes off the screen. "Nearly a dozen spherical drones from Pegasus have remained flying over Ramey's airfield and its surrounding airspace, though."

"Is that so?"

Ravena nodded.

"What about air traffic there?" the colonel asked.

"Limited, sir. Arrivals and departures are being granted only to small local aircraft and only on the free-landing area at the northeast of the airport, near the residential hangars. As for the rest of the airport and its surrounding airspace, it seems to be controlled by Pegasus."

Lanzard arched an eyebrow. "So Pegasus now controls ninety-eight percent of Ramey Airport? Clever move," he said as he took a step closer to the holo screen. "We'll have to reinforce our surveillance."

"Sir?" Captain Ravena turned to the colonel. "I don't think that will be necessary. Our intel contact at Ramey informed me that the airport's security is working to the fullest due to the upcoming event."

"True, but no doubt they are being controlled—at least at some level—by Pegasus, who we don't trust," Lanzard said. "What I wonder is how much exactly Pegasus is controlling Ramey's security. That said, we'll remain alert, from Ramey and from over here. Now, Captain, is your team assembled and ready for the infiltration operation there?"

"Yes, sir," Ravena answered, raising his chin. "Half of the team is already at Ramey. I ordered the rest to meet me in half an hour for a briefing before we leave."

"Excellent." Colonel Lanzard said. "Let us hope everything goes as planned."

Keithan returned to land thirty minutes after he had taken off. The test flight was a success. It went much better than he had expected. He spotted his friends waiting for him at the entrance of Hangar H11. Marianna was recording him with her hover camera, standing a few feet in front of Fernando, Mr. and Mrs. Aramis, and Laika. They all moved back as the *d'Artagnan* approached. Keithan kept the craft hovering five feet off the ground, moved past them, and stopped in the middle of the hangar, where he took out the landing pads and settled the craft down.

"Guys, I'll tell you, the *d'Artagnan* is going to *stun* everyone tomorrow!" Keithan shouted while he got out of the cockpit. "She reached 434 knots in less than sixty seconds! If that's not fast for the Pegasus Air Race, I don't know what is."

"Keithan, that's practically five hundred miles per hour!" Fernando exclaimed in disbelief, simultaneously turning to his father. "That's nearly twice her former record!"

Mr. Aramis didn't have to say anything. He simply extended his right hand for Fernando to slap it. Both had a look of satisfaction and pride on their faces. Meanwhile, Marianna continued recording. They were all gathered around the *d'Artagnan* while Keithan continued telling them how the test flight had gone. He even told them how much lighter and more maneuverable the aircraft felt now, thanks to the few external pieces Keithan and Fernando had been able to remove from her.

In the end, Marianna moved the hover camera around to get one final close-up of them and the aircraft. "So, with the last test flight completed," she spoke to the camera, "the *d'Artagnan* team is all set for tomorrow's Pegasus qualifier tournament."

"All set indeed," Keithan confirmed with a confident smile as he and Fernando slapped hands, ready for the great day that awaited them tomorrow.

CHAPTER 29

Finally. The day of the Pegasus qualifier tournament had arrived.

The thought was more than enough for Keithan to get out of bed without any struggle after he heard the alarm. He woke up feeling full of energy, which was unusual for him since he wasn't much of a morning person. Having spent the night at his house was part of the reason despite Fernando's insistent invitation to stay at his house again. It wasn't that Keithan didn't like staying at the Aramises, it was just that he had wanted to make sure he would rest well, and where better than in his bed?

The first thing Keithan did once he got up was look at himself in the mirror to check his new look, which he had worked on last night. It wasn't much; he had simply colored a neon-orange streak at the front of his short jet-black hair. Keithan wasn't sure if his friends would like it, but he didn't care. He thought the streak looked cool, especially since it matched the *d'Artagnan*.

Soon after that, he got dressed while he watched the TV screen projected over his desk.

"Good morning to all our viewers," ASC news reporter Mykeyla Strauss said to the camera. The shorthaired African American woman, who was in her mid-twenties, pressed her earpiece with one hand and held a small data pad in the other as she spoke, "It is seven in the morning, and we are transmitting live from Ramey Airport, at

Aguadilla, Puerto Rico, where there's action, excitement, and anticipation today for the Pegasus Air Race's qualifier tournament."

"Oh yeah," Keithan said while he put on his power-strapped sneakers.

"As you can see behind me, there is already much activity going on here inside the airport in preparation for today's event." The camera focused on the background while the reporter spoke. "There's a beautiful sky with few clouds and sunshine, and it's expected that the day will turn hotter later since there's not much wind. So today promises to be a great day for air racing."

The woman looked down at her data pad before she continued. "Unfortunately, the qualifier tournament won't be open to the public or other media, aside from us at ASC. We have been granted exclusive access to cover the event but only through the innovative and recently revealed flying camera drones from Pegasus Company. Nonetheless, that doesn't seem to have stopped many from coming. People from all over the island—and the world—are already beginning to gather outside to get a glimpse of the action throughout the extended fences that enclose the airport. As for those of you who are watching us from your homes, stay tuned to ASC news as we will continue reporting the latest about this exciting event, and hopefully, provide some footage later on."

Keithan was almost done. He'd just put on a black shirt and hung the *d'Artagnan*'s key over his neck when Fernando called him on his wrist communicator.

"Fernando. What's up?" he said, putting the call on speaker.

"Just wanted to let you know that Mom's planning to pick you up in half an hour."

"No problem. I'll be ready," Keithan replied. "See you in a while."

He pressed the End key and turned off the TV. He grabbed his racing leather jacket, but before leaving, he leaned toward the digital photo frame on his desk. At the moment, it displayed a picture of his mother holding a six-month-old Keithan in front of a green mountain range.

"Well, this is it," he murmured to the picture. After a short moment of thought, he left his room.

Keithan found his father in the kitchen, gazing out the window while he drank his customary coffee. Two mechanical arms attached to the wall kept busy over the stove, preparing French toasts and scrambled eggs with cheese.

"Keithan," said Caleb Quintero, turning to him with a gentle smile. He arched his eyebrows, clearly noticing the new orange streak in his son's hair.

"Hi, Dad," Keithan replied, heading to the refrigerator.

"So the big day is here."

Keithan glanced at his father, forcing a casual look. "Um, yeah," he said.

He could sense his father was having difficulty trying to start a conversation, and Keithan could sense where it was leading to. Most likely to try to convince him not to participate in the tournament.

"Son, I've been meaning to talk to you …"

And so it begins, Keithan thought, mentally preparing himself.

"I didn't tell you about Professor Dantés's call a few days ago. She called to tell me about what happened between the two of you."

Keithan had just served himself a glass of milk and instantly halted it in front of his mouth, not daring to drink or reply yet.

"She said she tried to convince you to not participate in today's tournament but that you refused to do it," his father said. "And, because of that, she asked me to try to talk some sense to you."

Keithan gulped. "Dad, I know you don't want me to—"

"It's all right, Son. I'm not planning to stop you from participating," said his father, taking Keithan by surprise. "I know how important it is to you. As you said before, it's for the Pegasus Air Race, and it's going to be held here in Puerto Rico. And … as hard as this is for me to say," he pointed out, "I have a feeling your mom would have been excited about it. That's why I decided not to tell you about the professor's call until now."

Keithan's face lit up. He hadn't expected this from his father. He couldn't believe it, either. Was his father okay with him participating in the qualifier tournament? Keithan didn't know what to say, but he needed to say something back. He opened his mouth, but before he was able to speak, a horn sounded outside.

Mrs. Aramis had arrived.

"Hold it," Keithan's dad said. "Breakfast first."

As soon as Keithan finished eating, he grabbed his leather jacket again and hurried out the front door. He saw Mrs. Aramis waiting with Laika inside her minivan. He was about to climb into it when he heard his father call out from behind.

"Keithan! Wait!"

Mr. Quintero closed the front door and activated the security lock before hurrying toward Keithan.

"Dad, what are you …?"

"What?" his father said with a shrug. "Just because I don't agree one hundred percent doesn't mean I won't support you."

Keithan shook his head. "Really?"

"Of course," his father said. He rested a warm hand on his son's shoulder. "And I would *not* miss your first qualifier tournament for the world."

Mr. Quintero looked past Keithan and nodded to Mrs. Aramis. "Hello, Lynora."

"Good morning, Caleb." Mrs. Aramis smiled back at him. "You're coming with us?"

"If there's room in there for one more."

Being a resident of the airport allowed Mrs. Aramis to enter the premises with Keithan and his father without any inconvenience or delay. Security check, however, took its time due to the day's event, but once they were given access clearance, everything else went on smoothly.

Now inside the airfield, Keithan gazed out the side window, trying to control his excitement. Everything out there confirmed that today indeed promised to be a great day for air racing, as the reporter Mykeyla Strauss had said on the news. The airfield was full of life but unlike it had ever been seen there before. Racers with their crews, as well as Pegasus officials, and even several of Pegasus's MA-7 robots could be seen moving all around. Digital and printed banners of Pegasus Company hung everywhere. Along the main runway ran an extended and multicolored row of waving teardrop flags with the Pegasus logo. And in the air, numerous spherical drones flew low from one end of the airfield to the other, as if patrolling everything from above.

It was a fascinating view, though it still seemed strange for Keithan to see the spheres flying casually over Ramey airspace when only a few weeks ago everyone had thought they were UFOs. Still, Keithan didn't let this distract him. Today was about the Pegasus qualifier tournament; nothing else mattered.

Upon arriving at the Aramises' hangar, Keithan found Fernando with Marianna and their father outside with the *d'Artagnan*, which was covered with an old, sand-colored drape.

"Hey, guys!" Keithan called, jumping out of the minivan.

"Whoa!" Fernando stopped his wheelchair when he noticed the orange streak on Keithan's hair. "What did you—?"

"It looks awesome!" Marianna cut him short, also surprised.

Keithan beamed at them, stroking his hair back from his forehead. "Are we ready for today?"

"Almost," Mr. Aramis replied with a peculiarly teasing tone.

Keithan approached them with a puzzled look. "What do you mean?" He looked from Mr. Aramis to Fernando and noticed Fernando was hiding something behind his mischievous smile.

"We have a surprise for you," said Fernando, looking eager to tell him. "It was Mom's idea, actually." He turned his wheelchair to his mother. "Now can you tell him?"

"Wait! Not yet …" Marianna said. She adjusted her camera headset and lifted her round video camera, which flew off her hand and came to stop in front of Keithan. "Okay. Now."

"What's going on?" Keithan asked.

Mrs. Aramis explained, "I am sure you, Marianna, and Fernando are ready for the Pegasus qualifier tournament, but a few days ago I figured you were still missing something."

Keithan stared, puzzled. "What could we possibly be missing?"

"Something every air racer and aircraft needs to have," Mr. Aramis said.

Keithan scratched the back of his head, becoming anxious. His dad, standing behind him, looked completely lost.

"You're gonna love this." Mrs. Aramis revealed a small bag she had kept hidden behind her back. She pulled out three black strap bands and handed one to Fernando, another to Keithan, and finally one to Marianna.

"Armbands?" Keithan said, now even more confused.

"Digital armbands," Marianna corrected him while she continued recording his face with her hover camera.

Keithan stared at the armband in his hands. The black piece was made of an elastic fabric and had a small flexible screen shaped like a triangular shield in the middle. He pressed the screen, deeply intrigued. It came to life, displaying the digital number eighteen in shiny orange with a silver layout.

"Wow!" Keithan gasped, instantly realizing the meaning of the number. He looked at his father with wide eyes and showed him the armband. Caleb Quintero gasped too.

"Every racer needs a racing number," Mrs. Aramis remarked with a smile of satisfaction. "In your case, Keithan, we thought you might like to wear that one in particular."

Keithan gazed down, trying to hide his emotions. Staring at the number eighteen, his eyes watered, but he held back a tear from trickling down his right cheek.

"Mom's number," he murmured with pride. He felt his father's hands rest on his shoulders.

"Nobody else could be worthy enough to use that same number, Keithan," his father said.

"Me and the *d'Artagnan* team," Keithan corrected him, looking at Fernando and Marianna.

"And that's not all," said Marianna, turning to her father with her hover camera.

Mr. Aramis nodded and stepped backward to the *d'Artagnan*. "Lynora and Marianna worked all night on this," he told Keithan and his father. With one strong swing, he pulled out the drape covering the aircraft.

Keithan gasped a second time. On the side of the *d'Artagnan*, next to her name, was the same shield with the number eighteen.

"*Now* we're ready for the qualifier tournament," Fernando concluded with a tight-lipped smile.

Inside a small windowless room that was hidden in one of Ramey's private hangars, Captain John Ravena finished suiting up. He had arrived there less than twenty-four hours ago. After he strapped on his high leather-and-rubber black boots, he pulled on his gloves and zipped them. Once he was done, he pressed a small button on his left sleeve and watched a green hologram appear around his entire forearm. It displayed different readouts of his vitals and body temperature. Since everything looked to be in order, he turned off the display and stood up.

Now fully dressed in his brand-new racing gear, mostly black and with red patches on his shoulders, waist, and calves, Ravena faced a full-length mirror to evaluate his new appearance. His red, short boxed red beard was gone, and he had to admit, not having it made him look so much different—and younger. This was part of the plan for his new identity, though watching his reflection he found it a bit hard to convince himself of this transformation.

There was a hiss, and the door behind Ravena opened. Through the mirror, Ravena saw a slender woman with a black pixie haircut enter. She wore a casual short-sleeved shirt and bootcut trousers that matched Ravena's racing suit. The woman stood before the door, a determined look on her face.

"Captain, it's time," she told him.

Ravena nodded in acknowledgment and grabbed the black racing helmet with twin red stripes that rested on the seat next to him. *This is it,* he reminded himself before he turned to face the woman.

"And so our operation begins," he said.

CHAPTER 30

Ramey Airport might have been closed to the general public today, but the people who were allowed inside were more than enough to pack it. The majority gathered on the south side of the airfield. It was there where Pegasus Company had established itself with different stretch marquees to carry out the qualifier tournament. Practically everybody who was anybody in the air racing industry was present aside from all the working officials from the airport, as well as the air racers, their crews, and the different emergency units, both terrestrial and aerial. Keithan, Fernando, and Marianna could tell by the large number of luxurious vehicles that were allowed to enter the airport—their passengers most likely former air racing celebrities and multibillionaire sponsors from all over the world.

It felt awkward at first to get into the line of luxurious vehicles, but it was the only way for Keithan and his company to reach the other side of the main runway. Mr. Aramis, who was at the wheel, drove the scarlet minivan to the west side of the airfield as if heading to Ramey Academy, then turned left, just as the other vehicles were doing. Pegasus officials were directing everyone to the designated parking area, yet when they saw the minivan towing the *d'Artagnan*, they allowed Mr. Aramis to continue straight forward to the area where the racers and their aircraft were gathering for registration.

"There's a good spot," Mrs. Aramis pointed from the front passenger's seat.

"Where?" Mr. Aramis asked.

"Over there. To the left."

Behind them, Keithan, his father, and his friends gazed out at all the different racing aircraft. Each crew included between fifteen and twenty people, all of them wearing brand-new outfits that matched the colors of their respective aircraft and racers.

"Is it necessary to have so many people in a crew?" Marianna asked while looking out the window.

"Not really," Keithan said. He didn't know what the deal of having so many people in a crew was. He and Fernando (and on rare occasions, Mr. Aramis) had dealt with the *d'Artagnan* without any problems, and so far, it had always been more than enough.

The minivan finally came to a stop, and everyone got out. Mr. Aramis and Keithan's father detached the *d'Artagnan* from the trailer. Meanwhile, the rest took in everything around them, letting the stimulating racing atmosphere infect them.

"Keithan, look!" Fernando pointed to a burly, bald man in a yellow racing suit who stood next to a matching one-manned aircraft. "That's Fritz Kelleher, last year's champion of the European Aerial Cup!"

"And look over there," said Keithan, pointing to another racer in a navy-blue racing suit. "That's Matthew McMillan, the ex-navy fighter pilot who broke the record in the national championship two years ago."

Unlike Fernando, Keithan did his best to control his excitement. After all, those other racers were going to be his opponents soon.

So far, there were seventeen racers with their aircraft and crews already settled, from well-known pros to a few rookies who Keithan didn't know much about. Of course, as expected, Keithan was the youngest, and as he kept gazing around, he began to sense he wasn't blending in easily. He could see many people there noticing him but with strange looks, clearly because he wasn't wearing a real racing uniform like the other racers, but mostly because he was just a kid. Keithan was able to hear some of them murmur scornful comments as they passed him by. They also gave the *d'Artagnan* strange looks, but that was expected. While most of the other aircraft there were shiny, sleek, and decorated with all kinds of sponsoring decals, the *d'Artagnan* stood there with her exposed, old, and tarnished parts and her weathered battered epidermis.

Let them be fooled by her appearance, Keithan told himself in his head; he couldn't wait to show everyone what he and the *d'Artagnan* could do once he could take her into the air.

"Keithan? Keithan Quintero, is that you?"

Keithan looked left and right, trying to see who had called him. A sleek young man in a two-piece dark-blue racing suit with orange sleeves came up to him. His brown, faux hawk haircut seemed to have so much gel it glowed like a racing helmet.

"No way. Aaron Oliviera?" said Keithan, recognizing the former student from Ramey Academy. "What are you doing here?"

"What am I doing here? What are *you* doing here?" Aaron said with an honest, pearly-white smile. He didn't expect Keithan to answer. Instead, he reached out and gave Keithan a firm handshake. "I spotted your aircraft from back there with my crew and couldn't believe it. I mean, I would recognize that aircraft anywhere—mostly because of its strong resemblance to the one your mother flew." He turned to Fernando. "And you're ... Aramis, right?"

Fernando moved his wheelchair closer and shook Aaron's hand. "Yes. Fernando Aramis," he said.

Keithan and Fernando remembered Aaron Oliviera. The boy had graduated from Ramey Academy last year. Not only was he one of the most outstanding students that had been in the academy's Air Racing Program, but he was also a cool guy, always friendly and sociable with everybody. Such personality had even earned Aaron the student council presidency during his senior year.

"So what have you been doing?" Keithan asked him.

"Air racing—a lot," Aaron said. "I moved to San Diego after graduation. I have competed in a few races in Reno, L.A., Dallas. I also participated in last year's Daytona Airshow. That was a great experience. And when I heard the Pegasus Air Race was going to be held here in Puerto Rico—and at Ramey—I had to come. I couldn't let the opportunity pass, you know."

"Neither could we," Keithan said with a grin.

"You can say that again. Man! It would've been awesome if I'd been able to participate in the Pegasus qualifier tournament at your age! And of all the students from the academy, were you two the only ones who were allowed to represent it?"

"Oh, we're, um …" Keithan started to say.

"We're not representing the academy," Fernando clarified.

"Oh," Aaron said.

"There *is* one student who'll probably be representing it, we think," Fernando added. "One of the seniors. Gregory Paceley."

"Paceley? Yeah. I remember him," Aaron said.

"Speaking of which, where is he?" Keithan asked.

He looked at all the aircraft gathered out there, expecting to find Gregory's somewhere among them. Surely the young senior should have a small team too, yet there didn't seem to be any other small team out there aside from the *d'Artagnan*. Had Paceley backed out? Keithan wondered.

"Oh, well," he concluded.

Drostan Luzier was the other racer Keithan didn't find among the other competitors, but Keithan knew Drostan wouldn't be participating in the tournament, for as last year's champion, all Drostan had to do was defend his title the day of the race.

Soon the inscriptions process began, and it was completed in less than an hour. Pegasus officials went through each of the racers present, registering them and their aircraft. Following that, they asked all the competitors to gather with their crews to begin.

All of a sudden, loud rock music started playing all over the airfield. The wide screen on the side of the Pegasus airship came to life, displaying the announcement of the upcoming Pegasus Air Race with its date: Saturday, May 1. The image, along with the music, got Keithan and everyone else all pumped up. The crowd, both inside and outside the airport, whooped and cheered. Seconds later, the music faded, and from beneath the airship's screen, a rectangular hatch swung forward, and the Pegasus CEO appeared.

"Good morning, ladies and gentlemen! Welcome to the 2055 Pegasus Air Race qualifier tournament!" Giovanni Colani's voice boomed through the multiple speakers mounted throughout the airport. The crowd went wild. Then he continued. "An exciting day awaits us. Racing pros and novices will test their skills and stamina to find out if they truly have what it takes to be in this year's Pegasus Air Race. We have a diverse group of competitors from different parts of the world. I would like to thank them and their crews in advance, as well as their sponsors, for being part of this extraordinary event.

"To all the air racers, I wish you the best of luck. And now, without further ado..." He stepped closer to the ledge of the platform, holding high a remote control. "...let the tournament begin!"

The music boomed a second before the spectators gasped and craned their necks as nine spherical drones shot up into the sky like bullets from behind the giant airship. They ascended fast and in a perfect diamond formation. At nearly five hundred feet, they arced downward and dove without reducing speed. All of a sudden, black, white, and yellow smoke trails shot out from them. And just when everyone least expected it, the nine spheres broke off in separate directions, leaving an astonishing, bomb-burst smoke design in the sky.

"Whoa!" Keithan exclaimed, completely blown away. He felt the hairs on the back of his neck stand up.

"All right, guys!" Mr. Aramis said. He clapped his hands together to get the attention of Keithan, Fernando, and Marianna. "It's time for you to go to the inspection session." He signaled to Keithan to mount the *d'Artagnan* before he stepped back with Mrs. Aramis and Keithan's father. "We'll be watching you from out here, okay?"

Keithan nodded. He took a deep breath and blew it out to release all tension in his body. He opened the *d'Artagnan*'s cockpit canopy and climbed in. The aircraft turned on smoothly with its roar. He could see the other racers mounting theirs and igniting the engines.

"Marianna and I will meet you at the inspection area," Fernando told Keithan, his voice competing with the sound of the engines.

"Got it," Keithan replied, nodding.

"Come back in one piece, Keithan!" Mrs. Aramis shouted to him from a distance.

"That's right. Be daring but be safe too," Mr. Aramis added.

"Come on, you guys, don't put more pressure on him," Caleb Quintero said. He hurried to the side of the *d'Artagnan* before Keithan would enclose himself in the cockpit and said, "Good luck, Son. And, um, whether you qualify or not, know that I'm already proud of you, as much as your mother would have been."

Keithan blushed at the unexpected words. He couldn't see himself, of course, but he could feel his heated cheeks. "Thanks, Dad," he said, beaming at him.

He waited for his father to step back. He was about to close the canopy when Marianna rushed to the *d'Artagnan*. She reached out to the cockpit with both hands and pulled herself up.

"You're gonna do great," she told him as she leaned closer to Keithan with an effort. And taking him completely off guard, she planted a kiss on his cheek.

Whether it was just for luck, Keithan didn't know. He had no time to react. He just stood there, speechless and stunned as Marianna stepped away. Not too far away, Keithan noticed Fernando in his wheelchair, also with a stunned look on his face. Keithan was careful not to make any gesture. He cleared his throat, closed the canopy, and put his helmet on.

He raised the aircraft, gradually increasing the antigravity plates' power, and retracted the landing gear. He'd just turned on his headset, and the first thing he heard was Fernando's voice complaining to Marianna, *"Why did you have to kiss him? Now he's not going to focus as he should."*

——(-o-)——

To be in the inspection area was like being inside a department store during a Black Friday. At least that was Keithan's first impression when he got there. It was the busiest area under the tallest of the stretch marquees. So many people were there trying to do so many different things at the same time, from Pegasus officials moving all around in a hurry to racers and crewmembers either demanding attention or trying to get somebody to explain to them what they were supposed to do. The glossy MA robots were the only ones there that weren't under any stress. They worked nonstop around a series of big mechanical arms and two scanning platforms where two racing craft were placed for inspection.

Keithan had just dismounted the *d'Artagnan* and left it with a group of Pegasus officials who would soon move it to one of the platforms. Fernando and Marianna waited for him not too far ahead. Neither of the two was denied access since no more than two crewmembers—preferably a chief aeroengineer and an assistant—were allowed to be there with each racer.

"The *d'Artagnan* is the sixth in line," Keithan said when he reached his friends. "Now all we have to do is wait to be called."

"Good," Fernando said. "Marianna and I just handed in the profile data to the judges."

They noticed a young man with a black-and-white Pegasus shirt and silver shades climb onto a small stage located between the two scanning platforms.

"All right, ladies and gentlemen!" the man said animatedly, his amplified voice heard through all the speakers. "The first two racing aircraft to be inspected are set on the scanning platforms. On the left one, we have the *Lightning Dragon*, belonging to the Australian air racer, Tony LeVier!"

He gestured for the fifty-two-year-old racer in dark-green racing suit to join him on the stage while the audience applauded.

"And on the right," the announcer continued, "we have the *Fiore Veloce*, belonging to the Italian air racer, Rosangela Sofio!"

Another round of applause followed as Rosangela Sofio, whose racing suit matched the green, white, and red of the Italian flag, stepped onto the stage. Like LeVier, she looked confident and comfortable up there, which showed she wasn't new to this type of protocolary presentation. It was the opposite of Keithan, who had chills just thinking that he would have to get up there when his turn came.

The two pilots' aircraft displayed at either side started to rotate over their platforms. At the announcer's signal, the big mechanical arms above them descended and moved around both aircraft, scanning them from top to bottom. Seconds later, a 3-D image of the green-and-black *Lightning Dragon* appeared on the wide screens for everyone to see. On the left side, it displayed its length, wingspan, and main features, while on the right side, it showed a picture of Tony LeVier, along with his racing profile.

"Wow! Twenty-seven first places! Two of them in the Pegasus Air Races!" Fernando exclaimed in disbelief while watching LeVier's profile.

"That's throughout his whole career," Keithan clarified, also gazing at the screen, impressed.

"Don't forget he's been racing for nearly thirty years," Marianna pointed out to make sure Fernando and Keithan weren't intimidated.

As soon as the mechanical arms completed their scanning, the announcer addressed the audience again. "Well, so far it seems the *Lightning Dragon* meets all the requirements and regulations. Still, let's see what the judges have to say." He gazed at a table not too far from the stage. There, a group of Pegasus officials corroborated all the information presented. Seconds later, the announcer nodded and turned to the audience again.

"And it passes inspection," he exclaimed, "which means the *Lightning Dragon* team moves on to the next session of the tournament!"

A round of applause followed as LeVier raised his fists in celebration.

Rosangela Sofio's turn came next. The applause died down again, and the image on the wide screens changed as soon as the mechanical arms on top of her *Fiore Veloce* began to do their work. The 3-D diagram of her aircraft appeared, accompanied by her photo and profile. Sofio's racing background was also impressive. Though not as long as LeVier's, it showed proof that Sofio was a worthy competitor with thirteen first places and numerous participations in a variety of aerobatics air shows and competitions throughout Europe.

"Looks like the judges are ready to reveal their answer, and..." The announcer held his breath, intentionally keeping the suspense in the audience. "...they approve! The *Fiore Veloce* team also moves on to the next session!"

Right after that, the two air racers stepped down the stage. The MA robots at the back took the two aircraft out of the scanning platforms and brought up the next two. Aaron Oliviera and Leeson Lancaster, aka "the Vampire," were called to the stage.

The same procedure followed. The Vampire's craft, the *Bat Fury*, had the first turn. As expected, it passed inspection without any problem. Yet its owner, whose pale skin looked as if it had never been touched by sunlight, remained with a cold stare while everybody applauded and cheered for him. It was kind of funny and weird at the same time to see that the guy didn't even seem the least bit amused by all this. With his gothic look, which included long dyed black hair, black lips, and black eyeliner—all of which matched his fully black leather racing suit—he just stared blankly forward and nodded slightly.

Aaron Oliviera, on the other hand, was the total opposite. Fully charismatic, he raised a tight fist into the air and shouted with excitement at the judges' approval of his aircraft and racing profile. Keithan, Fernando, and Marianna rooted for him.

By now, Keithan felt his nerves beginning to rise. His breathing also turned heavy and faster. He was even moistening his lips repeatedly without noticing it until Marianna turned to him with a worried look.

"Are you okay?" she asked.

"Yeah," said Keithan, trying to sound casual.

"You're sure?"

Keithan nodded. The two of them focused their attention on the front again when the people around them burst out with loud laughter.

It took them a moment to understand what was happening until they saw the *d'Artagnan* being brought onto one of the platforms.

"What is *that* thing?" someone in the crowd shouted.

"What a piece of junk!" another cried, making the rest of the people there laugh harder.

"It's a joke! Whose aircraft is that?"

Fernando and Marianna couldn't help but show their irritation by poking their tongues into their cheeks. As for Keithan, he tightened his jaw and nodded in resignation.

"Let's just wait until I show them what she's made of," Keithan reassured his friends.

The announcer on the stage was also taken by surprise when he saw the *d'Artagnan*. His expression was more of incredulity, as if he were wondering how such a rough-looking aircraft could have even been allowed to be brought up onto the platforms. He had already called the fifth air racer to join him on the stage: Daiki Tamura, the twenty-five-year-old Japanese rookie. As soon as Tamura appeared, the man went on with the presentation.

"And on the right," the announcer said aloud, shaking off his laughter, "We have the *d'Artagnan*, belonging to Keith—"

A man who had sneaked onto the stage interrupted him. He held the announcer's arm and whispered something into his left ear.

"He's what?" the announcer whispered; it was heard through the speakers.

Not far from the stage, Keithan and his friends stared at the announcer in wonder. They could see the man's expression now showing confusion. Something was wrong, but what? The audience, too, stared in wonder, waiting.

The announcer hesitated and was forced to look back at the audience. "Um … K-Keithan Quintero," he said finally, though now he lacked the enthusiasm he had had a few seconds ago.

Keithan glanced at his friends with a puzzled look. Fernando shrugged and gestured for him to go onto the stage. Keithan hesitated.

"Just go up there," Marianna insisted, and so Keithan made his way through the crowd and climbed onto the stage.

The audience's reaction was completely different from when the previous racers had been called. There was some applause, but confusion hung in the air. They just couldn't believe a thirteen-year-old boy had just been presented as one of the competing air racers.

"Are you Keithan?" the announcer asked, muting his microphone and leaning closer.

"I am," Keithan replied, not letting the awkwardness of the moment get the best of him.

"Come with me."

The announcer left the stage, leaving the audience intrigued. As Keithan descended, he gestured for Fernando and Marianna to follow as well. The announcer led him to the judges' table and stepped aside.

Three judges, all wearing black Pegasus shirts, sat on the other side. They stared at Keithan with unreadable faces. The most intimidating of the three was the redheaded woman in the middle. Her blue eye shadow and lipstick was too garish for the occasion and made her look like a life-sized doll rather than an actual person. Her companions were two men, one short with greasy blond hair, the other brawny with a brown, bushy mustache.

"I presume you're Keithan Quintero. Air racer number eighteen?" the redheaded woman said.

"I am," Keithan said, still clueless about what was happening.

"And is that your crew?"

Keithan glanced over his shoulder and found Fernando and Marianna behind him.

"Yes."

The woman glanced at each of her companions before she returned her gaze to Keithan. Leaning closer to him, her fingers laced together in front of her, she said, "I'm afraid we can't let you participate."

CHAPTER 31

This is a joke. This must be a joke!

It was the only thing that ran through Keithan's mind at the moment. Nothing else registered, not even what was happening around him. Keithan hadn't realized it, but he was staring blankly at the three judges seated in front of him at the other side of the table. The moment seemed eternal, as if everything around Keithan had frozen, except for the time. It wasn't until Marianna gave him a nudge on his left arm that he came back to his senses.

"What do you mean I can't participate?" he asked the female judge, doing his best to remain calm. "Is there something wrong with the *d'Artagnan*? She should meet all of the requirements."

"There can't be anything wrong with her," Fernando interjected, moving his wheelchair closer to the judges' table. "We checked all the required specifications and regulations for the race; she *does* meet all of them."

The redheaded judge turned from Keithan to Fernando with an awkward frown. "Excuse me, but who exactly are you?"

"I'm the team's chief aeroengineer," Fernando shot back with a challenging tone.

"*You're* the chief aeroengineer?" said the short man at the woman's left.

Fernando hissed, irritated. He took out his aeroengineer student license and held it in front of the three judges. Keithan remained silent with his arms folded over his chest, waiting to see if any of the judges would dare to throw a counterargument now.

"Well," said the short man, getting back to the matter at hand, "your aircraft exceeds our expectations to qualify even though its appearance gives the wrong impression."

"And most of its parts are old and rusted," the other man added scornfully, more to his companions than to Keithan and his friends.

"The problem, however, isn't the aircraft," the female judge interjected, taking control of the conversation again. "It's you, Mr. Quintero."

Keithan's eyes widened. He hadn't expected this. "*Me?* What do you mean 'me'?" he exclaimed, starting to lose his composure. Just then, he felt a pair of heavy hands fall on his shoulders.

"What's going on here?"

It was Mr. Aramis. Somehow, he had managed to sneak his way into the inspection area.

"Who are you?" the female judge asked.

Mr. Aramis hesitated. "I, um … I'm part of the crew."

"Is that so?" said the woman, looking skeptical. "Well, sir, I have just informed young Mr. Quintero and his friends that he cannot participate in the qualifier tournament."

"What? No disrespect, ma'am, but did you check his profile?" Mr. Aramis said. "I can assure you, Keithan here is an excellent air racer. Not just a jet-qualified pilot student, but also a member of the Air Racing Program at Ramey Academy."

"I'm the only one in my level who can hold five g-forces while flying," Keithan added proudly.

"And more than that," Marianna said, raising her voice, "he's the son of Adalina Zambrana."

At this, the three judges froze simultaneously. Even the announcer, who had been standing nearby all this time, listening to everything, gaped at Marianna's remark.

"Adalina Zambrana," the announcer said in disbelief, removing his shades. "The three-consecutive times and undefeated champion?"

"The very same one," Marianna reassured him, hands on her hips.

The judges seemed impressed by this fact. Keithan noticed they were not seeing him now as a mere youngster. Was being the son of the most famous champion in the Pegasus Air Races all Keithan needed to be allowed to participate?

"I'm sorry, but that doesn't change anything," the female judge said firmly. "Mr. Quintero still can't participate."

Keithan, who for a moment had gotten his hopes up, was right back where the argument had started. He took a deep breath but let it out slowly through his now-flared nostrils, keeping his lips sucked in, along with his irritation.

"May I ask why I can't?" he managed to say in a controlled tone.

The woman was straightforward. "You're only thirteen."

Keithan had no counterargument.

"Hold on," Fernando interposed. "There's no age limit for the Pegasus Air Race. That's one of the things that make this race unique. The only specifications stated in the rules for an air racer to be considered to participate are that he or she must be a qualified jet pilot, have an aerobatics certification, and a qualified aircraft."

"And Keithan meets each," Marianna added.

"People, please. We need to continue with the inspections," the announcer interrupted. He looked anxiously at all the people around them waiting, yet neither the judges nor Keithan and his friends seemed to pay any attention to him.

"It generally takes until the age of seventeen or eighteen for a student air racer to accomplish all those requirements in any ordinary flight academy," explained the judge with the bushy mustache. His droopy eyelids now showed signs that he was growing tired of this. "And you guys are saying Mr. Quintero has already accomplished them, being only thirteen?"

"Yeah, well, Ramey Academy isn't like any other flight academy, sir," Keithan clarified. "It begins to prepare elite students like me from the age of nine. Even Captain Colani knows that."

Despite his explanation, it seemed the arguing wasn't going

anywhere. Still, Keithan, Fernando, and Marianna weren't satisfied, which was why they weren't willing to let it go. They didn't care how much longer they stalled the inspections.

The two male judges leaned back in their chairs, unwilling to say more. It seemed to force the redheaded woman between them to take the reins and try to put an end to this once and for all.

"We understand your point," she told Keithan and his friends. "Unfortunately, the age factor is what prevails in this matter."

"How come?" Keithan asked.

"Because according to the Thirteenth Law established by the International Aviation Administration, any air racer under eighteen can participate in a competition, whether local or international, *but* depending on the rules of the flight academy from which he or she comes from. And in your case, Mr. Quintero, Ramey Academy has established that its students will be allowed to participate *only* if they are formally and fully represented by a licensed flight instructor, which you seem to lack."

That was the bombshell, to which Keithan couldn't answer back. He felt the weight of everyone's gazes, as if they were all waiting for him to reply. Still, Keithan remained stunned, once again staring blankly at the judges, his jaw slightly dropped.

"You do know who we would have to bring here, right?" Fernando told him in a dreadful tone.

Keithan gulped. He boiled inside with frustration. It made him want to burst out shouting, but just as he was about to, he compressed the strong feeling by tightening his fists and simply walked away.

"Keithan," Mr. Aramis called after him, but Keithan kept walking with a quick and heavy pace.

"Keithan. Wait," Marianna also called out. She hurried after him, making her way through the crowd. "*Keithan!*"

"There's no point in staying. Let's just go," Keithan shot at her without bothering to glance back or stop. He had just gotten out of the crowded marquee and stepped under the intense sun. "There's no way we're going to convince her to come and help us."

"Who? Who do we need to bring here?" Marianna asked.

"*Dantés!*" Keithan blared. He spun around so suddenly Marianna almost bumped into him. The look of shock on her face, however, made him think twice about his reaction. It wasn't Marianna's fault; he hadn't meant to take it out on her. Therefore, he took a moment to calm down.

"Dantés is my designated flight instructor at the academy," he said, seething. "And trust me, she would never approve representing me in this tournament. For crying out loud, she was the one who tried to tug me out—!" He was unable to finish the sentence. He was so full of shame and anger that he looked away.

At a distance, inside the inspection area, things sounded as if they were getting back into motion. Yet all that excitement Keithan had been sharing with everyone else there had drained from him.

Marianna glanced back over her shoulder, toward the area where the inspections continued, and returned her gaze to Keithan.

"Isn't there any way we could, you know, convince Dantés to …"

"There's nothing we can do about it, Marianna," Keithan exhaled. "It's … it's over."

And with that, he turned around and kept on walking.

It was so humiliating Keithan didn't even have the courage to go back to the area where his father and Mrs. Aramis waited. He didn't want to be with anybody at the moment. He just needed to get out of there, away from the qualifier tournament and out of the airport. He still couldn't believe what had just happened. After everything he had done, all the intense training and studying for this day, it had all been in vain. And just because of one stupid rule he didn't even know existed. Keithan was only thirteen, but he didn't need Professor Dantés to represent him when he had everything he needed to be in the Pegasus Air Race. Despite what Dantés, the judges, or anybody else thought about him, Keithan was certain he was prepared to qualify.

Keithan marched out of the airfield and not once did he look back. He didn't even slow his pace. He just kept on walking, not caring where he went. Submerged in his thoughts, he continued through the shiny green grassy area of Ramey's golf course and the dried terracotta terrain beyond it. He ended up at *Las Ruinas*, where he finally sat down. Keithan ignored his wrist communicator despite the insistent incoming calls from Fernando, Marianna, and his father. When he got tired of it, he simply sent each of them the same text message to let them know he was okay but without mentioning where he was.

Keithan now sat on top of one of the ruins' exposed foundations closest to the ledge of the coastal cliff. From there, he could still hear the roars and whirring of the flying air racers participating in the tournament. Keithan wanted so much to stop hearing them that he tried to focus on the sound of the waves that broke on the sand at the bottom of the precipice. At a distance, far in the open sea, he spotted a few people surfing, and while Keithan stared at them, he slowly let his mind clear, trying to relax.

Minutes later, he decided to go down to the beach. He had to take a narrow, steep path through rocks and sea grape shrubs to get there. He took off his power-strapped sneakers once he reached the bottom and continued meandering at the shore, letting the water reach him up to his ankles. Down there, Keithan felt much better. The beach wasn't too big. Secluded by rock formations, it almost looked as if humans had never visited it before.

Keithan took in everything the place had to offer: the fresh wind brushing his hair, the salty smell of the sea, the squishy feeling in his feet as they sank slightly in the wet sand. All in all, the setting presented Keithan with what he needed most now: a completely different environment. An environment so natural, isolated from all technology, and in which the sea seemed to predominate just as much as the sky, unlike when he flew.

It wasn't until the sun started to set that Keithan realized he should leave. He didn't go home, though. Instead, he headed back to the airport to visit Fernando and Marianna. The street lampposts were already lit by the time he got there, and seeing the Aramises' hangar closed, Keithan went around it and headed to the rear. This was actually the residential part of the hangar, which connected with the back of the armadillo's carapace shape that could be seen from the main runway.

Standing before the front door, Keithan pressed the doorbell. Marianna opened the door.

"Keithan."

"Hi," Keithan replied with a tired voice.

"Are you all right?"

"Yes. It-it's just been a long day for me."

He rubbed the back of his neck and did his best to keep eye contact with her. He opened his mouth to speak again but hesitated. "Listen, I'm … sorry for snapping at you this afternoon. I-I was just so upset—"

"It's okay," Marianna cut him off, seeing him struggling with his words. "I totally understand."

She gave him a warm smile, and for a moment they held each other's gaze without saying another word … until they both noticed the awkwardness of the moment.

"Um, would you like to come inside?" Marianna said, shaking her head and stepping aside.

Red-faced, Keithan nodded and entered.

"You know, what happened today was disappointing for all of us," Marianna said as she closed the door behind her. "I'm sure you'll get your chance to be in the Pegasus Air Race someday."

"I know, though it won't be here in Puerto Rico," said Keithan, disheartened.

Marianna led Keithan to the dining room where her family was gathered having dinner. Laika was with them. She was the first one to notice Keithan, and she would have run to him and raised herself to put her front paws on his shoulders, only she was much more interested in the delicious-smelling pot roast and baked potatoes that were served on the table.

"Look who finally showed up," said Marianna, getting everyone's attention.

"Keithan!" Mrs. Aramis said with a smile. "Sweetie, where were you all day?"

"At *Las Ruinas.*"

"*Las Ruinas?*" Fernando repeated, surprised. "You walked all the way there?"

"Yeah, well, all that walking helped me clear my head from today's events."

Mrs. Aramis brought Keithan a plate. "Surely you must be hungry, dear. Here."

Keithan didn't argue. He was starving.

Soon after they finished eating, Keithan, Marianna, Fernando, and Laika went outside to get some fresh air. They settled at the terrace on top of Mr. Aramis's dome-shaped office, which overlooked a great part of the airfield. Keithan leaned over the railing and gazed far at the other side of the main runway. Several lighted marquees could be seen with air racers and their crew teams celebrating. The giant Pegasus airship hovered silently behind them, illuminated only at the bottom by a series of spotlights on the ground.

"So how did the tournament go?" Keithan asked, more curious than enthused.

"It went well," Marianna said casually as she opened a bag of baked potato chips. "Fifteen out of twenty air racers qualified. Tony LeVier was one of them, of course, as well as Matthew McMillan, Rosangela Sofio, and the Vampire."

"Aaron Oliviera qualified too," Fernando remarked.

Keithan raised his eyebrows. "Really? Great for him."

"He delivered an impressive performance in the obstacle course even though he didn't do too well in the speed test race. Oh, and there was this new guy, John Ravena, who also did an impressive performance."

"John Ravena?" said Keithan, not recognizing the air racer's name. "I've never heard of him."

"We hadn't, either," Marianna said. "According to his profile, he has a short history of air races in Nebraska. Anyway, he and the rest of the air racers who qualified flew over the main runway in line formation at the end of the tournament so they could be presented to the spectators."

"Huh," Keithan sighed thoughtfully.

Looking back at the celebration going on at the other side of the runway, he wondered how much fun he could have had tonight if he, too, had participated and qualified.

"Man, those judges from Pegasus," he said, letting his frustration come out. "They should've let me participate. I swear, if they had let me, we would have been out there celebrating too."

"I know. It stinks," Fernando said. "Even after we worked so hard on the *d'Artagnan*."

"Tell me about it. And even after I raced against Dantés," Keithan said.

"Come on, guys. You shouldn't keep taking it so hard on yourselves," Marianna interjected. "It's like what Mom said. You're still young; you'll get plenty of other opportunities in the future." She paused. "If it cheers you up, Keithan, Dad said the three of us can help him with his secret project the day of the race."

"He's going to let us in on it?" Keithan asked.

"Only on the day of the race," Fernando clarified. "Dad told us only then can he tell us everything about the Daedalus Project. That's what he calls it, by the way."

It wasn't much, but at least it was something else to look forward to the day of the race. Who knew? Perhaps helping Fernando and Marianna's dad in the unveiling of the so-called Daedalus Project could lead to something interesting, like getting the chance to meet the owner of Pegasus Company in person.

Keithan's wrist communicator buzzed.

"Hey, Dad," Keithan spoke into the device.

"Keithan, where have you been all day?"

"Just clearing my head. Don't worry, I'm at Fernando and Marianna's house right now. I was about to head back home."

"Would you like me to pick you up?"

"Nah, it's okay. I'll just leave right now."

Keithan pressed the End button on the tiny screen and turned to his friends. "I better go."

"Would you like Mom or Dad to take you?" Fernando suggested. "I'm sure they won't mind, considering that it's nearly nine o'clock."

"Don't worry. I'll be fi—" Keithan never got to finish the sentence. He froze when, all of a sudden, in the middle of the main runway, a blurry and almost completely transparent object dropped out of the sky and made an incredible ninety-degree pull up—right before it could have impacted the runway. It happened in a split second, and just like that, the flying object shot out of sight, straight toward one of the private hangars to the right.

Keithan's hands flew to his ears, expecting to hear a thunderous crash, but to his shock, there was no sound whatsoever. He gazed at Fernando and Marianna over his shoulder to see if they, too, had seen it, but he didn't have to ask. Their gaping mouths confirmed they had. Fernando remained petrified, and so did Marianna, who dropped the bag of chips she had been eating. Even Laika saw it, and she immediately raised her front paws on the railing and barked toward the runway.

Keithan's mind instantly raced back to that Saturday afternoon a few weeks ago when he encountered something similar to what he just witnessed.

"What ... was that?" Marianna said with a trembling voice after a moment of silence. "That couldn't have possibly been an aircraft."

"Oh, yes, it was," Keithan replied, his eyes now wide as he realized what he had actually seen. "And I'm going to check it out."

He didn't waste time to give an explanation to Marianna and Fernando. He simply hurried down the terrace's outer staircase and took off fast, straight to the airfield.

CHAPTER 32

His father would be upset about having to wait for him longer than expected, but Keithan couldn't leave the airport now. Not yet. He needed to find out what exactly he, Fernando, and Marianna had seen appear and instantly shoot out of sight over the main runway. Otherwise Keithan would certainly have a hard time trying to get some sleep tonight.

He ran past the residential hangars, looking all around for any sign that could lead him to the mysterious object, but so far, he couldn't find anything. Apparently nobody else had seen what had happened. Aside from the crowd still celebrating inside the marquees at a distance, there wasn't anyone else out there at the airfield. The buildings nearby weren't even lit. The only visible illumination came from the small blue lights aligned throughout either side of the main runway and the moonlight, which, along with the cold air and the silence all around, created a gloomy atmosphere.

Suddenly, the sound of running feet behind Keithan made him stop and turn. Marianna was approaching.

"What are you—?"

"You think you're the only one who can go after it?" she told him. "I wanna check it out too."

Marianna had stopped running but didn't halt. She moved past Keithan, now taking the lead.

"Hey—wait up!" Keithan called, catching up with her.

Marianna had come prepared. She had brought her round hover camera and headset controller, which she had already turned on.

The two of them were now passing through a group of small private aircraft that were parked to their right when Keithan's wrist communicator startled them.

"It's Fernando!" Keithan hissed and took the call.

"Guys, you're gonna get in trouble," Fernando stressed. *"You're not supposed to wander on the airfield at this hour. There are security cameras—"*

"Shhh," Marianna interrupted, leaning closer to Keithan's wrist communicator. "Fernando, take out your laptube."

"What?"

"Take out your laptube," she insisted. "I'm going to transmit to you what I see through my camera."

She didn't wait for a response from Fernando. She lowered her headset's tiny screen lens over her left eye and adjusted the camera's settings.

Neither she nor Keithan stopped walking. Meanwhile, Keithan kept Fernando's call active on his communicator. Soon they left the group of small aircraft behind and reached three twin-fuselage airliners that were aligned in front of two hangars. Keithan and Marianna moved carefully underneath them, making sure that nobody from airport security was nearby.

"That thing must have headed straight toward one of those hangars ahead," Keithan said while he scanned the area.

"I don't think so," Fernando countered through the wrist communicator. *"That thing flew too fast to have been able to stop in one of the hangars. It should have crashed at the speed it shot out of sight. Most likely, it flew away over them— it makes more sense."*

It did make more sense, but Keithan didn't want to jump to any conclusions until he found out more. Marianna was probably thinking the same thing because she hadn't slowed her pace.

As they came out from underneath the third and last of the airliners, Keithan and Marianna noticed an area ahead on the ground illuminated by a bright white light. The light was coming from an open hangar. The two of them exchanged intrigued looks and continued moving but slower.

"Don't make a sound," Keithan told Marianna and raised his communicator. "Fernando, don't say a word. Stand by."

He took the lead again and headed to a tall stack of fiberglass crates nearby. He crouched and gestured for Marianna to do the same. They could now see where the light was coming from. Just as they expected, it came from the open entrance of one of the hangars.

The arched building, with no identification on it, was located approximately forty feet from where Keithan and Marianna were hiding. Inside it and near its entrance, Keithan could see some activity; about a dozen figures in dark suits were moving around busily. He could also hear a humming much similar to that of a jet engine coming out from there, but Keithan noticed something strange; there wasn't a single aircraft in the hangar.

"Do you hear that?" Keithan whispered.

Marianna grimaced. "It sounds like a power generator."

"No. That's a jet engine," said Keithan, convinced. "I would recognize that sound anywhere. But I don't get it. There's no aircraft there."

He stared at the hangar entrance through a crevice between two of the big fiberglass crates. Next to him, Marianna leaned closer to the edge of a crate and let go of her camera, which took off from her hand and remained hovering.

"Let's see if we can get a closer look," Marianna whispered. She returned to Keithan's side and cautiously moved her camera with her headset controller. The camera hovered slowly toward the front of the crates and faced the hangar.

"Careful. They might see it," Keithan whispered.

"They won't," Marianna assured him. "Fernando, are you still there?"

"Yes," said her brother's voice through Keithan's communicator. *"I can see what the camera is transmitting, but it doesn't look like much. Just some people moving around in an empty hangar."*

As he said this, Keithan and Marianna froze when the unthinkable happened. Right in the middle of the hangar, what looked to be a flying craft—a super-advanced craft—materialized out of thin air, hovering about six feet off the ground. It was just like in a magic act; one moment there had been nothing, then the next, the craft was there.

"Oh my …" Marianna started to say, but her words trailed off.

Next to her, Keithan stood openmouthed. He couldn't take his eyes away from the craft inside the hangar. The thing looked as if it had come straight out of a science-fiction book or movie. Most of it was made of a strange material, bluish and transparent, yet solid. Its fuselage was an elongated and sleek ellipse, and it was missing a cockpit, like a drone. Curiously, its vertical wings, as well as what appeared to be its front and rear stabilizers, were amorphous and made of a sort of semitranslucent metal. And at its rear, the craft had a small exhaust nozzle that still glowed blue and white.

"Now do you guys believe in invisible aircraft?" Keithan murmured.

"Definitely," Marianna replied, still gazing at the craft in amazement. "But where did that thing come from? And who are those people with it?"

Keithan drew his attention to the figures inside the hangar. Their dark suits were hard to make out from that distance. They were unisuits, but something told him they were more than that.

"They certainly don't look like airport employees," Marianna whispered. She zoomed in on the image on her small eye screen. "What do you think, Fernando?"

"I agree," Fernando said. *"Airport security wears royal-blue uniforms, and regular employees, neon yellow. The ones those people out there have, not only are black, but they also seem to be made of carbon fiber instead of the common fire-resistant fabrics. Those look more like military."*

"Well, they don't look like Air Force or Navy," Marianna muttered.

"That's because they're neither," Keithan whispered, his expression changing from deep wonder to astonishment at the new realization.

He saw all the pieces fall into place like a pile of digital files that had just been uploaded into his brain. The mysterious aircraft, the figures with the unusual dark uniforms, the UFO sightings rumored all over Ramey … they only meant one thing to Keithan …

"That's the Sky Phantom Legion."

Marianna turned to him with a frown. "The Sky what?"

"The Sky Phantom Legion. Remember, Fernando, the out-of-print book I asked your dad about?"

"Um, yeah?" said Fernando, sounding unclear about where Keithan was going with this.

"That book talked about a private, secret air force with highly advanced aircraft unlike any other ever seen, which were believed to have come from outer sp—"

"Keithan," Fernando cut him short, *"you're talking about a science-fiction novel.* Fiction, *as in not real."*

"Not all science fiction is just science fiction," Keithan insisted, remembering what Mr. Aramis used to say. "That hangar out there and those people with that aircraft have to be—"

But Keithan didn't get to finish the thought, for at that moment, a white spotlight fell on him and Marianna. It happened so suddenly they froze, holding their breath for an instant.

"Oh no!" Keithan gasped. He looked up but was blinded by the intense light that surrounded him.

"Guys! What's going on?" a confused Fernando said through the communicator's integrated speaker. *"Say something!"*

Keithan didn't reply. He pressed the End key on the wrist communicator and turned to Marianna with a look of horror on his face.

"We gotta go. Right now!" was all he told her. In unison, the two rose.

"Wait!" Marianna shouted.

She disappeared behind the stack of fiberglass crates and came back with her hover camera in hand. As she reappeared, Keithan also saw several figures from the hangar coming in their direction along with several vehicles.

Keithan reached out and grabbed Marianna's free hand. Together they broke into a panicked run. Not once did they dare to look back. They could hear the vehicles accelerating while the spotlight remained over the two of them with the deep humming of the hovering craft from which it was generated.

Running with all their might, they passed once again underneath the twin-fuselage airliners. They were about to get out from underneath the last one, but one of the chasing vehicles passed them and drifted. It forced Keithan and Marianna to change direction. It was a dumb move on their part, though, since they were trying to get to Marianna's house, but the two were now heading straight to the main runway.

Keithan felt a strong pull when Marianna stopped abruptly. He looked over his shoulder and saw that she had dropped her camera headset.

"Are you crazy? Leave it!" he urged.

"No—wait!"

"No! Keep running!"

He pulled her hard and forced her to continue forward. They didn't get far, for they weren't even close to the area of the residential hangars when two other vehicles blocked them. The vehicles, with single spherical tires on either end, were as black as the night itself and didn't seem to be identifiable. Their doors swung upward, and six armed figures wearing black high-tech suits, unlike any other Keithan had ever seen, got out and formed a circle around him and Marianna.

"Wait! We're not armed! We're just teenagers!" Keithan cried, fatigued. He instantly raised his hands to the sides.

The figures didn't say a word. They just stood in attack position, one leg bent forward with their weapons raised, which Keithan noticed were attached to their forearms like gauntlets. One of them came up from behind Marianna and snatched her hover camera.

"No! It's just a camera!" Marianna cried.

As she turned, two other figures stepped into the circle from opposite sides. Each one withdrew a weapon much stranger than the others held—like a green, glowing round gun with a grip at either side.

Marianna turned to Keithan, horrified. He glanced at her but returned his gaze to the new figures. One was a man, the other a woman. They paced around Keithan and Marianna, and without a warning, they fired.

Marianna shouted, but to her surprise—and Keithan's—neither one was hurt. The devices the two figures were pointing at them with were now projecting a horizontal green laser grid, which extended from one device to the other and moved slowly up and down through Keithan and Marianna, scanning them. Both Keithan and Marianna remained petrified, watching without even daring to blink.

Then every electronic device the two still had on them started to shoot out sparks.

"Hey! What the—! Ouch!" Keithan cried, struggling to take his wrist communicator off. He looked down and noticed his power-strapped sneakers also malfunctioning. As for Marianna, she took off her wrist communicator, which also shot out sparks, and threw it on the ground.

"They're clear," said the woman holding one of the scanning devices, and she and her companion turned them off.

"Good," said a cold voice nearby. "Bring them."

The bright spotlight that had been on them vanished. It took a few seconds for Keithan to adapt to the sudden darkness, but before he was able to see clearly again, a pair of hands grabbed his arms and dragged him to one of the vehicles.

"No—wait! Where are you taking us?" he shouted.

"We didn't mean any harm!" Marianna cried while struggling to get free.

They were no match for the strong figures who brought them to one of the vehicles and pushed them inside. Keithan and Marianna fell into the middle of a set of seats that faced each other like those inside a limousine. Then the door was shut. The vehicle roared and did an abrupt hundred-and-eighty-degree spin that threw Keithan hard against the glass window.

"*Ungh!*"

"Keithan! Are you all right?" Marianna cried while she tried to straighten up.

Right before Keithan could reply, he fell backward as the vehicle accelerated forward. It was as if a maniac were in control of the steering wheel, a maniac hidden in a separate cabin on the left side of the vehicle. The worst part was that neither Keithan nor Marianna had time to put on their seatbelts. The vehicle reached in seconds the inside of the hangar where the mysterious craft had appeared and stopped so abruptly it threw the two of them forward, slamming them against the opposite seats.

"Man! *Ungh!* Don't these people know how to slow down?" Marianna moaned, rubbing her forehead.

Keithan shook his head and felt it with both hands, expecting to find a bump or two. Outside, he saw the other vehicles arrive. He heard the loud noise of a machine. It was coming from behind. Keithan looked through the rear window and saw that the hangar's wide door was closing.

"Keithan, I'm scared," Marianna murmured.

"You're not the only one," he told her.

He had no idea what would happen next. Were they being arrested? Or worse, were they being kidnapped? Whatever it was, it didn't look like it was going to be pleasant.

All of a sudden, Keithan's thoughts drifted away at the same time his vision turned hazy. He became dizzy and started coughing. So did Marianna. By the time they realized there was gas sneaking through the air conditioning vents, it was too late. Marianna collapsed onto the seat. Seconds later, Keithan's eyes rolled into the back of his head, and he, too, lost consciousness.

CHAPTER 33

B lurry glimpses. That was all Keithan was able to see while he struggled to come back to his senses. The images were so unclear Keithan wasn't sure if he was seeing them with his own eyes or if they were just appearing in his subconscious. On the first look, he saw some of the figures in dark bodysuits pull him and Marianna out of the vehicle. Later, he saw the figures carrying him by his arms and legs through a tubular tunnel with dim illumination that came out of the corners of the floor base. How much time passed during this? He didn't know.

A white light switched on beneath Keithan. It was so bright it woke him up with a fright and forced him to shade his eyes with his hands. It was then that Keithan found himself lying face down on a cold floor, right next to Marianna, who also seemed to have been woken by the light.

"Are you all right?" Keithan groaned, getting to his feet.

"I-I think so," Marianna replied, rubbing her eyes. "Where are we?"

Keithan turned on the spot, disoriented. He was standing at the center of a small room shaped like a giant bubble, for its walls and ceiling were one concave, mirrored piece in which he and Marianna could see themselves reflected all around. It reminded Keithan of the wacky mirrored rooms found inside fun houses at carnivals. The only light there came from the floor, which was completely illuminated as if it were one giant lamp. Yet the strangest thing about the room was that there was no access door visible anywhere, which made Keithan wonder how he and Marianna had been brought here.

"Looks like we're in some sort of interrogation room," Keithan guessed.

"What makes you say that?" Marianna asked.

"Most rooms with big mirrors tend to be used for interrogation, which could mean..." Keithan moved closer to the wall. "...we're probably being watched from the other side."

He was staring in wonder at the strange, mirrored surface when his reflection vanished and a large viewscreen with the image of a man with a square jaw appeared right in front of him.

"Whoa!" Keithan cried.

The man on the viewscreen stared down at him and Marianna with a serious expression. He looked strong despite his white crew cut and his pale and wrinkled face. He, too, was dressed in a black tech suit, though unlike that of the figures that had brought Keithan and Marianna here, his suit looked more prestigious, with chrome shoulder patches and a silver aiguillette that hung from his right shoulder and under his arm. Without a doubt, this man was a figure of high rank.

"Look at his insignia," Marianna whispered.

Keithan lowered his gaze, and right away he recognized the insignia on the man's chest. It was just like the one he had seen in the old paperback book at Mr. Aramis's office: a triangle leaned slightly to the right, with each of its points enclosed in a small circle, and an art deco-style wing at the right. Keithan was about to tell this to Marianna, but the man on the viewscreen spoke.

"Who are you?" His voice was deep and full of authority. "State your names."

Keithan and Marianna hesitated.

"I-I'm Ma-Marianna Aramis."

"And I'm ... Quintero— Keithan. Keithan Quintero."

The man narrowed his eyes. "Why were the two of you spying on our hangar?"

Keithan chose his words carefully. He knew it was best for him to be honest. "We, um … We were just … intrigued," he managed to say, struggling with his nerves and glancing at Marianna in the hopes that she would back him up. "We saw a strange blur shoot past our hangar, over the airport's main runway …"

"W-we ran toward where we saw it disappear," Marianna added, deeply nervous. "That was when we found the hangar, and—"

While she explained, the man raised what looked to be a sleek data pad. He looked at it and cut Marianna off.

"Marianna Aramis," he said. He read it from the data pad now in his hands. "Age: twelve. Birthday: December 28. Studies at San Antonio School at Isabela, Puerto Rico. A current member of the students' audiovisual club two years in a row."

Keithan and Marianna exchanged looks of astonishment, for while the man spoke, Marianna's profile appeared on a corner of the viewscreen, along with her school profile picture.

"How did you get—?" she started to say, but the man kept on reading.

"… Home address: residential hangar H11, Ramey Airport, Aguadilla, Puerto Rico. Has an older brother: Fernando Aramis. Parents: William Aramis, an aeroengineer and private mechanic at Ramey Airport; and Lynora Aramis, who is a housewife."

"Who's spying on whom now?" Keithan muttered.

The man gave Keithan a cold stare before he gazed down at his data pad and tapped on it a few times. The next moment, Marianna's whole profile disappeared, only to be substituted by Keithan's.

"Keithan Quintero," the man started to read aloud again. "Age: thirteen. Birthday: September 18. A level-five pilot student at Ramey Academy of Flight and Aeroengineering and a prominent member of the Air Racing Program."

There was a short pause. Keithan noticed the man frown, impressed.

"A resident of Ramey, Aguadilla. An only child. Parents: Caleb Quintero, who works as a professor of mythology at the Aguadilla University; and Adalina Zambrana—"

The man hesitated. He checked his data pad to make sure he had read correctly.

"Adalina Zambrana?" he muttered.

Keithan waited with Marianna, not knowing what to expect. Neither one had a clue what was happening. Was there something wrong with Keithan being the son of Adalina Zambrana?

"Interesting," the man said thoughtfully. "Very interesting."

Keithan sensed the man studying him with his deep gaze, yet all Keithan could do was stare back at him. Then, without any warning, the viewscreen flickered and disappeared.

"No! Hey!" Keithan cried. "*What* is going on? *Argh!*"

Keithan threw himself at the wall and pounded on it. "What's going on?" he repeated louder. He was tired of all the waiting. He wanted answers, and he wanted them now.

Desperate, he moved around the room, feeling the smooth surface of the walls in the hopes to find an access door somewhere. Meanwhile, Marianna followed him with her gaze from the center of the room. Her eyes revealed deep fear and uncertainty, yet Keithan didn't notice it until she said, "Mom and Dad must be deeply worried by now."

Her words made Keithan stop. He sensed the fear in Marianna's voice, and so he turned around to face her, sighing.

"We're going to be all right," he told her, gradually calming himself. "We *will* get out of here. I just don't know when … or how."

Keithan thought about Mr. and Mrs. Aramis and his father. Without a doubt, Fernando must have told them already what had happened, and they must have informed the police already to begin a search for Keithan and Marianna. Keithan only hoped they would find them before it was too late.

Giving up, Keithan sat down on the illuminated floor next to Marianna. Ten minutes later, a small area on the mirrored wall started to melt, then disintegrate. It began as the size of a bullet hole, or more as if someone had thrown a pebble at it, making ripples around it. Slowly it became wider until it created a dark opening in front of them. When it reached the floor, it stopped.

From the blackness on the other side, two men, strongly built and with robot-like expressions on their faces, stepped into the room. Now up close, Keithan could see the details of their dark uniforms. They were some sort of high-tech unisuits made of black leather and carbon fiber, with a series of readouts and digital keys that glowed on their left sleeves, as if their entire forearms were data screens.

"Come with us," the man on the right said flatly, but he held out a hand as Keithan and Marianna got on their feet. "No, just you." He pointed at Keithan.

Keithan shook his head, not sure if he should go on. It seemed best for him to do as he was told and avoid getting into any more trouble than he and Marianna were already in, but instead, he stepped back. And gathering his courage, he replied in a defiant tone, "I'm not leaving my friend here."

He took Marianna's left hand and kept his gaze at the two figures. He felt Marianna pressing his hand in return.

The two men, practically twice Keithan's and Marianna's size, could have easily grabbed and dragged him out of the room—if not carried him out like a ragged doll. Yet they remained with their hands to the sides and simply exchanged annoyed looks.

"It's all right, men; the girl can come too."

The voice came from behind the two men who, in response, stepped aside and turned to face each other. Following protocol, they raised their hands in salute as a third figure, clearly of higher rank, entered the room. To Keithan's and Marianna's surprise, it was the man with the distinguished-looking uniform they had just seen a few minutes ago on the viewscreen.

The man's presence made Marianna and Keithan freeze. He stopped in front of the two of them, his hands behind his back and a serious stare that then disappeared and was replaced by a slight smile.

Keithan raised an eyebrow, confused. The man's smile seemed to show warmth, as if he were glad to see them.

"I am Lieutenant Colonel Codec Lanzard," the man said. "I am head officer of this facility, and, aside from the circumstances, it is an honor to meet the son of the bravest and most daring woman I have ever known."

"Huh?" Keithan shook his head. "Yeah, well, it's nice to meet a fan of hers, but I don't think that this is the time or place to—"

"Oh, I'm not a fan," the colonel cut him off. "I have much more respect for what your mother did when she was alive. When she ruled the skies."

"What do you mean?"

Colonel Lanzard was about to reply when a woman, also in a black tech bodysuit, hurried into the room.

"So it *was* you two they caught spying at the hangar!" she said in disbelief.

The woman barged in and stopped next to the colonel with an aura of authority despite Lanzard's presence. Her light-brown hair, tied in a bun, accentuated her hardened face. Keithan recognized her at once.

"Miss Dantés!" Keithan exclaimed in shock, as if everything else that had happened so far hadn't been hard enough to believe.

"There is just no way for you to stay out of trouble, is there, Keithan?" Dantés said.

"Calm down, Agent Venus," Colonel Lanzard said, turning to her. "Everything is under control."

"Is it, Colonel?" Dantés shot a deep look at him even though she was addressing a figure of higher rank. "These two civilians here have found out about this organization. These two *young* civilians, sir. That is more than evident proof that our security measures have been compromised, and we cannot—"

"Wait a second!" Keithan finally snapped. "She's part of this too?" All eyes were on him now, even Marianna's, but Keithan didn't care. He couldn't wait any longer to get some answers. "All right. What's going on here? Who are you people, really?"

Dantés didn't make a gesture or effort to answer. The colonel, on the other hand, gave a curious frown when he noticed Keithan staring with intrigue at their insignias. Lanzard glanced down at his before he looked back at Keithan and said, "Something tells me you already know

... don't you?"

Keithan gulped. "The ... Sky Phantom Legion?"

Dantés's jaw hardened.

Lanzard grinned. And with that, he turned to the officer on his left.

In return, the officer nodded and stepped forward. He pulled out a silver pen-like device, and pointing it at Marianna—*fffp!*—he shot a tiny dart at her.

Marianna shouted and grabbed her left arm where the dart landed. Keithan saw her lose her balance and grabbed her. Shocked, he turned from Marianna to the officer.

Then came Keithan's turn.

He felt the sting of the dart on his left forearm, close to his wrist. "What the—?" he cried but couldn't finish as he began to feel dizzy. And as it had happened inside the black vehicle with spherical tires, his vision turned blurry. Keithan lost his balance. Marianna already lay on the floor, unconscious. In front of him, Dantés, Colonel Lanzard, and the two other uniformed officers stood still, watching him.

"Don't worry, Keithan," the colonel said, the deep voice slowly fading. "Everything will be all right. This is for the best."

And for the second time that night, Keithan fell and lost consciousness.

CHAPTER 34

*I*t's so cold.

It was the first thing that came to Keithan's mind when he woke up. He opened his eyes slowly and allowed them to adapt to the light of the room. Fortunately, it was a soft light coming from a frosted window to his right. It made him realize he was not in his bedroom, where the window was opposite his bed. But where exactly was he?

The familiar smell of soft, leathery, and nutty cologne told him his father was somewhere nearby. Keithan found him on a chair next to the bed. His father's tired face showed that he had not slept well, yet Caleb Quintero's eyes lit up when he saw his son awake.

"Hey. How are you feeling?" his father said with a warm smile.

"Good. I guess," Keithan said wearily.

"Do you remember anything about last night?"

Keithan stared blankly, trying to remember. Then he opened his eyes wide.

"Marianna!" he exclaimed, quickly sitting on the bed. To his relief, he found Marianna at the other end of the small rectangular room, accompanied by her parents and Fernando. She was already awake, and she, too, was seated on a single bed. On her head, Keithan noticed several wireless electrodes, which monitored her brain activity and transmitted everything to a small control panel on her bed's headboard. Keithan touched his head and discovered he also had several electrodes.

"Keithan," Fernando said as he moved his wheelchair toward him. "Are you okay?"

"Yeah," Keithan nodded.

Mr. Aramis turned to him. "Are you sure you don't have any bumps on your head?" he asked Keithan.

Keithan gave him a puzzled look. "I-I don't think so." Still, he touched his head again to make sure.

"You know, you and Marianna are lucky after what happened to both of you last night," Mr. Aramis said.

"What exactly happened to us?" said Marianna, disoriented.

Keithan had been about to ask the same thing.

"You don't remember, eh?" Mr. Aramis said. "Airport security found the two of you lying unconscious at the airfield, near the small aircraft parking area."

"*What?*" said Keithan, more confused now. He had no memory of that whatsoever.

"We were told both of you were blown back hard by an aircraft's jet engine and knocked unconscious," Keithan's dad explained. "At least that's what airport security told us."

"It was they who brought you to the hospital," Mrs. Aramis added.

The story made some sense, but Keithan wasn't convinced. By the look on Marianna's face at the other side of the room, it seemed that she wasn't convinced, either. Keithan concentrated hard. He remembered being with Marianna last night. He remembered the airport too, but he couldn't remember anything else … until he saw the red sting on his left forearm.

It all came back to him in a flash. He raised his gaze at Marianna, and just as he had expected, he noticed that she, too, had a red sting on her left forearm, near her wrist. It was all Keithan needed to see to confirm that what they had just been told was a lie. Nothing more than a cover-up plotted by the Sky Phantom Legion.

It took Keithan a few days of rest to feel like himself again. After he checked out of the hospital, his father took him back home where he slept and slept, only with a few intervals of watching TV while he had something to eat. It wasn't until Wednesday, back at the academy, that he felt much better. Yet, despite the energy he had recovered, he was still troubled by what had happened to him and Marianna. Because of that, he only had one thing in his mind today: to talk with Fernando on the first chance he got.

Keithan hadn't talked to him or Marianna since they all had left the hospital. He met his best friend at the entrance of the hangar bay when Fernando arrived with his mom to bring the *d'Artagnan*. Once the aircraft was inside and Mrs. Aramis left, Keithan tried to bring the subject about last Sunday night, but Fernando didn't even let him begin.

"Not here," Fernando told him, raising a hand so Keithan wouldn't say more. He looked from side to side, as if to make sure that nobody was listening. "We have a lot to talk about. I found some stuff related to what happened to you and Marianna that you need to see. But we can't talk about it here."

For some reason, Fernando was anxious to get to class. Keithan looked up at the holographic time running continuously throughout the hallway and wondered why his friend was in such a hurry when they still had fifteen minutes before their first class started. He kept up with Fernando down the ground floor's main hallway then through the cafeteria to reach the courtyard. They were less than forty paces away from the hangar opposite to the academy's main building when Winston and Gabriel, who were also heading to Advanced Aeronautics, caught up with them.

"Hey, Keithan! Congratulations!" Gabriel said.

Keithan frowned and turned to him. "What?"

"Dude, you made the front web page of *Sky Daily*."

Keithan halted abruptly and forced Fernando to stop his wheelchair. "What? What are you talking about?"

"Um, Keithan …" Fernando started to say while Winston showed Keithan a data pad.

Keithan took it and his eyes widened. On the screen was the web page of the famous online newspaper with last Monday's date, but beneath it was a picture of him along with a title in big letters:

Son of Air Racing Legend Denied to Defend Title

"What the …?"

"I was hoping you wouldn't see that," Fernando said next to him with a look of regret.

Keithan stared at the data pad in his hands, speechless and in disbelief.

He felt somebody pat him on the back, right before he heard a pair of voices say, "Tough break, Quintero."

Keithan raised his gaze and saw Owen and Lance pass him along with their aeroengineer partners, Manuel and Gustav. Their smiles clearly showed that they were mocking him.

"Defend your mom's title? Against Drostan Luzier?" Owen added rhetorically, laughing.

"Keep dreaming," Lance finished for him.

"Forget about that," Fernando told Keithan as the twins and their friends continued ahead. "You have more important things to worry about right now—much more important things."

Keithan swallowed hard and shook his head. Fernando was right. Keithan handed the data pad back to Gabriel and continued to class with Fernando. As he went on, however, he set the alarm on his wrist communicator to remind him in the afternoon to look for the article. He would definitely like to know what it said about him.

Throughout the entire morning, Keithan tried to find the opportunity to talk in private with Fernando, but they didn't get a chance since they were so busy during classes. Even during lunch hour, they were unable to talk because of Genevieve and Yari, who practically invited themselves to their table to eat with them.

Fortunately, the opportunity came right after lunch, in their Aeronautical Chart Interpretation class. Their professor, Mr. Quill, was absent due to a medical appointment. Therefore, Keithan, Fernando, and their classmates were to go to the multimedia library instead.

Keithan and Fernando settled at the end in two of the cubicles with virtual computers.

"So how's Marianna?" Keithan went straight to the point as soon as he made sure no one was close enough to hear.

"She's all right," Fernando said in a low voice. "She went to school today. Mom didn't want her to go, but Marianna insisted, saying she'd been feeling fine since before she was allowed to leave the hospital."

"Did she talk to you about what happened to us? You know, what *really* happened?"

"Oh, she did. She told me everything."

"*Shhh!* No talking in the cubicles area," Mrs. Peebley's voice was heard from a distance.

Both Keithan and Fernando poked their heads over the cubicles to see how far she was. Mrs. Peebley had an impressive hearing ability. Even though the library was mostly quiet, she was far at the other end.

"I couldn't believe it when Marianna told me Dantés was involved in the whole thing," Fernando lowered his voice.

"Neither could I," Keithan whispered.

"By the way, have you seen Dantés today?" Fernando asked.

"No. And, honestly, I'm not looking forward to it. I'm pretty sure she'll want to talk to me, but I don't think I should."

"Well, whatever happens, just be care—"

"*Shhh!* I said no talking," Mrs. Peebley interrupted, her tone now louder and warningly.

Both Fernando and Keithan waited a few seconds before they continued.

"Anyway, there are some things I need to show you." Fernando reached for his bag hanging behind the back of his wheelchair and pulled out an old-looking book.

"The *Sky Phantoms* book!" Keithan said in a whisper and took it.

"I went to Dad's office and searched for it as soon as Mom and Dad went out to look for you two." Fernando leaned forward. "Dad doesn't know I took it. I was hoping it would help me find out more about the Sky Phantom Legion—and trust me, it did help a lot."

"Fernando, that was brilliant!"

"*Shhh!*" came from the other end of the library.

Keithan turned the book to face the back cover and stared at its illustration. The insignia there was the exact one he had seen on the lieutenant colonel's high-tech uniform.

"According to what I was able to read from that book," Fernando began to explain, "that so-called Legion has been operating since the past century, fighting in the most extraordinary sky battles the world has never heard about."

"And which the Legion most likely will never want the world to know," Keithan said thoughtfully, still staring at the insignia.

Fernando nodded. "Most of the book's pages aren't legible, so I was able to read only fragments. There wasn't much I could make out of them, yet..." He turned to the cubicle's computer and plugged in a data card drive. As soon as the holo screen and the projected keyboard appeared, Fernando tapped in some keys. "...I searched the internet for more info about the Sky Phantoms. I didn't find much about them, but I did find something interesting about that book. It seems it was controversial in its time, back in the late 1940s, when it came out."

"Controversial?" Keithan asked.

"Uh-huh. Apparently some people believed that what the author had written in the book was not science fiction, but true events that revealed the existence of a private secret air force. Here. Check this out."

Fernando reached out with a finger to a file icon on the left side of the holo screen and opened a digital document. It showed the image of a yellowish newspaper clipping from *The New York Times*. Keithan leaned closer to it and noticed the clipping's year of publication at the top right: 1950. Below it, centralized, was its title written in big black letters.

Sky Phantoms: Science Fiction or Nonfiction?

The title immediately intrigued Keithan.

"And check this one." Fernando scrolled down the document and showed Keithan a different clipping. This one had shiny colors, which gave Keithan the impression that it had been scanned from a much more modern magazine. Its title was also written in big black letters.

Science-Fiction Quick Best Seller
Is Mysteriously Taken Off the Market

"This one talks about a conspiracy against the book and its author, Hamilton Stargland," Fernando explained. "It informs that in less than five months after the book was released, its publisher unexpectedly discontinued it and removed it from all bookstores."

"What?"

"And that's not all," Fernando went on. "Read this line over here." He pointed to the third line of the article's last paragraph.

"'Nobody ever saw the book or Mr. Stargland again,'" Keithan read loud enough for only Fernando to hear. He shook his head and turned to his friend. "Wait a second. Nobody knows what happened to the author?"

"Think about it," said Fernando, keeping his voice down so he wouldn't upset Mrs. Peebley. "All the pieces seem to fall into place: a book that some people believed revealed the existence of a secret legion of fighter pilots but was disguised as a science-fiction novel, the book being unexpectedly taken out from all bookstores, *and* its author never seen or heard of again. It all seems like a conspiracy by the Sky Phantom Legion itself against the author—maybe to stop him from revealing the Legion's secrets. Why do you think it's so hard to find information about the author and the Legion even on the internet?"

Keithan raised an eyebrow. He couldn't believe Fernando had managed to come up with a deep theory about all this during the past few days.

"You and Marianna couldn't have been the first to have discovered the truth about the Legion," Fernando continued. "Hamilton Stargland must have been one of the first—if not *the* first—to have done so a century ago. It could be possible he camouflaged all the facts in a sci-fi novel to reveal everything to the rest of the world."

There was a moment of silence between the two. Keithan looked from the article in the holo screen to the book in his hands, then to Fernando.

"So, in this case, reality inspired science fiction instead of the other way around," he wondered.

Once the bell rang, Keithan, Fernando, and their classmates headed to Atmospheric Science: their next and last class of the day. Keithan and Fernando, however, were halfway there when one of the hall monitor robots halted right in front of Keithan.

"*Hey.* Would you mind?" Keithan said. He tried to go around the robot, but the HM unit didn't let him.

The robot, already having confirmed Keithan's ID on his uniform's insignia, said in its particular distorted voice, "Keithan Quintero, I have instructions to escort you to Headmaster Viviani's office."

"Huh?" Keithan was taken aback. "What for?"

"Geez, Keithan. What did you do now?" Genevieve said as she passed him.

"I haven't done anything," Keithan said with a shrug.

"Headmaster Viviani requests your presence right away," the robot said.

"Better do as it says," Fernando said. "Don't worry, I'll tell Professor Velazquez."

Grumbling, Keithan let the HM unit lead the way. They went together to the central elevator, which took them to the top floor. Once they reached the front of the waiting area of the headmaster's office, the robot took off. Sally, the headmaster's glossy white robot secretary, greeted Keithan.

"How may I help you?" she said, her womanly voice kind and metallic.

"I'm here on Headmaster Viviani's request," Keithan replied.

"Your full name, please?"

"Keithan Quintero."

Sally made an acknowledging beep. Then she said, "Mr. Quintero, Headmaster Viviani will be with you shortly. You may take a seat."

Keithan was about to sit down when the headmaster appeared from the sliding door at the other end of the room.

"Keithan, I'm so glad you're here," Viviani said. "Come in."

So glad? Keithan repeated in his head. He did his best not to react with an awkward expression while he tried to comprehend why the headmaster was in such a good mood.

Viviani stepped aside to allow Keithan to enter. "There's someone here I want you to meet. Well, actually, it is someone who wants to meet *you*."

Keithan gave him a questioning look. The headmaster directed him to look at the end of the office, and there, Keithan found a figure he recognized right away.

The man, whose raven-black beard almost looked perfectly squared, was standing before the desk and the wide, circular window. He was dressed in a fancy pearly white suit with golden epaulets and a white peaked cap with a gold-winged stallion brooch.

Keithan stopped instantly—not by shock, but by surprise. He couldn't believe who was standing in front of him.

"So you're the famous Keithan Quintero," the man said in an Italian accent, moving toward Keithan with an extended hand.

Half stunned, Keithan shook it. "And you're Captain Giovanni Colani, the CEO of Pegasus Company."

CHAPTER 35

Atmospheric Science must have started by now, and surely Keithan's classmates would be having a hard time trying to stay awake while Professor Velazquez drowned them with one of his usually boring lectures about meteorology. They would also be assuming that Keithan had gotten into trouble since he was still at the headmaster's office. If they only knew Keithan was far from trouble, standing in front of the CEO of Pegasus Company.

They would never believe him. Keithan was sure Professor Velazquez wouldn't, either.

Next to Keithan, Headmaster Viviani contained his excitement for having Colani in his office. No wonder he had received Keithan in such a good mood.

"Please, take a seat," Colani told Keithan, gesturing to one of the two red leather chairs in front of the headmaster's desk.

Keithan looked from Colani to the headmaster and sat on the chair to the left.

"I've been looking forward to meeting you since the qualifier tournament," Colani told Keithan as he sat next to him.

"You have?" Keithan said.

"Oh, yes. I first heard about you when you were denied to participate in the tournament. By the way, I'm sorry about that. Headmaster Viviani here tells me you even air raced against one of your professors to prove that you could be in the Pegasus Air Race.

However, it wasn't until the day after the tournament, when I read the article about you in *Sky Daily*, that I found out that the young air racer who had not been allowed to participate was none other than the son of Adalina Zambrana." Colani paused. "I just couldn't believe it. That's why I came here to meet you. It would have been an honor to have you in my air race. Imagine..." He turned to Viviani who was now seated on the high-backed chair behind his desk. "...the son of Adalina Zambrana defending his mother's unbeaten record. It would have been the main attraction at this year's race, don't you think?"

It sounded awesome, but the thought made Keithan bite his tongue to hold his disappointment. He had imagined the same thing long before he had been denied to participate in the qualifier tournament.

"Who knows? Keithan could get his chance someday, when he's older," Viviani said.

"Well, only time will tell," Colani said. He stood up and turned to Keithan once again. "For what it's worth, I would like to make it up to you, Keithan."

Colani reached into his suit and pulled out an envelope with a golden Pegasus seal and handed it to Keithan.

"What's this?" Keithan asked.

Viviani adjusted his coin-shaped glasses and leaned forward over his desk, deeply curious too.

"It's a dinner invitation," Colani said, "for you and your father to come to my airship this Friday night."

Keithan's eyes lit up. "Your airship?"

"Yes," Colani said. "You will love it. My professional chefs, who fly with me wherever I go, would prepare an exquisite menu, including desserts unlike any you have ever tasted. Plus, we could share great stories about your mother—that is, of course, if it is all right with you."

Keithan opened the envelope and pulled out the invitation card. It also had the Pegasus logo, along with all the details: date, time, even Keithan's name, all of which were centralized in the card.

"So what do you say?" Colani asked.

Keithan remained openmouthed, still staring down at the

invitation.

"He seems to be out of words," Viviani said with a snort behind Colani. "That is a great honor, don't you think, Keithan?"

"I— Yes, sir." Keithan finally found the words, and he looked back at Colani. "My dad and I *will* be there, Mr. Colani. It would be an honor."

"Oh, the honor is all mine," Colani told him.

"Congratulations, Keithan," the headmaster said. "Well, now, you better head back to class. I wouldn't want you to get into any trouble with one of your professors."

"Yes, sir." Keithan nodded to him and stood up.

He couldn't wipe the big smile off his face as he set off to Professor Velazquez's classroom, and he couldn't wait to tell Fernando what had happened. He gazed up at the moving hologram hovering above him on the ceiling. It showed that it was 2:25 p.m. He still had a half hour of class left. Keithan hurried down the stairs, but right at the bottom, he came to an abrupt stop when, to his shock, he found himself face-to-face with Professor Dantés.

Keithan wasn't sure, but by the look on the woman's face, it seemed she had been waiting for him. But how did she know he would be there?

Dantés stared at him with deep suspicion before she said, "My office. Right now."

That was it. She turned away without even waiting for Keithan to respond.

This time Keithan was straightforward. "Sorry, Professor, I'm not going to be able to make it. I'm supposed to be—"

"I'm not asking you, Quintero. I'm ordering you." Dantés hadn't stopped moving down the stairs. "So as I said, my office. Right now."

Keithan gulped. All the excitement he'd had since he'd left the headmaster's office vanished in that moment.

"Man, doesn't that woman ever even smile? At least say hello first?" he muttered angrily.

Keithan knew it was best to explain himself later to Professor

Velazquez than not to follow Dantés's orders. So instead of heading to class, Keithan went straight to Dantés's office. He could have taken the elevator to get there quicker, but Keithan decided to take his time since he had a strong feeling about the reason the professor wanted to talk to him.

Once Keithan got to the second level of the hangar bay, he stopped in front of the frosted glass door with the professor's name stenciled at eye level. He took a deep breath; he was certain the meeting wasn't going to be pleasant.

The frosted glass door became transparent and slid upward, as if it had sensed his presence. And as soon as Keithan stepped in, it slid down behind him and frosted up again.

Dantés watched him enter the office from the other end. She stood behind her glossy amorphous desk, arms folded and with the usual I-mean-business look.

"I hope you can explain to Professor Velazquez why I'm going to be late for his class," Keithan told her as he stopped in front of the desk. "You're going to get me into trouble."

"You might be already," Dantés replied, her expression as hard and cold as her tone.

"Now I know what you meant, Dantés. There's just no way for the boy to stay out of trouble."

The comment came from behind Keithan and made him jump. Keithan could have sworn there had been nobody else in the office, but when he turned around, he found himself facing the imposing figure of Lieutenant Colonel Lanzard: the leader of the secret Sky Phantom Legion.

Keithan's instant reaction was to look all around the office to check if there were any of the men in high-tech black bodysuits. The last thing he wanted was to have any of them shoot a dart at him again.

"Relax. We're not going to shoot any darts at you this time," Colonel Lanzard said, as if reading Keithan's mind.

Still, Keithan wasn't convinced. He kept a good distance from the colonel, making sure he could see the man's hands at all times. The

- 300 -

civilian disguise Lanzard was wearing didn't fool Keithan. Lanzard looked like an executive, wearing an ordinary black business suit. Anybody else would have bought that, but not Keithan.

"Why are you here?" Keithan dared to ask him. "I haven't told anyone what happened last Sunday, if that's why."

"I hope that's true—for your sake and that of your friends," the colonel said pointedly. "Still, don't think that we are done with you and Miss Aramis."

Keithan took a step back and gulped.

The colonel smirked. "Did you think we were just going to leave you in the hospital to make it all look as if you and Miss Aramis only had an accident after you found out about the Legion?"

Keithan opened his mouth to reply but held his tongue.

"That was just the first step of our plan, just to buy ourselves some time before we deal with you," Lanzard explained. "And we *will* deal with both of you since we can't allow anyone to reveal the existence of the Legion. There's no way you and your girlfriend can escape that."

"Still, we'll deal with that matter later," Dantés said, forcing the conversation forward. "Right now, we have something else important we need to take care of … with you."

She looked straight at Keithan. Keithan only frowned, lost.

"Which is exactly why I am here," Lanzard told Keithan. "You see, I came as soon as Dantés informed me that Giovanni Colani was here at the academy, apparently having some sort of private meeting with you and Headmaster Viviani."

Keithan shook his head. "Wait— Is *that* what this is about?"

"What did Giovanni Colani want with you?" Lanzard asked him, now turning more serious.

"Huh?"

"What exactly did Colani want with you?" Dantés insisted, moving closer to Keithan.

Keithan was caught off guard. All of a sudden, he felt like a crime suspect being interrogated. What were Dantés and Lanzard planning to do next, torture him if he didn't cooperate?

"H-he wanted to meet me," Keithan said. "Mr. Colani heard about me when I was taken out of the qualifier tournament, but he found out later that I was Adalina Zambrana's son. So he came to the academy to meet me."

Dantés grimaced. "That was it?"

"Not really," Keithan went on. "He also told me he was sorry I wasn't allowed to compete in the tournament, and he wanted to make it up to me."

"Make it up to you?" Dantés said.

Keithan nodded. "He invited my dad and me to a dinner party at his airship."

Noticing Lanzard's and Dantés's perplexed looks, Keithan showed them the invitation. Dantés took it and opened it.

"It says it's this next Friday night, at 7:30," she told Lanzard.

The colonel didn't reply; he simply narrowed his eyes, thinking.

"Is that a bad thing?" Keithan asked. "I'm sure there's nothing wrong with that. I mean, do you have something against the owner of Pegasus Company? Or the Pegasus Air Race?"

"That's not your concern," Dantés told him, still looking at the invitation.

"Actually, it should be his concern now," Lanzard interjected, "for his own good."

Dantés gazed up at her superior with a look of disbelief. "Colonel, I am sure you're aware of the seriousness of the matter. Quintero is a minor. You cannot possibly be thinking of getting him more involved than he already is. He even got himself more involved when he tried to participate in the Pegasus qualifier tournament. Luckily..." She turned to Keithan. "...I was able to prevent that."

"*What?*" Keithan exclaimed, his eyes wide in shock. In a flash, he realized what had happened at the tournament.

"You mean ... *you* influenced the judges into not letting me participate?"

"Yes, I did," Dantés replied in a soft tone that showed no remorse. She stepped closer to Keithan, showing him who the authority figure was. "It was I who told the judges at the tournament that pilot students from Ramey Academy would not be allowed to participate unless they were represented by a licensed flight instructor. Furthermore, *I* made sure that none of the students who were planning to participate would be represented by any of the academy's flight instructors."

"So that's why Gregory Paceley didn't show up at the tournament," Keithan said.

Having discovered the Sky Phantom Legion, and even meeting the owner of Pegasus Company, now meant nothing to him. He could only stare at Dantés in disbelief, anger boiling inside him. How could she be so mean? And what was her problem with the Pegasus Air Race?

"Please don't give me that look," Dantés said, as if sensing Keithan's frustration and anger. "I did what I had to do."

"Why?" Keithan insisted. He didn't take his eyes off her.

Dantés seemed to have no intention to answer. She sighed, but seeing Keithan's determination to wait for an answer, she said, "Because … we suspect there is a threat behind the air race."

The reply was nowhere close to what Keithan had expected, yet he gave her a skeptical look. "What are you talking about? Like a terrorist attack?" he said.

There was a moment of silence in the office.

Then Lanzard spoke. "Let's show him."

Both Keithan and Dantés turned to him, surprised.

"Sir?" Dantés said, incredulous.

Lanzard folded his arms, staring deeply at Keithan, but addressed Dantés. "I know you don't agree with me, Agent Venus, but young Mr. Quintero here knows too much already. I would rather use that to our advantage. Hopefully, it could even be the best way to keep a closer eye on him."

"Absolutely out of the question!" Dantés cried.

"I beg your pardon … *Agent?*" Lanzard said, his deep voice asserting his authority.

Keithan stared silently at Dantés. He couldn't believe she would dare to oppose a figure with a rank higher than hers.

"With all due respect, Colonel, I know what you're trying to do, but I'm afraid I can't allow it," the professor said, her jaw tight. "Three nights ago, he found out about the existence of a top-secret organization, and today you're considering making him part of it?"

"I am well aware of what it involves," Lanzard said, "but it so happens that I—well, *we* might need his help."

There was a long tense silence between Dantés and the colonel.

"What if I refuse?" Keithan interjected. "I don't think I like the idea of helping you people cancel the Pegasus Air Race. You don't even have proof of that 'threat' you think is behind it."

"Well, I don't think you have much of a choice but to do as we say," Lanzard told him nonchalantly. "Unless you would rather have your other option."

"And what would that be? You're going to have my memory erased for finding out about the Legion?" Keithan said.

Neither Lanzard nor Dantés made the slightest gesture, which made it clear they weren't amused. It was more than enough to make Keithan's cocky attitude vanish and his tone drop dramatically.

"You can do *that*?"

"I'd rather avoid it," Lanzard told him, his tone now warning. "It would be unfortunate to have you go through our memory-wipe process. Just imagine, not being able to remember how to fly anymore and not even remember your name. That said, I suggest you see it as if you have no other choice but to come with us. So what will it be?"

CHAPTER 36

Keithan had no convenient choice but to accept what Colonel Lanzard wanted him to do, and the first thing was to leave the academy with him and Professor Dantés. He had no idea why the colonel needed him so badly, but he trusted he would find out soon. The three of them were already leaving the academy even though classes weren't over yet. Dantés marched silently to Keithan's right, her face hardened. She hadn't agreed to this, but she seemed to have no intention to leave Keithan alone with the colonel. That, at least, made Keithan feel a bit safe.

Together, the three of them left through the hangar bay's entrance and continued walking until they got underneath the academy's bridge. There, under the bridge's shadow, waited a low black vehicle with twin spherical tires and tinted windows. As Keithan, Lanzard, and Dantés approached it, its passenger cabin opened, and Lanzard gestured for Keithan to get in.

Keithan obeyed but not without glancing at the sky first. He could hear the aircraft of the students who were taking flight class. Now, more than ever, Keithan wished he were flying too.

"Move over," Dantés said sharply, forcing Keithan to sit at the windowless side.

Lanzard sat opposite to him. The vehicle took off as soon as the door closed.

There was no point in asking where they were taking him. Keithan knew they were heading to the hangar where everything had started. They got there in nearly less than a minute, yet for some reason, when the vehicle stopped, neither Dantés nor Lanzard moved.

"Um, aren't we getting out?" Keithan asked them.

"Not yet," Dantés said.

The light inside the hangar dimmed as its wide entrance closed behind the vehicle. Keithan waited, though without a clue why. There was a heavy thud outside, and the vehicle shook. Startled, Keithan turned from Dantés to the colonel, but both still looked calm, as if they hadn't felt anything.

Then the weirdest thing happened. The walls of the hangar began to grow upward, or so Keithan thought before he realized it was the floor where the vehicle stood that was sinking. Slowly, it revealed an underground chamber with dark steel walls and dim white lights. There, to Keithan's surprise, he saw the mysterious aircraft he and Marianna had seen appear last Sunday.

The craft, still as intriguing as the first time Keithan had seen it, was stationed at a corner of the chamber with a series of cables and computers connected to it. Around it, a small group of men and women were working on it, all wearing glossy white lab coats and strange headgear with small data screens.

Keithan had just leaned closer to the window to get a better look when the vehicle roared again and turned abruptly a hundred and eighty degrees on the spot. Luckily, Keithan's seatbelt kept him in place, for in the next instant, the car accelerated and shot straight into an elliptical tunnel.

"Whoa!" Keithan exclaimed, straightening himself but holding on tightly to his seatbelt while Dantés and Lanzard simply remained steady and silent.

Now outside the window, the only thing that could be seen was an endless, neon-blue light line running throughout the tunnel, along with the intermittent blurs of the elliptical steel frames that they were passing by. Meanwhile, Keithan stared, gaping. He had heard rumors about tunnels that ran underneath Ramey Airport, but as far as he had known, they were supposed to be old drainage tunnels, not dry and shiny ones used for transportation.

Trusting in his keen sense of space and direction, Keithan figured he was being taken westward. He also had a strong feeling that they would soon pass the airport and continue underneath the golf course near the coast. Keithan was just wondering how much longer this whole trip would take when, all of a sudden, the vehicle shot out of the tunnel and drifted hard until it came to a stop.

Finally, the door swung open and Dantés and Lanzard got out.

"Let's go," Lanzard said.

Keithan hesitated, gazing perplexed at the new area they had arrived. It was a cavern hollowed out of limestone; the floor a metal grid platform, which creaked with every step they took. Lanzard went ahead, and Keithan followed with Dantés, who kept the rear. There was water nearby, though Keithan couldn't see it yet. He could tell by the coldness of the place and the smell of moisture in the air. The water gradually came into view, glowing turquoise nearly twenty feet below the platform. Keithan, however, wasn't able to contain his astonishment when he saw what was in it. Side by side and half-submerged in the water, floated two large and fully rusted submarines.

"Oh, my …" Keithan started to say, but his words trailed off as he realized that the legend was true. There *were* old submarines from the World War II era hidden under Ramey after all, just as he had heard many locals talk about for years.

"Is this … the Sky Phantoms' base?" Keithan asked, not taking his eyes away from the submarines.

"No. This is just a docking port," Lanzard corrected him while he continued walking.

The trio went down a narrow grid catwalk that descended to the submarines. In the end, four men wearing identical high-tech, black bodysuits met them.

"Prepare the transport capsule," Lanzard ordered as he approached them.

"Yes, sir," the men answered in unison, and immediately the group split. One of the men headed left while another headed right. A third, who stood on top of the closest submarine, went into a top hatch, and the fourth moved aside, allowing Lanzard and his company to enter the submarine's side opening.

It was pitch-black inside of the large, rusted watercraft, which forced Keithan to feel his way through in order to move and hope not to bump his head into anything. Lanzard's heavy hand rested on his shoulder.

"Watch your step now," Lanzard told him, and pressing down Keithan's shoulder, he forced him to sit down on what felt like an individual seat.

Soon after that, the men outside closed the hatch, taking what little light could be seen.

"All right, Keithan, strap yourself," Dantés said.

Keithan heard the professor right in front of him, and behind him, he heard the colonel already putting on his own restraints. It wasn't easy to do it in complete darkness, but Keithan managed. As he adjusted the restraints over his chest, he kept trying to make some sense of what was happening. Why were they going underwater? And then there was the matter of the two old submarines ...

"No offense but, you people own aircraft with advanced technology, and we are going to travel underwater? In this ancient and rusted submarine?" Keithan said.

Silence followed, which was why Keithan opted for holding his tongue for the rest of the ride.

A male voice came from a speaker inside the submarine. *"Initiating countdown for ejection. Ten ... nine ...eight ..."*

Everything around Keithan began to vibrate so violently he had to grab hold of his seat. Instead of feeling inside a submarine, he felt now more as if he were inside a rocket about to launch. At the same time, a strange and heavy whine began, gradually ascending with each second.

"...seven ... six ... five..."

"Is this normal?" Keithan yelled over the deafening noise.

"...four ... three..."

"Don't worry!" Lanzard yelled back. "That's just air compressing!"

"Air?" Keithan cried.

"*...two ... one.*"

SWOOSH!

The ejection threw Keithan's head back hard and kept him pressed against his seat. He, Dantés, and Lanzard shot out of the cave like a torpedo. Keithan saw that they were no longer inside the submarine, but inside a small capsule, traveling at incredible speed through a giant glass tunnel deep under the sea.

Finding out about the submarines had been incredible enough, but what Keithan could see now was breathtaking.

Outside the glass tunnel where the capsule traveled, Keithan saw an incredible world he had only seen in pictures and on television: the world under the ocean. Rocky hills, mountains, and valleys—all of them enriched with so many colorful kinds of underwater flora—extended as far as the eye could see. Sea creatures, from the most common fish and crustacean to the most unusual ones, moved all around. Keithan spotted a few great white sharks swimming dominantly among the rest of the creatures, as well as several large schools of glistening silver-colored fish performing curious movements in perfect synchronization. But that wasn't all. There was even a variety of old sunken ships and broken aircraft of different periods visible. Corals covered their rusty bodies, as if they had adopted them into their habitat, making the wrecked craft look now like natural underwater sculptures.

Keithan felt like being inside a gigantic aquarium while he watched it all in amazement.

Moments later, a series of wide pillars appeared on either side of the glass tunnel. They rose high all the way to the surface like colossal metal tree trunks. Keithan didn't know what they were at first. Luckily for him, his pilot sense of direction came in handy again. He had a strong feeling the capsule was going westward, far away from the coast of Puerto Rico by now. That meant the giant pillars could only be one thing: the heavy bases of a group of wind turbines in the open water.

And as far as Keithan knew, there was only one group of wind turbines close to the west coast of Puerto Rico.

Immediately, Keithan knew where he was headed. Lanzard and Dantés were taking him to Mona Island.

CHAPTER 37

So far the journey seemed like a field trip but unlike any other Keithan had ever been on. There was no guide to tell him about what he was seeing, and since Lanzard and Dantés kept to themselves, Keithan just watched in the hopes that they would explain everything to him soon. Their capsule transport arrived at a docking port inside another cave, and as soon as they got out of the capsule, they headed into a dimly lit tunnel.

So this is why nobody is allowed to visit Mona Island, Keithan realized while he continued quietly behind Dantés and Lanzard. It made perfect sense; Mona was known to be a natural reserve these days, isolated from civilians. It was the perfect place to hide a secret base.

The tunnel, mainly rock but with arched iron beams that sustained its ceiling and walls, hit Keithan with a familiar smell of moisture that gave him a feeling of déjà vu. Something there told him he had been here before, most likely when he and Marianna had been abducted. Keithan, however, began to grow tired of the tunnel after a while, for it seemed to have no end. It made him feel as if he were inside a giant earthworm hole, sometimes turning left, others turning right while it ascended slightly.

Finally, Lanzard, Dantés, and Keithan arrived at the end of the tunnel. There stood a wide iron hatch door with some noticeable rust. Lanzard tapped in a code on a panel, and the heavy hatch door swung forward, whining as it opened. Lanzard went through first, and Dantés gestured for Keithan to follow.

The sound of machinery mixed with the humming of a ventilation system filled the new area Keithan, Dantés, and Lanzard had entered. The three were now walking on an old metal catwalk that hung high over what appeared to be the main hangar bay. Keithan gazed down, and his eyes widened with amazement when he found, not just one, but a whole squadron of the semitransparent aircraft parked in line. Men and women wearing either black bodysuits or white lab coats were working on some of them.

"They're called Sky Phantoms," Lanzard remarked, gesturing to the high-tech aircraft below.

Keithan stopped when he witnessed one of the craft disappear and immediately reappear before his eyes. Apparently the people around it were checking its invisibility system.

"Keep moving," Dantés told Keithan.

He kept on walking, but fascinated and unable to hold his intrigue any longer, he had to ask, "Where did you people get those aircraft?"

"That's strictly classified," Colonel Lanzard said, still walking in front of him.

"What about this whole place?" Keithan said as he noticed that the rock wall at the far end of the hangar bay was actually a launch tunnel. "Is this part of the United States Air Force or something?"

"The Legion is not attached to any nation," Lanzard explained. "As its name implies, it is a *phantom* among them."

"What does that mean?"

"It means no one is sure about its existence, and we prefer to keep it that way."

This time Dantés had answered.

"So you're a legend to the rest of the world," Keithan commented.

"Exactly," said Lanzard, still moving and without looking back.

Keithan frowned and hurried to keep up with him. He glanced at Dantés over his shoulder and noticed that she was still close behind him.

"And what exactly does the Legion do?" Keithan asked.

"We protect the sky and the world when necessary," Lanzard said.

"Like superheroes?" Keithan asked.

"Secret agents would be more appropriate," Dantés corrected him flatly.

They went into another tunnel at the end of the catwalk. To Keithan's relief, it was much shorter than the previous one because soon they came to a metal staircase that descended to a more lighted area. Keithan found this new room even more impressive than the hangar bay. It was a warehouse filled with the most bizarre fighter aircraft and machines Keithan had ever seen. On one side he saw a half-beaten and rusted war tank, which resembled a German tank from the World War II era but with wide wings. Opposite to it, and resting against the wall, was a giant saw disk craft with twin cockpits in its center. There were also modern-looking craft, among them a giant squid-shaped machine with antigravity propulsors that rested sideways farther ahead, its metal tentacles tangled and broken, and many other flying oddities Keithan had no idea where they could have come from.

One way or another, each one reminded Keithan of Mr. Aramis and the similarly unusual inventions he kept inside his hangar. *If only Mr. Aramis could see this*, Keithan thought.

He kept on walking past the different machines, barely blinking and feeling like a kid in this aviator's wonderland. Meanwhile, Lanzard went on explaining. "Through the past hundred years, the Sky Phantom Legion has played its part fighting in the most extraordinary battles anyone could ever imagine, some of which the world has never even heard about. The machines you see here are a mere example of what we have been up against so far. Like that one over there ..." Lanzard pointed to the saw-disk craft with twin cockpits to their right. "That thing was the creation of a mad inventor who tried to take down the skyscrapers in New York back in the 1990s."

Keithan frowned. "I've never heard of that," he said.

"Of course you haven't," Lanzard said. "That's because we were able to stop the man in time. Now this one over here you might recognize."

Keithan turned his head to the machine Lanzard pointed at. He did recognize it. It was a monstrous, insect-like robot with three jet-propelled legs and a wide, armored light bulb-shaped body from which a pair of broken laser cannons protruded.

"That's from the Aerial War era," said Keithan, gazing up at it in awe. "Hundreds of those things were spotted in different parts of the world."

"That's right," said Lanzard, staring at the machine. "Taking them down was quite a handful."

"Which also cost the lives of many Phantom knights," Dantés added behind Keithan.

Keithan had seen old footage of machines like the one he had in front of him. They showed many of those things terrorizing major cities during the Aerial War. From what Keithan had heard, a mad engineer had built them to try to gain world domination, but he had failed and died in the attempt when the machines had turned against him as a result of some miscalculation.

Keithan continued following Lanzard across the warehouse. The two of them, along with Dantés, were now approaching a huge iron doorway, but Keithan stopped when he spotted a particular aircraft in a corner.

"Is that …?" He didn't even finish the sentence. Instead, he hurried to the craft, forcing Lanzard and Dantés to follow him.

The aircraft Keithan was looking at now didn't seem as impressive or intriguing as the rest. It was the smallest machine there. Yet it wasn't its size what caught Keithan's attention, but rather the fact that it was an old and ordinary Navy bomber airplane.

"That's a TBM Avenger," said Keithan, perplexed.

The dark-army-green plane, with its long cockpit made to fit three people, stood on top of a diamond mesh platform, which made it look more like a collector's piece than a captured craft. Keithan had learned about this plane in his History of Aviation class while studying about World War II aviation. The plane had been introduced at the beginning of the 1940s to be used by the United States Navy.

But what was such a primitive fighter craft doing here? Keithan wondered.

"That plane is one of ours. In fact, it is one of the oldest and most valuable objects of the Legion," Lanzard explained.

"*That* plane?" Keithan repeated, incredulous. "Isn't that thing like too old tech for you guys?"

"Not at its time," Lanzard said reassuringly. "The technology that was hidden in that plane, as well as in its brothers, made it special."

"What kind of technology?" Keithan asked, but quickly he understood. "You mean … *this* was one of the first Sky Phantoms?"

Lanzard nodded. "The squadron to which it belonged to was known by a different name, though."

He gestured toward an old bronze plaque screwed to the side of the plane's fuselage. Keithan approached the plaque and read its engraving.

In memory of Flight 19.
The flight that gave birth to a legion.

It took a moment for Keithan to make some sense of what he'd just read. *Flight 19*, he repeated in his head. He was sure he had heard about that flight somewhere. Then a gasp escaped his mouth at the realization.

"You gotta be kidding me!" It was all Keithan could say, yet neither Lanzard nor Dantés replied.

Every pilot in the world knew about Flight 19. It was the flight from 1945 in which five Avenger torpedo bombers disappeared while doing a routine exercise somewhere within the Northwest of the Atlantic Ocean. The event still intrigued many to this day, especially since it was the same that began the whole phenomenon about the famous enigma of the Bermuda Triangle.

Keithan found it hard to believe at first, for as far as he and most people knew, none of the five Avenger bombers had ever been recovered. Yet, seeing the plane right there, and thinking about all the weird things he had seen so far, it all started to make sense to Keithan. Flight 19 had been the first test carried out by the Sky Phantom Legion to hide their unique technology from the rest of the world.

Dantés cleared her throat and gestured to the lieutenant colonel, insisting to move along.

Lanzard shook his head. "Right," he said. He placed a hand on Keithan's shoulder and forced him to turn around so they could continue forward.

"As you can see," he told Keithan, now walking beside him, "our aircraft have evolved notably throughout the years, mostly because there are others out there who have also evolved in new and creative ways, but also because they have attempted evil schemes or caused terror … just as we have begun to suspect recently from Pegasus Company. Which brings us back to the reason I brought you here."

Keithan frowned. He still had no idea why Dantés and Lanzard suspected something fishy about Pegasus. *Why would Pegasus be up to no good?* he kept wondering.

The three of them passed through the tall doorway at the end of the warehouse and came into a much smaller area where a round iron door stood. On its surface, glowing in white, were the words "Sector 5: Research and Analysis."

Two uniformed men stood at either side of the round door. They straightened and saluted at the sight of the colonel. Lanzard saluted back. He didn't have to ask permission to be allowed to enter; he simply approached the door and reached out a hand to press it on a small scanner. The door divided itself into two, sliding sideways and opening to a new room.

It was a cave, Keithan saw, but a cave brimming with technology. It appeared to be some sort of mechanical engineering lab. Metal tubing ran upward and sideways all over its rock walls like artificial vines, and all around there were different workstations, each one with complex button displays and multiple holo screens that showed strange schematics and formulas. All the workstations were oriented to the center of the cave, where two big octagonal glass chambers stood. They reminded Keithan of the simulators room back at the academy, though a lot smaller. Yet what Keithan saw inside the chambers was what instantly caught his attention.

Each chamber was isolating a spherical drone from Pegasus Company. One of the drones was a total wreck, with most of its pieces lying on the chamber's platform. The other one was intact and sustained with three independent stands. From the chamber's iron top, a series of wires and cables hung connected to the second metallic sphere, like electrodes on a robot's giant head.

"We captured the one on the right about a month ago." Lanzard gestured toward the intact sphere. "We captured the other a few weeks earlier, before Giovanni Colani arrived at Ramey."

Keithan paced toward the chambers, deeply intrigued now. Then he turned to Lanzard and Dantés.

"So … this is why you're worried about Pegasus," he said.

"More or less," Lanzard replied.

"But … they're just auto camera drones," Keithan said. "What threat could they be? Colani introduced them the day he arrived at Ramey. He built them to broadcast the Pegasus Air Race from the sky."

Lanzard sighed. "That could be what Colani might have wanted everyone to believe. We, however, have reason to suspect the spheres have another purpose. Since they arrived at Ramey, we have noticed that they have been overflying, not just the airport, but most of the west coast of Puerto Rico too, as if they were searching for something."

"So? That still doesn't make them a threat," Keithan said.

"True, but what they are hiding does," Lanzard said and turned to Dantés. "Show him, Agent Venus."

Dantés, who still looked as if she were chewing her face—clearly because she didn't like the idea of Keithan seeing all this—approached the isolation chamber with the intact sphere. She stepped onto its platform and activated a bright-green laser wall behind the chamber's thick glass door.

"What's that?" Keithan asked Lanzard.

"It's an antitracking shield," the colonel answered. "Like the chamber, it prevents the sphere from transmitting or receiving any signal when the door is open. Now come, it only gives us a window of seconds to go through it."

He rushed Keithan to climb onto the platform while Dantés pulled down a lever on the glass door to open it. Dantés closed the door behind her as soon as the three of them got inside the chamber, and the laser wall deactivated.

Keithan could only stare in wonder now standing up close to the spherical drone. He held his breath while Dantés removed one of its metallic side panels. He leaned forward to get a closer look. He made out the hovering and rotating propulsion systems inside the drone and the integrated camera on its front. But right next to the camera, something else was installed that also pointed toward the outer lens. It was a much different type of mechanism, one that Keithan hadn't expected to find and which made chills run down his spine.

A laser cannon.

CHAPTER 38

I t didn't matter how long Keithan stared at the Pegasus spherical drone; at the moment nothing else registered in his head except the fact that the thing had a concealed weapon right next to its integrated camera. The big question was *why*. Why would Pegasus build an armed machine when the company was so well known for standing against exactly that? As far as Keithan knew, Pegasus built flying machines for a better future, not for war. It had been under that same philosophy Pegasus Company had been created in the first place.

"It's hard to make sense of it, isn't it?" Lanzard said.

Keithan nodded, scratching his head. "This thing was supposed to be just a flying camera," he said.

"We know," Lanzard said. "Still, this drone here, as well as the one in the other chamber, is not the only thing that has been worrying us about Pegasus."

Keithan turned to him, frowning. "What do you mean?"

"We have noticed other anomalies since Pegasus arrived at Ramey—most of which are related to its upcoming air race."

"What other anomalies?" Keithan asked.

He expected the colonel to answer, but instead, Dantés explained.

"Think about it," she told him. "Don't you find it strange how unexpected was the decision to make this year's Pegasus Air Race in Puerto Rico? The location of the air race tends to be announced a whole year in advance, and last year Colani announced that he was considering Canada and Argentina as the place for the next Pegasus Air Race. He never mentioned anything about Puerto Rico."

"There hadn't even been rumors," Lanzard added.

"Then, out of nowhere," Dantés went on, "digital poster ads began to appear all over Ramey Airport, announcing Aguadilla as the place for this year's Pegasus Air Race. And the incredible part was that neither Ramey nor the government of Puerto Rico knew anything about it. Not until Colani arrived in his airship."

Keithan recalled the time at Rocket's Diner, after he'd air raced against the Viviani twins, when he saw one of the digital poster ads for the first time. He had found it hard to believe at first. And he, too, had found it a bit strange how unexpected the announcement had been, but he would have never ever imagined a conspiracy behind the air race as the colonel and Dantés suspected.

"Despite all this, we didn't realize the seriousness of the matter until we found out what these drones were hiding," Dantés said.

Keithan took a moment to allow all the information to sink in. "Pegasus has a lot more of them. Who knows if hundreds?" he realized, turning from the sphere to Dantés and Lanzard. "And they're all going to be released the day of the race."

Dantés nodded. "Just imagine, hundreds of these drones flying all over Puerto Rican airspace without people knowing some of them are armed. You tell me if that doesn't worry you."

It was without a doubt a frightening thought, though it was still hard to believe.

"So now you understand why Dantés prevented you from being in the qualifier tournament," Lanzard said.

Keithan was convinced; it was more than enough reason for what Dantés had done to prevent him from participating in the tournament. It still upset Keithan, but he understood now that Dantés had to do it.

Keithan sighed. "What are you planning to do, then?" he asked.

"First, we need to get to the bottom of this," Lanzard said. "We need to find out more about what Pegasus could be plotting behind the race. That is why I need your help, Keithan. I need you to find out for us what Pegasus is really up to."

"*What?*" Keithan and Dantés exclaimed, eyes bulging.

Keithan shook his head, already overwhelmed with surprises. "Sir, how would you expect me to—?"

"Colani's dinner invitation. It's the perfect opportunity," Lanzard cut him short. His deep and determined look showed that he was dead serious.

"Sir, I-I don't think *I'm* the right person for the job. I mean—"

"He's just *thirteen!*" Dantés finally blurted out. Her look of shock was much more evident than Keithan's.

"Which is why nobody would suspect him," Lanzard insisted, his tone still casual, as if he were asking Keithan to undertake a simple task. He kept his hands behind his back and his eyes at Keithan. "The Pegasus Air Race will be this next weekend, so we are running out of time. We already sent a secret agent disguised as one of the air racers to spy on Pegasus. He confirmed that the company is indeed plotting something secret for the day of the race. Now, what I would like you to do, Keithan, is to try to get some information from Colani. See if you can make him give you a hint about what he's planning."

"Colonel," Dantés said, "don't you think it would be best if we wait for our agent to contact us again? He might give us more information later."

"He already contacted me this morning, Agent," Lanzard turned to her. "Unfortunately, the only thing he has been able to find out about it is the code name of the project."

Dantés narrowed her eyes.

"They're calling it the Daedalus Project," Lanzard concluded.

There was an intense moment of silence.

"The Daedalus Project," Dantés repeated thoughtfully. "Where have I heard that before?"

Keithan knew where *he* had heard it, though he still wasn't sure what it was. Still, he had a good idea where it was being built—and more than that, *who* was building it.

——(·o·)——

Inside his private workshop, surrounded by all kinds of scrap parts and tool machines, William Aramis worked nonstop with his robot assistant, Emmeiseven. William did his best to keep on schedule. He didn't waste a moment; he even ignored the time. Drops of sweat trickled down his forehead and over his welding goggles, which shielded his eyes from the sparks that sprinkled like tiny fireworks in front of him.

Then he stopped. So did Emmeiseven, which flipped its welding gun back into one of its mechanical gauntlets. And at that moment, a grin appeared on William's face.

"At last!" he exclaimed with satisfaction.

He stared down with pride at his latest invention. He couldn't wait to show it to the rest of the world: the Daedalus Project.

There was only one thing left to do. William headed to his laptube on a table to the right and opened a digital document titled "Daedalus Project 23-9-14-7-19: Unveiling Sequence." In it were the details about how the project's unveiling would be carried out the day of the race. William looked it over. With a single click, he deleted it and typed in his own plan to unveil his invention.

The plan would take everyone by surprise, William was certain. Not even Pegasus would see it coming.

AUTHOR'S ARTWORK AND DESIGNS

Inspired by the Novel

Pegasus Company Airship

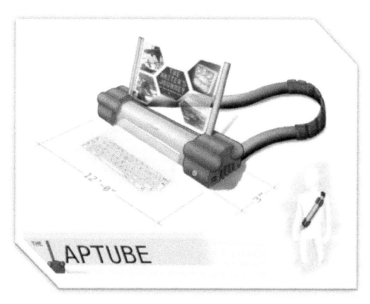

Laptube

Fernando's Wheelchair

Rocket's Diner

Inside the Mind of the Author:

Question and Answer with Francisco Muniz

How did your path to become a writer start?

My path started in my late teens, but it was strongly influenced by my childhood. It's funny because I never imagined becoming a writer when I was a kid. I'm embarrassed to admit that I didn't like to read and write much then. I did like to draw a lot. My mother used to say that I would end up working on animated films. At the time, I used to create stories for the characters I drew. Unfortunately, I only kept the stories in my head; I never wrote any of them down.

It wasn't until shortly after high school that I really got into reading a lot—and for pleasure. I guess it was because I got tired of watching too much TV, the same cartoons, the same movies. By then, a big bookstore had opened near where I lived, and the curiosity of what it offered led me to give books a chance. Next thing I knew, I was reading *Harry Potter*, *The Neverending Story*, the *Star Wars: Jedi Apprentice* series, among many other books. That eventually led me to think, "Hmm, what if I could create a good book too?" So I decided to answer that question by trying writing, and I began coming up with ideas from some of the drawings that I had done when I was younger. I liked it because I was creating again, and I wasn't doing it just for myself. I was creating stories to share them in the future too. And so the writer in me was born.

What inspired you to write *Keithan Quintero and the Sky Phantoms*?

I have always been fascinated with the idea of flying even though I'm not a pilot, nor I plan to become one … at least for now. For a long time, I wanted to create a story about a boy who could fly, but I didn't want to go for the Peter Pan approach, which I like a lot, but it's already been done. I wanted to create something new, something fresh and take my initial idea to another level. That's how I came up with the idea of a young pilot. More than that, of a young pilot who with his effort and the help of his friends would get to build his own aircraft and use it to study in the hopes of becoming a great air racer.

What was the most challenging thing about writing the book?

I would have to say showing a positive and fun vision of a future that's still imperfect but not dystopian. I wanted to create a future that readers would really like to look forward to, especially because of technological advancements, and that they might find hard to see in the real world today. Part of the idea was actually inspired by the hopes and vision of the future Walt Disney talked about when he designed the first Tomorrowland park at Disneyland, which opened in 1955.

What led you to set the story in Puerto Rico?

I remember I spent several months wondering where in the world I could set the story. Then, one day, I asked myself, "why not in Puerto Rico?" I grew up there, and I remember listening to stories about UFO sightings in different parts of the Caribbean island. Whether they were true or not, I was still intrigued by those stories while I was growing up, especially about how people made the whole UFO sightings a phenomenon. And as a science-fiction enthusiast, I found the stories very entertaining. Also, Puerto Rico has some very interesting locations that gave me a lot of ideas for the story. So I brainstormed with that because I wanted to include settings from the island that enriched to the plot. I think I accomplished that with Mona Island and, of course, Ramey Airport (which is known today as the Rafael Hernández International Airport) in the city of Aguadilla. There are more interesting locations readers will get to enjoy about Puerto Rico in the upcoming sequel like the Arecibo Radio Telescope and Lajas Valley, to name a few.

Keithan's best friend Fernando, who is in a wheelchair, is a type of character that unfortunately is rarely represented in fiction. Was there a motivation or inspiration to create him?

The very lack of representation of characters with disabilities in fiction was exactly what motivated me to create Fernando. However, I wanted him to stand out as a character through his great qualities. Fernando is an inventive and dedicated aeroengineer student. He loves to build things and solve problems. Everything he does by himself and with Keithan shows how intelligent and creative he is. His customized powered wheelchair is proof of that too. So I figured that going into details about his disability, whatever it may be, wasn't relevant to the story; his strengths and talents are.

Is Keithan Quintero a reflection of yourself?

Oh, I have mixed feelings about that. [Chuckles] In some ways, I have to admit Keithan is a lot like me. I mean, Keithan's cocky, and I guess I like to be like that too—but sometimes! And only in a playful way, not to be annoyingly arrogant. In Keithan's defense, he's cocky in a similar way, but being an air racing pilot student, he has to be because he needs to rely a lot on his confidence when he flies and races.

Keithan is also very daring like me, I think, and like me, he finds it very hard to say no to a big challenge when he knows what he wants and what he needs to do to accomplish things. Whether we succeed or not, we both do our best, always. Another thing Keithan seems to reflect about me is how important he considers his best friends in his life. Yes, Keithan wishes for fame as an air racer, but when it comes to friendships, he doesn't care about having lots of friends. His two best friends, Fernando and Marianna, are more than enough for him, and I guess he relies on them a bit to make sure they remind him to be humble. That's something I have appreciated from a few close friends of mine, and I wanted to show that in the relationship Keithan has with Fernando and Marianna.

What about a difference between you and Keithan? Is there one?

Oh, yeah. There's one big difference between Keithan and me: he's extremely competitive. I'm not.

In the author's biography, it's mentioned that your becoming best friends with an eccentric inventor was a big influence for the book. Would you tell us about that person?

That eccentric inventor is a very cool architect I used to work with during my twenties. He's my best friend. He's a huge science-fiction enthusiast too, and his designs and inventions show that, which is why I consider him eccentric. I learned so much from him. Our friendship always reminds me of the relationship between Marty McFly and Doc Brown from the *Back to the Future* films. The guy even has a DeLorean! I'm not kidding. One of the other things that I find very cool about him is his office and his workshop. They are full of collectible spaceships, robots, and aliens, among many other things. He even built the entrance of his conference area like the doorway from one of the spaceships from Star Wars. All that stuff about him was such an influence for me while I was developing the story that the character of Mr. Aramis ended up being a mirror image of my friend.

What do you wish readers gain from your book?

Pleasure first and foremost. Pleasure from reading it. I would also like them to gain motivation from the book to dare to follow their dreams, kind of like how the character of Keithan dares to follow his. I remember I reflected about that a few months after the first edition of the book came out. I've always believed the book has the potential to entice our inner child's desire to be daring sometimes to accomplish our goals, and I hope many readers can experience that when they read the book.

Do you have any advice for aspiring writers?

Write what you want. Write the stories or songs you would like to read and hear and that no one has created. There are no limitations when it comes to creative writing. If you aren't sure how to begin, just ask yourself "What if …?" and complete the question, then answer it. Another advice I would like to share to aspiring writers is to read as much as you can. Read stories like the ones you would like to write and don't limit yourself to that. Read about other things that you like and intrigue you. Also, write as much as you want whenever you can. Keep a journal with you or write your ideas on your phone, your computer, anywhere you can keep working on them. More importantly, determine yourself to finish what you write. I always say that there will always be room for a new story—including yours. And there will always be someone out there who would like to read it.

Don't miss the sequel

BOOK **2** Available Now

Lightning Source UK Ltd.
Milton Keynes UK
UKHW042011031220
374592UK00010B/827/J